The Kissing Circles

...to be or not to be extraordinary

Nitin Tewari

Invincible Publishers

First published in India in 2016 by Invincible Publishers

ISBN: 978-93-86148-03-2

Invincible Publishers
F-55, Sushant Lok II, Hong Kong Bazar Lane Sector 57, Gurgaon-122003

Opposite Kasturba Ashram, Radaur Distt Yamuna Nagar, Haryana- 135133

Dedicated to
The Engineering Universe, E.U.

कर्मण्येवाधिकारस्ते मा फलेषु कदाचन।
मा कर्मफलहेतुर्भूर्मा ते सङ्गोऽस्त्वकर्मणि॥

You have the right to perform your action only, but never to the fruits thereof.
Let not the fruits of action be your purpose, nor let yourself be attached to inaction.

Disclaimer: This is not a treatise on engineering colleges. Definitely not concerning the IITs. Not by any stretch of erotic imagination. But it does involve engineers; the B.E.s or B.Techs or whatever is mentioned in their institute's brochures or their degrees, irrespective of how much land such institutions have ruined and the rank they hold in DataQuest surveys. Engineers, the good ol' fellas who form the core inhabitants of this vast Engineering Universe or E.U. as they fondly or frustratingly call it. And there is no EXIT!

Introduction to Karma.

The Big Bang or the Big Phusss!

****

Good afternoon Mr. Manoj Bansal, she said as my eyes rested on her hair. Her jet-black hair with its soft, loose curls that framed her face perfectly. Her smouldering kohl-rimmed eyes stood out on her oval visage, enticing me to brush my lips against hers, especially her pouting lower lip. Not just brush. Chew. While the exotic floral fragrance of her perfume and her intoxicating demeanour was enough to leave an indelible triple-X effect on my body. Dressed in a traditional Indian suit with churidar pyjama that flaunted her shapely legs, the HR manager was a beauty – a dusky beauty.

Yes, in a brief ten-second long sneak peak when she had stood up to receive me for my interview, I had encountered the most beautiful 5D experience of my life that still lingered in my eyes.

'Bansal *bhainchod*, how's it going?' Chaudhary croaked in his night pyjamas and a crumpled shirt and waved at me; enough to break my reverie. The facade around me, on the other hand, was in stark contrast to his unkempt spectacle. Roughly two hundred screwed-up soon-to-be engineers had flocked to the auditorium of our Regional Engineering College of Delhi, *Dwarka* on a muggy August afternoon.

For past three years we'd lived in this Engineering Universe or EU as we fondly called it. We had prayed, engaged in warfare and cannibalism and mugged our holy books - the *Balaguruswamys*, the *Oppenheims*, the *Sawhneys* - or even the Idiot's guides. Or, at best, we'd burned daylights and midnight lamps on Counter Strikes, Age of Empires, MSN or Yahoo chats and of late, cyber-slackers' then new-found passion called Orkutting.

But that day, we had marshalled out of our wells, spruced up in formals topped off with ties and leather shoes for our "rise and redemption" during our final 'fall' in our final year.

While our personas, all of a sudden, had taken a new charm, Gods – the leading IT firm, TCSL - had descended with open arms in a large winged Vessel as the first mass recruiter for our *Kumbh* Carnival - the annual placement season. To offer us the IT nirvana.

I was certainly not ready and highly unsteady to go.

'I heard the HR is *hawtt*,' said Chaudhary, wearing a lickerish grin on his unshaven face. His mouth odour avowed he hadn't brushed his teeth either before he came rushing from the hostel in slippers. So aghast he had been on skipping the interview.

Yeah, this sucker had skipped it.

Despite being an Instrumentation and Control Engineer, this guy had guts to skip the IT companies and wait for the core Giants. Bloody topper! And why not? People like Chaudhary were an absolute deal; *a breed that never cares which engineering college or discipline they are reared in, post IIT JEE debacle.*

My breed couldn't be farther from his. We were like opposite ends of the solar spectrum. If Chaudhary was Violet, I was Red. Actually, he was Ultra-violet, and I was Infrared. Yet, I was one up on him, as far as this hot HR was concerned.

'Hot is a gross understatement,' I said and proudly described him the dusky celestial nymph I had met an hour ago during my HR evaluation. He heard each word with intent.

'Corporate life transmogrifies these females, isn't it,' said I. Chaudhary agreed with a sigh, leering at the Electronics, ECE girls chattering near the window, perhaps picturing their similar corporate mutations. 'Yeah, man. They look so desirable.'

So much that I forgot what an ordeal my day had proved to be.

'How many?' Prof. Dhillon, our placement in charge, had given me the most belittling and spiteful stare of my life. Misfortune had befallen me when out of the blue one of my mark sheets had gone missing. It always happened to *me*.

'Just one sir, second sem.'

'Just one? Bravo boy,' he snarled. 'If I were in their shoes, I'd have rejected you outright. But see? Our reputation saves your bum,' he had minced no words in reminding me the greatness of the Institute and my shit-worthiness before handing out the NOC. But nothing matched the screw up I had managed in my first round of interviews.

'Being a Manufacturing and Automation Process engineer, why do you wish to join software industry,' the two interviewers had asked.

Good Question. 'Actually, I don't feel comfortable dealing with a laborious job where I need to be on my feet the whole day. I'd rather prefer a sitting job like working on a computer. I feel that's how I can offer maximum output,' I had said.

Straightforward, honest and dumb. Oh, yes. A pothead without smoking any cannabis.

'So you're a cool dude, looking for a white collar job, eh?' said one while the other scanned my *kewl* six-foot bespectacled toothpick frame. LOL erupted somewhere instead of *Sabu's volcano.*

'But why TCSL?'

'Well, I have gathered some feedback from my seniors,' I threw in a desperate fib.

'Feedback?' they sounded curious.

'They say the organization is quite a government like. *Ekdum Sarkari,*' I uttered, hell-bent on a self-destruction.

The two interviewers sat upright. Perhaps, waiting for a 'hic' to escape my mouth; it would confirm whether I was stoned or drunk. Irony sure died laughing at that moment.

I cleared my throat. 'But personally speaking, this semi government structure is the USP of your company.'

'Oh fuck? Semi-government structure?' Chaudhary was in splits when I narrated him the story. 'Man, you seriously said that? This is the best thing I've heard today.'

I felt better. Proud too.

'I can imagine them glaring at you like one-eyed Crime Master Gogo, unable to fathom whether it was a compliment or an insult,' he said, invoking Bollywood characters in his speech – his trademark. 'And then?'

Then? I said:

'The other IT firms believe in slog culture and push their employees to the hilt. Now if we cannot be American loungers, we cannot be Japanese workhorses either who toil for hours and hours like precision machines. We are Indians.'

They gawked at me like menacing Hawks, ready to pounce on any minute.

I continued, 'Consider this. We have families that turn *multiple* families when we marry. We need time for each of them, and then space for our personal growth too. Your company, sir, provides exactly that. A middle ground! A perfect environment for an Indian to work, thrive and deliver!' and concluded my theory with a conviction I wished I had exhibited in my term viva. Exhaling a deep breath, I looked at their smiling faces. Hawks had metamorphosed into patrons. Mighty impressed patrons.

'Oh *Amar*, I'm proud of you man,' Chaudhary said, fighting back the tears of laughter. *All is well that ends well.*

'Fuck dude, I was fucking screwed. *Bhenchod*,' we heard Bhavesh Kaul howling at the other corner as soon as he walked out of the interview hall.

'Why is he always so hyper?' I asked Pulkit, his hostel neighbour.

'Cry wolf and create panic for others, simple,' he explained.

Cry Wolves is a breed of engineers who pretend to be hell scared in demanding situations when the truth is, they are the most confident bunch of all.

While the wolf cried, my nervousness grew and chilled me to the bones. I waited like a sacrificial lamb yet to die after two hard blows, checking out other aspirants. Near the stairs, Vivek Bathla, from Computers, pored over 'Yes You Can' by Shiv Khera.

Oh dear, do I really have a chance? 'I should've waited for the second round,' I said, feeling tired, unsure, and irritated. A week prior I was fixed upon skipping the first round of companies, altogether. But Preetika had insisted. *Screw you Ghissu.*

'Always a better idea to try at least. Look at what Murthy did. He moved a mountain bro,' Pulkit stated the matter of fact.

I nodded, wondering if I had shaken off some dust at least, from the barren mountain if not moved it already. The final round would be 'Management Review' and I was sure I'd crack it. Making business decisions based on real life case studies came naturally to me, thanks to my *baniya* genes.

'Dude, this MR was a freaking mess, but somehow I survived,' said Kaul, joining us and as usual, shared his case studies in the most over-excited mien.

For all his histrionics, his style of talking always impressed me. At times, I'd find myself mimicking his dramatic pauses and stressing on individual syllables by pulling my lower lip below my upper incisors; the way he spoke. But in all honesty, it was his English skills I envied the most.

If I want an IIM stamp on my forehead, I must learn from him.

'You'll do good Bansal. You're a born manager. Just act like one,' Kaul pumped self-assurance back into me. Man, I felt taller. After all Kaul, whose sole mission in life was to crack the IIM, regarded me a born manager.

Brimming with confidence, I sat before the interviewer, ten minutes later. Bring it on, Monsieur. I smiled.

His lips moved too and following words escaped his mouth: Which subjects did you study in the previous semester?

My wide grin exposed my *Dabur-Lal-Dant-Manjan* teeth.

Subjects, eh? Could there be a dumber question in the whole Engineering Universe? *We had five.*

'Microprocessors…Mechatronics…and…and…fuck…no, not fuck…I mean…Fuck,' I blanked out.

Laughing my guts out, I nearly fell off the stool I was sitting on, as *Manoj, the Bansal* narrated me the story of his first interview fuck-up. 'Yeah, man. And you know what was the date that day? 08-08-2006. Could you beat the combination?' he added.

'Now I see, why you're so worked up with 2015,' I chuckled.

Well, that is how our "Rum pe Charcha" had started; with his numerological assessments and astrological analysis of our future in the forthcoming year as we warmed our heals, perched on the terrace of my father's Sarkari accommodation on New Year's eve. Though my primary aim had been to share with him few ideas, I thought might turn into a decent fiction.

But before we could come to that, he demanded my opinion over his new start-up idea – "The Kissing Circles Ice-Cream Hub", downing his second Patiala peg. Ice cream, I could understand but what was 'Kissing Circles'?

'That's an unusual name,' said I. Manoj smiled at my conjecture. 'But what is it exactly?'

'A long story,' he refilled his glass. 'A true one, though.'

'We have an entire bottle to finish.'

Manoj picked up the bottle, 'You underestimate this poor wretch, dear Watson. It is, what set the whole story in motion,' he said and began.

Forget his interview, the narrative, which followed thereafter, left me brimming with emotions. Hiding beneath the appellation was an enthralling tale of four zeros that had changed their lives forever. I decided to forego my other ideas and asked if I could turn the chronicles of these circles into a full-blown novel, instead.

'You have the rights,' he said, emptying his glass for the fifth time.

'I think, I should include multiple, unique point of views.'

'Different perspectives! Sounds interesting but how'd you define its hero?'

'Does it have a hero?' I smirked. 'Let the story decide.'

June 3rd, 2007

At the zenith of Economic Boom...
& Confusion...

The God's own Country

****

Kerala Express slowed down and crawled towards Trivandrum Junction, fifty-three hours after it had left New Delhi.

Some other day, Rajesh Pandey would be a martyr, braving a journey of such exhaustive measures. But today, the breath-taking emerald green landscapes, bewitching pristine hills and tranquil backwaters that beckoned him with the first ray of the rising sun, had reawakened his dying spirits.

On a new day, he was in a new world; the God's own country.

A typical Kerala summer afternoon – hot and sultry, greeted him as soon as he shifted his luggage from his compartment to the frontal vestibule of his coach. He stood there. Waiting for the train to come to a complete halt and watching the coolies take their reserved spots, ready to barge in. He prayed they did so with little more civility than their North Indian counterparts. Stepping into the most literate state in the country sure had raised his expectations. A loud thud brought his attention to Manoj Bansal who struggled at the door with his baggage.

'Easy man, easy. This is the end,' he said, helping Manoj adjust his luggage. Three enormous boxes he carried, and Rajesh was curious to know what lay inside.

They had serendipitously met at the New Delhi station two days earlier. Not for the first time, though. They had known each other since their first semester at REC Dwarka. They were in the same batch - Manufacturing and Automation, before Rajesh opted for REC Rohini following an upgradation to Mechanical Engineering. Three years ago, he had felt proud. Today, he cared a dime.

In the EU, their institutes, the two RECs of Delhi, formed a unique binary star orbiting around a barycentre called Delhi University and yet, shared a queer animosity.

For some incongruous reasons, their inhabitants would raise spears and unsheathe swords every time they'd spot a chance to prove their 'supremacy'. Be it their huge sprawling campuses, their job packages, the number of selections in the IIMs or the US varsities for M.S. or even something trivial like the sex ratios in various engineering streams...*wait! That isn't trivial.* Anyways, these younglings derived orgasmic pleasure in every other useless factsheet.

Not today, when the verity of life stared at them. Its name was DigiSys. And tomorrow, they'd begin the Corporate Learning Program or CLP on their first job. It would've been an ordeal of two months, the usual tenure. But a new corporate policy had stretched their agony to three, given DigiSys' recent acquisition by the French giant CapVirgo. Though he wasn't sad, the breathtaking Kerala had ensured. Despite an almost-breakup with *her* – the love of his life, a week earlier.

Things would just be fine, he promised himself as he alighted to the platform number three. The coolies had behaved as per his expectations. So far so good.

Behind him, still reeling from the trauma of extension, Manoj lumbered down like a dead log. Unlike Rajesh, the sight of backwaters had failed to revive his soul. Yes, it had been a year of heartbreaks; Indian cricket had team exited the world cup in the qualifying round. Yet, Rajesh found his despondency bizarre. Throughout their journey, Manoj kept pulling back with a grimace and stayed put on the upper berth most of the time.

Quite contrary to how he'd been in college, Rajesh recounted.

He vividly remembered the car racing competition Manoj had organized during their Tech-fest in the third year; one of the most well-managed tech events he'd ever been to. The only one he had won. Despite discovering right before the contest that his design didn't satisfy a crucial norm.

Wouldn't have been possible without this dude, he fondly called Bansal. He'd been so assuring and forthcoming that day, soothing his frayed nerves, enabling Rajesh to make one last minute change to his design to clinch the top prize.

And today, he saw the same Bansal struggling hopelessly while talking to the coolies that hovered around him.

With a sigh, Rajesh glanced about the medium sized station. The four platforms were mostly empty, and apart from the usual suspects – locals dressed in their traditional white lungi and shirt, he could spot a few young outsiders too. Mixed emotions on their faces revealed their true identity. Trainees for sure.

'I give up, man,' Manoj threw up his hands in exasperation. 'I cannot stand their gibberish anymore Negotiating with Malayalam speaking heads that understood neither Hindi nor English, had proved too much for him.

'Sugamalle,' Rajesh cut in with a smile. While Manoj stared at him in disbelief, the coolie looked floored hearing the greeting; an easily discernable fact by the broad grin on his face.

In less than a minute, an emboldened Rajesh exhausted all the Malayalam he had learnt in past two days from a benevolent Malayali co-passenger and convinced the coolie to knock fifty bucks off the fare. Manoj slacked his jaw, impressed.

'I told you. Malayalam is our key to having some gala time in *Mallu-Land*,' Rajesh gave out a proud laugh, brightening up Manoj a bit.

For fifty-three excruciating hours, Manoj had sulked in the train loaded with *Madrasis*, unable to accept his fate. His father's words had kept ringing in his ears; *had you worked a little harder, you'd have a fetching job at least. Look at Mishraji's son. He is on US deputation with TCS.*

Manoj had never cared for a job. All he coveted was an MBA from a top institute. But an unmentionable percentile had not only dashed his IIM hopes, it had rendered him useless for the second rung B-schools as well. That was his third failure; missing

IIT being the first and a low rank in REC entrance, his second. DigiSys had been a bright spot. But then, not the future he had envisaged for himself.

How'd he escape? He wondered as he traipsed behind the coolie. His gaze swung to Rajesh. An Infosys reject, Rajesh shared the same boat. But unlike him, Rajesh was one of those 'engineer' engineers.

He still remembered the indigenous car Rajesh had designed for the competition and the last minute heroics that won him the top prize of ten thousand rupees. Also that eco-friendly car prototype as part of his B.Tech project; it had grabbed newspaper headlines too.

'Same crap we churn year after year,' Rajesh had sniggered during a brief smoking-stroll at Bhopal Junction. 'And you know the best part? The majority of us think we're going to be the Steve Jobs of the automobile industry. Like I always thought I'd design a flying car one day. Such deluded *Chutiyas* we are.'

'I always assumed you'd pick a Mech job.'

'Are you kidding me? Where are the Mechanical jobs? Each year, the institute pulls one twenty halfwits like me into a Goddamn course where the industrial demand isn't even ten percent. That too, only for toppers. Hail the booming economy.'

A grim reality it was but Manoj couldn't agree more.

A fractured and misbalanced manufacturing industry fulfilled only limited desires and those too, were reserved for the best – the great devotees. And here, these two weren't even average. They were mediocre. *Sinners*, that is to say and their fate was alike – the IT hell.

Almost, Manoj corrected himself. At least Rajesh had a girl in his life. Could it be the reason he was so relaxed about his situation? In an instant, the solution to his life's troubles flashed before his eyes. He was glad he had that 'wonder book' tucked away in his luggage.

He must dust off his inhibitions and start hobnobbing with the lungi-clads right away. A matter of just three months.

Manoj raised his chin and purposefully, fastened upon the Malayali gentleman plodding ahead of them with his two heavy suitcases.

'I like this lungi. Where do you get these?' Manoj pointed at the white *lungi* wrapped around the man's waist. The gentleman – a menacing lookalike of the typical baddies Manoj had seen in the South Indian movies, glared at Manoj but not for blocking his way.

'First time in Kerala?' he scowled in a thick accent. Manoj nodded with a confident smile. 'This is not lungi. This is *mundu*. Never ever call it lungi,' the man snarled indignantly and resumed his walk towards the main exit.

'That was commendable,' Rajesh tried to stifle his laughter. Manoj couldn't hold back a smile either, repeating the word "Mundu" softly. The book would come in handy in the Mallu-Land, he concluded.

Vashikaran works better on truculent selfs. Mallu girls should be more fun.

As his smile grew wider, his mother's precept echoed in his ears. *Son, you are still very young. Focus on making a name for yourself and not waste your life, chasing frivolous things,*

Frivolous, it is not, mom! Manoj argued.

'Taxi,' the coolie called out. And soon after saving hundred more bucks, courtesy the coolie, they were merrily on their way to the final destination – DigiSys Consulting Services.

Rajesh Pandey's

The First Step

****

Touted as the largest IT hub in India, Technopark was situated on the outskirts of Trivandrum. Launched in 1990 the lush green site housed nearly two hundred IT companies, including DigiSys Consulting Services. With more than ten thousand software professionals by the end of 2006, the mini town had truly seen a gargantuan growth since its inception, and the moment we entered the grand gate, we were in awe of its grandeur.

'That's the DigiSys hostel,' said Manoj as we proceeded to the entrance of a midsized building. The guard on duty directed us to the administrative office - a small cabin located on the periphery of its north corner where the assistant-in-charge greeted us in thick South Indian accent.

'Your names, please,' he enquired, turning to his small desk to pick some papers and a pen.

'Rajesh Pandey,' I said.

'Manoj Bansal,' said Bansal.

'One by one, please,' the person said with slight irritation, his eyes never leaving the papers.

Snubbed, we looked at each other and then at the stout middle aged official with a curly oily mop of hair on his head. His ID dangled on his neck with an ugly mug-shot; a worthy rival to a DTC bus pass, I supposed. I read the name - Dolphin...Delphin Perumbavoor and grinned. *I'd stick to Dolphin.*

Searching out our details, Dolphin requested us to produce our joining letters and asked us to sign on a pink register as soon as we handed him the documents.

'You two are going to stay together?' He picked another register, green, while we both set our signatures on the pink one.

'We would prefer separate rooms,' Bansal said and paused. 'We'll get individual rooms, right?'

Dolphin glanced up, looking not too pleased. 'This is a hostel. Not some hotel. Each room has double occupancy,' he told Bansal in a cold, sarcastic tone. *Poor Bansal.* I guess today was his day to pick the wrong Malayali guys.

'We'll stay together,' I said impatiently, wanting to lie down on a bed as quickly as possible.

'Only third floor has empty rooms available in that case. Take "301",' Dolphin offered.

'Could you check if "305" is unoccupied too?' Bansal asked.

Why? I threw him a puzzled glance

'"301" adds up to 'four' which is ominous. I'm an eight born so "305", which is also an eight, would be favourable for my profession,' he reasoned.

What crap? Had he lost his mind? I stared at him, dumbstruck. *Or was he suffering from multiple personality disorder?* I mulled over my decision to share a room with him but then made up my mind to go along anyway.

'Ok, I don't believe in numerology but should I tell you my lucky integer as per your hypothesis?' I adduced. 'It's nine.'

Bansal cleared his throat, looking uncomfortable. *Gotcha boy!*

'Technically, 306 should be the one,' he uttered. 'But whether it favours you or not, depends on your expectations and your temperament as well,' he added shortly.

'Shouldn't we go for "306", then?' I smiled.

'"306" is not vacant,' Dolphin interrupted, seemingly peeved at our ongoing parley. '"305" is. Decide, please.'

'Well, in the absence of nine, eight would work. It'll reorient your life's direction. Mark my words!' Bansal prophesied and turned to Dolphin. 'Give us "305".'

'One more information,' Dolphin said, sliding our room keys

across the table. 'We have water shortage at present. The supply may be cut on some days.'

And I thought things would just be fine.

'Don't worry, we will arrange water tankers, but you have to make sure that you participate in water conservation,' Dolphin added. 'At times, the tankers may not be available too.'

'What are we supposed to do if there is no water?' I asked.

'Don't worry. Monsoon is almost here. Our hostel is equipped for rainwater harvesting,' Dolphin said with a hint of pride. His "Don't worries" worried me the most now.

With his best wishes and few more suggestions we headed to the hostel – an imposing three-storey building, and it looked beautiful. Built in traditional Kerala architecture, it had two separate blocks, each having a square courtyard in middle. Spanning over two acres, it could accommodate two hundred residents at any given point of time.

'A state-of-the-art structure, indeed,' I said.

'A world without barrier,' exclaimed Bansal, leering at the girls roaming and chatting around in the corridors. 'I've never seen such a high sex ratio in anything related to engineering,' he said with a glint of a *Tharki* stalker. 'Must be two is to five. What do you think?'

Man, where was this weirdo hidden all these years? He is sure going to be fun. He was statistically correct, though.

'Possibly. Our room is on the third floor right?' I asked as I glanced around for the elevator. There was none.

Things would just be fine, I reminded myself with a painful sigh and prepared for the torturous ascent.

The Coconut Theory

****

'Dear associates,' Col. Menon began the orientation in a solemn voice with thick accent. A retired army officer from Engineers Corps, he was in his mid-fifties and appeared incredibly 'fit' to the two hundred young trainees who sat in front of him in the main auditorium; half of them still floating in the moana of their dreams while the other half, indifferent and resigned to their IT reality.

In Col. Menon's court, though they were equals.

'Yes, *associates*. That's how we address each other in DigiSys,' he continued. 'No juniors, seniors, sirs or mams because you're past your college. Not employees for sure as none of us own DigiSys. Simply *associates* because each of you is our companion in this organization.' He paused to let his words sink in.

At DigiSys Training Campus, Col. Menon's sole task was to give the newbies a sense of belonging right from the day one. With a broad frame and gleaming eyes, he possessed a natural aura of effortless authority to keep the required discipline. Yet, it was his whip-smartness - a Malayali attribute, he'd often jest - that made him the administrative in charge of one of the largest training facilities in the country.

'Welcome to DigiSys,' he announced.

A thunderous applause erupted, bringing a smile to his face. The ice was thus broken.

'I'm hungry,' grumbled Manoj, sitting beside Rajesh in one of the middle rows – a step closer to their radical professionalism against a liberal backbencher's status in college.

Rajesh nodded in agreement, feeling the hunger pangs too.

It hadn't been a salutary morning for both. First, they had

barely managed to scramble out of their beds by seven and by the time they answered the whistling calls of nature, the taps were already running dry.

'I had read the theory of cost cutting measures but never expected these guys to conduct a practical on our first day. This is so cheap, man,' Rajesh had kept growling. 'We need an extra bucket.'

To exacerbate their situation, buses were already packed and ready to leave while the canteen also drew to a close when they reached downstairs. They had to choose; a bus-ride with an empty stomach or a two-kilometre footslog on a half-filled gut. They had picked the former.

And now both sat, crunching their stomach and listening to Col. Menon, praying for the session to end. Fortunately, Col. Menon skipped the vision-mission statements of DigiSys and its history. The new CapVirgo management hadn't set the new guidelines yet. He moved straight to the training schedule.

The CLP was divided into three phases of one month each, he told them. The first comprised of fundamentals and included theory for most part. The second was dedicated to the group applications and presentations and the third, which was introduced this year focussed on actual industry projects.

It'd prepare the associates joining the live projects well in advance, thereby decreasing the on-project learning time, the management had claimed. In reality, it'd screen the recruits before tagging them to a particular vertical or as a matter of fact even retaining them in the company.

'And before I wind up, let me tell you a story, a real story,' Col. Menon said. He loved spinning yarns, long drawn out ones – another of his Malayali traits.

'You all have seen coconuts trees – the slender, unbranched ringed trunks capped by the king sized featherlike leaves that gift us what Marco Polo called an 'Indian nut'. "*A nut that is a meal for a man - both meat and drink, he said.*" The same nut which

Sinbad, the sailor fancied and sold during one of his voyages,' said Col. Menon.

Manoj and Rajesh clutched their stomach tighter, growling with hunger at the mere mention of food.

'But picking that fruit is not easy. You require a certain technique to climb the giant tree,' he continued. 'Now, hear the story. Two young associates a couple of years ago, fascinated by these fruits, set their sights on the tree. They talked to a few locals and learned the technique. On one beautiful Kerala evening after a few unsuccessful attempts, they both managed to climb up while their local friends watched from the ground and clapped at their astonishing feat.'

He paused and glanced over the audience. The curiosity on their faces told him they were hooked.

'Now as I said, *it was one fine Kerala evening*,' he said in a singsong tone, showing another glimpse of his trained vocal chords. 'By that I meant, it might rain any minute. So while they hi-fived each other at the top, it started to pour. Heavily! In a matter of seconds, our associates were deserted. Their friends were gone.'

The audience chuckled.

'Not our fault,' he shrugged. 'For all our love for the rains, we don't appreciate getting drenched. Our *mundu* takes too much time to dry. Anyways, fire brigade had to be summoned to bring them down.' The audience burst into laughter on his concluding remark. 'So, what is the moral of the story?'

Hushed murmurs began as associates exchanged confused looks. The humour had vanished like the spirit from an open liquor bottle.

'I know where this is leading to,' whispered Manoj.

'You gentleman, please tell us,' Col. Menon pointed towards an associate in checkered shirt, in the third row.

'Moral is that we all must learn how to climb down before we climb up,' said the *checkered shirt*.

Col. Menon rolled his eyes and shook his head, ominously.

'My suggestion would rather be, don't even try. Because if a coconut drops, it doesn't break but if you fall, you are definitely going to crack open,' he said, leaving his audience further confused.

'I knew that,' Manoj mumbled.

'And if you do crave coconuts, there are plenty available in our canteen,' he completed and chortled at his own aphorism.

Their orientation was over.

DigiSys corporate learning centre was an opulent building, three storeys high. Its interior was akin to a mini-sized mall with a large oval shaped arena built at its centre.

'Certainly, for the IT gladiators baying for each other's blood,' whispered Manoj. Rajesh chuckled.

The building roof was in form of a glass ceiling that allowed natural light to filter through, thereby illuminating the entire facility and cutting down the electricity bill. Its premises had thirty midsized rooms, five spacious computer labs and one sizeable library with most of the books focusing on various IT disciplines. Though, Rajesh and Manoj found their respective favourite sections - 'Mechanical Designs' and 'Management', too.

Post hoc an hour-long tour of the facility and submitting the copies of necessary documents, they received temporary IDs and rationed meal coupons along with handouts detailing their daily schedule and curriculum. Due to increased load, the campus operated in two shifts, and they were assigned the morning one – from eight to two.

Their final task of the day was to fill out details for a new bank account. Once the formalities were completed, each of them received a kit, enclosing a debit card, a chequebook and sealed pins.

Exhausted, they headed to the canteen to grab some food.

'You think by coconuts, he really meant coconuts?' Manoj scratched his chin, waiting in the long queue.

'What are you talking about?' said Rajesh, puzzled.

'Colonel Menon,' he said. 'Did you not see how he stressed on the coconuts of DigiSys canteen?'

'I'm not sure, if he did,' Rajesh rummaged in his pockets for the meal coupons.

'But I am convinced. There was a hidden message,' Manoj leaned forward. 'All he meant was that if you're considering leaving DigiSys in search of better opportunities, do not. Be happy with what you're offered here. They want to fucking enslave us, man.'

Rajesh broke into a faint laugh, but Manoj didn't change his expressions. Rajesh pursed his lips and moved to the counter.

'*Sugamana,*' he greeted the canteen manager.

'*Sukhamalle,*' grinned the manager.

'*Kai kyane inde,*' he asked further.

Baffled, Manoj let out a harsh breath. He was famished and felt no necessity to delay feeding his starved tummy. But before he could protest Rajesh's linguistic show-off, the manager rose to the bait and ran through the entire menu in their common gibberish.

'Hold please,' Rajesh stretched his palms, lost *and* bewildered in translation. The manager noticed the pain on his face and with a broad smile, pointed towards the menu board. Manoj chuckled at last.

'That tete-a-tete out there was mind-blowing, dude,' Manoj smirked, picking his spoon as they sat to eat. He threw a quick glance at the food items on his plate. The gravy looked nice, thick and yum. Smacking his lips, he scooped a spoon full of gravy into his mouth.

'Rapidex Malayalam speaking course.'

Manoj coughed and almost choked. Rajesh pushed his glass of water towards him.

'Rapidex? Seriously, you're playing around with those *jalebi* letters?' said Manoj, with disbelief. The Malayalam script in the form of North Indian dessert *jalebi* danced before his eyes while the Rapidex jingle rang inside his ears. 'Where did you find it?' he said, mixing his gravy and rice and scooping a mouthful.

'In Kozhikode, when you were sleeping', Rajesh winked.

'Oh man, this crap tastes so nice. Someone has rightly said it's the stomach and not tongue that tells the taste of a morsel of food,' Manoj said.

'Said who? You?'

'Can I sit here?' an accented voice spoke from behind.

Tilting his head, Manoj noticed a five and a half feet darker, past version of himself albeit with a small set of eyes wearing an expression of astonishment on his face. *A Southie associate,* he thought.

Why does he seek their permission? Besides, shouldn't it be 'may I' and not 'can I'? He pondered. His GRE prep guide mentioned something similar. Time to resume his revisions if he intended to lift himself out of this slimy muck and mire, he reminded himself.

'Of course, you can,' offered Rajesh. His "can" wasn't lost on Manoj either.

The associate, oblivious to his deliberations, took a chair beside Manoj and unleashed a blitz in Malayalam. Manoj shot Rajesh a shut-him-up-or-I-will-break-his-teeth look, wanting to have his scrumptious lunch in peace.

'Sorry, we don't understand Malayalam,' said Rajesh.

The associate paused and laughed hysterically. So weird it sounded that Manoj wanted to now smack Rajesh for interrupting him.

'I *yem* sorry. I saw you two *tawking* to the canteen manager so I thought-' he continued laughing at his confusion, 'Never mind, I am Adish. Adish Mathew.'

Adish Mathew's

Edavapatthy

****

Coincidences are strange at times. At 'all' times. But when they occur, they invariably seem inconsequential to our lives. Ditto, the day I met those two Northies.

Frankly, I had never had high regards for Northies as we were taught to be sceptical about them. Not that we viewed our other Dravidian fellows in a better light. In fact, our Malayali cynicism extended to everything classified as Non-Malayali under and above the sun. The sun included. But Northies! They kind of deserved it.

My first interaction with Northies transpired in NEMIT - a Madrasi Institute they often called it. They formed separate groups, hardly mingled with us, never forwent a chance to mock our English by mimicking our accents and always talked in Hindi. Such callous attitude they had towards us. But the worst was their remarks about our food. They frowned upon our South Indian dishes and yet always relished them. Hypocrites, I tell you!

But these two seemed unusual. Especially the one sitting across me; a typical dude with a gym-toned physique. Or else how many would strive to learn our language on their first day in our country.

'Never mind, I'm Adish Mathew,' thus I introduced myself. The dude was Rajesh Pandey, as he told me and the one beside me chomping and slurping was Manoj. So tall and yet so thin; he resembled less a human and more a coconut tree. And the way he looked at you through his thick glasses, you'd think his eyes would pop out and drop to the floor any instant.

'Which batch?' I asked.

'I'm in D5 and Manoj is in D12,' said Rajesh.

'I'm in D12 too,' I exclaimed, but sensing a lack of enthusiasm in Manoj, shifted my focus to Rajesh, 'in fact, half of our batch comes from my college, NEMIT,' I boasted. And why not? Forty engineers had been recruited from NEMIT that year. A record. And a definite achievement for an institute that didn't even exist six years back.

'NEMIT?' Manoj repeated.

Sure, he didn't know its whereabouts, and I didn't blame him. Though I wished it was Rajesh in D-12 instead.

'Isn't it in Bangalore?' he said.

He was aware. Jesus, he was noteworthy too.

Both these exclusive beings belonged to the RECs Delhi, as they revealed. I'd been to their institutes once. To participate in their tech fests. Huge campuses they had, two hundred acres each. Not to mention their rankings as per the annual Dataquest survey; they would rank invariably in top ten. I had always dreamt of rubbing shoulders with IITians, but I guess, RECians were cool too.

'So, Adish…Adish right?' Rajesh re-confirmed. I nodded. 'You are a local?'

'Kind of. My family lives in Cochin,' I said.

'Great! We have a local with us now. I guess our lives would be much easier, and I won't have to learn Malayalam anymore,' said Manoj with a sigh of relief.

I wished I had the patience to evince the light of Malayalam to his ignorant mind. Rajesh seemed a better bet.

'Any help you need, let me know,' I assured them.

'Thanks, man. Actually, we need to buy few things. Is there a market close-by?' asked Rajesh.

'And, a good restaurant,' Manoj demanded.

'Well, Kazhakuttam is the nearest market. Just a kilometer from Technopark. It has few restaurants too. Yummy, delicious food, you get there. Particularly the Kerala specialties, cooked in coconut oil and special spices. You will find everything; chicken, mutton, fish, beef. Oh yes, you must try *chilli* beef,' I summarized in one single breath while they stared at me. I realized they didn't eat beef as it was prohibited in their culture.

'I'm fine with chicken, mutton and fish. No beef please,' said Rajesh. Manoj, however, dealt me the sucker punch.

'Any vegetarian restaurants?' he asked.

It was my turn to stare back. 'Vegetarian?'

'He is a veggie,' Rajesh revealed. Fuck! A veggie!

Honestly, nothing was more dreadful than 'Vegetarianism'.

I feared this breed more than the Northies. Their real purpose was never to relish the food on their plate but to guilt-trip non-vegetarians, my father would often say. 'Vegetarians are the freaks, the oddities.'

And this guy was a *Northie vegetarian.* An unspeakable demon.

'A few serve Dosa, Idiyappam, Idli, Vada and Sambhar,' I said, indifferently.

'North Indian vegetarian,' Manoj stressed. A pin drop silence fell between us as we locked our gaze. The herbivore had pushed it too far.

'Let's go and check for ourselves.' Rajesh proposed.

'You don't even eat eggs?' I asked. My mind still grappled with the fear of dealing with a vegetarian on the prowl.

'Pure veg. Is it so difficult to grasp?' Manoj pleaded.

Jesus, he was real. But why would I be bothered? I nodded and retreated to my food.

Not too long ago, Kazhakuttam used to be a quiet three-way junction. But now, numerous eating joints and apparel shops had opened up in its various lanes. One lane, though, had old customary stores intact where one could purchase groceries and other daily requirements at cheap rates.

'Ask him the price.' said Manoj, holding a large black umbrella. We had stopped by a small garments shop on my suggestion as the rains could arrive any time. The shop had plenty of customers, and since the shopkeeper didn't understand English, it was my turn to take the centre stage.

'Four hundred,' I said after checking the price.

'I can read the price tag,' Manoj growled. 'But how much does he want for it?'

'Four hundred,' I gulped, dreading his next step.

Manoj shrugged and scanned the umbrella to reconfirm if it was worth the price. 'Too high, man,' he said. He was ready to bargain.

Now, Northies are experts in bargaining and the first step in the process is to offer a counter-quote that must sound not only unjustified but ridiculous too. Though, more or less the exercise stays harmless, unless...

'Offer him two hundred and fifty. We'll buy two,' he interrupted my ponderings.

...unless someone urges me to do it!

Two hundred and fifty? My jaw dropped. His mere suggestion that I say aloud that quote stalled my breath. Why was this fiendish soul hell bent on testing my faith on God?

Sensing my hesitation, Manoj gave me a piercing, quizzical look. I rather wished the earth would disappear beneath my feet.

'Are you sure? Isn't it too less?' I stuttered.

'Less? Are you serious?' He guffawed at my plight. 'Oh boy, let me teach you some tricks of business. Ask him if he would sell three umbrellas for two hundred each,' he revised his bid.

'Two hundred!' It had gotten worse. 'And three umbrellas! But you need two,' I protested.

'Don't you want a new one?' he frowned. 'Now, don't waste time. Ask him.'

With no escape in sight, I turned towards the counter where other customers were negotiating too, albeit politely. Mustering all the courage I could, I cleared my throat and uttered that despicable quote. Murmurs vanished, silence shrieked, and the shopkeeper's eyes bored into me. I was sure, if he had magical powers, he would've shot lasers from his brown orbs and burnt me to ashes for my transgression.

'*Sugamana*,' interjected Manoj. The shopkeeper responded with a smile. Manoj raised three fingers, telling him he required three pieces or so I believed.

'Three hundred, final price,' said the shopkeeper.

Manoj grinned. The deal was struck. Scoundrel had used me as bait. The three fingers meant three hundred rupees.

'Look, what I found,' Rajesh flashed a cigarette pack outside the shop. 'See, that's branding,'

'Kerala Lights,' I identified the cigarette as one of the most famous brands of Kerala.

Manoj took the pack and inspected it curiously. 'Marlboro?' he narrowed his brow.

Rajesh winked and drew on the cigarette he held in his other hand. 'It tastes amazingly strong,' he said, exhaling a thick cloud of smoke.

'You got the SIM cards?' enquired Manoj.

Rajesh nodded. 'You bought umbrellas? But where are the rains?'

'Edavapathy is reaching today,' I said.

'Edava...what? Who?' Manoj said.

'Oh sorry. *Edavapathy* means Southwest monsoon. Every year we greet Edavapathy at the harbour.'

'Harbour? Is it coming by ship or boat,' Rajesh quipped while Manoj laughed. I laughed too but at his sheer ignorance. In reality, Northies never realize how special of an occasion Edavapathy is for the populace of Kerala.

'Let us go to there and see for ourselves.'

But Manoj shook his head vehemently and reminded us of

the pending items such as milk, sugar, toothpaste and a pair of shorts.

'We can pick them tomorrow. The market isn't too far. But the way Adish is describing this Edava…thing, I say we go and have a look,' Rajesh said.

'I need milk every night,' Manoj protested, albeit weakly.

'We can pick milk on our way back. The shops stay open till eight,' I offered that serpent an option. If he wouldn't agree, I'd turn a rebel. At no cost would I miss the first raindrop.

'Come on Bansal,' Rajesh coaxed, stubbing out his cigarette with his shoe toe. 'Months later when you bag an IIM call, and God forbid, it's not IIM *Cosy-code*.'

'*Korrhi. Korrhikode*,' I interrupted. I had to. His pronunciation of 'Kozhikode' was all over the place.

Manoj glared at me, not pleased at my interruption.

'Yes, thanks, *Korrhikod*,' Rajesh continued, 'Anyways, then you will realize that you have one story less to share from this place, the story of Edavapathy,' he stamped like a *Chavittu Natakam* artist with all the right notes.

And his pronunciation was spot on.

Manoj caved in, and agreed while I thanked Rajesh in my heart. He had indeed saved me from an imminent act of discourtesy.

Housing the famous Vizhingam lighthouse – a prime tourist attraction - and with a facility of more than hundred anchors for all kind of boats, be it fishing or passenger, the harbour was a major spot for commercial activities. When we reached the port, the boats were on either on retreat or had already moored. A possible storm, predicted by Met department, had forced them to prepone their scheduled return.

Typically, first of June would be the appointed day for South-west monsoon to break over Indian mainland through Kerala.

But a four-day delay this year meant it'd be arriving today. To welcome it, the Malabar shore was already brimming with people under a rumbling and darkening sky. Rain clouds they were.

Astonished at the immense crowd, both Rajesh and Manoj had their mouths wide open.

'Must be around five hundred,' said Rajesh.

'More than a thousand is my guess,' said Manoj.

'It's going to swell further,' I added, 'Let's go to the beach.'

'What if it is a false alarm?' asked Rajesh as we jostled through the thick crowd, towards the narrow red sand beach.

'We have a local saying, *Chakki mukha chakrai vachonam karu*, which means, "when clouds acquire the shape of Jaggery, rain shall arrive",' I said, pointing upwards and began to hum a poem my arts teacher is school had written once:

Longing hearts look up and behold
with fears, thunders and lightings instill,
Jaggery conjures up in the clouds
and smiling Gods are waiting still;
Swaying palms-

'Looks shapeless to me,' Manoj interrupted my train of thought. *What was his problem?* 'Oh, yes. I can see something. Let's click pictures man,' he exclaimed.

As we adjusted for the perfect frame, the first raindrops fell on our heads. We paused and looked skywards. More globules rapped our faces. We clicked our pictures in eager haste, though, Manoj seemed pleased with the outcome, particularly the one with Yo expressions and his arms making a cross.

'This is going to be my Orkut profile picture,' he declared in triumph. *Orkut!* I was delighted too. By adding him to my friend list, I'd reach 678 friends - twelve less than Venkat, our batch topper. Since he was also in CLP, I had to be on constant prowl to beat him.

The rain gods oblivious to my plan, however, moved faster and opened their gates. While Manoj and Rajesh unfurled their new umbrellas, I gave them my phone for safekeeping and stood under the pouring clouds transfixed, getting soaked in Adam's ale that spilled in gallons from above.

And why not? I hadn't savoured the moment in four years. And today, I didn't wish to let it go. I yearned to soak in every drop that fell on me. The drumming throb of *Chenda*, rose and fell nearby as if Elijah himself was calling out:

Go up, eat and drink;
for there is the sound of the roar of the heavy shower.

Hiding under umbrellas, the Northies looked mesmerized; for the first time, tasting the aboriginal flavour of the God's own country and witnessing the incredible Kerala unfold in front of them. The celebrations had begun.

I started to laugh. And laughed and laughed.

'Your phone Adish,' Manoj yelled. 'Your *Dad* is calling.'

The Routine

Thirteen compilation errors! His eyes bulged at the desktop.

Sitting in the programming lab and floundering against his arch-foe - the C++ language, Rajesh's worst nightmares seemed to come true. He tried to figure out the error source, but his brain had ceased to function. His logic was fine, pseudo-code appeared faultless and yet, a working code, as usual, proved to be a harrowing quest. Carrying water buckets from the ground floor to his room looked to him, a far more lucrative option.

He could never grasp the nuts and bolts of the popular language that was developed by Bjarne Stroustrup during the 1980's at the renowned AT&T Bell Labs - founded by the Alexander Graham Bell who invented telephone and brought the world closer than anybody else, in the history of humankind.

Ugh! He was aware of the history. But that didn't help him an iota to unravel the mystery of C++ that began during his second engineering semester. Forty! He had scored forty marks, the minimum required to pass the subject. Though his actual score must've been lesser, he was sure, and felt profusely indebted to his pretty prof for giving him a lifeline.

Could he phone a friend, Adish? He wished he could trade Adish for his window-side bed that Manoj coveted so much. *Such a lucky ass, Bansal is for having Adish in his batch!* He cursed.

Darting nervous glances around like a cornered mouse to find an exit and save his life, his eyes instead, hit upon her captivating sight. Gracefully dressed in formals, dusky, five and a half feet tall perhaps, with a lean proportional figure, Shelja Thomas arched onto Manjot's desktop, examining his code in the far corner of the lab.

Didn't she resemble Sangeeta Kashyap, the enchanting prof of C++ programming and his first crush? *Oh, she was some woman.* He remembered the day Sangeeta or SAK – as they called her, had first stepped inside their classroom.

Every heart had skipped a beat. Writing the introductory problem on the board, SAK had sashayed to the rear wall and had spent rest of the session loafed against it. Sitting in the second row, it had caused so much inconvenience to his neck, swivelling each time his eyeballs wished to behold her. To save himself further agony, he had shifted to the hindmost row the next session. He never went back to the front.

Rajesh rubbernecked at Shelja with renewed interest. Her black, ponytail hair with streaks of burgundy complimented her roundish face, bearing a piece of innocence that enhanced whenever she smiled. And she smiled always.

'What the hell is wrong with me? I'm in a serious relationship, damn it,' he chided himself, feeling guilty. It reminded him that he had forgotten to call *her* in the morning.

How could he? How the fuck, could he? Ever since he reached Trivandrum, he'd barely spoken to *her*. The fact that she was on a family vacation hadn't helped his cause either. *Her* authoritarian parents kept *her* under constant vigil, so for a week they'd have limited opportunities to talk, *she* had informed him. But that didn't mean he should go astray and ogle at other females. Ravishing females. No, never.

He prodded his forehead and gandered back at his notepad to recheck his pseudo-code. Satisfied, he resolved to have one more swing at the code. Frantically, he typed a few commands on the screen and ran the compiler.

Fifteen errors found.

His shoulders dropped. Dispirited, his sight again wandered off towards Shelja.

No way could he proceed further today.

'Let us analyse a case study,' said the management faculty, Arvind Acharya, drawing seven rectangular blocks on the board.

'Management is the top bet because this IT bubble is going to rupture sooner or later, trust me,' Manoj whispered to Adish with a curious smile.

'I know it's difficult for you but don't worry. You'll get used to the coding slowly but surely,' Adish retorted, listlessly.

Filling the empty blocks with the available verticals of Finance, Soft Drinks, IT, Services, Medium or Heavy Scale Industry, Agriculture and FMCG, Arvind turned to the class.

'An entrepreneur wishes to venture into a new business. Capital is not an issue with him. What would you suggest?'

Wasim Dost Khan raised his hand from the second row.

'I would recommend that he invests in FMCG as it'll never be down. Not even during a recession because we cannot do away with our day-to-day essentials. We can further narrow it down to, let's say, soaps,' he said with confidence.

'Yes, but for you to use any soap, your hostel must have water,' said Arvind, setting everyone off into bursts of laughter. Once the class cooled off, he presented his analysis:

The operating profit margins in FMCG are lower than the technology domain by three percent. Though the real contrariety lies in the growth rate. For FMCG, it is around half a percent in preceding two years whereas the figure is over three for IT.

'Then IT Technology *saar*. It's booming,' another voice said in a thick South Indian accent.

'The IT bubble can burst anytime. I'd propose agriculture,' one more cut in, to counter.

'Agriculture is rain dependent,' a fourth one reasoned.

'Has he invested before?' said Manoj.

Arvind narrowed his eyes, 'What did you ask?'

'I want to know if he has invested before. I mean the capital he has - did he earn it as profits from a business or is it inheritance?' Manoj detailed out.

'Does it matter how he procures the capital?' Arvind looked intrigued. A few laughs, though, were let loose misconstruing his interest as sarcasm. 'Quiet, please. It's a legitimate question,' he clarified, 'but why is it legitimate?'

'Because it gives an indication of his business acumen, his ability to tolerate risks and his expectations from the venture in the short or long term, realistic or fantastical,' Manoj explained in a single breath. Arvind grinned and rubbed out everything he had scribbled on the board.

'That's your first lesson. You are not *that* entrepreneur. You're merely an assist to help him build his business or later manage it,' said Arvind. 'So, until you get a firm understanding of the client and his business, you cannot propose the purchase of even a single commodity,' he concluded and sent a nod of appreciation at Manoj.

Smiles followed from various quarters, including the one from a girl. Manoj heard chimes ringing in his ears. *Never miss the chance when fortune smiles at you,* Michael Holding would say whenever someone dropped a catch of Tendulkar.

He acknowledged her back with a toothy grin.

Rajesh squinted at the girl talking animatedly with Manoj in far off corner of the canteen. Manoj hadn't joined them for lunch today. But that wasn't his main concern. It was *the girl* who looked so familiar. *Where had he seen her?*

The girl with the bucket! It struck him

Wasn't she the one? Carrying...no not carrying but lifting. Not that either. Dragging! Yes, dragging her bucket through the corridor, half filled with water in the most cloddish technique he'd ever seen. He had spent a few wicked minutes to study the statics and dynamics and yet, couldn't figure it out an iota except for...her curves peeking out of her water soaked clothes.

She was the one. What had Manoj christened her when he'd described her? Ummms!

'Lucky bastard,' he mumbled as Adish sat down with his plate.

'She is today's prize,' Adish revealed.

'Today's prize?' Rajesh couldn't contain his laughter, 'Did he win your *Sthree Shakti* lottery or what?'

Adish guffawed. 'Looks like it. Our dude totally ruled the management class,' he said, making explicit gestures with a clenched fist. 'He was so impressive, seriously. I almost fell in love with him. But she staked out her claim, first.'

Rajesh laughed even harder. 'Crazy or what? God! I knew this guy was a number one *tharki*,' he said, scooping up another bite from his plate.

'Tharki?' Adish asked, puzzled.

Rajesh looked up to elucidate the riddle but then, something brewed inside his head. 'Ever wondered why Bansal is so tall unlike you?' he said with a smirk.

Manoj Bansal's

The Complexity of Engineers' Lives

****

Tharki roughly means Satyromaniac; as per the dictionary, a male who has an excessive desire for sex. Funny, isn't it? I mean which male doesn't? Anyways if Rajesh did insist to discriminate against me, I had no qualms about being called a Tharki. Nor would you, if you happened to be the person who:

* *had no sister, even in the entire extended family who could introduce him to her female school or tuition friends.*

* *spent ten years in a Government Boys School of Meerut except for two years when he slogged in a boys hostel to ensure a '10+2' from Delhi and could never find the time, a girl and the courage to bunk and go on a Priya date.*

* *got into an Engineering college where the ratio of girls and boys was inversely proportional to the cube of its institutional ranking in the Dataquest survey;*

Then you, my friend, you'd know how much complexity the other sex added in us engineer's lives,' I vented out the interminable monologue at an otherwhere Pandey, who had planted that diabolic formication inside Adish's puny brain.

Struck with a discreet silence as I lay on my bed post dinner, I became aware that I was alone in the room. Forthwith, I felt a strong urge to access my forty gigabytes of *pondies* that laid wasted in my brand new eighty GB USB hard disk.

Yes, you heard it right. I was the proud owner of forty GB of porn! The most exhaustive porn collection in our entire institute. People would swarm around me in search of the divine bliss and beg me like quintessential addicts. And I'd be the peddler wearing a checkered coat and an English hat with a Cuban cigar between my lips unlit as I didn't smoke. Leaning against a colonial lamppost on a lonely moonlit street, I'd be gloating and blowing imaginary smoke rings.

There lay the answer to his second query, my lanky structure.

Well, my past hadn't been rosy. Until my tenth standard, I was amongst the shortest in my class and hence, a subject of frequent lampoons. So depressed I'd be that even when I hated Hrithik - the new kid on the block, posing a challenge to my favourite Shahrukh, yet I couldn't help hankering after his Greek-God built.

A miracle happened then. A brand new Pentium-IV along with a dial up Internet connection arrived at my home to assist in my studies. Soon I unearthed an exercise that burned body fat and increased height. *Eurhythmics.* A system of rhythmical physical movements to sound and music for therapeutic purposes.

Fat or no fat, I decided to put the internet to its prime use. Rest became history and history turned legend as I stepped into the college, standing over six feet.

Curiously, our hostels had a tradition to honour the masters of Eurythmics with the sobriquet of 'Shaggy' aka 'Mutthals', depending upon whether you were a hipster or a desi. An ordinal number would be suffixed to mark the generation as well. In total six 'Shaggys' and three 'Mutthals' had been christened hitherto and hence, I became 'Mutthal – the Chaturth, or the fourth'.

I had to buy a Laptop.

A Celeron on monthly installments would be an excellent idea.

Idea. Wait! I had few clips on my phone. One of them was titled 'Skin Deep'. 'Thank you, papa,' I mumbled and grabbed my Moto-razor for the final act. Before playing the clip, I lowered my boxers and covered myself with a bed sheet.

That's how I roll.

The clip was soft porn, starring a slinky Latino model and her Afro photographer. I preferred softer versions. They had a story and unfolded gradually, like the way she undressed for a steamy bath, bit by bit and tit by tit. It was the last simile my mind had concocted ahead of shifting its egomaniacal abode inside my head to a more humble clime, above my balls. My heart pounded fast; pumping down as much blood as possible to ensure my rapt mind didn't suffer from the lack of oxygen. My hands moved under the sheet and my eyes closed as I replaced her Afro partner. Almost at the dwam of ecstasy…

…a click broke my reverie.

My eyes opened and legs bent in reflex as the door flung open, and Pandey sailed in, humming an old Bollywood tune.

I had forgotten to bolt the door. *Fuck…fuck…fuck!* Petrified, I uttered a yelp, 'What?'

Pandey stopped mid-stride, 'What what?'

'You were…talking to your girlfriend, right?' I stammered and without him noticing, bent my legs further to hide any evidence of the little game I was playing. My right hand was still stuck on the joystick, though. Taking it out could attract attention.

'Yeah, we had a quickie. Her dad summoned her,' he said and walked over to his bed and lay down, his gaze fixed on me. 'A quick phone call, I meant.'

That's not a quickie, asshole. Quickie is…

'I don't understand,' he shrugged. 'She is beautiful, I mean. Intelligent, loving and caring - she is everything you can ever desire in a girl. Then why does she behave so…so complexly?'

Telling me about 'complexity' at this juncture was like apprising Rahul Dravid the complexity of staying in the Indian ODI cricket squad.

Yeah, douchebag. You've already labelled me a tharki, and if you knew what I was up to, I would be ruined. And girls? I just want that Latino and five minutes for my quickie, asshole.

'You are so lucky, man,' I said. 'People like us could only behold and fantasize about those gorgeous doctors in the Fashion Parade. But you have one for a girlfriend.'

'You know, I met her in your Fashion Parade,' he grinned.

What the fuck? Words dried up on my lips, as a gust of memories rushed to me; young alluring undergrads in flying miniskirts, a rare sight during our cultural fests. These damsels from Delhi's prestigious medical institutes would pay us an annual visit and unlike NIFT girls, who were too occupied flaunting manmade designs, these considerate and compassionate fairies (later joined by women's engineering colleges too, in their solidarity march for our desperate cause) showed off God's creation.

It was no brainer whose '*oeuvres*' gave delectation to our eyes or NSP. *Nain Sukh Prapti.*

He met her in our Fash P! Anger returned to my throbbing veins. How could God be so cruel? *Our college, our fest, we invite those girls, and these Rohini guys get to enjoy the fruits. Assholes. Fucking, freaking assholes.*

I looked daggers at him while he directed his gaze at my bed sheet.

'Is the bathroom tap leaking?' I asked. Forget the Docs. Time was running out on me.

'Why don't you go and check?' he suggested.

'I think it is fine.' My ploy had failed.

'Why are you covered in a bed sheet? Weird you are,' he said with an impish smile and shuffled on his bed. An opportunity beckoned me. But before I could act, the doorknob clicked once again.

'Urgent group meeting for tomorrow's presentation. Venkat is calling,' Adish stormed in wearing a mundu, folded at knees and stood by my bed.

'I've already given my inputs. What does he want, now?' I said, irritated. I hated this Venkat idiot. And this Adish too.

'That's what. They are debating on your points. You are a hit boss,' he said, and stared at my bed sheet, lifting his mundu further up. 'What's with the bed sheet? It's so hot and humid. I am not even wearing an underwear inside-.'

'I don't want to know,' I screamed. 'And lower your lungi, *bhenchod.*' Pandey couldn't resist a snicker.

Scoundrel. This guy laughed a lot which reminded me of an old proverb – 'Those who laugh in excess cry in excess too'. Let IT confiscate his life; all his laughter will dissipate, and he'll yelp a cry for liberation.

'I've to make an urgent call. You go. I'll come in two minutes,' I said. Adish nodded but stood there still, smiling at me. I glared back.

'I'm off to my paternal village this weekend,' he cleared his throat. 'We have a small ceremony for paddy plantations. You guys wish to join?'

'Paddy Plantation!' Pandey bolted upright. 'Count me in,' he said, giving him an instant thumbs-up. 'Where is your village?'

'Mevalloor. Around hundred and fifty kilometres from here.'

'One fifty? Too far, man. Let us catch some sleep on Saturday and visit Kovalam beach on Sunday,' I protested. Frankly, I didn't care if they regarded me a tharki. I wanted my beauty sleep.

'Come on dude. You forgot our Kerala *Darshan* plan?' stressed Pandey, leaning towards me. I had no idea how to escape.

God showered his mercy upon me, and his phone rang. Sensing an opportunity, I asked Adish to go and check the tap as soon as Pandey rushed outside. With them gone, I pulled up my boxers in a jiffy.

'The tap is working fine,' Adish declared and came out.

'What the hell is wrong with this girl? She gives me a missed call, and when I call her back, the line is busy,' Pandey flashed his phone. 'Oh shit, I'm such an idiot. She must be trying my number,' Pandey deduced. His phone rang again, and the smile reappeared on his face. Jumping onto his bed, he answered the call. 'Hey, baby.'

'Come,' I told Adish, striding out. Venkat will pay, I vowed.

It was well past midnight when I returned to the room, furious on that idiot Venkat, to have wasted everyone's time by calling a pointless meeting. But seeing my wheatish complexion in the mirror – the one thing I hated about my baniya genes, I was now upset too.

'Why are you whining?' asked Pandey, hearing my mutterings.

'Whining? Meet this scoundrel Venkat, once. And you'll learn what a worthless pinhead he is,' I spat, applying the fairness cream on my face – my daily beauty regimen. 'Everybody was fine with my inputs but this guy! No, he had to thrust his own ideas. And what for?' I said.

No response came from Pandey.

I turned towards him. 'To impress some girl in our group. Such a retard he is.' Lying on his bed, Pandey gave me a mute stare.

'The same girl, you had lunch with?'

How the hell did he know? 'Y…Yes,' I said sheepishly.

'Ah. She is the one you nicknamed "Umms" today morning,' he said with a wicked grin. 'God, she is ubiquitous.'

What! I recalled our morning conversation and resolved to be present the next time the water tanker arrived.

'That's not the point. The point is how could one be such a fool not to see what is right there in front of him. If she were interested in him, she'd be taking lunch with *him*, not me. And besides, she has a boyfriend,' I said.

'She has a boyfriend?'

'Yeah. But that is also not the point. The real point is, don't turn your work into a personal competition,' I said, easing onto my bed.

'Oh man, you are a pro, now,' he chuckled.

'Why are you up so late?'

'What do you think?'

'Waiting for her call?'

He shrugged. 'I guess she must've slept.' I had noticed that his pillow-talks were shortening with each passing day.

'How long have you guys been in this relationship?' I asked.

'Fourth of July is our first anniversary.'

'Almost a year. Are you guys serious?'

'Dude, we are madly in love. Two break ups and yet, going strong.'

Two breakups! Shouldn't he be worried? But how would I know? I had never had a girlfriend.

'You're a lucky man. Job, girl and no worries. What a peaceful life!' I was in a pensive mood. We had spent only few days staying together, but I was sure of one thing. Pandey was a genuine guy.

'Not as peaceful as you think. Girls can be difficult sometimes. In fact, most of the times,' he turned philosophical too. 'Besides, there is a continuous vying for your girl by other guys. It gets scary man, especially when you're away.'

I heard him with purpose. His insightful *gyan* on such topics was no less than Upanishads for a novice like me.

'But then, there is Love. True love. It resolves everything.'

A sudden silence fell in the room as he grew quiet and stared at the ceiling fan while I speculated if this complexity existed only in an engineer's life. The forever depressed and unprivileged soul. Considering Pandey's tribulations, it seemed to worsen ensuing one's induction into this privileged section – The Couple's.

'Just a matter of three months, Bansal and things will be okay,' he concluded in eternal hope and rolled over to the other side.

I waited for few seconds to double-check he'd dozed off. Once confirmed, I grabbed my phone from the side table and muted its audio before playing the Likewise, Latino clip. Visuals would suffice.

'Are we going to Adish's village?' he asked.

'Tomorrow man, tomorrow. Good night,' I shut him up and pressed the play button, pulling on the bedsheet again. Additional thoughts of *Uums* filled up my head. *Uums* – the sex bomb.

The Rice Bowl of Kerala

****

Historically, paddy cultivation has been an integral part of Kerala's culture and life. Where the spices put Kerala as the most sought after business destination in India on the still evolving world map, it was rice that often determined the strength of its many kingdoms. And the most prominent of its rice producing regions was Kuttanad – the 'Rice Bowl of Kerala' of olden times.

Kuttanad comprised of the present day expanses of Alappuzha, Pathanamthitta and Kottayam; three of the state's fourteen districts. Where Alappuzha boasts of the rustic backwaters - the site of world-renowned Snake boat races; the majority of Pathanamthitta consists of highlands and is synonymous with pilgrimage owing to its venerable Sabarimala temple.

Yet, it is Kottayam that has a distinct legacy altogether. Its unique features like its history of kings, the scenic stretches of canals – including the great Vembanad lake, vast acrid blankets of rubber plantations and being the nerve centre of newspaper industry of Kerala have conferred on it the enviable title – 'The land of letters, legends, latex and lakes'.

Kottayam has five taluks, and one of them is Vaikom, the site of the momentous Vaikom Satyagraha – a movement against untouchability in pre-independence India. Belonging to this taluk, seventeen kilometres away from the Mahadevar temple and along the banks of river Muvattupuzha, lies Mevalloor. Inhabited mainly by Syrian Christians and the people of Ezhava community, it was Adish Mathew's paternal village.

On the auspicious day of Paddy plantations, Mutthur Sankunni's main task had been to separate and arrange paddy sprouts by noon for the committee to proceed with the ceremony.

Crouched on his knees, Mutthur checked his watch. It was nine. Nearly two-thirds of their assignment was already over. *Not bad, considering they began at six,* thought Mutthur. He was thankful that the morning drizzle had turned the weather mild and pleasant or else they would be bathing in sweat by now.

Realizing that his handymen must be craving for tea, and a deserved breather, he announced the break and strode out of the warehouse. A vast sweep of the empty fields lay flooded in front of him under a clouded sky.

It was the alternate Virippu season and rest of the taluk had already sown paddy at the hint of pre-monsoon showers two weeks ago. Only forty acres of land under community farming, cumulated by a committee of eight families residing in the adjoining colony, remained unsown. The reason had been the new hybrid seeds Vasudevan, his elder brother and the appointed head of crop management, had proposed for the trial. With shorter rearing period, these seeds responded to wet cultivation. And since, Edavapatthy had been delayed, they had to wait a week longer.

Mutthur peered back at his resting labourers. In past few years, emigration of local Malayalis to the Gulf nations of Oman, Saudi Arab and UAE had skyrocketed in search of better opportunities. It had created a void in the state for menial jobs, which these labourers from Bihar and West Bengal now filled.

'Things are changing, Mutthur. You should also go to Oman,' Vasudevan had suggested him on many occasions.

'And what would I do there, chetta?'

'You're a graduate. Shibu has promised so many times he will find you a good, respectable job. But you don't listen and just squander your time here.'

'Here I have the fields and the boat.'

'The boat? Oh yes, Captain Mutthur. Do you think anyone cares? Have you forgotten the fate of our father?'

This had been their conversation for the past three years, ever since Mutthur took the reins of Maruthi Vallam in his hands.

Unlike the other younglings of his village, Mutthur believed in his ancient legends like a devout. His impetuous passion for their customs particularly, Vallamkali - the boat race had won him several admirers. Yet, as skipper, he had failed to galvanize his crew and their boat, Maruthi vallam towards a better result. For three years in a row now.

This year, Paddy had also added to his vexations. He wondered if it could be the last time he'd see green shoots swaying in those fields? A debate had occurred during their previous committee meeting when Dubai returned Ramanathan Cherian had floated an idea to appropriate half of the paddy land for rubber estate in the upcoming season. Ramanathan was recently married.

'Rubber doesn't feed us. Rice does,' old Basheer Kutty had argued.

'Basheer, we cultivate rice to sell and not to eat,' uncle Eappen had sallied, breaking into a hearty laugh.

'True, rubber doesn't feed us. But it does make our pockets deeper,' Vasudevan had spoken with deliberation. 'We can feed better, provide our children with better education and save for our future too.'

Vasudevan had been tilling ever since he was a boy. And now when he was married and had a child, he faced the same dilemma that farmers not just in Kerala but across the country faced too. Food crops were becoming less economical with each passing year. While the minimum selling price had remained stagnant, the cost of cultivation had risen manifold in contrast. Add to it, the way monsoon patterns had altered and the frequent news of farmer suicides in other parts of the country, peasants of Kerala would've felt the undercurrents someday.

They did, and needless to say, cash crops like rubber now

looked more rewarding by any standard. *But shouldn't we be mindful of the balance between 'need' and 'want' that had been Mother Nature's primordial dictum?* Mutthur had asked himself. And what would Lord Parashurama say? As per the legend, He had reclaimed the ancient land of Kerala from the sea and bestowed it to his ancestors, to nurture and protect. Since then, Malabar's had been an agrarian civilization and regardless of one's faith, every soul here was a peasant; either in his farmland or of some well-off neighbour.

But who'd listen?

At last, the new and the old lines of thoughts had settled on a mutual plan of action to let the Virippu season pass and take out an additional harvest with the new hybrid seeds before they committed anything for the following Mundakan season.

Once they had sown the seeds, he'd be free of his farming duties to concentrate on the following Vallamkali season, he told himself. This year he had too much at stake.

While Mutthur's mind was profoundly engrossed in Mevalloor, the superfast KSRTC bus carrying the three engineers came to a brief halt at Kottarakkara amidst torrential rains that lashed the small town; the birthplace of Kerala's most famous art, Kathakali.

'Adish, fetch me something to eat, man,' Manoj pleaded.

'We shall eat at Kottayam,' said Adish, unwilling to step out in the rain. 'Two more hours, please.'

'Such insensitive jerks you're. First I get no sleep because you guys wake me up at seven and now, I get no food either,' Manoj ranted. 'I said I wasn't interested in this trip.'

While they quarrelled, Rajesh ignored them and instead, concentrated on the bus window that had no glass panes. He had noticed the strange convention first during their trip to Vizhingam harbour. Here, the windows had metallic slabs that operated vertically as opposed to horizontally as was the norm in Delhi state buses. There were other dissimilarities too.

It was a state transport, and yet the conductors abandoned their seats to sell tickets and oddly enough used neither whistles nor banged coins on the panes to signal the driver. Rather, a rope dangled overhead across the length of the bus and attached to a bell above the driver's head. Similar to the chain system in trains, it could be pulled by anyone.

Rajesh had loved the idea. Simple and uncomplicated. Such simplicity was typical of Kerala, Adish had explained, except for their occasional *hartals*.

'You can eat banana chips,' Adish pointed towards a semi-drenched hawker who had boarded the bus.

'Banana chips? Have you no shame? You guys had puffs at Kazhakuttam, and you're offering me Banana chips,' Manoj spat.

'There were no veg puffs,' Adish reminded him.

Manoj recalled the morning incidents. They had searched around the Kazhakuttam station for half an hour but the only availability was a *beef puff* that Adish picked, and *egg puff*, which Rajesh grabbed. Bananas were available too, but they were orange in colour, and he'd been too afraid to eat them.

'And what's the point of this hundred percent literacy you guys keep harping about,' he sneered. The whole communication exercise had piqued him further. 'Get me those chips. I don't have any patience to decode his Malayalam,' he said.

Adish whistled up the hawker and bought two packs. Manoj jumped to grab one, ripping it open in no time and stuffed several pieces into his mouth at once.

'I hate these banana chips. I bloody hate them,' he continued to rant, on the verge of crying yet, crammed more down his maw as the bus kicked into motion once again.

Mevalloor was still too many hours away.

Rajesh Pandey's

Pal Payasam

****

Nasranis belong to the sect of St. Thomas Christians - the first Christian sect of India. The apostle himself established it when he set foot on the port of Muziris around 52 A.D. Some Jews who were already a part of Kerala's ethnic mix that time adopted the message of Christ alongside a few local Malabaris. A small number of Namboothiris too, came under the umbrella of Syrian Church, to form a closely-knit orthodox community. For next one and a half millennia they resided, united in their litturgy, and flourished, confining themselves to Malabar. Until the arrival of Vasco Da Gama at the harbour of Calicut in 1498.

Vasco da Gama who had anticipated a grand welcome for his Latin beliefs by his East Indian brethren, had felt sorely disappointed when he discovered, to his consternation, that the amalgamation of Indian culture to the western ideas with Jewish traditions had forged a disparate identity for Nasranis. *Quite divergent to our European brethren,* he wrote in his memoirs.

'It was the sort of union amongst its different cultures that moulded Kerala into world's first melting pot of many faiths,' Adish's grandfather stated proudly as we sat on a sumptuous sofa in their palatial living room, listening to their history.

It was a two-storey redbrick house of the Palakkappilly family – one of the eight homesteads in the colony where Adish's family greeted us with warmth and eagerness. It comprised of Adish's parents, elder sister Sara, grandparents, his two uncles, their wives and five cousins. They belonged to the Achayans, which in their native language, meant "elder brother" but now primarily referred to the Christian rubber plantation community of Kottayam. While Adish's father, P S Mathew, ran a rubber mill, his younger brother Eappen facilitated the supply of raw rubber. Though their elder sibling Cherian, a retired government insurance officer, had been an exception

Throughout the noon the brothers kept debating on Kerala's economics and politics, switching back and forth between English and Malayalam. The little I could comprehend revolved around how the Communists' rule and their policies were impeding the state's growth. *His rubber business particularly*, Adish told us, revealing further that Politics and Socio-economics were the favourite topics of a Malayali.

'Why do we never see you discuss the same?' I asked him.

'I am an anomaly in my family,' he said.

At half past one, a reverberating conch called out for the residents of the colony to assemble at the nearby temple for the offerings. They had already visited the holy family church in the morning and had prayed, a fact that brought a look of incredulity on our face, admired by a faint smile on Adish's lips.

The temple lay across the paddy fields on an embankment of Muvattupuzha and appeared quite old as evident from its half-timbered structure. The temple framework was constructed of dense, robust wood and its pyramidal ceilings were covered with copper plates. In the middle of the temple courtyard, stood an archetypal wooden flagstaff coated in brass. Looking at the emblem of *Garuda* at its top one could identify the presiding deity as Vishnu.

Inside, Adish introduced us to Mutthur – his friend and the young captain, preparing the offerings of paddy sprouts in a brash ashet. Adish had given us his brief overview – to be specific, how their boat team had been finishing a dismal last for past three years under his command. Well, we had gladly anticipated our meeting with a fellow no-hoper.

'Welcome to our village,' Mutthur greeted us in good English and a corporate handshake with an affectionate smile. 'I hope you enjoy here.'

Mutthur was as tall, dark and reasonably handsome with sharp facial features and a thick crop of straight hair on his head that were swept back tidily. Wearing a *Chandan-tika* on his forehead, he came across as a cheerful person with a genial smile that never deserted his face.

Ringing the chimes, the priest soon summoned everyone to gather in front of the deity. Holding the ashet, Mutthur excused himself and minced towards the head assistant of the priest.

The prayers soon began and for next one hour, we witnessed the intonation of mantras and hymns and a repeating process of offering palmful sprouts to the idol until all of them were exhausted. A long never-ending *aarti* followed, culminating the ceremony.

'Time for the grand feast,' said Adish.

'I hope vegetarian,' pleaded Bansal.

'Obviously. Are we not in a temple?' Adish winked.

An hour later, it was dawned upon us, what 'grand' meant. The meal, *Sadhya*, was nothing short of an actualization of the mythical Hindi phrase '*Chhappan Bhog.*' No one could be more ecstatic than Bansal. The mere sight of twelve food items served on a large plantain leaf had exulted him, but the feast had only commenced. With five types of curries, five types of chutneys and six types of vegetables dished out so far, Bansal had to keep adjusting his belt. And the fact that it was served by Sara, Adish's sister, hadn't helped his stomach either.

A management postgraduate student, Sara was quite unlike Adish, I couldn't help notice. While he was an imitation copy of his father, though lacking his father's rotunda in place of a torso, Sara definitely inherited more of her mother's genes that gifted her fair complexion and long straight hair. Yup, we had noticed her mother too, discourtesy Bansal.

'Rice?' Sara offered again, carrying the rice bowl.

I refused, shaking my head, but Bansal couldn't. 'Yes, please. And some of…that red curry,' he struggled.

'Rasam,' she said, pouring rice on his leaf. 'I'll bring it for you.'

'I hope you are enjoying,' said Adish as Sara left.

'Are you kidding? I love it, man,' he said, stealing a quick glance at Sara. He could fool Adish but not me. 'All your sins of keeping me hungry are forgiven. Nothing can now stop your ascent to the heaven,' he said and burped. Adish and I erupted into laughter albeit for separate reasons.

The *plat du jour*, however, was reserved for the end. Pal Payasam.

'It is made of rice, milk and cashews,' said Adish.

'You mean a *Cashew Kheer*? Why the f…' Bansal stopped midway. 'Why didn't you tell me earlier?' he cursed, blinking at the extra rice.'

'So, you won't eat Payasam?' I asked.

'Says who?' he snickered, adjusting his belt further. 'I'll manage.'

'Your diet defies your physical structure. Where does it all go?' Adish asked, incredulously.

'I have my own methods to burn excess energy.'

'And how long do you plan to be in the bathroom?' I sneered. Bansal glared at me. 'What? You're more famous than Gabbar Singh in REC Rohini, man. Every hard disk in our hostels bears your mark,' I laughed.

'Such impure thoughts in a temple. Shame on you man,' he chided me, making a disgusted face.

'I get it how you feel when you cannot follow Malayalam,' grumbled Adish. 'I guess it is the same when I can't figure out your jokes.'

'Isn't it incredible that you can prepare so many exceptional dishes from simple grains of rice?' I commended, as Payasam was served to us on a fresh leaf. Mutthur had joined us too.

Adish smiled. 'As you mention grains of rice, something just popped up in my head,' he said. 'There is a legend attached to Pal Payasam, which relates to grains of rice.'

'What's that?' I asked.

'I can't recollect the entire story. Mutthur must know it. He remembers all folklores by heart.' We tilted our heads towards Mutthur like ever-expectant hungry puppies.

'I can narrate, but in only Malayalam.'

'Don't worry. Adish will translate it for us,' I said. Adish glanced at his father, sitting in a corner with a forced smile on his face.

'Go ahead Adish,' spoke Basheer Kutty, from the same corner.

Mutthur and Adish began:

'Long time ago, the region of Kuttanad was ruled by the Namboothiri Chempakassery kings who had assumed the title of 'Devanarayana'; they were the devotees of Krishna. At its peak, the Chempakassery kingdom with its capital at Ambalapuzha controlled not only the rice bowl but also the backwaters and the ports of Aleppy. Through them, they exported rice to the neighbouring kingdoms. With time, they grew wealthy and powerful and so swelled their pride and arrogance too. They presumed if they wished they could exert their authority over the other kings by cutting off their rice supply.

Now it so happened that the King was fond of the game of chess, which he played every day in his court. He was a master at it. He'd invite men he considered wise and took pleasure in defeating them. Soon there was none left in the whole of Kuttanada who hadn't lost to the king.

'Is none born in this land who could win against me? Come forth anyone if you think you can. I promise I shall reward you with anything you wish for,' the King would brag and announce after each triumph.

Nevertheless, he would give a purse of gold coins to the losers as well.

One day a sage, returning from an urgent errand down south, reached his court. The king received him with great gusto and requested him to spend the night in his palace. The sage agreed, and the king ordained his ministers not to have any slack in his service.

Next day, the sage entered the court to give his blessings to the king and take his leave. The king, at the moment, was engrossed in a game of chess.

'He doesn't take too long to finish the game. None has ever come close to even challenge him, let alone defeat him,' the chief minister boasted. 'So we request you to wait a little. The king would really appreciate a proper farewell for you.' The sage smiled and settled on a divan to observe the game.

The king, as expected, emerged victorious in the sixteenth move. 'Is there none who can go beyond sixteen?' he mocked thereon.

'Sixteen is still too many, O King. Had you stayed alert, you could've finished the game in ten moves,' the sage said, rising from his seat.

'Ten moves?' the king raised his brow. 'Impossible.'

'It is possible,' the sage claimed, 'I can show how.'

The king looked at his ministers. A hushed silence enveloped the court. 'It seems you have a firm grasp on this game, O wise sage. Why do we not contest, then? If you win, you may claim any reward you desire from my kingdom,' the king spoke with pride.

The sage smiled. 'You forget the story of King Bali, O king,' the sage said. 'Pride destroys a person.'

The king let out a mirthless laugh. 'O wise man. Who is so unfortunate in this land not to know the story of our beloved Lord Bali? But a story it is and I say to you, mine is not a blind promise. Seal your victory not in ten but in twenty and you shall earn your reward.'

'I accept your magnanimous offer, O king. Let the God's will prevail. But as you see, I'm an ascetic. My needs are measly. A few grains of rice would be all I seek.'

'A few grains?' the king chortled. 'Where you stand, is Kuttanad, the rice bowl. How much rice do you ask for? One sackful? Two sacksful? Let me offer you twelve sacksful for twelve months.'

'No King. Don't offer me sacks. Pledge only the quantity of grains which satisfies my precondition,' the sage said.

The king was puzzled. 'Say it,' he said.

'As we participate in this game of the Gods, let their divine seat – the chessboard decide the quantity I should collect from you,' the sage proposed. The king scratched his chin and nodded at his peculiar demand. The sage explained thus:

One grain for 1st square, two grains for the 2nd and four grains for the succeeding one. Likewise each subsequent square will double the number of grains in the previous one. When we reach the 64th square, Gods will reveal the eventual number of grains you shall owe me.

'That's it?' the king was baffled. 'This is nothing. Ask for more.'

'This is all I need.'

The king gawked at his ministers who were equally bemused.

'Pray be seated, O wise Man. Let us begin,' the king offered resetting the pieces.

'Please ask your ministers to go ahead and arrange for the rice. It is going to take time,' he requested and took his place across the king. The king guffawed at his suggestion and commanded his chief minister to do the needful.

As a courtesy, the king invited the sage to commence the game, readjusting the hourglass kept beside the board. But as soon as the sage moved his first piece – a knight, the king perceived it was going to be a tough match. He didn't have to wait for too long, though. At the tenth move, he was defeated.

Muffled whispers flew amongst his courtiers as the King flopped against his cushion, much to his chagrin. He, however, quickly regained his composure and clapped. 'I've been outdone today,' he said and turned to his chief minister. 'Is the reward ready?'

'No, my king. We need more time to arrange the grains,' the chief minister said.

'What? How much time does it take for a few grains of rice?' the King curled his lips. 'The venerable sage can't be left waiting,' he thundered.

'It is fine with me. I can wait,' the sage said

'Very well then. Shall we play an additional round?' asked the King. The sage smiled and nodded. 'And, please do not be worried. Your reward shall be intact even if you lose this time,' the king forced a laugh and picked the pieces.

This time, the King opened. However, he couldn't alter the result. Once again, at the tenth move, the sage put him in check-mate. The king deduced it had been no fluke. Engulfed in doubts, his mind whirled around in a nebulous haze. Who was this sage? If he was so proficient, why hadn't he ever heard of him?

The chief minister entered the court empty handed again, and the king wasn't amused.

'What's the matter?' he asked.

'We have run out of rice in the royal granary, and yet we have just reached the 40th square,' the chief minister said.

40th square! The King stared at the chessboard and realized the folly he had committed. He had been outwitted, and all his pride had vanished - all thanks to those 64 squares.

Ekai, dahai, saikda, hazaar, dus hazaar, lakh, dus lakh, crore, dus crore, arab, dus arab, neel, dus neel, padm, dus padm, sankh, dus sankh, maha sankha, I counted the final figure.

1,84,46,74,40,73,70,95,51,615.

It'd reached the utmost limit of Hindi numeral system. And if I assumed twenty-five milligrams as the basic weight of a single rice grain, the number would've amounted to close to two Arab metric tonnes. The king could never have fulfilled the Sage's demand. He was humbled forever.

The sage had revised his proviso and instead, told the king to distribute Pal Payasam every day, to pilgrims at Ambalapuzha temple; a custom, he believed, would keep humility intact in Mahabali's land till eternity.

Shuffling in my bed, I wondered how these age-old legends carried such deep messages. More amazed, though I was on how Adish had almost reproduced the prosody of the original story that Mutthur spoke. Enthralled, we had felt as if we'd dived into the ocean of Kerala's myths and history and discovered an underlying world of colours and life's eternal truths.

As an ardent follower of history and mythology and a participant of drama workshops, I held an opinion that knowing an epic was one thing; weaving it efficaciously to invoke an audience's interest, quite another. And such ability chose its cradle in those who took pride rather than a critique of their culture. Only this pride could transform the story telling into a lyrical *piece de resistance* and coerce the audience into suspending their beliefs. I had no doubt that despite his modern and materialistic milieu, Adish was still rooted in his culture and that made him a compelling storyteller.

In his mother tongue, he must be incredible.

Bansal's snores and my extreme dizziness brought me back to the real world. The rain lashing against the windows and the roof sounded less of a melody and more of static from a radio.

Inside, it was a fairly large and well-decorated room with wood veneered floors on the upper storey where we rested tonight. On one wall, hung a large portrait of Saint Thomas – the apostle, presided by an arm-sized holy cross having four equal limbs, as in a plus sign, unlike the regular Christian one. A Nasrani cross, I assumed.

Beside me, Bansal slept like a log in the wake of his daylong efforts; ample travelling, gorging and of course, orkutting. Friend requests had been sent, received and accepted, particularly from Sara. To avoid suspicions, Adish and his two cousins were also a part of his Orkut list now.

As for me, I had a chat with Ruhika after a long time. She'd be coming to India for her brother's marriage around mid-July. But she'd be staying mostly in the vicinity of Bhopal.

Meeting Ruhika wasn't a possibility.

Struggling to keep my eyes open, my mind drifted back to my love. *She* could call any minute. I had to stay awake. I grabbed my phone and browsed through *her* pictures. An ethereal beauty *she* was; so effusive and full of life while I was an undemonstrative hopeless romantic. *Her* round, luminous eyes would cast such a magical spell over me that every time I clocked at them, I felt I was melting in; like iced vanilla ice-cream on a hot brownie. *Her* favourite. *She* was everything to me; my friend, my lover, my soul mate. And I missed *her*.

I dialled *her* number. Switched off. Enough for tonight, I decided.

The Fall

****

'Each day they select one portion of the farm to pluck ripe fruits for the market,' explained Adish as they walked through dense coconut woods, soaking in the sweet, evocative petrichor. It'd be their second and final excursion in Mevalloor, following the Sunday mass at Holy Family Church with the Mathews.

Rows after rows of palm trees, roughly fifteen feet apart, stood tall on all sides for tens of acres. At the end of their sight, they could see large yellowish-green mounds being piled up by a couple of labourers. As they drew near they discovered, to their astonishment, one of the stacks was orange in colour.

'Aargh. First orange bananas and now orange coconuts', Manoj cringed.

'King coconuts,' Adish pointed upwards. Manoj and Rajesh followed his finger to the top of the tree and noticed similar bunches hanging. Meanwhile, an almost naked lean and muscular brown figure in intermittent white had appeared before them. Holding a large harvest knife in one hand and two loops of ropes in another, it grinned as their gaze dropped back to the eye level. Panic-stricken, the two stepped back, letting out a collective gasp.

Mutthur! What happened to him?

'They wish to see how you pick *Thenga*,' said Adish.

Manoj laughed while Rajesh looked at his thumbs, puzzled. '*Thenga*? You are getting a *thenga*,' mocked Manoj.

'Thenga means coconut,' Adish said.

Rajesh's grin grew wide, almost touching his ears.

'Come, I will show you,' Mutthur said and slipped the knife carefully into his mundu. He led them to a tree and glanced up at the sagging fruits. Beside them, some pots dangled too, attached to ropes. 'This one', he declared.

Rajesh slid his hand over the wet trunk and pondered if the morning drizzle had turned it slippery.

'First you wear these loops.' Mutthur flashed the ropes at them. He wore one loop around his ankles and pressed his feet against the base of the tree. Wrapping his arms around the slender girth of the tree next, he coiled the second loop over his wrists.

Taking a deep breath, he slid his arms upwards to their maximum height and moved his feet up along the trunk, holding it firmly. Locking his position, he gave his torso an upward thrust like an agile frog and in one swift motion, climbed up by two feet. He continued his vertical hops and within a minute was sitting atop waving at them.

'That is how Colonel Menon's associates climbed up,' Rajesh gaped at Mutthur, mesmerized. 'It sure looks tempting.'

'He will now check if the fruits have ripened,' Adish said.

Above, Mutthur drew his knife and with its hilt, knocked the base of the coconuts, plastering his ear to the fruit. Satisfied they were ripe enough, he shouted at them to step back.

Adish promptly complied while Manoj and Rajesh grinned, looking upwards. As Mutthur wielded his knife to knock off the bunch in one stroke, Adish realized he had spoken in Malayalam. But it was too late. The coconuts plummeted at them like a missile and in a split second, crashed to the ground right next to them. A few feet away, actually.

'Jesus Christ,' muttered Adish.

Rajesh and Manoj stared at the bunch in horror as blood curdled in their veins. Had those *coconut-sized* coconuts landed on their heads, they would've ascended direct to heaven.

With or without discovering the gravity again.

They stood there dazed, listening to their palpitating hearts while Mutthur lowered one of the dangling pots to his handyman. Putting his knife back into his mundu, he slid down.

'You nearly killed us,' Manoj stuttered, still traumatised.

'I told you to step aside,' Mutthur said with a deadpan face.

'You spoke in Malayalam,' Adish retorted.

'You were the translator,' Mutthur grinned. 'Don't worry. You are my guest. I will make it up to you,' he reached for the pot and peeped into it.

'Adish. What's in the pot?' said Manoj.

'Kallu. I mean toddy. It is basically-,'

'Spare the details,' Manoj interjected Adish. 'Who the hell doesn't know Toddy,' he said, enlivened. He no more regretted staying put at the village, and being almost crushed under the coconuts.

By the river, the four men were perched on a palm trunk that had bent and grown horizontal over the water body; lost in their musings and imbibing the tranquility around them.

'This feels like heaven, man,' Manoj mumbled, laughing in spurts and gulped down one more glass of the sweet palm wine. One full bottle he had downed so far, and loved the unwinding effect toddy had on his mind now. With heightened senses and answers to the mysteries of universe unravelled before him – including the theory of invisibility - one thing that still mystified him was why Rajesh had refused the magical potion.

Agreed, he also feared getting tipsy during the day, but that was because he didn't want Sara to form any wrong impression. And when Adish assured him that fresh toddy wasn't too strong and turned devilish only by the sunset, he'd jumped on the offer.

But this dude! He was still stuck on coconut water.

'You say I don't know what I miss by not eating non-veg? I tell you mister, you do not know wha…what you miss by not having this t…toddy,' Manoj slurred and laughed again.

Rajesh continued to sip his orange coconut, gazing at the river surface that glittered like pearls in the sunlight keeking through the rifts in the retreating rain clouds. The slow current was in stark contrast to the Himalayan rivers; with strong currents and mostly non-navigable in their upper course, except by rafts. By the time they emerged in the lowlands and became traversable, they would be scattered wide, surrounded by barren stretches and hence, completely unsuitable for a romantic boat ride.

But today, he yearned for a romantic trip in this idyllic setting with his love. They'd always met either in malls or restaurants except when she visited his institute and thereupon, his hostel room - the place where they had exchanged their first kiss. Other than that, they had to keep their canoodling restricted to the secluded rows in dark movie theatres or the parking lots where she'd station her car.

A paradisal experience it'd be, he pictured; entwined in each other's arms, traversing through the blissful river, sipping king coconuts. She loved coconut water; it was her daily indulgence and boy, it worked because her skin was baby smooth and flawless. *Oh! How much he wished to be with her and feel the rub of her skin against his body.*

'When does your practice start?' Adish asked Mutthur, two feet away on the same trunk.

'In the coming week,' said Mutthur.

'I'm sure this year would be a turn-around.'

'It has to be. I don't have a choice.'

Adish gave him a quizzical glance.

'Past nine months have transformed my life, Adish,' said Mutthur, gazing at the far end of the river where rowing boats ferried people across the stream. 'I want you to meet someone.'

'Wait. I need to pee,' said Adish, getting up. He rushed to an isolated spot behind a plantain tree nearby.

'Mister Colonel Menon! When there's so much fun at the top...who...who the hell cares to climb down,' Manoj chortled hysterically, his arms raised towards the sky. But before anyone could share his merriment, he disappeared with a cry. A moment later, the two men remaining on the trunk heard a splash.

Startled, Adish swung his neck, still busy taking a leak and looked at Mutthur while Rajesh had his eyes riveted on the ripples in the water, clutching to the tree in horror. He couldn't swim. What should he do?

He heard one more splatter. Mutthur was gone too.

Seconds passed like hours as Rajesh prayed and waited impatiently for them to rise to the surface. Mutthur emerged soon, grabbing a hapless Manoj by his collar who clung to him with all his might. Without zipping his fly, Adish too, went into the river to lend his hand. Together, Mutthur and Adish, carried Manoj ashore while Rajesh climbed down the tree and reached the rescue spot.

Looking pale with fright, Manoj huffed and puffed. His lips quivered, but no words came out. His spectacles were gone too, sunk to the riverbed. Suddenly, he began to weep that soon grew into a howling.

'I could've died, man. I could've died. It was so deep and cold and dark,' Manoj stuttered and shivered. He stopped wailing, and his eyes grew wide, 'And then I saw a hand. It pulled me out and showed me the light.' He paused and surveyed the three faces around him, then tilted his head up, towards the sky, 'I'm sorry *Bajrang Bali.* Thank you for saving me.'

'Oh Jesus, you are so kind. Thank you for blessing him,' Adish closed his eyes and prayed as well.

A smile broke across Rajesh's face, in relief that Manoj had chosen the ten-feet deep calm shallows of Muvattupuzha, and not the fiery rapids of the Ganges.

'Are you all right?' Mutthur said.

'Yes, I am,' Manoj hugged Mutthur. 'All because of you "my friend in need friend indeed" friend.'

It drizzled once again, both from the heavens and as well as his tear ducts.

DigiSys

****

DigiSys was founded as Digital Computer Systems (DCS) in 1979, the same year Macintosh project was launched. It was an age when organizations across the globe were coming under the promising grip of efficient Electronic Data Management Systems (EDMS). As a result, the immense physical data that existed in the form of handwritten papers needed to be digitised for a smooth transition.

A fresh postgraduate from MIT while experimenting on the digitisation of such documents sensed an opportunity and established a small outsourcing firm out of his one-room apartment in Boston. Creating a unique proposal based on Relational Data Management System (RDMS), he soon approached key financial institutions in the US. Within a week he had converted one of them into his first client. Hailing from Tamilnadu's Kongu Nadu region, the medieval seat of Pillai aristocrats, Gooty Sunder Pillai was on course to create history.

Sunder Pillai successfully ran and expanded DCS for half a decade, before extending focus towards India when in mid-eighties, the erstwhile Prime Minister of India promised to bring an IT revolution. Pillai sought his brother, T. Ramaswamy Pillai who quit TCSL, and began their operations from a new company office on the outskirts of Pune. They straightaway ventured into selling mini-computers and attached services. Foreseeing an enormous potential in software consulting, almost prophetic, Sunder Pillai hired top engineers to form their IT division – DigiSys.

For next decade and a half, DigiSys made a steady progress. However, it lacked aggression. Perhaps, for want of a top manager like Manoj. As a result their top dogs quit, either to make hay of better opportunities or to found their own start-ups, unwittingly kick-starting a boom that changed the whole IT map of the world. When mankind entered the twenty-first century, DigiSys weren't even among top three Indian IT companies.

Though in past five years the organization opted to be aggressive and took giant leaps. It soon boasted of more than one lakh employees worldwide, grabbing eyeballs from across the globe. Speculations of a merger and acquisition ran rife, stonewalled on every occasion by Sunder Pillai. However, post his retirement in the second quarter of 2005, the talks turned reality. The French giant CapVirgo - one of the world's largest corporations, had acquired DigiSys in a whopping $ 4.5 billion deal.

For undergraduates like us who'd been recruited by DCS in past twelve months, it came as a shot in the arm. We were now the envy of the engineers across the country. This year, I gathered, CapVirgo-DigiSys was going to recruit the IITians.

Ah, IITians as my junior associates. Could you imagine!

Despite being Tamil, Sunder Pillai had always been my idol, but now I was falling in love with his eminent French connection as well.

Signed: Adish Mathew

The near-drowning incident brought one mutation in Bansal – a fast on a Tuesday. Besides waking up at six and taking a morning bath, lighting *agarbatti* and reading *Hanuman Chalisa*. I was sceptical, though, that he'd complete the abstention considering how big a glutton he was. But to my bemusement, the bugger had pulled it through. Well, he had astounded me on so many occasions now that I was certain more was in the offing.

I guess, I was beginning to admire this fellow.

'What session is this?' Manjot interrupted my thoughts.

'Some software development,' I said.

With an 'hmm' he dug back into his phone.

I inspected the other faces in my class. Most of them were South Indians. Actually, the entire lot of trainees consisted of people predominantly from the south of Vidhyanchal. Since, our batches had equal representations of computer-based and non-computer engineering streams, it meant the few North Indian non-C.S. guys were scattered equally into the sea of South Indians. Our batch had six. Not that I had any issue with Southies. But on many occasions, I found their over-competitive attitude quite suffocating. Curiously enough, the remaining five Northies seemed more relaxed than I.

Anyways, the second week of the CLP hadn't proved to be any different from the first. Just, ten minutes ago I was all at sea, struggling with the confusing programming loops. I had used a 'do-while' loop but as per Shelja, I should've used 'if and else'. I failed to comprehend why.

Manoj got lucky, though. He had Adish, the C++ champion with him. Together, they'd been selected as the Business and the Technical skill leaders of their class, owing to their performance in the first week. So buoyed was Manoj by the achievement that he had freed his GMAT and GRE books from the confines of his luggage and decided to embark upon his CAT preparation journey.

For me, it was neither here nor there. The tech leader was a Tamilian whose name I couldn't pronounce. Not that I ever wished to. I was fine conversing with Manjot Singh Bhullar, the Business Skills head of our class. For he possessed one super quality; he had no delusions. Unlike most of our Northies - the epitome of deluded showoffs.

Yesterday only, when we, the wretched non-IT souls discussed our engineering disciplines, he'd been blunt and straightforward. 'Guys, we all are going to write stupid codes and not design a building or an instrument or as a matter of fact, a car. Codes! Do you get it?' he had said, with a finger quote. Though, it had brought a chuckle in us. No, not our depressing debate but his intermittent Punjabi locutions dipped in thick Amritsari accent. I loved the Surd.

Bansal liked him too but for more orthodox reasons:

* *Surd had promised him that he'd find a Punjabi Dhaba and*
* *Gurleen - the gorgeous female and Surd's girlfriend who was also a part of the CLP.*

As expected, our tharki had taken a fancy to her.

People like Surd were so fortunate. At peace with the eventualities of their lives. And why shouldn't he be? He was a guitarist, had a rock band and best, had his girlfriend's company 24x7.

I couldn't fathom why but I felt insanely ethnocentric today, comparing myself to the Northies and Southies alike, yet it was always me who emerged the loser. Or perhaps, I felt unnecessarily agitated because I'd been away from *her*. God, *she* made me feel like a hero. *Her* hero.

'*My name is Orindom Bhottawcharjee, and I'd be condocting your software developement session*,' a voice boomed from the front in a thick Bengali accent, rattling my reverie.

'DigiSys has Bongs?' Manjot spoke in his typical accent and turned towards me. 'So, by Col Menon's Godavari rule, it makes us seven non South Indians in this room now. Quite optimistic.'

I didn't care for Col. Menon's rule. For my obnoxious brain, needing an urgent distraction, he was a Easterner.

'*Before whee get deep into the sobject, we shall first deciphor bharious cycles of software developement*,' Arindam who quite resembled his namesake 'management guru' with his long ponytail hair, picked up the marker and drew a flow chart while I girded myself for a barrage of Bengali and Punjabi intonations in a sea of suffusing Southie twangs.

My racialist day was made.

Signed: Rajesh Pandey

Our choices were simple - German, French or Japanese as these regions had most of our clients and business centres besides the usual English countries. We had to choose one.

I had already ruled out Japanese. Too difficult. And between German and French, I was more inclined towards German. Adish however, hankered after French. He was fascinated by the French lifestyle and French movies and wanted to learn the language, he told me. I wondered what he fancied in French films unless of course he watched them through my eyes and as far as their lifestyle was concerned, his food etiquettes could not be farther from the French.

'If you also enroll for French, we'll be able to practice between ourselves. Imagine how proficient we shall be, in two months bonzor,' said Adish.

'Bonzor? What's Bonzor?' I asked, puzzled.

'See. That's French for 'mister'. Had you known the language, Bonzor would sound familiar,' Adish mocked me.

'It's Bonzhwoh Mehsyur Tsemenick,' Mady's voice echoed somewhere in my mind.

Mady or Mahaaditya Purnendra Birje was my engineering classmate, friend and the weirdest name in the Institute. Arghh! His mere thought depressed me. Fucker was a dayski i.e. a day scholar and yet, managed a BLACKI – the onc with all the six IIM calls. Whereas I got to rot in IT. He was a stud, though. *Saala!* And he spoke French and had a French girlfriend too.

'Bansal, it is *Bonzhwoh Mehsyur Tsemenick,*' Mady said correcting me. I read the line again, 'Bonjour Monsieur Zemenick'.

Bonjour, in Adish's Southie accent, had become the Bengali version of '*banjar*' or barren. I looked at Adish and saw my redemption right in front of me. *Watcha saying that day, pal? Korrhikode, eh?*

'It's *bonzhwoh,*' I pronounced it for Adish. 'And it is a greeting like a hello and not a translation for 'Mister'. We use *mehsyur* for that,' I explained, adding the word "Monsieur". Adish gawked at me in awe. His lips moved to repeat *Monsieur.*

'Mysore, you are a stud bro,' he snickered. Mysore would do. At least it wasn't Chennai. Nevertheless, it was settled that we were opting for French. French porn would make more sense, it had struck me in time.

'I wish I had a Laptop to access my French videos,' I thought aloud.

'You have French videos? They could be a great learning tool. You think I should ask my father for his Laptop? He is leaving for Oman for two weeks,' said Adish.

'Can you do it?' I held his arms, yet trying to hide my own excitement. Mady, you rock buddy.

'I think so. Let me try.'

Happy, elated and excited with the sea of opportunities that lay before us, we next assembled in a huge hall with two long tables at the centre. On one table were arranged many glasses all-distinct. While on the other small ceramic dishes were placed, accompanied by a set of spoon, knife and fork along with a bowl.

A five-course meal with dining etiquette awaited us.

'I love continental food,' Adish remarked.

'Of course, you do,' I said, imagining him eating curd rice mixed in Ratatouille with bare hands.

'Welcome associates. I'm Namrata and today we learn the art of fine dining,' a graceful sari-clad lady made her presence felt. Seemingly in the late thirties, she had straight, cropped hair, fair complexion, a medium stature and a confident gait.

Must be a North Indian, or else she would be *Namratha.*

'Let us begin with the drinks,' she motioned at us and minced towards the table with the glasses. We followed too and made a huddle around her. 'You all know the two wine types, don't you?' she said. Each of us nodded, flashing a broad smile. *Which one opens today? Red or White?* We gaped as she picked one glass. 'Which one is this for? Could anybody tell us?'

I couldn't at least. Being an engineer, the only liquor I had ever consumed, was either beer or Old Monk Rum. Champagnes, Wines were only fantasies that I had read about or seen on TV. Yeah, during the IIM treats I did try cocktails. But then, you don't care for serving glasses when you gain access to a bar during happy hours and someone else is footing the bill.

Santhosh Pandit Venkat raised his hand. Sucker.

'Red wine,' he said. Namrata smiled and picked another glass. Similar but slightly bigger and tapered at the bottom. 'And this one?' she asked, keeping it beside the first.

'For white,' Venkat was at it again. Adish had rightly named him *Santhosh Pandit*, a Malayali slang for an idiot. Huh! Loser preferred the girly stuff. I doubted if he'd ever wetted his whistle with Rum that could be slugged in steel or plastic tumblers or in the worst case, poured into soft drink bottles - the way we indulged mostly.

Namrata smiled and exchanged the positions of the two glasses. 'It is a that mistake you cannot afford to make any more. You're with a French major now.'

Venkat was embarrassed. Uums giggled, and Adish's chest swelled at the mere mention of the 'F' word while I smacked my lips and waited for the sound of the cork popping out of a wine bottle. *Wines had corks, right?*

'Let us move on to the food etiquette now,' she announced and transferred to the next table where a small, cold cutlet and a soup bowl tittered at us.

Signed: Manoj Bansal

'What is he doing exactly?' Rajesh asked Manoj, confused as they sat around me in the canteen for Friday dinner.

Manoj hadn't noticed it earlier; Adish was engaged in a battle with a Malabari chicken piece, trying to eat it using his knife and fork. He had stained his entire plate and had splattered rice onto my plywood surface too.

Manoj wasn't sure if laughing would be a good idea. 'He learned how to dine today,' he winked.

'Dine? This is heights yaar. Here, I'm unable to code a basic program which is a pre-requisite to stay in this company and now of all the things, we have to learn how to dine as well?' Rajesh threw up his arms, totally flustered.

'When in France, you have to behave correctly,' said Adish, calm and composed like a Zen monk. For a moment, both Rajesh and Manoj suspected if he had already booked his tickets.

'Dude, you believe this shit?' Rajesh asked in utter disbelief.

Adish ignored and continued his mission. His crowning glory soon arrived as he separated some flesh out of the bone. Like a crane he gobbled it without a chew and turned to them, wearing a winner's smile.

'So what's your weekend plan?' he asked, holding the fork and knife upwards like a pro.

'No idea. Why don't you suggest something?' Rajesh said while Manoj concentrated on my plate.

'You can go to Kovalam beach or-.'

'You means?' Rajesh cut him short, and his eyes widened. 'You're coming along, right? You had promised,' he reminded Adish. Manoj nodded in agreement.

'I'm going home for the weekend,' he said, unexpectedly putting down his knife and fork aside and grabbed the battered chicken piece into his hand.

Enough practice for the day, he had decided.

'We'll go to Kovalam,' Rajesh decided too.

Over his sleeping body, Manoj decided three.

Signed: The Canteen Table

Adish Mathew's

The Shadow of The Past

****

'These people shall never understand Progress,' said my father, peering at the narrow roads of Kochi. Today, we were affected by a few jams due to the agitations of Labour Union while en route to Cochin International Airport for his outbound flight to Oman.

For his rubber business, my father regularly flew to the Gulf, especially Oman where one of his partners resided and looked after the operations. But for past four years, he had restricted his travelling, almost grounding himself. Its genesis lay in me.

Four years ago I had been a let-down, securing an abysmal rank in AIEEE. Hence, despite my above average +2 percentages, admission into a decent engineering college had remained a pipe dream. Facing a prospect to be admitted to an obscure institute, I had made up my mind to rather drop a year on my father's behest and join IIT-JEE coaching classes.

But then, life doesn't unfold the way you plan it. Few things happened with me that threatened to bring shame, not just to my family but our whole community.

My mother deplored the situation, blaming it on my father's perpetual absence from the house. Consequently, he committed to spending more time in India and monitoring me strictly. My future didn't alter, though. The way I had been sent to a boarding school in Kodaikanal for my +2, I was sent to Bangalore this time; to a newly-founded institute. However, my father did ensure me a Computer Engineering berth under the 'management quota'.

For four years, I put in an unremitting slog to erase my past and make my father proud. The gamble paid off when I landed a job in DigiSys and bagged one of the most lucrative IT packages in the country on offer; a deal he deemed ideal for his son.

'But I appreciate, how DigiSys is teaching you to gain control of your life, and I'm glad you're working towards it,' he said. His rare smile promptly earned my obedient nod.

'Dad, I was wondering,' I said, 'if I get a laptop, I could utilize my time at the hostel. Most of the tutorials available in the library are either in CD or DVD form.'

'Good, you reminded me. I was thinking the same,' he said. I grinned in my heart, expecting a brand new laptop. 'Do one thing. I'm not using my old laptop. Take it. I'll bring a new one from Oman for myself,' he added before I could list down my specifications.

'Those North Indians, what are their names?' he asked abruptly.

'Rajesh and Manoj.'

'Yes! Be careful of them.'

'Careful? Why? I mean what's wrong?' I was perplexed.

'Oh, don't take otherwise, Adish. You are a professional now. You should make colleagues and not friends. In any case, three months later you will be posted in Bangalore and they will be back to...some place up north,' he asserted.

Lord, I detested having a conversation with him. His own set of opinionated assertions always turned it into an ordeal for me. Always.

'But I don't intend to go to Bangalore.'

'Don't be stupid. Bangalore is the IT destination. And you have so many of our Malayali people there. Where else if not there?'

'I don't know.'

'I know,' he raised his voice and peered at me as if trying to read and wipe every trace of nonconformity from my face. 'You have wasted enough time on friendships. By the grace of Lord Jesus, you're on the right track now. Stay put.'

I nodded and gazed outside. I was still undecided on visiting Fort Kochi after dropping him off. Mutthur would be there waiting for me with 'someone' he hadn't revealed who. Quite odd. He had never kept anything from me before.

Our friendship went back as far as I could remember. Whenever I visited Grandpa, I'd meet him too. We'd run around the paddy fields throughout the day; the coconut water being the secret of our energy. Mutthur even tried, in vain, to teach me how to climb palm trees. Though my best memory was of the small boat, we'd row in Muvattupuzha. He sculled it with fiery passion, bearing the hallmark of his father - the onlookers would often reminisce.

As we grew up, our boats grew too. Toddy replaced coconut water while disparate futures beckoned us. But before our fate could seize us in its claws, the day came when we rode the big boat together. Our Maruthi Vallam. It was four years ago:

I had been at my Grandpa's house, still overcoming the trauma of my engineering entrance results. I needed to spend some quiet time before I began my IIT coaching. One of those evenings, Mutthur took me to meet Antony, our village boat captain. Our boat singer, Hashimudeen had left the shores, seeking riches in the Gulf. And without him, they couldn't hope to participate in the upcoming vallamkali season.

'This is your hour - join the big league, my friend,' Mutthur said. 'Be our Bhagavatar. The deity needs you.'

I felt nervous and unsure. But Antony turned out to be the warmest soul I had ever met; his burly looks that intimidated me earlier, now seemed reassuring. He had heard me performing in the Church choirs and believed I could do it. He was in love with my voice, he even joked. True it was, though. So comforting and encouraging he'd been that within a week, I rode the grand boat under his command, singing and motivating our crew in the waters of Muvattupuzha.

The year had been so good. Until the day when the wheel of misfortune rolled over me. Antony had gone to the sea and never returned. Soon, I lost everything else too.

'I'll be back in two weeks. Be careful with the laptop and God bless you,' my father said as our Innova halted in front of the new international departure gate. Without adding another word, he clutched his luggage, got off the car and walked in while I lolled onto the back seat, relieved at last.

'Home, sir?' the driver asked, pulling away.

'Fort Kochi.'

1341 A.D. was a watershed year in the annals of Kerala, literally.

While the great Periyar flood obliterated the historic port of Muziris from the map of Malabar Coast, it also left a newly formed natural harbour behind; at Kochi, a fishing village then. So instinctively, when Chinese arrived here, the first thing they did was to install Chinese fishing nets all over the region that made it resemble China. Henceforth the name, 'Co-chin', meaning 'like China' stuck with the traders from Europe, Arab and China who later visited the land. The flood also brought in from Muziris to Cochin, its Cochin Jews, who settled in the area called Fort Kochi.

Manoj and Rajesh must visit this place, I reckoned ambling along the Synagogue lane in the Jewish town. Mutthur was at the folk theatre, watching Mohiniyattam with a friend. Having an hour to kill before the show wrapped up, I decided to visit Jacob in the meantime. Jacob Moses - my art teacher in school, was amongst the few elderly Jews who still resided in what at best, could be described as a relic of Indian Jewish kibbutz.

Well, Jewish colony used to be a bumbling commune, Jacob often reminisced. But now, it had reduced to a mere tourist spot; a narrow stretch of a street market with its shops mostly selling antiques and souvenirs from Kerala's history. One could see

Portuguese furniture, Victorian dresses, clock imitations of the Synagogue, scale models of old European ships and Chundans - the serpent boats alongside famous Kathakali masks that hung from the shop windows. And Jacob owned the largest of such shops. Started by his father in 1952, it was a museum in itself.

I peeped inside and noticed half a dozen tourists, attentively listening to their guide.

'And that, my dear friends, is a hundred-year-old object *de virtu* straight from the glorious past of Kerala,' the guide spoke in well-polished English. He stood beside a regal boat, I hadn't seen before. A new addition!

Jacob's eccentric and obsessive interest in art and history had expanded his collection to enviable levels in the neighbourhood. Particularly, after he quit his job as a professor of history at the prestigious Cochin University and joined Knanya Convent high school; to teach children his favourite subjects. And the first time he had interacted with us, I had developed an instant liking to the old man. It was Jacob indeed, who had exposed me to the history and myths of Kerala.

'Now you will hear more about the boat from its owner Mr Jacob, one of the few remaining Jews in India,' said the guide, giving way to Jacob who sauntered out like a mysterious national treasure.

The visitors shifted their glance from the boat to Jacob, wondering which one was the bigger surprise - seeing a live boat whose likes they had seen on TV or witnessing an old living Jew with a trademark black Jewish cap.

'Odi-vallams played a crucial part during the wars in ancient Kerala. These were used for speedy transportation of manpower through the backwaters,' Jacob began in a gentle, convincing tone. 'Being the fastest boats ever designed, soon after the war period ended, Odi-vallams became the most potent carriers of the famous Kumarakom pirates. This one, in front of you is a real pirate boat, made in 1905 by a great Asari,' he said, earning 'oohs' and 'aahs' from the visitors. They were hooked.

I could sense that the ones, who had watched the Pirates of the Caribbean, had already visualized their Kumarakom version of Captain Jack Sparrow; a mundu-clad toddy drinker, flashing his sword at the swarming army of Kalariyapattu warriors while his Jack-tars pushed the vallam through backwaters.

'It pulled off at least fifty piracies between 1905 and 1917. And nary a time was it caught. But one day, an old Dhoti-clad fellow turned up and all the pirates became Satyagrahis, forsaking their beloved for nonviolent and peaceful usages like – sports,' said Jacob, with utter disdain.

The audience sighed at the anti-climax. Although it dealt with good winning over evil, I could bet my life that the visitors would've taken more delight if he had added a decade more of piracy; and a couple of encounters with British in which the pirates could've looted, killed a few whites and become martyrs later. That would've been a perfect story. But Jacob, it seemed, was in no mood to offer them the pleasure.

'It set about to conquer the traditional boat races and won not less than twenty trophies till 1962 when it won its biggest prize and retired,' Jacob concluded with a grin.

'What is the cost of this boat?' one visitor asked.

'Forty Lakhs,' said Jacob.

Realizing they were late for the evening prayers at Santa Cruz Basilica, the visitors feigned disappointment and followed their guide to exit the shop one by one.

'Adish Mathew, have you lost your way, my child?' Jacob leapt at me as soon as he saw me peeking from the shop entrance and hugged tightly.

'I am here to meet you,' I said.

'Are you?' Jacob laughed, 'I'm glad you came by. God bless. Come, come inside.'

He led me to his small cabin where we seated ourselves,

overlooking the entire shop. 'It had been a long time,' he laughed again. He hadn't changed a bit except for few more wrinkles on his bespectacled face that still exuded his quaint charm.

Jacob was not white like Europeans. Rather, he belonged to a community of Malabari Jews, which had a darker complexion and features like the Yemenites. European Jews termed them as 'Black Jews' during the sixteenth century; while keeping the title 'White Jews' for themselves.

'How are you?' I asked

'What do you think?' He laughed louder, 'Doesn't matter. What matters is how you are, my young boy.'

'I've completed my engineering.'

'Oh, wonderful.'

'Yes. And I've joined a company called DigiSys.'

'Ah didn't you try for those Tatas?'

'They didn't come for the placements.'

'Ah, what a shame! But you must try. Those Parsis are excellent folks and even better employers I've heard. Though the best ones are the Jews, mind you. Unfortunately, they have all sailed away,' he winked and chortled at his own joke.

I could sense his underlying pain. After the independent nation of Israel was established, the Jews who had arrived and put their roots down in Kerala in as early as sixth century B.C. had gradually abandoned the town and had migrated - to Israel, UK and US. His own sons, two of them, resided in Birmingham while his only daughter was married to a businessman in Tel Aviv. But Jacob had stayed here. Alone with his shop.

'When did you acquire this Odi-vallam?' I asked curiously.

'The one outside? Six months ago from Purakkad. Those idiots were dying to dismantle it, said it wasn't in use for twenty years,' he revealed. Purakkad was the neighbouring village of Mevalloor.

'You saved it,' I smiled. 'Looks pretty solid.'

'You bet. Your generation doesn't recognise that everything is not for use. Some things are memories, and pride. They must be preserved,' said Jacob. 'I am happy they sold it. I'd been looking for it for years,' he paused. His gaze darted around to ensure no one was at a hearing distance. Satisfied, he turned to me and bent closer.

'I closed it for two lakhs,' he chuckled.

''Two!' I almost shouted. 'And you are selling it for forty?'

'I am not selling it.'

'You are not?' I was confused.

A wide grin spread over his lips. 'Let me show you something.'

He led me back to the spot where the boat rested.

'See, what is written there,' he pointed at a carving beneath the front or perhaps, the rear hood of the boat.

'Jacob and Sara, 1962', I read, astonished.

'Memories, my boy and you don't sell memories,' he smiled and began an incredible story.

'I'm sorry for being late,' Mutthur apologized as soon as we met outside the folk theatre. A girl accompanied him. A pretty girl, in fact, dressed in a sari. Quite a surprise. A pleasant one, though.

'Stop being formal because you're with a girl,' I mocked. He looked embarrassed while the girl blushed.

'Actually, the show ended late,' the girl spoke.

She had a sweet and courteous ring to her voice.

'Adish, she is Kala and Kala, he is Adish,' Mutthur finally remembered to introduce us.

'Good to see you.' Kala said to me. 'I've heard a lot from Mutthur.'

'I see. But how come I am yet to hear a single word about you? I said in a tone of mock anger.

'I should've told you earlier,' he said apologetically. I knew he felt guilty. In their eyes, I could discern a longing for each other. I had no doubt that they were deeply in love and honestly, I couldn't be happier for Mutthur.

With a warm, congratulatory hug, I dismissed all his fears.

'So what brings you here?'

'The Shiva temple isn't exactly a romantic place,' Mutthur winked. Kala blushed again. 'I am here for the blessings.'

So God had chosen today for all my emotional upheavals.

'Would you join us?' Mutthur asked. I nodded.

'Where are we going?' asked Kala.

'To meet Antony,' I said. Her expressions told me she knew him.

We walked till the end of the harbour through the small red sand beach and climbed the large rocks that formed a zigzag path along the periphery of the shore. As waves struck against the rocks beneath while we trudged on the stony path above, he shared his tale of love with me.

'It was during the last year's boat race when I first saw her in the Kumaramangalam temple. She had accompanied her father, Medavoor Nair and their village boat team.'

'Medavoor Nair?' I gawked at Mutthur. He shrugged.

Medavoor Nair was no ordinary man. Son of the most famous Thachan of Kottayam, he was the legendary captain of Perimar village and incidentally, the arch rival of Mutthur's father when he led Mevalloor's team.

'Is he aware?' I asked. He nodded.

'He has said in clear terms that he won't agree to our marriage if we lose to their team this year,' Mutthur revealed.

'It's an open challenge. Couldn't she convince her team to finish the race behind yours?' I suggested jokingly.

'Not possible. Their captain, Gopalan, covets her too. So now, it is kind of a *Swayamvara*,' he said, smiling at Kala who nudged to shut him up.

'Ayyo, the story has a villain too. Mind blowing blockbuster,' I said as we all laughed. Inside, we knew it was quite a humourless and disconcerting situation. I had known Gopalan. His very name discomfited my soul.

'That's where Antony rests,' Mutthur pointed to a spot some distance away into the sea.

A wave of mixed emotions swept over me, reminding me of the painful memories as I stood at the rocky edge, gazing into the sea towards the same spot.

It was where Antony had met an unexpected end four years ago when his overloaded trawler had capsized during a fishing expedition.

I inched ahead, hoping Mutthur and Kala wouldn't notice the tears that had welled up in my eyes. We stayed there for some time, sitting on the rocks in quiet. While Kala and I gazed at the dark clouds gathering overhead, throwing pebbles into the sea, Mutthur scribbled on the gray rock he sat over.

'Would you join them for the practice?' Kala asked me.

'I can't. We have presentations due next week. I have to work with Manoj. Manoj is the guy whom Mutthur saved from drowning by the way.'

'You saved someone from drowning?' she turned to Mutthur with a 'you haven't told me' expression.

'I forgot,' he said.

'Your man is a hero,' I whispered to her and winked. Kala blushed at the compliment. 'And they haven't forgotten, unlike you. They rave about you all the time.' I said to Mutthur.

'Is it so? Why don't you bring them to Mevalloor again? I am sure they'll take a shine to the boat race and cherish a trip down the river.'

'I don't know, but they do wish to revisit the place. I'll ask,' I said, not committing on behalf of Rajesh and Manoj.

'Why are you scratching on the rock?' Kala rose and walked up to Mutthur who stepped aside to reveal an inscription. Her eyes gleamed as she read, Mutthur and Kala, 2007. 'I thought you had forgotten me,' she said.

'What?' Mutthur let out a hearty laugh, 'How can I ever?'

While they hugged, I looked once more into the deep sea. All love stories were not supposed to have a happy ending. I prayed that Mutthur and Kala's had one, in 2007.

Just like Jacob and Sara's. In 1962.

Manoj Bansal's

Painful Week

****

This Sunday proved to be quite rewarding. Unlike the previous one. So much that I felt a strong urge to write an essay, like we did in our primary school:

A visit to Kovalam beach with my batch mates presented me an ample opportunity to be around Uums as long as I wished to. Including our hour-long playful beach sessions. Surprisingly, she also offered me an unwavering attention throughout the evening. Much to the dismay of Venkat, who as per my sources, was so traumatised that he turned to food for solace and overate; only to end up with an upset stomach.

Poor chap. He didn't realize it wasn't the food but my private photo op with Uums atop the Lighthouse that he couldn't digest. Well, I felt both empathy and sympathy for that fool. I hoped he had learned his lesson.

Never ever mess with a Meerutiya.

The evening arrived riding on a wave of overwhelming emotions as I spoke to my parents after a week.

'Look, Sarita. In today's age when other kids are forgoing their customs, traditions and religion, our son is upholding them all,' my father sounded exhilarated on hearing I had observed a fast on Tuesday. Teary eyed, I doubted if Mishraji's son had made his father proud in the similar manner.

'Bajrang Bali shall definitely reward you with the fruit of your devotion soon,' my mother added. She wouldn't have, had she known the prophecy would come true in less than two hours. Adish, my bro, finally showed up with a shiny laptop.

It was the best Sunday of my life. If such weekends were the upshots of dull, boring weekdays, I'd never mind them at all.

Essay over. New week rolls in. DigiSys vows to make a hash of not just our days but our nights too, third week onwards. Reality bites!

'What is 'Systems Thinking'?' Adish squinted, as he read the heading on the white-board, feeling hopeful.

'Must be some crap related to computer systems,' I said.

It was one of the three short courses that had bludgeoned our schedule – 'Unix' and 'Programming Skills' being the other two. I had braved one 'Unix' session along with its 'simple' assignment, but it had proved no less than a monstrous dragon, straight out of the Chinese mythology that had devoured an entire night.

Tonight didn't promise any respite either.

Adish on the other hand seemed thrilled, or it wouldn't be wrong to say, aroused. So impassioned was he in the matters of computers that I was sure he could've had an orgasm without even turning them on.

Meanwhile, hopelessness swamped my mind as I prepared for the next assault of the IT Orcs, on an empty stomach. Damn Tuesday! However, the air of desolation vanished as soon as the subject line, "How to be a good consultant" appeared on the board in bold letters.

'Be it compilation errors, functional specifications, delivery issues, a sudden bug or merely a communication gap between you and the client,' the faculty said, underlining the situations we could face while working on real industry projects. 'Every snag demands you to have a thorough knowledge of your system.'

'I thought he would discuss Operating Systems,' Adish yawned.

'Do you wish to keep fixing windows from a pirated CD, forever?' I mocked him and ignored his groans for the rest of the session.

'CPC? What's CPC?' I asked a beaming Pandey as he joined us in the library and told us about his new discovery, CPC.

'Copy, paste and call,' Adish said.

'You know CPC?' asked Pandey, puzzled.

'You didn't?' Adish looked puzzled. I was puzzled ditto, having no idea what these guys discussed. Though, it was hard to tell who was the most puzzled amongst us.

'Fucker, I'd been struggling with coding for so long and you never told me,' Pandey scowled at Adish, agitated.

Hmmm, it had to be something imperative.

'How would *I* know that *you* didn't know? You should've asked,' Adish was timid in his defence. All his aggression was reserved for me, I guess.

'I guess I'm the only one here who understands the meaning of true friendship,' Pandey loured at us.

Sucker. I knew why he looped me in. I had said no to another visit to Mevalloor. Come on guys, Uums had propounded a trip to Ponmudi on Saturday, I yelped without a sound.

'And I'm the only one who can't decipher what you guys are squabbling about,' I reposted.

Adish shrugged. 'Basically, you don't need to create anything from scratch. All elementary problems have been decoded and coded already and put into the library in the form of functions. You can just copy, paste, add your lines or call them directly. CPC. That's how easy it is,' he explained.

'Easy! Whoa, and fucker you're telling us now when half of our brain cells are defunct, coding non-sense after non-sense?' I was furious, unfazed by his monk-like calm as well as by the Library's decorum. 'You want to hit him? Count me in,' I said to Pandey.

'Exactly,' said Pandey.

Rising from our seats, we were on the brink of thrashing the traitor when his saviour wafted past smiling at us or rather

Pandey, instantly putting a halt on his aggression. True to the rumours these Mallus did have some unity, man.

'That's Shelja, our C++ faculty, right?' I said. 'Why did she smile at you?' I asked Rajesh.

'She didn't smile. She *acknowledged* my smile.'

'When did you smile, fucker? And why?' Now, I was really, really pissed at both of them.

'She is the one who gave me CPC,' said Rajesh, as if CPC was some mouth-to-mouth resuscitation or so I pictured.

'Details, Pandey. Details,' I demanded, banging my fist on the table. I wanted an answer.

'Okay. I was stressed and frustrated, unable to compile my program when she came and peeped into my desktop,' Pandey began his story.

I imagined the missing details: Shelja bending down over his shoulder, her fragrance blended with her body's infrared radiations palpitating Pandey's heart. She was extraordinarily hot to resist, and the only reason I'd never ogle her much in the lab was Uums occupying my adjacent seat.

'She asked if I tried the library,' Pandey continued while I pictured them making out behind the shaking bookshelves, books falling all over them. 'Of course, I didn't know that either, so she explained me the concept of library too.'

'You didn't even know library?' asked Adish.

'Shut up fucker. We will test your programming skills in the room tonight. Let him finish the story,' I said impatiently.

'She then reviewed my pseudo-code and guess what, she found it perfect,' he squealed. Meanwhile, in the fantasyland, her chin touched his head. She found it perfect. Really?

'What did she find perfect?' I asked. Did I miss something?

'Don't tell me that you don't know what a pseudo-code is,' Adish interjected again, turning to me.

'I swear I'll break your head if you utter another word, dumbass.' Adish had pushed it too far.

'Well, she sat beside me and opened few files. Then she added some data, called few programs and, it was done. Compiled for the first time,' Pandey whooped. 'She then shared with me, the mantra to succeed in IT. CPC.'

'She must have sat quite close to you,' I said. Both of them stared at me.

'*Bhenchod*, such a tharki ass you are,' Pandey said.

'Satyromaniac ass,' Adish translated, and before I could turn and lay my hands on him, he had vanished.

The waterfall model of Software Development Cycle had transformed into a flooded river of programming that threatened to drown us all. But courtesy Rajesh Pandey, we had attained the mantra to stay afloat. Adish had also realized his fault and offered his penance in the form of an extended personal tuition on 'how to code professionally'.

For the first time, I couldn't help but thank my stars for having Adish and not Pandey in my batch. Imagine the unmitigated disaster: Pandey and me on adjacent systems, unable to figure whether Shelja had any flaw or the Compiler had any trace of beauty.

'Do you think it is going to work?' asked Pandey. He had finished his day's last chore - his pillow talk over the phone. I too had had - my beauty regimen.

'It requires time and patience,' I said, crawling into my bed. A month had passed and I was yet to see the results of this fairness cream. But I knew patience was paramount. It was an undoing of twenty-three years, after all. And I trusted Shahrukh. 'I think it will get better.'

'Better? It is getting worse, man,' said Pandey.

Worse! Fuckshit, now this was unexpected. I rushed to the mirror and scanned my face. He was right. I was shattered. 'All because we are here.'

'That is what,' he banged his fist against the pillow, 'and we are here for two more months, fuck.' God, he cared so much for me. I was shit scared now. No, not because Pandey cared but because, I had considered fairness cream as my last resort.

'What should I do?' I asked. 'Should I stop using this cream altogether?'

'Cream? Why should you stop?'

'Because you said it's getting worse.'

'What's the link between my relationship and your fairness cream, *bhenchod*?' he said, irritated. 'Wait! You think I was commenting on your stupid cream?' Pandey broke into laughter.

Couldn't he be specific? He had this annoying habit of placing ambiguous *objects* in his speech. 'It's easier for you because you have a girlfriend,' I said, wishing I were someplace else.

His laughter grew louder. 'You sound like Adish,' he said.

Like Adish! Now, I was depressed.

'Sorry, I didn't mean to ruffle you. But this distance is getting on my nerves. I had never tried so hard before,' Pandey said, in a worried tone.

Though he meant physical distance, I had noticed the growing emotional distance between them too. To make matters worse, they were barely conversing. Either she'd be busy or he'd be caught up in our hectic schedule.

'But why are you making so much effort?' I asked

'Who else will?' he said, throwing up his hands. 'Boss, if you're seriously serious about having a girlfriend, then you ought to learn this by heart. It's you who has to make all the effort. It's the *lule*.'

'Lule?'

'Sorry, I meant rule. Just her baby talk.'

'Baby talk? Lule?' I couldn't hold my laughter. Pandey turned pink with embarrassment. 'Ok, *rule*. So, they don't participate?' I asked. He ruminated over my question or rather, my proposition for a while.

'Well, they do. I mean two people are together only when they both itch to be together, right?' he tried to explain.

'And how would you know when one of them stops feeling that itch?' I was curious. His invaluable lessons might come handy in decoding Uums' behavioural patterns too.

'Perhaps, when you don't talk to the other person and yet, you don't feel miserable,' he said with a forlorn expression as if evaluating his own relationship.

'But you feel miserable.'

'Wretched,' he said and went quiet.

Love, I suppose, was painful and I could see that pain on his face. It prompted me to reflect on my own future, in a disturbing silence. Until it was ruptured by the Screamy Surd.

'Congrats suckers,' Manjot stormed into our room and broke us the news. A new Punjabi Dhaba had opened right outside the Technopark gate.

We goggled at him in total disbelief as if he was a Tolkien's elf. Magically our spirits lifted, shoulders rose, and stomachs bawled to quieten the diatribes of our hearts and minds. When in pain, eat and eat a lot, the nearest mosque seemed to vocalise.

Nothing could stop me tonight.

'Bring me one, just one bucket of water and I shall bring you two. I swear. Please, I beg you,' I pleaded to Pandey.

There was no way I could go downstairs, drag the bucket to our room and yet, not liberate the three states of matter that had built up inside my stomach, midway.

His last night's desolation and a virgin dhaba had forced me to devour four giant *paranthas*, one plate of *rajma-rice* and a large bowl of *raita*; by morning, it had proved too much for my intestines to handle. For the first time in Kerala, I had abandoned my bed at 6:30. To compound my agony, the taps had transmuted into an air-blowing machine as if mocking my arse.

Nah, mine won't give up. Not yet. Unimpressed, my bowels groaned. *Fuck, fuck...Ah, softly fuck.*

'For friendship's sake, man,' I implored. 'For your sake.'

'I'm going,' he relented and left with the bucket.

With utmost care, I reposed my torso on my bed, in the least uncomfortable position. Waiting for my saviour I coiled uncoiled, trying to release pressure in form of sulphurous emissions that soon converted our room into a toxic gas chamber. Now, sulphur could just be a neighbour of oxygen in the periodic table, lying in peace right beneath but its interaction with hydrogen could have wiped out the entire human race in this room.

Pretty much in stark contrast to the resultant of hydrogen oxygen bonding – the only friendship that could save us now.

Ten minutes. Where the hell was Pandey?

'Your Uums was in the queue too,' he announced, carrying the bucket inside. 'I swear if it hadn't been an emergency, I would've stayed there, watching her pull -,' his words disappeared into the invisible cloud of gas particles that wafted up his nostrils.

'What the fuck? That is how you thank someone?' he flinched with disgust.

'I'm sorry,' I rose to my feet with caution and reached for the bucket. It was too heavy. 'Could you put it inside please? For humanity's sake, man.' He glared at me, holding his breath.

I shot back a threatening look. *The more he delayed, the more perilous it would become.* He understood and capitulated.

'You are never ever going back to that Punjabi dhaba. Period,' said Pandey, moving the bucket into the bathroom.

'Don't you get it? My stomach just realized the kind of shock it was in for three weeks. Courtesy this Southie food,' I posited, going inside and shutting the door.

'Then, why did it not affect me?' he contended from outside.

'Exactly my point,' I said, adjusting my arse over the toilet seat before it exploded.

I spent harrowing minutes inside, emptying my bowels

and braving hydrogen sulphide. It had nearly killed me, but I couldn't take a chance. Ponmudi trip was at stake.

'Did you spare some water for me?' Pandey was sitting still on the bed when I came out.

'Not really. In fact-.'

'You are such a selfish jerk. I told you it was Punjabi dhaba,' he yelped, clutching his tummy. The calamity had struck him fifteen minutes late. 'Your turn now.'

'But I haven't washed my hands,' I said, putting my hands forth.

'Keep them off, *bhenchod,*' he said, stepping away. 'I don't care. Fetch me a bucket or I'll strangle you to death before this gas does.'

It was the Hamlet moment of my life - to go or not to go.

'Okay, but dare you tell anyone that I brought you water without washing my hands. You know I would be touching a lot of people...and things on my way,' I said, picking up the empty bucket.

I had reached the first floor when I finally stumbled upon the phenomenon Pandey would often describe; the anecdote of Uums, lugging the water bucket!

Usually lifting, pulling or pushing a bucket is a simple process. Well, usually. But not for Uums. What she was doing couldn't be termed simple. She was bent on her knees, with arms thrown to her left towards the bucket and face turned to her right. Her torso was straight, its geometric plane parallel to the direction of motion and her palms held the rim of bucket firmly, dragging it forward. Inexplicably weird and stupid.

But she looked damn hot – the kind of go-to-your-room-imagine-and-jerk-off hot - at the same time. Her wet, transparent clothes clung to her curvy hourglass body while her posture ensured her assets were nicely exposed.

Frivolous, Mannu. Frivolous, my mother's voice echoed in my ears. My hands covered them to block the noise, and when I removed them, Bryan Adams knocked my head.

*I wanna be the T-shirt when you're wet...*and I stood there transfixed, feasting my eyes on the lascivious sight. Although as a gentleman I should've offered my aid, I was in a dilemma, struggling with my second Hamlet moment of the day; to help or not to help. Shakespeare must've been a genius to devise one liner for all of the world's conundrums.

It's you who has to make the effort. It's the lule, Pandey screamed this time. My body jerked and flung to undertake the pain and misery and invest into its future, and my hands snatched the bucket from her.

'No, it's ok. I will manage,' she protested meekly, loosening her grip at once.

'Oh come on. What is my use if I cannot be of any help?' I said, holding the bucket as we walked – she sauntered while I trudged – up to her room.

'Are you going to Ponmudi?' she asked.

Did she say 'going' instead of 'coming'? 'Of course, didn't I tell you, I'd be tagging along,' I said nevertheless.

'Shit yaar. I will miss it.'

'What? Are you...*not* coming?' I put the bucket down at her door. Not a step more girl, not before you spit out the remaining details.

'I'm off to Aleppy backwaters. Samarth made plans. I told him it's hectic, but he misses me, yaar,' she blushed.

Tricksters! Why didn't she get her loser boyfriend to come and lift this bucket for her? 'Wow! That's great. Have fun,' I said with a perfunctory nod. 'I might drop my plans too. We got an invitation to watch Kerala's famous boat race practices. Such gigantic boats I tell you,' I gestured. I had to say something.

'Seriously? I have seen those on TV only. I wish I could join you,' she made a sad "aww" face. *Awww.*

'It's a boy thingy you see. Anyways you get ready. I'll push off.

Need water for my room as well,' I said, slipping my befouled hands into her bucket quietly and thoroughly.

Monsoon offer for you, ass! This weekend, have her with my indelible imprints.

'Where the hell were you, fucker? I almost died,' Pandey yelled as I entered the room.

'There was too much rush. Such a *Chindi* company, I tell you,' I grumbled. 'Misers can't even afford a continuous water supply. I don't care what Col Menon says. We're bringing the large container that Manjot has.' Pandey didn't bother replying and disappeared with the bucket.

'By the way, are you going to Mevalloor?' I asked.

'Yes. We'll miss you.'

'You won't. I'm in,' I said. Silence. 'I mean since he has invited both of us, he might feel bad if you go alone.'

The door opened with a creak. 'That's called friendship, man. Welcome aboard,' he patted my shoulder and shut the door with a thud. 'Sorry, I didn't wash my hands either,' he screamed from inside.

Arrghh!!

Maruthi Vallam

****

'What is this forest?' Rajesh asked as the four plodded through a narrow berm alongside the river, towards a looming grove.

'Rubber,' said Adish. 'Most of it goes to my dad's mill for processing, and then to Sultanate...I mean Oman. You know he plans to open a rubber factory there as well since he is free now.'

'Free from?' Rajesh said.

'Me,' Adish said.

As they invaded the murky wood, the first thing they took in was a peculiar acrid odour. Latex, Adish told them as they beheld hundreds of tapped rubber trees spread in all directions. Fresh milky white latex exuded from the tree barks and seeped through the incisions drop by drop into large collecting cups attached to the trees. The odour wouldn't be so strong but for the rains that had made the air denser.

'Amazing, isn't it? Just plant the trees and wait for few years. Then, tap them, collect the sap, process and mould it into solid rubber, and earn forever. Secure and comfortable,' Manoj exclaimed, inspecting the milky froth formed in the cups.

'People don't realize it is a trap,' said Mutthur.

Alarmed, Manoj withdrew his hands. 'What trap?'

Mutthur simpered and began to walk again.

'It tempts you because it is easy, convenient and more giving. And what you do? You let go of food farming for rubber. You reap the rewards for a while. But then technology steps in and environmental issues crop up. Now rubber is no good anymore. It stops fetching you much, and you are clueless what to do with it. You cannot buy food as well because the gap between demand and supply has pushed the prices up too. At last, you migrate and become a labourer, either in someone else's land or a factory far away in the Gulf. That is the trap.' Mutthur said.

Heavy, grim socio-economics but not too complex, thought Rajesh.

'But you need money for a better lifestyle,' Manoj countered, clearly in a mood to debate. 'Look around, man. I mean for all that hundred per cent literacy rate, not a single multiplex exists in whole of Kerala.'

'Multiplex? What is that?' Mutthur asked.

'It's a place where you have multiple cinema screens and a super-market in one single building,' Adish explained. 'By the way, there is one coming up in Kochi.'

'Odd, it is. All of it in one confined space! Why would you do that?' Mutthur was bemused.

'Because it's easy and more convenient,' Rajesh smirked. 'And, more giving too.'

'Yeah, man. Heavy discounts all year around,' added Manoj.

Mutthur scratched his chin. Then grinned. 'Ah, I get it. A trap,' he said and moved ahead, leaving Manoj confounded. Rajesh and Adish were smiling, though.

The narrow path soon opened up into a grassy clearing separating the vast river from the forest. Some forty odd people, a mix of young and middle-aged, waited there. To their left were moored several fishing boats alongside one long, very long boat.

'That is Maruthi Vallam,' Mutthur said. 'Named after Lord Maruthi; popular as Lord Hanuman up your North,' he smiled at Manoj who bowed his head to acknowledge the divinity.

'Hanumanly huge it is,' said Rajesh, wide-eyed at the astonishing piece of woodwork in front of him. Sixty-five feet in length, the boat was barely four feet wide even at its broadest point. Having several small chambers, fifty Mutthur told him, for the crew to sit, it was symmetrical on both sides with ends in a shape of hoods spiralling inwards. A pretty strange over all dimensions for such a long boat. With his limited knowledge of hydrodynamics, he knew it would be damn difficult to balance this boat in the water.

'How many today?' Mutthur asked Dhaniya, his broad and tall deputy as soon as he joined his crew.

'Forty-six, excluding you,' Dhaniya grinned. His front two teeth were missing.

Mutthur tapped his shoulder and turned to his men. 'Today we ride Maruthi Vallam at full strength,' he spoke.

'Jai Lord Maruthi,' the forty-six men cheered in unison.

'Come, dear oarsmen. Let's step aboard,' he said to the three engineers. Dhaniya brought the spare oars that Rajesh and Manoj accepted readily, their expressions turning from jovial to euphoric. Holding the oar, they toyed with its long flat blade. But Adish hesitated.

'*Achan* won't appreciate,' Adish muttered.

'He won't know,' Mutthur assured. 'And it's just a ride. How'd he find out?

'Okay,' said Adish, looking at the oar and still pondering over his choices.

'Don't you remember, Dhaniya. He is not the oarsman, he is *Nilakkar*,' Manoram spoke in an excited vein.

Manoram used to be an oarsman, Adish recalled. But when the previous Nilakkar unexpectedly bid goodbye to the shores of Malabar and headed to the Gulf last year, he was assigned the role of the boat singer. What was this fascination of boat singers with the Gulf, Adish wondered, finding in Manoram's story a parallel to his life.

'I don't remember the boat song,' said Adish.

The other oarsmen booed, 'What a shame! He is an Engineer now. Why should he care for our traditions anymore?' Adish stayed quiet.

'What is happening?' Manoj asked, unable to understand any of the Malayalam that flew around, over their heads.

'Nothing,' said Adish and grabbed the oar from Dhaniya. 'You have a boat singer. Let me be an oarsman today.'

Mutthur roared out instructions to his men as they boarded and arranged themselves in two rows along the length of the boat. Rajesh and Manoj sat in the middle alongside Adish while Mutthur stood at the rear with his long oar.

'The captain provides the backward stability and direction to the boat,' Adish explained. 'It's the toughest job of all as he needs to stand and balance his body firmly on a slender rear. Look at how Mutthur has positioned his legs.'

Rajesh noticed the sturdy legs of Mutthur, bent slightly and at different angles to each other. His torso leaned in such a way that it lowered the centre of gravity of his body, besides keeping it at the centremost point of his final stance.

'Are we ready?' Mutthur thundered.

'Yes,' the crew responded.

With further chants of 'Jai Lord Maruthi', the crew rowed to the middle of the river and aligned the boat to the flow, ready to sail downstream Meanwhile, Adish demonstrated to Rajesh and Manoj, how to use the oars.

'*Paranja thangane thanney,*' Manoram clapped and shouted in Malayalam, standing in the middle of the assembly.

'*Thei thei thakathei thei thoy,*' the oarsmen followed and pushed their oars into the water and made a complete circle. The boat trudged forward.

'That's the boat song,' Adish said.

'What's a boat song?' Rajesh asked.

'It defines the oaring rhythm.'

'How?'

'Well, it keeps each oarsman in sync with each other. So that they row the boat efficiently and gain the maximum speed,' said Adish. The deadpan face of Rajesh indicated he didn't follow a thing. 'See, it is similar to dance choreography, where all those dancers match their steps to the musical beats. Here, oarsmen sync their rowing to the beats of the boat song,' Adish explained further.

'Ah, it means a boat singer is the most crucial element of this assembly,' said Rajesh, bringing a faint smile on Adish's face. *Paranja thangane thanney, thai thai thakthai*, he repeated.

In sync with boat song, the oarsmen traced perfect circles with their oars, propelling the boat. The combined roar of fifty people suffused vigour into the atmosphere as Maruthi vallam gathered speed gradually. Just listening to the lyrical cadence Rajesh and Manoj felt their adrenaline levels rising even when its words were beyond their comprehension.

'It's moving so fast,' exclaimed Manoj.

'I never imagined I'd be an oarsman one day,' Rajesh said triumphantly and rowed with more intensity.

'Faster, faster. We are nearing the first mark,' Mutthur said as they now headed to a river bend ahead.

'The manoeuverability of these Odi-vallams is almost nil and hence, this curve becomes the most challenging part of the race,' Adish explained. 'Lock your legs under the front thwart and hold the gunwale firmly. Sometimes boats flip when crew is not able to control their speed.'

'What did he say?' Manoj stared at Rajesh who looked equally scared at the revelation.

'I cannot swim, man,' both screamed together as the boat fast approached the bend. The speed hadn't dropped yet. Instead, their pulses shot up.

Mutthur barked orders to his crew. The right row leaned towards their left while the left row stopped sculling and sat upright, holding their oars stationary, immersed at a particular angle. Their momentum dropped quickly but the boat wouldn't turn much, and drifted towards the outer edge of the river.

'Lower the speed', Mutthur uttered. The oars on both sides changed their movement and angle again, dropping the speed further. The boat turned further. 'Not enough. Lower, lower.'

Bending satisfactorily this time, the boat gradually aligned with the stream. Once the river straightened, the crew began to row profusely. It wasn't too long when they crossed the finish mark as well. The oarsmen cheered and chanted, raising their oars over their head. Season's first practice lap was over.

'What was our timing, Manoram?' Mutthur asked.

'Eight minutes twenty-four seconds.'

'That means on our first day, we have equalled our last year's timing. We've been blessed today,' Mutthur was elated. Closing his eyes he murmured a silent prayer. 'Everybody, switch your positions,' he commanded again. The oarsmen stood up and turned around.

'We shall return now,' said Adish, getting up.

'You won't turn the boat?' asked Rajesh, curiously.

Adish smiled. 'That's the uniqueness of Odi-vallams. We never reverse the boat because it is too tough to change its direction. You saw that on the bend. So, we switch ends.'

'Like a shuttle. Interesting,' Rajesh was intrigued. 'Making full use of its identical ends.'

'That's what pirates did,' holding his oar, Adish stood up too.

'Who're they?' Manoj was still seated when he spotted the boat that approached from downstream.

'Another practising team, I guess,' Adish craned his neck.

The boat song emanating from the other boat grew louder as it neared them, speedily.

'Gopalan?' Mutthur muttered under his breath as it slowed down and came to a standstill right next to Maruthi Vallam. He hadn't expected his nemesis to be making excursions in this region.

'Full on practice, huh?' Gopalan spoke in a sarcastic tone. 'And that too, with a full crew. Let us congratulate them,' he said to his oarsmen and laughed.

'What do you want?' Dhaniya asked in a raised voice.

'Shush Dhaniya! When the head is present, the tail should not wag,' Gopalan hissed. 'So, who are your passengers this year?' he said to Mutthur, scanning their boat and saw Manoj and Rajesh seated amongst the crew. 'Oh Lord Bali, what do we see here? Two *Hindikaars*?' He spat into the river in disgust. 'You don't have any shame, right? Is that how you hope to win her hand?'

Don't drag Kala into this, Mutthur clenched his fists, his entire body seething in anger, but kept his calm. Gopalan, though, continued his barrage. 'If you had asked me, I would've lent you my oarsmen. But you accepted help from those who ridicule us.'

'They are far better than a scoundrel like you,' Adish couldn't hold back anymore.

'Oh! Mr Engineer. Big boss Adish, eh. Nobody offered you a job or what?' Gopalan sneered while his crew tittered along. 'And does your father know you are idling here in Muvattupuzha with captain Mutthur?'

'Dare you speak to my dad you odious soul,' Adish bawled at him. 'Or you sure will burn in the inferno of hell.'

'Hell? Is that where Antony burns too, after his shenanigans?' Gopalan burst into a fit of laughter. Then, all of a sudden, grew quiet. 'You misunderstand me Adish. I'm not evil. I'm a good, God-fearing man. And why would I put you in trouble? You're already knee deep in it, my friend. May Antony bless you.'

Gopalan bawled at his oarsmen to propel upstream and within minutes, they disappeared beyond the curve.

Rajesh and Manoj exchanged a bewildered look. The body languages of both Adish and that six-foot, brawny *Mallu* on the other boat had appeared hostile. But since the whole argument occurred in Malayalam, they had no clue what passed between the two teams. Though, they could sense the disdain that now filled the air around them. They decided to wait and ask Adish later.

They had to unearth the secret.

Adish Mathew's

A Wish

✶✶✶✶

'I was part of the team four years ago, and that was the end of it,' I said. The quiet of the evening mixed with my silent anguish slowly engulfed our little boat as it moseyed along the stream under the cloak of darkening clouds.

Taking a swill of toddy, I ruminated on the outlandish calm Mutthur had displayed throughout the day, especially after that villain, Gopalan's appearing act. Mutthur of the yore would've beaten him to a pulp then and there. Not this one. This Mutthur was in love. True words, someone said:

Love is forbearing, love is kind. In a mysterious harmony, a soul it doth bind.

'Be careful,' I cautioned Manoj who had dangerously leaned away from the boat. 'Toddy turns devilish by evening, I had told you.'

'Thanks, man. I didn't realize,' he said, shifting to the centre with his oar.

'Do you miss the boat, Adish?' asked Rajesh.

I took in a long breath, going over the riddle once more. In past one week, I had done it many times, but failed every time to decipher what I sought in my life. 'Honestly, I don't know.' I told the truth.

'But why should your dad have an issue with you riding a boat. I mean, come on. Look at you. You're an engineer, with a real job. And you're learning French too. Of course, you're not going to give up on your career and ruin your life for a race?' said Manoj and paused. 'Or would you?' He peered at me dubiously.'

'It is not just the boat race,' I said.

'Then?'

'You won't understand,' I said, deciding to close the chapter.

Good, they didn't follow Malayalam, for their queries remained restricted. In any case, I didn't want them to learn the underground remnants of my pitiable past. Rather, I wanted to be in my burrow - my hostel room, as quickly as possible. But the boat continued to lumber at a snail's pace.

'You guys put so much effort and sentiments into one race. Quite amazing, isn't it?' said Rajesh.

'Well, it's not one single race. We have an entire season dedicated to Onam, which kicks off with the Nehru Trophy,' I said.

'What's Nehru Trophy?' asked Manoj.

'The most remarkable water sports carnival in India. Maybe, in the whole wide world. We have more than twenty kinds of boats, and each of them participates in the regatta.'

'Wow. So you need to defeat Gopalan in Nehru Trophy?'

'Not really. I have to defeat him in the most prestigious of all,' Mutthur spoke. 'The Kumarakom race - the singular honour for our Odi-vallams.'

'Sounds like we are going to have fun,' said Rajesh.

'Not me. Oh, wait! I can be a cheerleader,' I suggested and chortled at my own ridiculous idea – no doubt a toddy effect. 'It is easy for people like you but for us – life is a bitter truth.'

'Yeah, people like us,' Manoj sneered and looked at Rajesh, 'So Mr Design Engineer, you're going to design a pirate ship next at DigiSys shipyard, aren't you? Damn easy for you.'

This sucker was an asshole. He'd always be like - come on, let's poke fun at Adish Mathew.

'Yes, I guess. And are you not going to transform this boatrace season into the water F1 or even better, the water Olympics, Mr Brand manager?' said Rajesh.

Jump Adish! Jump into the river. Chuck it, I can swim.

'And I'm going to win the race and marry Kala in the most lavish wedding Mevalloor has ever seen. Such an easy life, eh?' Mutthur added sarcastically, and all of them broke into a laugh.

I didn't know how troubled these Northie minds were, but Mutthur's case was definitely worse than mine. Yet, he behaved so off-centred today. Earlier, he had let that rascal get away. And now, he cracked self-deprecating jokes. Was it to cheer me up? My emotions began to choke me.

No dad, you're mistaken about my friends. You have no idea why I couldn't make a single friend either in Kodaikanal or in Bangalore where people had turned into cannibals from the day one. Unlike these three who have no reason to laugh at themselves other than just to cheer me up. It's a human bond so few can forge, and even fewer may fathom. I so wish you understood, dad. Your son and the people he believes in.

'Oh my, a shooting star,' Manoj pointed upwards. We all glanced up but couldn't spot anything.

'Where dude? It isn't even dark yet,' said Rajesh.

'Oh man, you think meteors would wait until the night to enter the atmos, in India?' Manoj said. Rajesh chuckled at his own stupidity.

'You know what it means?' he cocked his head up, enthusiasm returning to his veins. 'Law of *"Kuchh - Kuchh Hota Hai, tum nahi samjhoge,"* states that our wishes are going to come true.'

'That's from *Liar Liar*, fucker,' said Rajesh.

'My bad. But that's not the point. The point is, it means Adish will be a cheerleader, and we are going to have lots of fun,' said Manoj and everybody shook with laughter.

Everybody as I joined them too. For, such evenings were a Lord's gift to one's life. And I sincerely hoped for our wishes to come true.

Engineers' First Salary

For their Fathers

****

A ripple of anxiety ran through Manoj as he listened to his father over the phone. Tomorrow, being the twenty-ninth of June and a Friday, he'd complete his first month in a job. Many months had passed by in his life. But on this instant, a departing month would mean a salary. His salary. A reality just a few days away.

'Ok son, take care. Let me know if you need any money,' his father said before he hung up. His tone seemed different today; uncertain and anticipating unlike the usual indifferent kind, the one Manoj was used to.

Manoj remembered how his family would sit tight and await his father's arrival on the first evening of every month, like any other service class household. With a distinct air about himself, he'd walk through the front door, well aware that his wife had prepared the monthly budget and his two sons were ready to present their pending wish list; the one they concocted a week before but never shared.

One more 'Bansal' would be added to 'the bread earner's roll' soon. Closing his eyes, he pressed his right hand to his heart and murmured, 'Thank-you Bajrang Bali.'

Relieved, he cudgelled his brain about his future. One month into a job and he was convinced that he lacked the ability to follow his father's revolutionary footsteps, which was - sticking to an occupation for too long.

His father had already done the unthinkable, spending thirty years in his maiden job – an accomplishment unheard of in the entire Bansal clan that ran 'Bansal Sweets & Snacks Corner' - largest such joint in Meerut. While, the two brothers of his father had adhered to their family business, and managed its two verticals 'Sweets' and 'Snacks', Shri Mahendra Bansal had broken the tradition by choosing the 'service class'.

Manoj could never comprehend why. To him, defying his baniya genes seemed a daunting task as he found it extremely painful to breathe an IT engineer's life. An MBA from IIM and a business venture, later, had become his, what they referred to in that movie as, yeah '*Lakshya*'.

'Have you heard the good news?' said Rajesh, breezing into the room. *What good could there be?* Manoj wondered and shook his head. Rajesh tilted his head sideways and grinned.

'Dear associates,' said Col. Menon and paused as usual to gain complete attention of his audience. 'Today, we have completed four weeks together. The first phase of the CLP is over.'

The audience clapped customarily, though genuinely happy, on the completion of one-third of the training.

'We advance to the second phase, which entails extra focus, determination and commitment. Therefore, your daily schedule has been extended by two hours.' No one clapped this time. Col. Menon sighed.

'As you're aware, we're racing towards our vision 2010. Markets look bullish. The Sensex has breached the 14,000 mark, and 15,000 isn't too far. There lies a great opportunity for us to fulfill our mission, which is to make our venture a joy for each stakeholder.'

The associates listened to him intently, though it sounded odd. An ex-army turned administrator speaking on the surging markets! Well, it was odd.

'And how do we ensure that?' he asked. 'By working together,' he continued. 'In the next phase every batch shall divide itself into smaller groups of six each. The only criterion is diversity. , Half of it should be from IT and C.S. and half from the other streams. Also, we prefer a healthy mix of both North and South India.'

One arm raised in the third row. 'What about East...West Bengal?' It was Sudipto.

Col. Menon rolled his eyes, 'Find a physical map of India, trace the river Godavari and mark the two halves as North and South if anyone has any confusion. You will have your answer,' he said. The audience burst out into a roar of laughter.

'And to broaden your smiles further, today happens to be the last working day of the month,' he said and paused, creating an utmost suspense like an archetypal TV show host, to heighten the drama before revealing the big secret. 'Congratulations on your first salary.' A thunderous applause erupted in the auditorium.

Sitting in one of the middle rows, Rajesh and Manoj shook hands ecstatically while Adish was quiet, with his head hung low.

'Adish! We're rich,' said Manoj.

Adish raised his chin. Tears complimented a broad smile on his face.

'Fantabulous feeling, isn't it?' Rajesh licked his lips, putting down his half empty mug with a thud, and stuffed a chicken 65 piece into his mouth. Manoj and Adish exchanged a grin.

Sitting at the Hawwah beach in an open air restaurant against a crimson setting sun and seeing Rajesh embrace beer, had rejuvenated their minds while the cool, light breeze blowing across had provided their aching muscles with an icy massage.

'What a great week it has been! Our codes compiled and ran, taps had water, and we got enough Moolah too,' Manoj buried his fork into another piece of chilli paneer. 'But the best part is, Pandey lost his *alcohorginity* today. Fucking unbelievable, man.'

'Who said I lost my alcohorginity, *today*,' said Rajesh.

Manoj was dazed; his mouth wide open, showing the remnants of what he chewed last, and the next item hanging an inch away. The day's surprises weren't over yet. Not by a close margin.

'It's been years. Nine, I guess, since I had my last drink.'

'Nine years? When did you exactly quit?' asked Adish.

'Fuck that. When did you actually start?' asked Manoj.

'On my eleventh birthday,' Rajesh eased into his recliner, holding his beer mug.

Eleventh birthday! Manoj and Adish exchanged a rapt look.

'Two years later, I drank a little too much at a New Year party. Someone informed my father, and he got senti. All middle-class fathers get senti.'

'Not my dad', said Adish.

'Because he is a baron, rubber baron,' Manoj teased.

'He will, someday,' said Rajesh, matter-of-factly.

'So, what did your father do?' asked Manoj.

'He played his emotional card. I wasn't prepared. He said I should drink the day I become responsible, basically in double-quotes, "the day I start earning",' Rajesh slapped the cigarette pack and popped one out.

'Dude, it was a great sacrifice', Manoj said and picked the last piece of paneer. 'You didn't quit smoking.'

Rajesh shook his head and lit his cigarette.

'He never asked you to?' Adish was puzzled.

'He never found out,' Rajesh picked up his glass.

Adish was impressed. He gaped at the knife and fork lying beside his plate with strange determination.

Made famous by the Hippies who arrived in hordes from Europe in the historic Hippie Trail during the sixties and seventies, Hawwah beach didn't have too many visitors now. Even the local traffic, over the years, had mostly shifted to the Lighthouse beach; the more commercial and famous part of Kovalam. Their other associates, including Uums, too had chosen to go there, but these three had consciously landed here, seeking calmness.

'Your girl is around and yet, you are not with her?' said Rajesh. Manoj lounging with them hadn't been less surprising for him. 'What's the matter? Broke up?' he winked.

'Friendship, man,' said Manoj. Rajesh narrowed his brows. Manoj turned quiet and kept masticating the paneer until he had swallowed it. 'Have you ever gone shopping with a girl?'

'We barely get time to talk, let alone shop,' Rajesh pondered over his curiosity. 'Not really, never in fact.'

Manoj took a deep sigh, 'I once accompanied Supriya and Preetika. They wanted to buy skirts, the long Fab India types. So, we went to Sarojini market. Three hours! Three hours we spent gallivanting, circling that square market four times for one damn skirt. In the end, we returned with two pairs of earrings. If not for Sarojini's *Dahi Bhalla chaat*, I might've shot them both with a Meerut brand *Katta*.'

Rajesh chuckled. 'Thank God, it never happened to me.'

'It will, because your dad is not a baron,' Manoj sniggered, turning his gaze to Adish who was busy fighting his chicken once again. The chicken hadn't capitulated yet.

'Why don't you eat with your hands and spare us the horror?' pleaded Manoj.

'Shoot me if you want,' Adish said. 'But I have to master these French ways. It would be a surprise to my father when he returns.'

'But he has gone to Oman, not France dude,' Rajesh reasoned, but Adish continued his struggle unabashedly.

The chicken leg though frustrated by his repeated assaults, resurrected and flew into the adjacent table. It had taken refuge on the plate of a probable Hippie, who glared at them, apparently not amused at an intrusion of his privacy. He uttered something that Manoj recognised as French.

'Lo behold, his chicken has made it to France before he could.'

Ignoring him, Adish rose from his chair and uttered, '*Je suis desole, monsieur.*' The Frenchman stared at him and so did Manoj and Rajesh.

'Oh boy, you don't assault someone's national pride so brutally,' said Rajesh. 'Especially, when it is French or Malayalam.'

'And you definitely don't mix them as if they're curd and rice,' added Manoj.

Unperturbed, Adish walked up to the Hippie and repeated, trying to sound better. '*Je suis desole.*'

The Hippie smiled. '*Tu parles francais?*' he asked. Perhaps, he had anticipated 'Hare Rama Hare Krishna' from an Indian.

'*Francais...oui oui,*' Adish nodded fervently.

'*Wee wee,*' Rajesh and Manoj repeated the sound, wondering how long he'd continue but Adish had decided it to be his French practical class. 'Adish Mathew,' he pointed at himself, '*Comment vous appelez vous?*'

'That Frenchie is going to punch him in the face,' Manoj said.

'I doubt. French people are ostensibly obsessed with anything *Francaise*. See, pride has swelled his chest. It's funny. I'm betting on Adish to get his chicken back,' Rajesh said laughing.

'*Alphonse*'

Adish was at a loss for more words. He had said 'sorry'. He'd asked 'his name' too which was Alphonse. What else? His sight fell on the Hippie's plate.

'*Mon chicken,*' Adish aimed his finger at the chicken.

'*Poulet?*' said the Hippie.

'No, not plate. Chicken, mon chicken,' Adish pleaded nervously. The Frenchman grasped that Adish had exhausted his French vocabulary. He smiled and gestured to him to take back his chicken piece.

'*Merci,*' Adish exulted at the stroke of his luck and returned to their table to resume his battle.

'I'm now friends with a North Indian Malayali and a Malayali French. Awesome,' said Manoj.

'Oui Oui,' Rajesh and Adish said in unison.

The day had been perfect. So far.

The Heartbreak

****

'I need the webcam,' Rajesh told the Internet cafe manager.

D-12 batch had planned a weekend Backwaters trip wherein they proposed to book large houseboats to celebrate their first salary, partying in the lap of the mother Earth. Naturally, Manoj had wanted to make the most out of the opportunity.

'Try to understand man. We are spending the night in Aleppy. I have to set things on course by helping her pick a dress for tomorrow. Something sexy,' Manoj had revealed with a hint of excitement.

'*Bhenchod*, you should be ashamed. You said she is in a serious relationship. Where do you fit in the picture then?' Rajesh had chided Manoj.

'She knows where to fit me. And dude, real desperate men don't say *no* to such divine interventions. Rather they jump on it,' Manoj had winked, and left to meet Uums to finalise the details.

He'd take an hour, his text had arrived later. So, in the interim, Rajesh had decided to spend his time surfing the internet while Adish headed to the local flea market, to buy gifts for his family.

User id: Honey_rajesh
Password: 16031985

Rajesh entered his login details on Yahoo Messenger.

The offline message window popped up soon, with messages from the id Ruhika_4u2:

'It was great fun chatting with you.' 'Hope to see you online soon.' 'Hey wassup? I will be online on Friday evening.'

Rajesh read Ruhika's messages and minimised the box to check his friend list. The yellow smiley against angelica16 meant *she* was online. He double clicked on the id and opened the dialogue box.

'Heyyyyy babyyyyy,' he typed, switching the webcam on.

'Hey baby. Was waiting for you. Now leaving in five.'

'Why? Stay and talk to me love. I wanna see you', he typed and sent *her* a 'view webcam' request. *She* accepted and appeared on his screen, wearing a bright-blue spaghetti top. His heart skipped a few beats as he drooled over *her* cleavage and pouty lips that matched the pink of *her* glowing skin. It had been a month. He zoomed back and saw *her* complete face; innocent and blushing, *her* hair tied in a ponytail.

'You look so hot, baby. Give me a kiss, no.'

She blushed, and *her* eyes danced over her screen. An alert notified Rajesh that Ruhika_4u2 was online.

'Hey how are you?' he typed to Ruhika.

'Why are you so slow, baby?' he asked *her*.

'No I'm not. You are only quiet,' *she* replied. 'Ok tell me. You remember my senior Rohan right? Tomorrow is his birthday. Suggest me a gift, no.'

'Gift? How do I know?'

'Hmm okay. Will figure out something.'

'Hey, guess what! We got our first salary today.'

'Hey. I am gud. Wassup with you?' replied Ruhika.

'I am good. Going to a party. My first salary is in account,' Rajesh wrote to Ruhika.

'Wow! Cool ya. I am so, so happy for you', *she* replied.

'Two more months and then, I am back in Delhi with you.'

'Hmmm. Cool', *she* typed, 'Hey gotto go. Will catch you laterz. Love!'

Before Rajesh could respond, *angelica16* was offline. *Her* webcam was closed too.

'What the fuck, yaar?' he cursed and opened Ruhika's dialogue box

'Hey congrats. Where is my treat?'

Rajesh felt his muscles quivering. *She* had again left without a proper goodbye. *What's wrong with her?* He was baffled. *She* had been making excuses not to talk to him. *She* had all the time for movies, friends and seniors but none for him, and had lately been avoiding his calls during *her* college hours too. Even the news of his first salary hadn't enthused *her* a bit. It was bizarre.

'You there?' Ruhika pinged.

'Oh yeah! Sorry, was on call. We'll celebrate when you are in India.'

He knew *she* loved him. Maybe *she* wasn't keeping well or *she* might be PMSing. He wasn't sure.

'Cool! I'll be in India next month. Are you on webcam?'

'Yes I am. Wanna see me?'

'I won't mind. Hope, you have your clothes on ;-).'

'I am in a café.' Rajesh sent her the webcam invitation.

Was he overthinking? An unusual nervousness surrounded him. Rajesh wiggled the mouse, moving the cursor round and round with an impassive stare on the screen. Resting it finally on the Firefox icon, he inhaled deeply and clicked open the browser. 'Gmail.com', he typed in the address bar, and once it loaded, filled the details on the login page with a pounding heart:

'Gmail id: angelica16.'
'Password: 6258530186'

Her password was simple, her phone number. Invading her inbox, he scanned her emails. Most were the forwarded crap like photos and links and notifications from Orkut. *Nothing here. Next,* he clicked on the chat hyperlink.

'Looking cool today. But why are you not smiling? Smile na. Please,' Ruhika pinged again. Rajesh smiled and winked at the webcam. 'You look cute,' she responded, promptly.

Minimising the chat-box, he returned to *her* Gmail chat history. The topmost entry was from Rohan Malhotra. *Double click.*

Rohan: Hey my love! Why are you not answering the phone?

Me: Oh shit! Left my phone outside. Was talking to Rajesh. He was calling nonstop.

Rohan: Why don't you tell him about us?

Me: Arre I will baba. But it's not easy yaar. We broke up just before he left but he refuses to accept it. I don't want him to turn into a psycho.

Rohan: Don't you worry babes. I'll handle him.

Me: Ohho! Forget about him, na. Lemme call you.

Rohan: Will talk later. I wanna see my sexy angel, first.

Me: Ahaan! What do you wanna seeee? ;-)

*Rohan: What I saw last night baby :-**

Me: You liked what u saw? ;)

Rohan: Loved it, mah love. I love everything about you angel.

Me: I have a naughty gift for your bday. ;-)

*Rohan: Come on skype and show me. :-**

*Me: Okay :-**

Last message 5:45 p.m.

Staring vacantly at the screen, Rajesh remained seated on his stool. His hand moved slowly into his pocket and pulled out his phone, which, all of a sudden, had grown heavier. With trembling fingers, he pressed the keys and dialled her number and held the phone to his ear. 'The person you're trying to call is busy on another call,' he heard on the other side.

Coldness hit at his core, a twinge rolled through his stomach, and a barrage of emotions flooded his brain. Fear, anger, humiliation, resentment, defeat - name any gloom-ridden emotion that could rip apart a person's heart, and it was right there.

His legs quivered, tears trickled down his cheeks, and he felt the whole world would collapse upon him. Realizing he was in a cyber cafe and might disintegrate any time, he wiped off his tears and quickly logged out of Gmail. He didn't bother replying to Ruhika either and closed his yahoo messenger as well.

At the moment he felt extreme hatred for anything remotely close to a female.

She hadn't answered any of his calls except for a text she had sent in response to his flurry of messages; to confirm what he read was indeed true. Her exact words, though, lacked any empathy. Instead, she had accused him of spying on her.

That had infuriated him.

'How could she do this to me? How could she cheat on me?' Rajesh muttered angrily, sitting at the deserted beach with his two hobbits – they'd call each other the three hobbits, courtesy Manoj, a diehard fan of the Lord of the Rings.

'The tides are rising high,' Manoj ignored his whimpers and kept an eye on the waves hitting the rocks.

Half an hour back, he and Adish had footslogged through the entire area in search of Rajesh who had suddenly gone missing. Fortunately, they had located him soon, shambling along the beach weeping like a lost child.

'You know why the fuck did I come here?' said Rajesh, 'I had a better job offer in Bangalore. With a higher salary package. 3.25 per annum.'

'3.25 Gross or CTC?' Manoj asked.

Rajesh paused from crying and stared at him. 'Gross.'

'Did you hear that?' Manoj exchanged a bewildered look with Adish. A package of 3.25 Lacs per annum was too good to leave and believe. 'Why…why the fuck did you join DigiSys?' he painfully asked Rajesh

'Because I loved her. I love her,' he corrected, 'and I wanted to be with her, in Delhi. She said she loved me too. Now she says she doesn't. How's it possible?'

Neither Manoj nor Adish had any answers. For, their minds were occupied more with the thought of him discarding an offer, which, in gross terms, was almost a *lakh* more than theirs. That too, in the city of opportunities, Bangalore. Feeling utterly insignificant in front of a real *stud*, they reprimanded their deluded selfs for ever comparing themselves to him.

'You two said, I was lucky. Did you not?' said Rajesh to both Adish and Manoj, his voice shaking with disdain and broke into a hysterical laugh. As one more tide struck the rocks, he abruptly went quiet and stared into the gathering darkness. Then, erupted into desperate sobs. Manoj cursed himself for having ever said those words.

For next one hour, Rajesh kept oscillating between these two extreme emotions like a pendulum. Manoj was thankful that at no point, it turned into a howling, though bringing him back to the hostel proved to be an enormous task:

Clutching his arms, first, they dragged Rajesh to the Auto stand. Midway through, it began to pour heavily, and they weren't carrying any umbrella. Soaked to the skin, and bearing his Tarzan wailings the whole way, when they finally reached the hostel, they had to repeat the same isometrics to push him up the stairs. To make matters worse, Uums had kept ringing and Manoj couldn't pick up the phone. Considering the situation a tad too delicate, he did not wish to upset Rajesh further.

Depositing Rajesh to his window-side bed, an unusually mute Adish left for his room. Changing his clothes, Manoj too reckoned it better to leave Rajesh alone for a while, and warily scuffed out.

The rain wore a gloomy appearance altogether, thought Manoj, leaning against the railings in the corridor. Lobbies were teeming with high spirited chatter of the associates, barring a lone ranger Sudipto belting out doleful Kishore Kumar songs at the second floor. It seemed the accounting system had skipped his salary. Perhaps, because it couldn't decide in time whether Sudipto was a Northie or a Southie. The Easterner was melodious, though.

Bengali genes, no doubt. He must request Manjot for a jam session. Someday. Not today. They were on the third floor and he couldn't risk Rajesh jumping off. He had read stories of deranged, jilted lovers, taking extreme steps. *Men in most cases. Driven to the brink by girls.*

His thoughts turned inwards. He had just planned a trip with Uums where she'd hinted at sharing a room on the houseboat, the next night. This was on the heels of a weekend in Aleppy with her boyfriend. Not that he complained. But just for his future's sake; was it so precarious with girls? In hindsight, Rajesh's case was certainly obverse to his own, though.

Manoj rang up Uums to know her whereabouts. She was in her room and asked him to come downstairs to have a little chat, her voice suggesting otherwise.

'Where the hell were you? I called so many times,' she said, her hands firmly placed on her hips as Manoj walked into her room.

'Pandey's girlfriend broke up with him. He is in a real bad shape,' said Manoj.

'Oh. That's horrible,' her hands shifted to her face to cover her mouth. 'But why?'

'She got someone else.'

'What? Seriously? Girls are evil, I tell you. I hope you are not too worried.' She came near and stroked his hair.

'No, I'm good,' he said, feeling her fingers running through his scalp.

'Hmm. But you guys are coming to Aleppy, right?'

Aleppy! He almost forgot. 'I'm not sure,' he shrugged. 'I don't think Pandey would even step out of the room. And somebody must be there to watch over him.'

'Oh, no. I was hoping you'd come or else I will get bored,' she twitched her face. 'And I personally think, your friend should come along too. It will distract him.'

'I guess you're right,' he said, knowing well that he could neither leave her alone to be pounced upon by Venkat nor abandon Rajesh in such indisposition. 'I should go and check on Pandey.'

'Okay and don't worry. He'll be all right,' she said, putting her arms around him.

Manoj hadn't expected Uums to hug him. But now when she did, he too wrapped his arms around her. To his surprise, she didn't pull away. Forgetting Rajesh for a moment, he homed in on Uums, touching the soft fabric of her dress and her equally soft skin underneath. The warmth of her body, kindled his every pore, and within seconds, he realized he wasn't prepared to deal with his hopped up hormones.

Should he let go of her?

Precisely then, Uums pulled away. Manoj couldn't tell if she did so because she too felt his hardness. But he did notice a smirk on her face as her eyes glanced down briefly before saying goodbye.

His heart was still palpitating, trying to burst out of his ribcage when he walked into the room and saw Rajesh in the unitary state of a sobbing.

Manoj let out a wistful sigh. *How would he convince Rajesh to go to Aleppy?*

Manoj Bansal's

Fire outside

****

Curled up on his bed, with puffy red eyes from a nightlong session of crying, Pandey was still glued to his phone, going over her texts for the umpteenth time. It was seven thirty already, and Adish waited at the door, for us to move; for reasons unknown, he had acted all hushed up since the last evening.

'I know it is ill-timed, buddy but given the situation, shouldn't you rather be with your friends,' I said to Pandey.

'Shouldn't you stay back, then?' he snapped, 'Prove how good a friend you are.'

I hated Pandey. Didn't he just have a painful, horrid breakup? Logically, he shouldn't be thinking or talking sense, let alone putting forward cogent arguments.

'This DigiSys room and hostel will remind you only of her,' I reasoned. 'You need fresh environment. The party will take your mind off things.'

'My whole life has turned upside down, and you want me to party? With DigiSys fellows, celebrating a DigiSys salary. And that won't remind me anything? Yeah, right. Genius!' he spat.

Asshole. The bus was at the gate, and this guy was wallowing in an unnecessary and logical debate.

'I've always accompanied you, whenever and wherever you have asked me to. Today is my turn,' I pleaded in a soft, desperate tone. If the previous night had taught me anything new about Pandey, besides his hidden *stud-ness* and his dream package, it was that he surrendered logic to exhortations. Well-soused with emotions. 'Would you not do it for me? Please come.'

He looked down and chewed over his options. 'Ok but forgive me if I do something wrong,' he agreed and rolled out of the bed.

'Nothing will go wrong,' I assured him.

'And I forgot to mention. Mutthur is in Aleppy,' said Adish.

A web of backwaters and lakes entangled into the vast fields of paddy and coconut forests, Alappuzha was nature's celebrated canvas, uniquely decorated with various shades of a single colour – green. And the houseboat? Well, it was enormous.

Double-storeyed, it had ten rooms on each floor, all fitted with a queen-size bed, air conditioner and an attached bathroom. A staircase connected the floors through a large unrestricted balcony on the foredeck. Furnished with tables, sofas and comfy chairs, it lent us a sweeping view of backwaters. A sizeable kitchen existed at the rear to prepare meals. Booze had been arranged as well and stashed into its two refrigerators before we commenced. At eight hundred bucks per person, it was a real bargain and closest to a cruise ship I ever got.

Our afternoon was spent munching and meandering through the marvel that unfurled before us; mesmerizing criss-cross waterways, Cormorants lunching on small fish, floating water hyacinths - an invasive species, gambolling kids, marble-white churches, wooden gabled-roof temples, primary schools, even a State Bank branch with an ATM. Aleppy was truly a biome.

Despite my pleas, Pandey stayed confined to our room albeit, stepping out occasionally to just stand and stare at the lake from the deck. Thankfully, Adish kept him company, which disencumbered me to spend time with Uums without feeling unduly guilty.

After a sultry show, weather turned pleasant towards the evening as rain arrived in heaps and cleared up in an hour, leaving us with a cool breeze and a majestic setting sun, its rays filtering through the palm fronds. That's how Kerala monsoon had been.

All we craved now was some liquor, but the boatmen insisted upon waiting till they had safely moored the boat.

'Three people fell into the lake last week, drinking too much, and drowned,' one of them said. Reminding me of my drowning incident, an impossible fear shook me to the core.

What if Pandey decides to drink and slips into the water accidentally? Or intentionally? He couldn't swim in either case. I had to keep a watch.

'I'm tired,' said Uums. 'Off to my cabin to rest. Are you coming?' Her invitation stressed me further.

'Yeah, I'm tired too. Let's go,' I said.

She switched on the air conditioner as soon as we entered the room. 'Close the door. A.C. is on,' she said and flumped to the bed. I noticed her white spaghetti top and knee-length maroon skirt that had risen a few inches, revealing more than a little of her waxed thighs. An old Hindi song played in my head as I obliged and closed the door.

Hum tum, ek kamre mein band ho...ting ting ting ting...

'I hope your friend is feeling better,' she said.

'Not really and I'm worried. Not sure if bringing him here, was a good idea. The water is too deep,' I said

'What?' she opened her mouth to laugh but her expressions changed the moment she registered my gaze locked on her. 'Sorry, but you think he is going to jump?'

'No, not that. But you see-,' I didn't know how to put it.

'Oh, my god. Don't worry baba,' she got up and hugged me in a repeat of last night. I played along and tightened my hold, and warmed my body against hers. Then, my hands moved. Inchmeal, over her back.

'Have you ever kissed someone?' she leaned away, wearing an impish smile.

God, she was under my charm and I could hardly breathe. Or wait, was *I* under her command? I cared a damn. All I saw, like Arjuna, was her juicy red lips as my sole objective and my answer, hidden in them. Somewhere deep inside me, a meditating beast unshackled himself and in one swift motion, pulled her closer to offer my hungry lips, which her burning lips received with equal zest. She didn't stop until I was about to faint out of breathlessness.

'Now I have kissed,' I let in deep, satisfied breaths and my lungs expanded to their fullest, filled with both air and pride. By the grace of...not Bajrang Bali but Lord Vishnu - his Superior, I had earned my first kiss before my twenty-third birthday.

'You wish to enroll for a common learning program.' She bit her lips.

'Right away,' I said and grabbed her waist; in a hope to clear the beginner's course and move to the advanced level. But guess what? There exists, a demon called exam in between. And exams are meant to screw you. My phone rang as soon as she shifted to a more sensual position. It was Adish.

'Mutthur has arrived,' he said.

'Mutthur? What is he doing here?' I was irritated.

'I told you he would come.'

'Oh yes,' I recalled. What perfect timing! Why didn't he let me drown that day? 'I will come.' I hung up and turned to Uums. She was fiddling with her phone.

'Sorry, it was Adish.'

'No, No. Good, he called. Let's go out or else people will start imagining…things,' she winked and laughed. Things would have to wait.

It was a long night of wild celebrations. From Bryan Adams to Pink Floyd, from MJ to Shakira, from Sonu Nigam to Sukhwinder – all and sundry carolled and with them, the music soared, our heads banged and hips shook. Booze dampened our parched throats, hefting us to the cloud nine. But soon, our first corporate carouse threatened to derail as our liquor ran dry. Our Genie Mutthur, however, saved our night with the 'Evening Devil' he had brought along, filled in bottles to the brim.

Pandey stuck to beer and quietly gulped down three pints, grieving inside his cabin. It performed a sort of miracle, though, and loosened him up as he came forth and joined us on the dance floor. Whistles flew all around when he held Mutthur's hand and improvised an amalgamation of North and South Indian dance steps on the song "Chak de India". Soon every pelvis was gyrating on their moves.

Minutes later, Pandey was nowhere to be seen as the music changed from chartbusters to the romantic melodies; his recent-most memories perhaps. We tracked him back to our cabin where he was weeping, ensconced in a chair, with a Rum bottle clutched to his chest. *Beer to Rum in a single day.* Devdas must be proud.

We settled ourselves on the bed, unsure where to begin. In a hope to distract Pandey we discussed assorted topics intermittently, and soon switched to Maruthi Vallam anchored not too far from our houseboat. Incidentally, Asari - the boat architect in Aleppy - had carried out crucial modifications to improve its performance; the reason behind Mutthur's stopover.

'It would gain at least six seconds,' Mutthur told us.

'Quite close to Gopalan's,' said Adish

'Hopefully. At a little cost, though,' Mutthur shrugged. 'I spent all of my savings.'

'You think it is worth the risk?' I asked.

'Yes. Anything for love,' Mutthur said.

'You spent every single penny on your love. And it seems you aren't too happy about it,' Pandey spoke, his eyes fixed on his phone. 'But that's not Bansal's point. His point is, what if it betrays you?' He snickered, looking at me. 'Don't you worry, boy. The best thing about possessing a boat is that it will always stay by your side, no matter what. Tied firmly with a string,' he gritted his teeth and took a swig from the bottle. *Neat.*

'At least pour some coke or water, man,' I pleaded.

'Today is his birthday,' he continued, ignoring me. 'And the thief must've nabbed his prize,' his jaws clenched and gaze flickered from one person to another, pinning at me at last. His *gollumesque* stare pierced through me as if I had snatched away his girlfriend. His precious!

'That fucker must be...,' he broke his utterance midway in disgust. 'Why the fuck she dumped me, *bhenchod*?'

Why? I still had no answer.

'I tell you why,' he said, uncoiling from his chair like a cobra. Even in this emotional and inebriated state, he wouldn't forgo his theatrics. 'Because I'm a loser and *he* is a doctor. His father is also a doctor, and owns a bloody nursing home. And I! What am I? *One* of the *millionnsss* of middle-class IT engineers of this country. What *aukat* do we have, Bansal?'

I knew why his anguish was aimed at me. For, I alone knew its roots. We came from the world that was perceived as *almost* the best, inhabited by people who *almost* got into the IITs. Initially, the difference between "the Ones" and "*almost* the Ones" seemed infinitesimal, its limit tending to zero. Then, we realized the *tag* of an IIT had already pushed it towards infinity. So, we cribbed and cursed, which in next couple of years, turned into a delusion - our fool's paradise - where we aimed for a top Co. or an IIM for our redemption. *Start-ups? You kidding me?*

First, we needed to be extraordinary. For Once, at least.

'See,' Pandey said, 'Mutthur can't get his love being an ordinary, so he must defeat Gopalan. Adish longs to be ordinary but no, his progressive father won't let him be.'

'Progressive!' Adish mumbled, letting out a suppressed laugh.

Mutthur smiled too. 'And Bansal, my friend...' the words trailed off in a fit of laughter as he staggered to his feet holding, the rum. 'Where is the country for ordinary men?' he said, throwing at us a long, pained stare and proposed, 'I'm going to find that country,' and advanced straight to the bathroom, shutting the door behind.

It was a grave situation. Yet, we laughed uncontrollably. We waited for him to come out but he lingered inside for too long. We agreed to leave him alone and decamped. While Mutthur and Adish chose to chit-chat on the lower deck, I joined Uums on the upper floor where the pig-headed Venkat was trying to woo her. Perhaps, motivated by Bryan Adams' "Let's make a night to remember", blasting from the speakers.

I so wished to tell him the details of our little escapade; Uums' and mine. I was sure he'd jump off the boat. *Jump!* I gasped, and looked at Uums, swaying her waist under the flicker of portable disco-lights. Red, blue, green. She glanced at me. My heart skipped a beat.

I love the way you dance tonight,
your gaze burning me in hearth of sweet desire.

I gasped again and hoping Pandey held his horses, plunged myself into the frenzy.

By the time we wrapped up and came downstairs, Adish and Mutthur were gone, happily snoring and roaring in their room. I peeped into our cabin and found it empty. The bathroom light was switched on, which meant Pandey was still lodged inside.

'Hold me Manoj,' said Uums, stumbling. We were hammered and tired, and she kept falling over so I held her safe and guided her into her cabin. The one with a double bed and sole occupancy rights tonight; for two bodies and one soul.

The ice had melted in the evening, and now the resultant water was on a fifty-degree boil - the temperature of our bodies. Shedding the last shred of inhibition, our bodies fused the minute we closed the door. Her lips parted at once.

Testing and tasting, all possible lip-locks I'd learnt from my *films*, we decided to go for broke, pulling each other's tops off.

The sudden sight of a well-endowed half naked female sent shivers down my spine - marking my life's eureka moment. My trembling palms moved on her soft mounds over her pink, lacy bra and squeezed a little. She let out a lustful moan.

'Easy tiger, don't be a brute,' she grated seductively in my ear, teasing my earlobe with her warm breath and took my specs off. 'I don't want any barrier,' she folded them and slid them behind the pillow.

The wild beast would see less. Fine with him because he'd listen to you no more, girl. He'd only feel now. Off went the hooks of her pink barriers, and I submerged myself into the bliss of her bosom. Eight years since discovering my manhood, I was on the verge of rediscovering the process of procreation.

Isn't it why a man and woman were created?

'I don't think you have protection,' Uums asked, closing her legs momentarily. *Okay, no procreation tonight. Suits me but please, don't shut the shop.*

'I forgot,' I said, tapping my head. 'It's in my bag. I picked it along with booze.'

'You were expecting this?' she mocked me, with a come-hither smile as her breast heaved with a sigh of relief. 'Oh God I love this. Go, get it tiger and quench my thirst,' she said. I had read such lingo in erotic stories but hearing them live was plain out of this world.

'I'll be right back,' I promised her, wearing my tee and stormed out.

Praying her phone to remain dead meanwhile, I was about to enter my room when my sight fell on it. Fire it was; huge flames erupting from the lake before me. I went closer to take a good look, and let out a squeal clutching at my chest. For, what I saw tightened every muscle in my body. There could only be one thing in our vicinity that resembled the long, narrow object that burned before my eyes. Maruthi Vallam.

Time moved both in slow and fast motion, as we desperately

tried to put out the fire and save the boat. But our rescue efforts had started too late. The fire had engulfed and gutted the whole boat. When Lord Hanuman's tail was set on fire, he had burnt down the entire Lanka and escaped unscathed. But today, his mere name couldn't grant that immortality to the boat branded after him. The irony had struck hard. Standing over the blackened remains of the charred boat, I cast a glance at the faces around me.

Adish was inconsolable, Pandey was stunned and I was aghast but Mutthur…Mutthur was paralyzed. He stared at the boat with vacant eyes, his arms hanging numb at his sides. I wondered why his fate had desired such a catastrophe for him. As he wept over his incinerated hope amidst the deafening crackle of the dying embers, Pandey's words rang up inside my head.

Where is the country for ordinary men?

Rajesh Pandey's

A Fire Inside

****

'I am going to find a country for ordinary men,' I said and entered the bathroom. Settled on the commode, I began to introspect, but alcohol had started to cloud my mind.

I felt a strong urge to smoke. But my cigarette pack was lying in the cabin and I wanted to avoid any interaction with the three. I got up and pressed my ear against the door but heard nothing. I quietly opened the door. The room was empty. My "friends" had left. And why not? They had a fucking party to attend. Assholes.

Disappointed in my "friends in need" and unable to bear the Bryan Adams track that played outside, I picked my rum and cigarettes, and disembarked the houseboat at the rear. I couldn't go far, though, as it was pitch dark outside. Even the moon had no desire to accompany me in my grief. Finding a solitary boat anchored nearby, I stepped aboard. Alone at last, I put the bottle down, leaned back and lit a cigarette, savouring its strong flavour. It always helped clear my clogged mind, and filled it with new thoughts.

What if the boat flipped and I fell into the water? I'd die, and none would discover until my body rose above the surface. Not even *her*. My heart raced, and I took out my phone.

Rajesh, it's over. I don't want to be with you. I love Rohan, I read and re-read *her* message. Clear and brutal.

How could love become so shallow? How could something so sacred wither away in a matter of months? How could she severe me from her life so easily? It was so different from the way they portrayed love – *true love,* in movies. Those *DDLJs* and *Dil hai ke maanta nahis!* From the countless films I had watched over the years, I recalled that the pattern of these heroes had reversed. Instantly, my whole life panned out before my eyes, and truth dawned on me.

I was not the hero. I was the *supporting* hero. Basically, a guy who unwittingly helps a girl consummate her life's true love. A loser who is invariably ordinary.

Right, so a typical new age story would read like this:

At the outset, the girl likes this "Supporter" or takes him as a shoulder in her transit, claiming to love him. To his credit, he does win few hugs and kisses but nothing more. He screws up his life, fights the world in hope that one day, he'd unite with her and receive more of her passion fruit. And just when he is about to, she realizes she loves someone else, a hero. She jilts this sidey-loser on a bus or a train and joins her prince charming at an altar of a five star hotel.

Hah! Claps!

Perhaps, the filmmakers' wanted to impart us the inane truth they had ascertained. Ordinary beings never stood a chance. It was inscribed in their *Kundali*. One thing didn't change, though. Heroes still had names like Rohan aka Raj Malhotra and not Rajesh Pandey. Damn, I hated my name.

No-one ever cared for 'Rajesh'. I was always called Pandey, be it school or IIT coaching classes or the Institute. Ten years later, I'd be promoted to Pandey ji, like my father. *She* was the only person who addressed me by my first name, Rajesh. That too, only recently. Earlier, I was *her* endearing *sweetu, janu, baby.*

Had *she* been hinting at the inevitable by calling me Rajesh of late? Of course, because *she* had Rohan, a name that even smelled like a hero. No matter how hard I tried, even I couldn't bring myself to call him 'Malhotra'.

'Bastard, bastard, bastard! And that B…' Damn! I couldn't abuse *her*. I loved *her*. 'I fucking love her.' Tears spilled from my eyes, like an incessant rain and dripped my pinnae wet. Irritated, I kept wiping my ears, but the seepage didn't stop.

Sleep came over me and I drifted into a dream. *Her* dream: Her naked body resting on the boat, glimmering under the full moon. I nuzzled her hair, smelling the green Apple scent. Then, teased her with wet kisses all over. Closing her eyes she moaned and bit her lips. Making intense love, we exchanged the heat of our unbridled passion over the *phone*.

She loved hearing the idea of my thrusts matching the rhythm of a rocking boat, erupting into orgasmic moans and took a promise that I'd be as wild in real. *Come here and fuck me right now*, were her exact words. I told her I'd be a horny beast the day we make real love and she'd experience an ecstasy like she had never. Aroused again, she said she'd like to ride me. Coming on top, she jiggled her body...

A mighty shake woke me up.

Music had stopped playing on the houseboat but I could still see few hazy figures hanging around. Perhaps the party was over. I checked my phone. It was eleven and yet, there were no missed calls or new messages. It seemed everyone had abandoned me. My head spun. No it was the boat that shook again.

I warily looked around but saw nothing. Fear petrified me as I imagined a monstrous creature writhing underneath the boat. In movies they always ate losers; the real reason they perish in the end. Loser meat was useless too.

What was I supposed to do? Should I let him rip me to shreds and devour me? It'd be a horrible way to die. The boat was calm again. I shook off the feeling with a deep breath and lit another cigarette.

She'd realize her mistake only when I was dead. *She'd* cry and feel guilty and pray that it was nothing but a nightmare. Dying, I fantasised, was a *good* idea. *Yes, I must die.*

Slowly I rose to my feet, trying hard to keep my balance. My legs trembled and hit something. The rum bottle had toppled. I stood still and waited lest someone heard the noise. Satisfied I was alone in my grief, I readied myself to take the leap of death into the silent lake. The water seemed deep. Twenty feet, they told us. I was under six.

I closed my eyes and mustered the strength.

My phone beeped.

'Bro all okay? I'm going to stay in Uums room,' read Bansal's text. Asshole turned out to be the 'blessed one' tonight. I was furious, less at him and more at Uums for deceiving both him and her boyfriend.

'What the fuck is wrong with girls?' I needed answers. I had to talk to *her*. I had promised myself a great life with *her* and I ought to know where I fell short before I jumped to my end. Drawing a long puff, I threw my cigarette, held the anchor rope and alighted.

As expected, the cabin was empty. Suspecting someone might come, I went into the bathroom and dialled *her* number. It rang for few seconds and unexpectedly, *she* answered. *Her* voice was soft but distant and cold.

'Why…why did you cheat on me?' I said with hitching sobs.

'I didn't cheat, Rajesh. We broke up, remember?'

'You broke up. I didn't,' I said. She remained quiet. 'I cannot live without you. I love you.'

'Rajesh, you're a great person. I'm sure you'll find someone better. Someone nice. Who'd love you.'

'I want *you* to love me, damn it.' I blurted. My throat felt sore, and my mouth ran dry.

'I love Rohan,' she said, definitely.

At that point neither she had anything to add nor did I. 'I'll talk to you later. Rohan is calling. Bye.' I heard the busy tone.

She had unceremoniously dumped my call too. My body went limp, and my phone fell on the floor. Sitting on the commode, I had no idea for how long, I wept. So lost I was in my anguish that

I failed to notice, when the door opened, and Bansal appeared gesticulating. His voice seemed to drop at me.

What the fuck was he saying?

'Mutthur's boat is burning,' I heard him then. Was he joking? He wasn't, I found out as soon as I stormed out on the deck and saw it myself. The boat was in flames.

That was my story of last night.

But how did the boat catch fire? The puzzle had troubled me ever since. The visuals kept playing in a loop inside my mind as I lay in my hostel room, prodding for answers. It was fine when I had left. As I stitched together the pieces once more, an impossible possibility struck me. The missing piece finally showed up, sending a shiver down my spine.

I had spilled three-quarter-full alcohol on the boat and thrown a fully lit three-quarter length cigarette into it.

'How do you feel now?' Adish asked. I ignored his query and kept staring at the only chapatti on my plate. My forlorn body felt no appetite after I had come up with the three-quarter hypothesis. It had trapped me in a condo of guilt but I had no guts to share it with anyone. Still I had followed Manoj to the canteen on his insistence. Yeah, *Manoj*.

He too, hadn't believed his ears, when I first called him by his first name while waking him up in the morning. A delicate moment it was, for both of us as it had jolted him out of the bed. He thought it was his father. Initially, my lips also refused to go against the law of names. But then, *'Be the change you wish to see'* quote of Mahatma Gandhi had never been a cakewalk in practice. He, however, had the undying love of Kasturba.

'Mutthur is in similar state,' Adish said, nibbling from his plate.

Mutthur has lost just a boat. I have lost my love. Fucker.

'It wasn't just a boat. It was Maruthi Vallam. His deity. His dream. His only chance to marry Kala. You know, everybody blames him for being careless, but none realizes it is him who has lost the most,' he added, catching my thoughts unintentionally.

Quite frankly, I was irritated and didn't care about Mutthur and his boat right now. What I needed was to feel good about myself and yet, all these guys could throw at me, were pitiful looks and a constant reminder of the ugly truth – an incinerated boat, an inconsolable Mutthur and his hopes reduced to ashes.

In hindsight, you were equally culpable. If only you hadn't left me alone. Friends!

'They found a charred rum bottle on the deck,' whispered Adish.

The ground sank under my feet. They knew.

'They believe it was some drunkard who dropped the liquor. And where there's a drunkard, there is always a *beedi* and a matchbox. That might have caused the fire,' Adish explained.

No, they didn't know.

'Rum is quite inflammable,' Manoj opined.

'It could be foul play,' Adish suggested.

'Who knows? What is Mutthur's view...'

I told you. Drink only when you are responsible enough, my father's voice rebuked me while they debated.

Clearly I wasn't. With one irresponsible act, I had destroyed Mutthur's one and only hope.

Perhaps *she* was right in dumping me.

I was the culprit, and that was the truth.

The Story of Mutthur & Kala

****

Mutthur had never felt so debilitated. Not even when his father lay dead before him; a long battle against throat cancer was lost.

But that one night in Alappuzha changed everything. A rum bottle and a beedi had mercilessly crushed his hopes and had reduced his life to a cruel joke of destiny. His entire savings were gone too. But the worst of all, his village had lost its prestige. This year, for the first time in known history, Mevalloor wouldn't participate in the Vallamkali. A matter of utmost shame for the whole Ezhava community, which held Sri Narayana guru so dear to their heart.

Back in 1903, when Sri Narayana Guru had wished to set up a school at a backward village of Kumarakom, it hadn't proved to be an easy task. Born into an Ezhava family, which was considered Avarna, he had fought against casteism throughout his childhood. Yet, that never deterred his faith. Neither in God nor his religion. True, he was an educationist, but he also believed that education alone couldn't uplift the downtrodden. Social and spiritual uplift was equally necessary. And for that, people had to be given uniform rights on the Gods they put so much faith in. Hence, when he was requested to consecrate the idol of Sri Balasubramanya Swami at Kumaramangalam temple, he agreed on one condition; the temple must treat each of its devotees as equal.

Without any debate, it was accepted and henceforth, came into being a tradition that celebrated this equality each year; also the sole reason the main competition for Sri Narayana Guru Trophy centred on Iruttukuthis or Odi-vallams, and not Chundans.

Chundans were the warrior class; the grandeur and pride of Kerala that reigned the battles of yore. Churlans and Veppu were used for passengers and material transport and hence, found application in modern business whereas Odi-vallams – once the vehicle of ordinary soldiers and then of smugglers, lagged. In present times, they couldn't find much purpose and hence, faced discrimination.

Perhaps, giving relevance to them was a way to remind people of the core teaching of Sri Narayana Guru – "Equality." It was what Mutthur had sought this year, for himself.

Slouched against a wall, in the warehouse, Mutthur contemplated on how to reverse his situation. Six weeks remained for season's first race, and eight to the festival. The previous boat had been dismantled. So there was no way he could go back. A new one could not be built. Not so soon. And if at all, by any means, it could be, where would he find the money?

Mutthur had always faced life's snags, small or big, with brevity but today he was trounced by his own fate. He loved Kala deeply and now, hopelessly. He knew Kala felt the same but given their culture and society, what choice could she have if her father indeed, decided to marry her off to Gopalan.

He had heard so much of *Tharavads*, the legendary social order of the Nairs that consisted of large joint families. But unlike other communities, they were matrilineal, liberal and unrestricted, and bestowed unique rights on women. Best of all, the right to choose their men. *One of its kinds in the entire country.*

For once, Mutthur wanted Kala to rediscover her inner Nair woman of yore, and challenge the orthodoxy that had crept into their Malabari society. But wouldn't it be expecting too much? Irrespective of the role reversals, a Nair woman loved her family. And for Kala, her father was her family. She'd rather die than elope, he knew.

Death seemed the only solution. But could death be trusted? He didn't believe in the next life and deemed the present one too sacred. No, he couldn't die. He shouldn't even let the thought cross his mind, let alone consider it. This was no movie, but real life. His life. And people had expectations from him. Especially his brother.

Staring vacantly through the door at the severe downpour outside, he could see someone talking to his labourers. *What would Kala do if they don't end up together? Could she live without him?* He had no answers.

'I'd been looking for you all over, and here you're,' Vasudevan stood at the door with an umbrella. 'Come, lunch is ready.'

Mutthur tilted his head up, but didn't budge. He simply patted his stomach once and shook his hand, implying he wasn't hungry.

'What will you achieve by not eating? You'll fall sick and turn weak. And there is much work in the paddy fields. I cannot do it alone,' he said, annoyed at his mulish brother.

It'd been three days, and Mutthur had barely eaten a morsel. At first, it hadn't worried Vasudevan much. He knew Mutthur had always been resolute and would eventually pull himself together. But things seemed different this time, and he was beginning to fear for his brother's well-being. Vasudevan waited for a response, but Mutthur kept staring at the fronds wall. Folding his umbrella, he stepped in and sat down across Mutthur.

'Ever since father passed away, I've never let anything bother you or affect you. But today I'm afraid,' said Vasudevan. His tone was soft and pleading, like an old friend and not an elder brother, Mutthur noticed. 'Tell me, brother. What eats you from inside?

Vasudevan was six years elder to him, and yet a time existed when the two brothers were more like friends; sneaking out to catch a show of Mammootty's latest release, going fishing together, climbing palm trees. It was he who had taught Mutthur how to climb and pluck coconuts.

On his part, Mutthur had never met a person more skilled than his *Chetta*. But twelve years ago, when Vasudevan took up the reins of Sankunni household following their father's diagnosis of Cancer, their relationship underwent a sudden change.

'I've lost my chance. I can no longer prove my worth to Kala's father,' Mutthur said. Vasudevan shook his head in disbelief.

'I had always prided myself on having a brother like you,' said he. 'Do you know why?'

Mutthur looked up

'Because you always put others before your own self. Village folks love you, respect you, and today you are bent on giving it all up, brother,' said Vasudevan.

'How?' asked Mutthur.

'By being parochial and selfish,' said Vasudevan. 'Ask yourself Mutthur. Would Medavoor Nair ever accept you and our family, irrespective of what position you achieve in the Vallamkali? You know the answer, don't you?'

Mutthur remained quiet. He knew what his brother hinted at.

Vasudevan took a deep sigh. 'Brother, better do something good with your life if you are so intent on being selfish, instead of misspending your youth on a frugal pursuit like some woman's love,' he said and stood up. 'Come. Amma is waiting.'

Today's Sadhya bore a pleasant taste for both families. And now, sitting in his house courtyard with Gopalan's family, Medavoor Nair discussed the upcoming Vallamkali season. While his daughter Kala helped Lakshmi, her sister-in-law in cleaning the kitchen. In olden days, a century ago perhaps, this scene in a Nair household would've been at least different if not antipodal.

'Mark my words, Velu. Your son is going to rewrite history. If anyone can surpass Medavoor Nair, it is Gopalan,' said Medavoor to the old, lean and bald Velu who laughed with paternal pride. Velu used to be Medavoor's deputy, but now, his son Gopalan commanded the Puranjal Vallam, the village Odi-vallam.

'You've been the real hero for us,' said Gopalan.

Kala's father Medavoor Karunakaran Nair had an interesting past; he had led the best finishing Odi-vallam in the history of their village – an eighth spot in the Kumarakom competition, twenty years ago. A feat Gopalan wished to outdo at any cost to win Kala's hand.

Not that Medavoor wasn't impressed with the fierce young skipper. In fact, he had pretty much made up his mind to marry Kala off to him. The only thing that kept him from making any formal announcement had been his daughter's transient affair with Mutthur. Though, Medavoor disliked Mutthur, the younger son of Mohan Sankunni and would never approve of him.

Why? Kala had asked on many occasions. However, Medavoor couldn't quite put his finger on the *why*? Surely, not for Mutthur's Ezhava caste. Even when Nairs had come a long way from their unique matrilineal system to an orthodox patriarchy in modern world, yet they hardly cared for the social caste system.

Could it be that, at times he saw Mohan's image in Mutthur? Or because at other times, Mutthur behaved like an antithesis to his father. Whatever it was, with Maruthi Vallam charred to ashes, Medavoor Nair had no reasons to be foreboding anymore.

Gopalan, on the other hand, had assumed a different perspective. He believed he ought to beat Medavoor Nair. For, if he succeeded, his future father-in-law who carried immense pride on his head would bow down to him. Ensuring that Kala didn't bring her father's pride into Gopalan's house.

'I have a proposition to make,' Gopalan said.

Alarmed, Kala appeared at the kitchen door. A smile broke across Gopalan's face, much to her dismay.

Kala had known Gopalan since their childhood. Well-built and tall, Gopalan was the eldest of his four siblings. He wasn't much educated – a metric pass, but was clever and smart, a trait that had kept their family business of fishing and agriculture thriving. He wouldn't talk much but regardless, carried a fierce reputation. He'd always been interested in Kala and believed he'd marry her one day. Kala too, believed the same until Mutthur trespassed and whisked her away. She was certain that Gopalan knew how steadfast was her love for Mutthur, yet it hadn't deterred him from coveting her.

A quick glance from Gopalan filled her with mortal fear - the one a sacrificial lamb might feel, tethered to a peg outside the butcher's shop. Could he be asking for her hand? She murmured a silent prayer to Lord Krishna.

'Why don't we put the deity back into the water once again?' said Gopalan. She gaped at him. He had put forth a proposition that no-one had anticipated. Velu and Medavoor too, stared at him as if he had opened a can of worms.

'Pardon me for my words but isn't it a shame that our Chundan rots in some unknown corner, devoid of the pride she is entitled for?' he added.

'He is correct, Medavoor. It's been six years,' Velu said, mulling over the conundrum, Perimar village had never stopped discussing. 'What are we leaving behind for our next generation? A shame indeed.'

'Was there no shame when year after year we disappointed our deity by below-par performances,' Medavoor spoke, his gaze fixed on the scale model of Chundan placed in the middle of the courtyard. It was created by one of the most famous Thachans of his times – his father, Narayanambhu Nair.

Thachans are Kerala's traditional boat architects. In the bygone era of the kingdoms, they garnered immense respect and value. Known with the title of "Asari", their knowledge, insight and skills would often decide victories and defeats in the long drawn battles for the supremacy of the backwaters.

But when these kingdoms declined and Kerala was ushered into the modern democratic world along with the rest of India, their boats became a part of leisure sports. The combative spirit of the Malabaris though, soon turned these sports competitive and boat craft assumed a new dimension altogether.

The designs changed to gain more speed as boats acquired a status that went beyond just being a deity; they were a mark of sporting pride for every village. Amongst all, the snake boats - the Chundan Vallams, captured most of the people's imagination owing of its glorious past. Medavoor's father, though, held Odi-vallams closer to his heart.

A devotee of Sri Narayana guru, he'd treat them as his own children who craved for his personal attention. Not before he reached the sixtieth year of his life, the village council could convince him to construct a Chundan. He had obliged under one condition. That, its reins be accorded to the worthy ones who offered their respect and virtue to his beloved Odi-vallams, first.

'But I agree with you, Velu,' Medavoor said after a long pause, putting his hand on Gopalan's shoulder and smiled. 'Now, I have hope. And I believe this year's race will resurrect our deity,'

Kala's heart sank. Gopalan had cleverly trapped her father in the inextricable web of pride and ego. He was the new promising hero who had pledged to take the village honour to newer heights. As for Mutthur, he had no way to partake in this game now where Gopalan seemed to be its sole player and winner too.

Gopalan grinned at Kala. She could sense that he was trying to read her mind through her expressions. He was ready to play his little game. Or perhaps his *little game* had already begun.

Rajesh Pandey's

The Purpose

****

Robin paced, back and forth. 'I see many young engineers obsess over exclusive jobs. Why? Because they think, it is exclusive,' he said, turning to his audience - our D5 batch. Robin was today's faculty to discuss our future in IT; his third such session in past two weeks.

True, DigiSys had entered the big league under CapVirgo, yet, their management was aware that Indian engineers continued to perceive Indian IT majors in a discreet way; barring TCS - a 'Tata' company, and Infosys - the biggest desi entrepreneurial IT success, none exuded reverence among the engineering graduates. DigiSys knew if they were desirous of retaining talent in their pool then what they offered, had to be lucid. And hence, an interactive session had been arranged right after the 'Communication Skills' session where every limit of ridiculousness had already been surpassed with topics like:

* *how to wear a groomed expression on your face?*
* *how to conduct yourself on an outing with your boss?*
* *how to entertain an employee from the client organization?*
* *how to draft cordial emails?*
* *how to receive a friend of your best friend, working in the US, at an airport?*
* *how to rebuke a restaurant manager for unhygienic food?*

'But what's wrong in being exclusive,' asked Raman. Heads turned in his direction.

Raman would be flying to the US next month for his M.S., and the only reason he came to Trivandrum was to amuse himself with a paid vacation. So all he'd do was, ask counter questions.

'Tell me first. Looking at the skeleton of a Dinosaur, could you verify whether it is Shahrukh Khan, or the pharaoh of Egypt or the great Picasso, if such eminent personalities existed among them? In fact if any of them were Hindus, you wouldn't even find their skeletons because their bodies might've been burnt to ashes, right?' said Robin, and the whole class cracked up. 'Nothing is wrong in being exclusive. It is the obsession with exclusivity that is disturbing.'

'But look at Microsoft, Adobe, Yahoo and Google and others. They make unique products,' Manjot said. 'Where are we?'

'We make products too. We have world's third largest banking software,' Robin said.

'But their innovative products like Yahoo messenger and Orkut have changed the world. They are a rage. Connecting lost friends and people world over,' said another associate.

Robin smiled, unperturbed. 'Let's consider a scenario. We have two products - FinSoft, our banking software and Orkut, your favourite social networking platform. What if both disappear?'

Silence and gasps. Because not having Orkut was an unbelievable scenario. Imagine a "single" engineer, unable to check profiles of a friend's friend's friends – patently females, or send messages and friend requests to random girls, put crappy scrap entries. Harrowing. Forget these hunters, what about the wretched heartbroken hunted souls? Personally, I was thirsty for Orkut Buyukkokten's blood. If not for him, it wouldn't despair me to stalk *her* on Orkut, delving into *her* scrapbook entries and photo albums. Yeah, I was still on *her* friend list and *her* blithe smile in *her* recent pics did make me miserable.

On the contrary Yahoo messenger, I firmly believed, was one of the greatest inventions. It provided you a cloak of anonymity; so essential for an isolated, personal conversation with someone you weren't familiar with. Without him or her being judgemental. It didn't matter whether the info exchanged was correct or not. What mattered was that you'd always get a listening ear without having to utter a single one, which at times seemed the most painful activity.

'And without banking you'll be back to much longer queues and delays in financial transactions, lesser security and chances of frauds that may affect your salary accounts as well,' Robin reasoned, pointing at us. He had a valid point. Two months back, we would've unanimously picked Orkut. But today was a changed reality. At least for me.

'Associates, I agree our task is different and our products are no fun, but they are essential. They are certainly not cool because they are a necessity. Be proud,' Robin concluded the session.

'Are you okay?' he asked as we dispersed.

'Yeah, I'm fine,' I said. He had heard my silence.

'Good then. You were exceptionally quiet so I suspected you weren't well,' he said. I smiled. 'Going for lunch?' he asked. I nodded, and we both headed to the canteen.

Robin began his professional career with DigiSys and spent seven long years in the company before switching to Infosys where he worked extensively on Finnacle - their core-banking product. He returned three years later when DigiSys acquired Finsoft, a similar banking platform. Homecoming proved to be a sweet experience and within a year, Robin was promoted to the position of Europe delivery head of Finsoft.

Astounded, Adish stopped eating and tried to digest the info first as we sat in the canteen. 'Wow! And where do we develop it?'

'Mumbai,' replied Robin. 'It's a real good project. We have recently signed a deal with the biggest of the French banks,' he added.

Adish gaped at Robin.

'Do you have consulting or business development too,' Manoj asked hopefully. He had skipped his customary lunch with Uums today. Robin was the man of the moment.

Bansal always had his priorities sorted.

'Not really. All of that is under CapVirgo.'

'Nothing for non-IT guys like us,' I smiled feebly at Bansal... *Don't. Don't tread into the forbidden territory. Control the urge,* I chided myself. Manoj looked dejected. In contrast, Adish had picked up his knife and fork once again.

'I'd say, IT has more to offer a non-computer engineer rather than a computer one,' Robin said. Adish straightened his back. 'You see, computer engineers are tech experts. They can use the tools in the smartest and most efficient way. But what they often lack is the instinct to identify a real industry problem. That's where the role of other engineering streams becomes crucial,' Robin made a double quote with his fingers.

Adish's tools - the fork and the knife, paused in mid-air while Manoj and I cocked our heads forward. Robin realized his session wasn't over yet.

'Let me site an example to elucidate,' he said. 'Suppose, we're called to provide support to the design industry, let's say, on a Ship building project. Now, what would happen if a computer puritan interacts with a marine or mechanical pundit at the client side?'

I got what he meant. On probability index, the event of both arriving at a common understanding was an implausible one.

Robin smiled. 'So, to understand it first from each perspective, I must have Mechanical, Marine and Automation engineers on the same board. They are our bridges which connect the two sides,' he said. It made sense. 'And now, a very important question, 'What's there in it for you?'

Indeed. As he put the most important issue for consideration on our table, I keenly observed the faces floating around us. Initially, each of them bore an enthusiasm of a newborn, but now many of them felt utterly insignificant. Perhaps, they all shared our common doubt - where are we going to end up?

'My advice to both of you,' he said, pointing at Manoj and me with purpose as Adish retreated to his food with his hands, no more interested in the topic. 'This bridge has the capabilities and the possibilities to become a destination. And they're right beneath the surface. But you have to scratch it to find it. And for that, you need a purpose,' he concluded on a cliffhanger.

A purpose! Manoj and Adish already had one.

Fuck it. Where would I find mine?

Manoj Bansal's

A Hope against hope

****

'Can't you build a new one?' Pandey repeated the same trifling question for the umpteenth time. None of us bothered responding and continued sipping toddy. 'I know, man. I know. That is impossible,' he retracted and quietened again.

We were atop the same tree I fell from, into my almost watery grave. Today, I was cautious and sat close to the base. The situation seemed grim and despondency had crept into our mood following Mutthur's revelation of Gopalan and his family's visit to Kala's house.

In a way, it reminded me of the fellowship in the Lord of the Rings sagged against the rocks outside the mines of Moria; their hope Gandalf succumbed to the fire of Balrog. The union of Mutthur and Kala seemed to me as daunting as the fusion of the ring and the fire of Mount Doom. Yes, doomed we were.

Gopalan, the dark lord, must be laughing his ass off.

'You look distraught. Here, try some toddy?' Adish offered the bottle to Pandey who shot him a look as if asked to perform a striptease.

'Take it, man. It is not devil yet. You won't do anything irresponsible,' I teased him. 'Watch out for the slippery trunk, though.'

Pandey glared at me while Mutthur kept looking at the retreating fishing boats.

'I shouldn't,' Pandey said. His soft reaction was brief and puzzling.

I had advised him not to step out and instead, rest in the hostel or catch a movie if indeed he wished a change of air. But he'd been adamant about meeting Mutthur.

'I feel like a total failure right now,' he spoke.

'And who do you think we are? Shaktiman?' Adish retorted. *A Shaktiman fan, he was.* I wasn't surprised. 'You know how lucky you are? It is so much easy for you,' he said. The ominous signs of his usual rants gurgled out of nowhere. Pandey's self-pitying virus had transmitted fast. Shaktiman would be dead soon.

'Easy what?' I asked.

Adish gasped. 'I believed, for me, DigiSys was *the* place, but I was so fucking wrong.'

'What crap, man?'

'Crap? Don't you remember what Robin said? You non-IT people, you are the bridge. And you are the destination as well. Who are we then? Labourers who forge the bridge?' he said and gulped the remaining toddy in his glass, down his throat.

Oh God, I saw daylight. Adish was a *mahapurush.* I was dying to grab his feet and shove him into the water.

'No-one cares what *our* purpose is. And if one does, we have no freaking idea what it is. You know, we think we rule our well. but the moment we swim out into the ocean we become nothing but a small fish,' he blurted out the whole zoology he knew, in one single breath.

'You mean frog?'

'Eh?' he gaped at me in confusion.

'Yeah, you said fish, but it is frog that lives in the well.'

'You Northies are so fucking insular,' he scowled. 'You might have frogs in your wells. We don't,' he spat further. 'In fact, we don't have wells either.'

'Remember Adish, how we used to catch frogs?' Mutthur spoke.

'You caught frogs?' I asked.

'Yeah, it's one of the favourite past times for kids. Hunting frogs during monsoon,' Adish explained.

Did he say hunting?

'Hunt for?' I dreaded the answer.

'To eat. What else?' said Mutthur.

'Of course, you're a fish then,' I almost threw up. 'A small fish.'

'You think it's funny?' Adish retorted. 'You know the face I have to confront in the mirror every day?'

Okay, I understood why it wasn't easy for him.

He carried on, 'People like us have two mirrors - one plain and another, a large concave. The plain mirror shows us our abject reality, forcing us to look into the concave one that transforms us into an inordinate giant.'

He had transposed to Ray Optics now. Couldn't there be a more outrageous way to describe your wretched life? Though my mirror was convex - the one that diminished your size.

'But you're such a great storyteller, Adish,' voiced Pandey.

'The best in our village,' said Mutthur.

Yeah man, I scratch yours. You scratch mine. And together we have toddy. I kept drinking.

'That's the thing. The best in the village,' Adish snapped back.

'Well, you could pursue your exceptional talent and be the best,' Pandey said with such a mix of tiredness, depression and motivation that I made a mental note to check my GRE guide for one word to describe his peculiar combo-motion.

Adish was quiet. Was he contemplating what Pandey said? I had no clue. But I was sure of one thing. The loser had managed to hog away the limelight from Pandey.

'I don't intend to be the best storyteller,' he said. 'That's not my pursuit. My pursuit is to know why everything should transmute into an exercise to prove your worth. I want to ask why...why two people who love each other so dearly, cannot be together.'

Didn't Pandey ramble about the same stuff that fateful night? *Copycat loser.*

Pandey chuckled as if he interpreted my broodings. 'I don't know. Neither have I pursued what I desired nor has anyone chosen to love me the way Kala loves Mutthur. So if you sincerely wish to see a frog, take a look at me. I'm the certified loser,' he gave one last shot to prove his frog-loser-worthiness.

Everybody kept mum which meant Pandey had won the final round. 'Why the hell can't we build another boat?' he cried once again.

I gestured at Mutthur to refill my glass. I had had enough.

'What happened to the previous boat?' I asked.

'The council dismantled it. They needed the wood for other purposes,' Mutthur said.

'I assumed you guys preserved your memories,'

'How many shall we preserve? Times change, demands change. And after a while, old memories do become a logistic issue,' he shared a perspective.

'Get a boat and at least participate,' said Pandey.

'What's the point? They were rejected precisely because they couldn't compete with modern boats,' Mutthur said.

'Survival of the fittest, that's what I was talking about. The not-fits don't stand a chance. Run, Lola run. The bloody nature is against you,' Adish barged in, shifting from Optics to the theory of evolution via Hollywood.

I wondered if he too, studied Biology in his +2. The subject was a nightmare. Adish was damn accurate, though. Nature was dead against our peaceful ramblings. From nowhere, the rain started to pour in buckets.

'Let us leave,' I said, unwilling to get drenched.

'The house is too far,' Adish surrendered.

Ignoring him, I pointed to a small hut at a distance. 'What is that place?'

'That's-,' Mutthur paused and stared at the hut for few seconds. 'Let's go there,' he said.

We'd almost reached the hut when Adish gave out a desperate shout, 'We cannot outrun the nature. It will consume us.'

Pandey came to a halt, having taken the deadly blow.

'What happened?' I yelled.

'Adish is correct. It is our destiny. We cannot escape it. That shed is an illusion,' he said and dropped to his knees, weeping. Shrouded in a helpless uncertainty, we stood around him while rain continued to drench us.

Then, someone spoke in Malayalam from the hut.

We swirled around and saw a lean, frail figure standing on the narrow verandah.

'Who is he?' I asked.

'Narayanan,' said Mutthur. More Malayalam words were hurled in our direction, sounding like a desperate plea.

'What does he say?'

'He is inviting us inside,' he explained, 'to join him for toddy.'

Adish Mathew's

Jacob

****

'I agree. The situation has been unfavourable to you two,' said Manoj to Rajesh and Mutthur. He was in the middle of his sermon spree. I had stayed quiet, lost in the conundrums of my own life.

The fifth element Narayanan, on the other hand, did speak once; when he wished to borrow toddy from us having emptied his. And while he hummed a grief-stricken poem, un-sharable from its very premise, my curious eyes surveyed his one-roomed hut, having an attached kitchen and a bathroom. It had minimal furniture and nothing much of value except an overflowing old but large bookrack, placed in a dim corner. Comparing it to the decrepit, fragile frame of a toddy-bibber; its presence was beyond me.

'He looks sad. What is he singing?' asked Rajesh, showing more interest in Narayanan's pain rather than Manoj's empathy.

'A verse from Ramanan,' said Mutthur and translated him the verse.

And the woman, She is the root;
benefits and fulfilment are her aim,
A woman's love is selfish ever,
possessions, riches secure her fall;

'Who was Ramanan?'

'A fallen poet,' I opened my mouth. 'He loved Chandrika, the daughter of a wealthy Advocate who promised him her eternal love but later betrayed him and chose an affluent youth Rajan. He hanged himself on the day of her marriage.' I had to share.

'Ramanan, Rajan...Rajesh, Rohan...Advocate, doctor. All same. Even Cha...fuck man,' laughed Rajesh, and picked up the glass finally. 'Could I get its Hindi-' he paused and laughed louder, 'sorry, English translation?'

'Stop this nonsense fucker,' Manoj, I guess, had had enough of their moronic prattle. 'You, Adish,' he turned to me, 'trust me. You looked beautiful when you were quiet.' I gasped. 'And Mutthur, I don't know about this Devdas, but *you* cannot give up so easily.'

'Finding a spare boat in a good enough condition is highly improbable,' Mutthur said.

'Humara boat use karo,' Narayanan broke his silence. Our eyes widened, not because we realized that he followed our conversation, but because he had uttered the forbidden language.

Gauging the expressions on the two Northie faces, I could tell that they had lost every hope to meet a native who could speak Hindi. Let alone finding a person confined to a hut in the middle of a Coconut forest that was forsaken by its own village. Well, I couldn't blame them. Mutthur and I had just started on our Hindi tutorials. Though I was equally surprised at Narayanan.

My sight again fell on the large bookrack. There were Hindi titles too. He was a secular reader, I suppose. Feeling proud to be a Malayali, I smiled at Manoj who curled his lips to acknowledge the fact. He'd later reveal to me that *we* defied the norms of rural capsules of the rest of the country where one knew only their native language. Well, Kerala was a wonderland, I rediscovered that day. Anyways, staying on the subject; Narayanan wanted us to use their boat.

'Your boat?' Mutthur frowned.

'You have a boat?' I said and turned to Narayanan.

'What is he talking about?' Manoj asked.

'Some old boat,' I clarified.

'Best boat in the history of Mevalloor. It defeated Medavoor Nair,' said Narayanan, proudly.

'Who is Medavoor Nair?' asked Manoj.

'Kala's father,' I said.

'Wow. Was he the captain?' Pandey looked at Narayanan with astonishment. 'He could offer us tips.'

Narayanan didn't speak further.

'Where is this boat? Demolished again?' I asked Mutthur.

'No one can demolish Thiruneelakhandam vallam. Robust and intact, she rests in peace. Somewhere,' Narayanan spoke in Malayalam now.

'But where?'

'Doesn't matter,' Mutthur said. 'The boat is unusable. The worst ever made. That's why it was retired twenty years ago.'

'And sold off to some crack heads for a pittance. To build a new boat that won Mevalloor the championship for three years in a row,' Narayanan scorned. 'Thank God a Jew saved it and thank god you got rid of that ill-fated junk.'

'It was Thiruneelakhandam vallam that was ill-fated. Just like its name, it was poison,' Mutthur thundered, his eyes locked with Narayanan's.

'Wait, did you say? A Jew saved it?' I asked. Narayanan stayed quiet but I had already cracked it. 'The boat is in Kochi,' I told Mutthur.

'No point discussing that boat,' he said.

'There is, Mutthur. Go and reclaim what is yours. Your father will be proud,' Narayanan beseeched. His emotions indicated there was more to the precious. Something deeply emotional. Perhaps sinister too. Like that *magical ring,* Manoj often spoke about, *which consumed every person who held it dear to him.*

Mutthur pondered over his words.

'What's going on?' Manoj pestered. I realized our conversation had shifted to Malayalam. I briefly explained the new discovery to him and Rajesh.

'We must go to Kochi,' Pandey rose to his feet. 'If that Jew understands love and its pain, he might recognise our plight as well.'

'In that case, I'd say, none understands it better than Jacob,' I got up as well.

Somewhere, the dark lord Gopalan stopped laughing, Manoj would say. 'The fellowship is ready. To claim the sword of Elendil,' uttered Manoj soon. The guy never disappointed me.

Our one-day schedule had turned into a two-day sojourn as we accompanied Mutthur to visit Jacob's shop. The history behind the boat had been one reason. Thiruneelakhandam was the same boat that had achieved the legendary result for the village twenty years ago, under his father's command; also the same boat, which overturned in Muvattupuzha during their return. Mohan Sankunni had lost a leg, but worse, he had lost his zeal for life.

'This place looks quite old. How many Jews live here?' asked Rajesh looking curiously at the Jewish town.

'Near about fifteen families,' I said, noticing that many of the shops were still closed.

'They have awesome stuff, man,' Manoj peeped with into the antique shops, wonderstruck.

'Wait till you see Jacob's shop. It is by far the largest.'

It is quite refreshing to revisit a place with a fresh pair of eyes, Jacob would often say. He was right, I learned as I ambled along the Jewish lane, with two sets of Northie eyes; marvelling at the different colours on the famous Graffity wall and the rough textures of the stony artefacts placed outside the houses.

'Wait, I need to buy cigarettes,' said Rajesh, as we passed by a cigarette shop. He'd been searching for "Kerala Lights" the whole way but every time met "Disappointment" that said a *hello* with a toothy grin. This shop proved worse.

The factory was shut, the vendor broke the news. Kerala Lights had been discontinued.

'What do you mean, "the factory is shut"?' Rajesh was baffled. 'Who, fucking shuts down a cigarette factory? It means eternal profits,' he lamented. 'One good thing in my life and that is gone too.'

'They are contemplating smoking bans too,' I said.

'No kidding, seriously?'

'Nope. Just the other day I heard their government is considering prohibition too. No wonder all Jews have vanished. These Mallus are crazy, I tell you,' Manoj chuckled and winked at me. 'Except for you, man. Let us go and check on our Jew.'

The shutter of the shop was still closed which was unusual. We weren't alone, though. One more gentleman stood there, waiting for the shutter to open.

'I hope he is alive,' Manoj whispered.

'Lord! What is wrong with you?' I snapped, and realized why the shop was closed. 'Damn, I forgot. Saturday is Jewish Sabbath day.'

'So it won't open?' Manoj squinted at me. 'Fuck you Adish.'

'But can we meet Jacob or not?' said Rajesh.

'Have you come to see Jacob Moses?' The stranger spoke to us, adjusting his gold-rimmed spectacles.

'Yes,' I said, scanning him from toe to head. He reminded me of Uncle Suresh, my dad's partner. Possibly in his forties, neatly dressed and speaking with a faint Malayali accent in his otherwise polished English. *Not one of our regular folks; surely an NRI.* Somehow, his presence seemed inopportune.

'Oh! I guess you don't know, then,' he said or rather stated. We looked at each other, trying to decipher his words. 'His fears are right,' he added, walking closer with an impassive face and pointed at Manoj. 'The old man is no more.'

No more? Dead? Jacob Moses was dead? My legs trembled.

'How's it possible? He was all fine when I met him four weeks ago,' I blurted out.

'It takes only a moment for someone to die,' the stranger said matter-of-factly. Our hearts filled with sadness, confusion, hopelessness, and mystery depending on what expectations we had built before coming here. 'Jacob suffered a heart attack and passed away in his sleep two weeks back,' he revealed.

'So the shop remains closed?' Rajesh asked. He was still able to think at least, while my mind had gone numb.

'Not really. His son will be here any moment. We have a meeting,' the man said.

'His sons live in the UK,' I remembered.

'Oh yes. But Jacob's dying wish was to be buried here alongside his wife, Sarah. So there was no question of him being flown to Israel. His sons had to fly down,' he revealed.

That's why Jacob never left India.

I had immense respect for the old man, which had grown manifold after he had narrated to me his exploits to win the love of his life. But never could I imagine that his love for his wife was so earnest.

'What happens to the shop now?' I asked.

'They wish to dispose of it. Not interested in running it anymore,' the man explained. 'There he is, Mark, his younger son,' he pointed to someone at the turn of the street.

Two men marched towards the shop. One of them, I recalled, was the caretaker, which meant the other person was Mark. The stranger rushed to greet Mark on his way, perhaps wanting to keep his business with him concealed from us.

'Are you here to meet my father?' Mark approached us after a brief conversation with the stranger. Speaking with a faint British accent, he was fairer that Jacob, lean and balding, with patches of gray hair. Jacob had died a peaceful, old man's death. *Rest in peace, master.*

'Yes, actually, but received the dreadful news from this

gentleman. It is quite a setback. Jacob sir was my art teacher at school,' I said, paying my condolences to Mark

'Oh, I see. So you were his student,' Mark said.

'Yes. Adish Mathew.'

Mark prodded his head. 'I think I've heard your name. Well, he passed away twelve days ago, to be precise. May his soul rest in peace,' he said, closing his eyes while I muttered, *amen*. 'Please come inside,' he invited us, and entered the shop with the stranger.

'It is still here,' I said, pointing at the boat. A collective sigh of relief washed over us, including Mutthur who even smiled upon seeing the regal blue boat. Rajesh nudged me to begin the talk.

'We wished to speak with you about the boat,' I said.

Two pairs of puzzled eyes bored into me; one each of Mark, *and* the stranger. 'What about the boat?' the stranger asked. I found him poking his nose quite odd. Nevertheless, I continued and told them the history of our legendary boat and how it was sold off in the hour of need five years ago. While Mark heard me intently, the stranger's gaze digressed, and pinned on Rajesh and Mutthur who moved about inspecting the boat.

'So you wanted to see it once more,' Mark concluded.

'Yes, but not just that,' I hesitated, and looked at Mutthur who gave me a nervous nod. I cleared my throat, 'We wished to borrow the boat for the Vallamkali season.'

Mark and the stranger exchanged an uncomfortable look.

'I see,' said Mark, turning to me, 'Well yes, I do plan to get rid of this boat as I wish to close this shop and go back to England as early as possible. But to say that I'm willing to lend it when I have someone interested in buying it outright, would be a plain lie.'

'Who is buying it?' asked Manoj.

'I am buying it, gentlemen,' the stranger stepped forward.

The Stranger

****

For two months, Vazhoor Chandy fervently cast around for a mascot for his new venture, travelling across the state; but unable to find anything that could appeal to him. Until he arrived at Jacob's antique shop and saw the majestic boat; regal blue, at sixty feet long, it rested in the shop shimmering like a celestine vessel. It's spiral hoods, larger and with more rings (seven, his lucky number) than the modern boats, were a rare craft. Vazhoor had fallen in love for the third time in his life. His wife, Frankinsence and now, this Odi-vallam.

Jacob, though, had asked an enormous price of fifty lakhs to part with his beloved. Vazhoor went back empty handed but kept his pursuit intact to convince the old man. He failed in each instance.

On his fourth attempt, however, he learned the news of Jacob's passing away. His son had decided to dispense with the shop and its artefacts but, fortunately for Vazhoor, other shop owners hadn't shown interest in the boat, which led Mark to believe it wasn't worth in gold.

Still, Vazhoor chose to play waiting game for a couple of days before sealing the deal at eight lakh rupees - one fifth of the Jacob's quote. The mascot had proved its worth even before he could own it. And now, it was going to change his fortunes. He knew.

'I am buying it, gentlemen,' he said to the four young men, vying for his prized possession.

'But Jacob sir never intended to sell the boat. He wanted to preserve it. It was his greatest memory,' Adish said to Mark. 'It was the same boat, which united your parents.'

Mark was quiet, his gaze fixed on the boat. His emotions though couldn't stay hidden from Vazhoor. Could Mark afford to be emotional at the moment? No, he couldn't, Vazhoor decided on his behalf and spoke in Malayalam.

'Mark, should we go inside if you're not comfortable counting the cash here? I have to leave for an important meeting in Aleppy,' Vazhoor said. Mark nodded and excused himself.

'What did he say?' Manoj asked Adish.

'Nothing. It's futile. Mark is in a hurry to close down the shop,' said Adish. His eyes followed the movement of the two men who entered the cabin where he had shared his last conversation with Jacob, and rested on Jacob's portrait that hung inside. He sighed, 'I don't think Mark has any idea what the boat meant to Jacob sir.'

'These NRIs, I tell you. The moment they leave the country and set foot abroad, they discard every sentiment. Be it our culture, tradition, or our history,' Manoj said.

They both walked up to the boat where Mutthur and Rajesh stood, gazing at the inscription, Jacob and Sara, 1962.

'Reminds me of the inscription I drew on the rock at Fort Kochi beach, remember?' Mutthur said to Adish.

Adish nodded. 'I wish you had met Jacob,' he said with regret. 'I should've brought you here, last time.'

'Will it work if you get it?' asked Rajesh, oblivious to their one-to-one in native tongue.

'I cannot say,' Mutthur shrugged. He had only heard the boat-stories from various people, including his own father when he was alive. 'But yes, something is always better than nothing.'

'We can talk to this new owner. Yes, he looks dangerous but who knows he might lend us the boat for the race. Let's offer him rent.' Manoj proposed.

'I agree. Our chances aren't bright, in fact almost nil, but I see no harm in trying at least,' said Rajesh.

Inside, Mark flicked through the wads of five hundred rupee notes while Vazhoor gazed at the smiling portrait of Jacob Moses presiding alongside Jacob's father. Could it be Mark who put it up, he wondered. But Mark was too disinterested in the matters of the shop. *No, not him. Definitely not.* Then who? *The servant,* he deduced as the caretaker brought over tea in two disposable glasses and set them on the table.

Mark had finished counting two of the four bundles. Vazhoor glanced at his watch. It was twelve already and now he had less than two hours to reach Aleppy. Sipping tea from the glass, he peeped outside and saw the four strangers still orbiting the boat like hungry Sharks. Two of them were North Indians.

What purpose could *they* have with the boat?

Vazhoor turned his attention to Mark. His fingers had stopped counting and he was peering outside too.

'Done Mark,' Vazhoor asked.

'Wait a second, Mr Chandy. I think I should talk to these boys once,' said Mark and stepped out.

'This Odi-vallam has been lying here for last twelve days since my father passed away. Nobody showed any interest. At least not with such urgency, except for you four and the gentleman inside,' Mark said to the boys. 'I know why he wants the boat. I know his motive. But I wish to know yours.'

'Our pride and life depends on the Kumarakom boat race, the most prestigious race for Odi-vallams,' Mutthur spoke and narrated how an accidental fire destroyed their boat and his father's history with Thiruneelakhandam - the boat lying in the shop. 'It is our last hope. And like you, the last memory of my father as well.'

Watching them from inside the cabin, Vazhoor hadn't missed the purpose in their eyes either. Mark had been a far easier prey than his father. But these four miscreants were ruining his prospects of owning the boat. He had to intervene.

'Look boys,' Vazhoor strode out of the cabin. 'I sympathise with you and your problem, but you're barking up the wrong tree. I cannot help you. This boat is going to my factory.'

'Can you not wait for two months?' asked Manoj. 'Please.'

'No!' Vazhoor said brusquely. 'I've waited enough. I have a business to run and other things to attend to.' His temper was now flaring up.

'This is our ancestral boat. And today we need it. But if you wish we can pay you the rent,' Adish offered.

Vazhoor stood there speechless for a while. For him, they seemed straight out of children's fiction, pinching and pulling him from every direction, as they'd do to a circus clown.

'Enough of this non-sense. I don't need your money, and if you wish I can offer you some to buzz off. This boat shall adorn the grand entrance of my Trivandrum factory. Now will you excuse us, please? I'm in hurry,' Vazhoor blurted out in Malayalam and turned to Mark. 'When do I send my men to move the boat from here?' he asked in a pressing tone.

With their heart in mouth, the four looked at Mark, their eyes pleading for one last time.

'I'm sorry Mr. Chandy. But if you wish to own the boat, you will have to wait for two months.' Mark said.

'What? Have you gone mad?' Vazhoor widened his eyes. 'You promised me. And now you refuse.'

'Please relax Mr. Chandy. You misunderstand me. I'm not saying a *no*.'

'Mark, enough. If I don't get the boat now, the deal is off and, you know how much you're going to lose.'

'I've already lost my parents,' said Mark, with a long sigh. 'What more can I lose?'

It was a point of no return, Vazhoor knew. With a heavy heart, he picked his money from the cabin and walked off, giving a cold stare to Mark and the four kids.

'My father greatly believed in love,' Mark said. 'He never left India because he wanted to live where his wife, my mother, lived and died. He chose to be buried here, alongside her. This boat is the symbol of their love and it should also live with the people who recognize this bond. I'm glad you came here to save me.'

Feeling tingling warmth in their limbs, and having no words to express their gratitude to a proud son, the four young men shook hands with Mark. Mark wished them luck and threw a brief glance at the boat for one last time, and mumbling something, he strode out.

'Your proposal has little complication, Mr. Chandy,' said John Mundassery, rifling through the documents Vazhoor had submitted to the Nehru Boat Race Council, NBRC. Today would be the last day for allotment of sponsorship spaces for the annual event, which was a month away.

'What complication?' he asked, sounding worried and still upset over the deal gone sour in the morning.

'The name,' said John.

'But it's just a name. The product is different now.'

'We understand,' he said. 'But people don't care. Or rather care too much to disassociate the brand from your previous product.'

'This is ridiculous. This is no reason. Please reconsider,' he pleaded but the oxymoronic smile on John's face told him that he shouldn't waste council's more time. The 'application window' was closed and those who'd been rejected would be considered only next year.

As Vazhoor got up and turned to leave, he shot one final glance at his proposal and the name and logo of his company printed over the top sheet. 'Kerala Lights,' he muttered and turned back.

'There has to be a way,' he made one last plea.

'There is,' John said with a smirk. 'Find your own boat team.'

The Law of Averages

****

'I must say, you've made considerable progress,' said Shelja, complimenting Rajesh on the code he had compiled with zero errors. 'It looks perfect.' She moved to the next desktop.

Rajesh beamed at his computer screen. In their sixth week of the C.L.P., he had more or less attuned to the new environment. Most of the topics they studied had been doddles. But 'programing' to him presented a threat; more real and dangerous than a nuclear strike by the neighbouring country. *How nervous he had felt on his first day in the lab,* he recalled. He had no idea how to cope. But slowly and steadily, he had improved his skills. Shelja had played a big role in his success, he believed.

He must do something to show his profound gratitude towards her.

Rajesh glanced in Shelja's direction. Her ethnic Indian wear - a paisley printed kurta and white churidar pyjama, had taken him by complete surprise today.

But how'd he cross the thick dotted line between a trainee and a trainer?

'Okay guys, one important announcement,' she spoke. Every head in the lab turned in her direction. That was her best trait, thought Rajesh. She could turn the laziest head with her sonorous voice.

'Thursday will be our last session,' she revealed. A deafening silence erupted in every young heart sitting in the lab. 'On Monday, there shall be a programming test, and its score will be attached to your mid term review exam the following week.' On Monday, they'd have heartbreak.

'Don't worry. It won't be tough,' she said, misinterpreting the mood of the class by a long hop.

'So the programming ends?' Vivek asked with mixed emotions in his heart. Shelja raised her eyebrow.

'Unfortunately, you're in IT. So, don't expect any respite,' she chuckled. 'Your next six weeks are dedicated to Java.'

'And who would be the faculty?' Rajit Nair asked, hoping Shelja would continue.

'Not much idea guys but you will find out by the end of the week. See you on Thursday then.' She had addressed enough queries for the day.

Thursday, the line would dissolve. Could he ask her out for a coffee then, probably over the weekend? Rajesh mused as he waddled out of the lab. Outside, he saw Shelja's fellow faculty Nikhil Lal, exchange sweet nothings with her.

What if her term ended and she left the CLP after the test? Should he be bothered? Wait, why the hell was he thinking so much about her? He had no clue.

Mutthur stared at the boat that shook constantly as waves in the overflowing Muvattupuzha rocked its bottom. At sixty feet, it'd be one of the smallest the competition might see this year. Provided the council agreed to its participation. And right now, he couldn't see any likelihood of that happening.

The return of Thiruneelakhandam had led to deep apprehensions from all quarters of Mevalloor. The village boat council itself had shunned the idea. A boat once relinquished, could not re-enter the periphery of the venerable temple.

But that should be the case only in presence of a presiding deity; Mutthur had countered.

The village had none at present, the council agreed. But then, the past three years that had seen them stuck to the last position became his biggest contention. With a forty-year-old discard, the possibility of the village becoming a laughing stock was suddenly a bigger concern.

Mutthur's hopes now rested only on Mohammad Kutty, Basheer Kutty's son and his father's old friend. A council member himself, Mohammad Kutty empathised with both - Mutthur and the boat, and at the moment, was trying hard to convince his fellow council members.

'Don't bring the dead back, Kutty. The judgement day is not yet here,' Therumal Chekavar, one council member, chuckled.

'The council has already burnt its hands along with the boat,' Rajagopalan, the head of council said with a certain disdain. 'His father lost his leg for the love of the sport, Kutty. But Mutthur is different. A good for nothing lad from this deluded young generation. It is for the best that we don't participate.'

From the corner of his eye, Kutty noticed Mutthur skipping a stone across the river. Irrespective of what Rajagopalan said, Kutty had always admired Mutthur for his boundless zeal and deep passion for their traditions, often citing Mutthur's examples to his son Adil. In Kutty's eyes, no-one could lead the village better, and that was why he always backed him.

Kutty had his limits, though. The council had nine members who collectively determined the fate of such matters and today, Mutthur's odds were one against eight.

'We've ridden on that elephant called Thiruneelakhandam. Don't you remember? We were part of the history,' Kutty said. Logic and reasoning had no place in such debates, he understood well. He must evoke the emotions to stand a chance.

'Don't you think we should be gracious towards this boat and give it a fitting farewell? We know of his father's sacrifice. We know how Narayanan lost his mind when council abandoned the boat?' Kutty paused and watched their agonized faces. The council members clearly hadn't anticipated an assault of the long forgotten disquieting memories, and chose to be quiet.

'Let us not hand out a chance to Mutthur. Instead, let us grant it to ourselves, Rajagopalan. We have nothing to lose. That is all I have to say,' Kutty concluded, hoping against the hope.

Rajagopalan mulled over his suggestion for a while and with a wave of his hand, invited the other members aside to discuss.

'I don't think they'd agree,' Mutthur said.

'Let's see,' Kutty shrugged.

'We sympathise with your emotions Kutty, but the council has to abide by certain rules,' Rajagopalan turned to them once more. 'I cannot yet permit him and the boat to participate, but I can do one thing,' he paused and looked at his fellow members for their final approval who nodded their head.

'Guru's birthday is fifty days away. We can lend Mutthur forty days, starting from today. On the fortieth day, the council shall meet here for an inspection. If Mutthur, his boat and his team can match at least last year's timings, they'll have Mahabali's blessings. But if they are even a second slower, there shall be no participation,' he finished.

Mutthur let out a deep breath, relieved at least for forty days. He knew, however, that Rajagopalan had made a near impossible demand of him. He had clocked a few practice sessions with the boat before presenting their case to the council. They were ten seconds off the previous year's count.

Mutthur however bowed his head to accept their decision as Rajagopalan and his committee marched away without adding a word further.

Could there be a way to crank up this old boat's maximum speed and make it competitive so that they could at least participate? He wondered.

'But the point is, how would someone fix the boat?' Adish shook his head. 'Had it been amendable, it wouldn't have been discarded in the first place. Besides, once a boat is trashed, no Asari will ever touch it. For them it is merely a piece of dead wood, relinquished by the deity's spirit. The council has already gone out of their way but don't expect anyone else to do it.'

'Bizarre. It is just a boat.'

'Not for our folks.'

Rajesh seemed in pensive mood, his eyes fixed on the waiter approaching them. Ever since Mutthur had called and shared the events at Mevalloor, he'd been pondering over his next action. There was no way he could leave Mutthur in the lurch. But it seemed each day had decided to throw a new challenge.

'What if we know the exact details of modifications to fix it? Could we then, find someone? Like a woodworker or a carpenter who can make those changes?' he said as the waiter put down a plate of *Aloo Paranthas* on their table.

'Dude, you are tripping without toddy. This Aloo Parantha must be the devil,' said Adish, and briefly put his focus back into the *rajma-rice* he savoured at the moment. 'This is yummy, man. Thanks.'

'I'm serious. Your people won't touch it. But what if I do? I mean what if I redesign it,' Rajesh proposed. Adish stared at him, astounded at the improbable thought. Applying butter on his paranthas, Rajesh continued, 'I've been studying the designs of this old boat and Mutthur's previous boat. Structurally both are similar, but their overall proportions are different.'

'Is it?' I could never notice,' Adish admitted.

'Try this,' said Rajesh, offering him one of the paranthas, which Adish dutifully accepted. Manoj was conspicuous by his absence, having chosen to stay at hostel for an unknown reason. 'I think we can try out few modifications which may boost its speed.'

Adish swallowed hard. 'What if it doesn't work?'

'Is it working otherwise?'

'No. But we are no experts, and we have borrowed the boat from Mark. What if...'

'Let us be real, Adish,' Rajesh cut in. 'Nobody gives two hoots to anything other than your snake boat souvenirs which sell like hot cakes at a toy shop or an antique shop,' he whispered. 'Listen, few minor design changes are all I'm proposing. We're certainly not going to break it.'

'But where is the money for all this? You know Mutthur has spent almost his entire savings on the previous boat.'

'I've decided to contribute my next month's salary. If you two chip in too, we can raise a decent sum and help him.

Adish smiled. The respect he had for Rajesh, amplified many folds today. A call from his father interrupted their discourse. He excused himself and nipped to a corner to answer it.

Odd as usual, Rajesh mused and continued to devour his food, deliberating in the interim to figure out a starting point. Ever since he had returned from Kochi, he'd been spending his evenings in the library and Internet café, studying design basics. But whatever little he could unearth, it'd been vastly different from the traditional engineering employed for the boats.

'Boat design project in DigiSys? What rubbish, Adish?' his father sounded aghast on the phone. Adish noted the rhyming between the two words - rubbish, Adish. 'It's an IT company for God's sake. Not some random logo design firm.'

'He wants to join a design project,' Adish lied.

'I don't care,' barked his father. 'I have no liking for these North Indians and their attitude. They lack discipline, and always indulge in pointless debates and worthless pursuits. And worse, they force you to enlist or else you're not good enough to be in their *league*. Look at your new food habits, if you don't believe me. I mean how could you otherwise nosh on *rajma-rice*?'

'Dad, it is nothing like that. They are brilliant. I learn a lot from them.'

'Learn? What the hell did you do with your computer engineering?' his father interrupted. 'You should be ashamed, Adish. Being in IT, they should learn from you and not the other way around.'

'But dad-'

'Enough, Adish. Telling you anything is like pouring water into a pot placed upside down. I didn't send you to Bangalore so that you ruin your future now,' he said.

'Dad.'

'Listen carefully, son. You'll stay away from their foolish ventures and until your training gets over, you'll stay away from Mevalloor too. Do you understand?'

Adish was quiet.

'I didn't hear you boy. Do you understand or not?'

'I do.'

'Good. Now go and concentrate on your job. Good night,' His father concluded and disconnected the call.

'All ok?' Rajesh asked as Adish took his seat, back at the table.

'Yes.'

'Anyways you said Kala's grandfather was a boat architect, right?' Rajesh asked. Adish nodded. 'Cool. There're two things I need from Mutthur, then. One, ask Kala to bring us her grandfather's books and notes. And second, I want close photographs of Gopalan's boat as well as last year's winning boats.'

'What is your plan?'

'We are going to defeat Gopalan.'

We, Adish took note. His father's words echoed in his ears.

'You ruined things in Aleppy, and then you were untraceable this weekend as well. Where the hell were you?' Uums had been upset since Saturday but chose today to reprimand Manoj.

They were back in hostel - in her room, working on an urgent assignment after a hectic day in the campus.

'Nowhere. A friend was in trouble,' said Manoj.

'Yeah, you and your friends. They're always in trouble. Can they think nothing beyond *gurlz* and *love*?' Uums said. The catch in her voice surprised Manoj. His mother sounded the same way when she rebuked his father. Had Vashikaran potion worked on her?

'Let us make a plan for this weekend.'

'Not possible. Samarth has plans,' Uums said, opening her Almirah. She was back to her original tone.

'Samarth? Again?' The potion wasn't strong enough, he guessed.

'What do you mean by again? He is not in some remote corner of India. He is in Kozhikode. How far is that?'

'Yeah, but doesn't he need to study?'

'What would you know about IIMs?' Uums spat, pulling out a towel from the wardrobe. 'Besides, he is quite chilled. Doesn't worry much,' she stepped into the bathroom, ignoring him and shut the door with a big thud. For a moment, Manoj felt as if he had been kicked in the groin.

What did she say about IIMs? He knew a lot about IIMs. He had friends there, Mady, Kaul and others. Manoj stared blankly at the door. *It was his friends, not him.* Uums was right. He was a mule; designed and destined to work in IT whereas her cool-dude boyfriend was an IIM brand manager in the making.

His heart quivered, and feet went numb, reminded again of his worthlessness. How could he overlook the grim reality of his bleak future and let Toddy brainwash him? The darkness of doubts shrouded his mind. His face stiffened, and body trembled.

'How dare she speak to me like this?' he muttered. 'If I'm so worthless, what am I doing in her room? If she was a topper in her below average Institute, I was also a-.' The answer struck him as his gaze fell onto the wardrobe mirror. A *plain* mirror.

He was a mediocre from a top college. Indeed a Loser.

'I'm going to my room,' he said aloud.

'Shut the door properly when you leave. See you at the dinner baby,' Uums spoke from inside.

Manoj paused in his steps. She had called him *baby*. There must be a reason. Should he wait for her to come out? Sure, his situation wasn't as good as he had imagined earlier but it wasn't too bad either. Whatever it was he must gain control of his life, he told himself, and with firm determination strode out of her room.

'I'm leaving for Mevalloor tomorrow evening. I'll be back on Saturday night. Are you in?' said Rajesh as soon as Manoj entered his room.

'Take Adish along,' said Manoj.

'Can't. He is grounded by the baron.'

'Good for him. I too won't be going to Mevalloor anymore.'

'What? Who will research with me?'

'I have to study for CAT and for the test,' said Manoj in a forceful whisper. 'And it's good Adish is staying back as well. We need to concentrate on our professional lives this weekend.'

'Professional lives? Over weekends? What do we do on weekdays then? College?'

'What you're doing is what people do in college, Pandey,' Manoj sneered.

'What do you mean?'

Manoj laughed. 'What do you think you're designing? Some *Jalebi* or *Samosa*? It is not even a car that runs on a road, Mister Mech. It's a damn boat in the water. And you got no fucking idea.'

'At least I'm trying to help Mutthur,' Rajesh retorted.

'You're not helping him. You're selling him an impossible hope. Better sell him an elephant. Because this hope is bound to shatter into a million pieces when reality strikes.'

'What is wrong with you? You've been acting strange of late.'

'Me, acting strange? Hah! Look who is talking. Ever since your break up you are acting crazy, and you are accusing me?'

'I am acting crazy?'

'Of course. Isn't it madness? That you want him to believe he'd get his love because *you* couldn't. Wake up and smell the coffee man. You just want to feel good about yourself.'

Rajesh stared at his roommate in disbelief. He had proved to be such a reprobate and Rajesh had no idea why? That girl must be poisoning his mind. Okay, let us fight venom with venom. 'Is it for Uums that you're slogging your rotten ass here?'

'Cut the crap, asshole,' Manoj almost jumped at Rajesh upon her mention. 'She has nothing to do with it.'

Rajesh laughed. 'Then, I know why you're pissed. Her boyfriend is in town. Isn't he?'

Manoj squinted and shook his head in disgust, 'Fuck you.'

'It is you. You need to wake up from the reverie my friend.' Rajesh chortled and before he nipped out to the mart, added 'And if possible, shake Adish up as well.'

Rajesh Pandey's

Reverse Engineering

****

A circle is a set of points in a plane that are at a constant distance called radius, from a given point, called centre. We all are circles; with no beginning or end, we keep rotating around one or the other point, our whole lives.

The analogy had hit me while I zeroed in on a mathematical problem, the Kissing Circles, to code during the forthcoming Monday test. And realized our whole lives could be summed up as a circle. While Mutthur rotated around his boat, Manoj around an IIM (of late around Uums and her beau), and Adish around his father, my centre had been *her* for the past one year. Yet, *she* hadn't bothered to check even once whether I was alive or not in the two weeks since...

Had I been such a meaningless chapter in her life? Or had she been sure that mine would be the meekest protest in case she ever dumped me? That, she'd face no trouble. That, I'd fail to be a sinister, psycho ex too. Damn! Rambling like a centre-less circle or rather a directionless straight line in dark vacuum, I searched for the gravity to pull me towards a new centre.

What if I never find it?

Gripped by a sudden melancholy, I felt hollowness creep into my chest and strangulate me. I couldn't be alone. Fuck! I missed Manoj and Adish. In hindsight, they spoke the bitter truth. Hope was always a dangerous word, as someone had put. I remembered the day right after my final semester exams when *she* had broken up with me. I had pleaded *her* so much to come back. We did patch up a week later but deep down, I had foreseen the torment. I knew our relationship was on a ventilator ever since, waiting for either of us to pull the plug. Yet, I had taken a gamble with "hope."

Throughout my way to Mevalloor, I vacillated whether or not to hand out the same dangerous hope to Mutthur; it was a gamble that might put someone's life at stake. But the moment I saw him at Vaikom, I knew I could not turn back.

'Did you get Gopalan's boat?' I asked Mutthur, going through the photographs of last year's winner and runner-up boats on his irritatingly slow Pentium 4 machine. It was in stark contrast to the core 2 duo machines at our training centre.

'Boat? You said photos,' he said, nervously.

My bad! 'Sorry, I meant photos only.'

'Oh yes. Photos were difficult, but Kala managed,' he said with a proud grin. 'I have sorted them for you in a folder. It is there on the desktop.'

I was impressed. For all his traditional job and attire, he was quite skilled technologically.

'Thirty pictures of one boat?' I held my breath as I previewed the contents of the folder; Kala and her friends starring in half of them. Unbelievable!

I could imagine her elaborate set-up now; first, she and her friends praised Gopalan and his team, posing with the boat as if it was Superstar Mohanlal or Mammootty. Then, she got a few pictures clicked with the real star too – a gloating Gopalan.

Poor Gopalan! He must've mistaken her ploy as her growing interest in him. *Suits that scoundrel,* I grinned. 'She had to lie,' Mutthur smiled sheepishly, rubbing the back of his neck.

I carried out a diligent inspection of the boat. It had a slightly different design than the two winning boats, which also didn't have identical hoods at their ends. Though it bore a striking similarity to Mutthur's new, I mean, older boat.

'Who made Gopalan's boat?' I asked

'Kala's *appooppan*...grandfather created the Puranjal Vallam.'

'Oh, I see.' The puzzle was solved, and my happiness knew no bounds. 'Could she get her...appooppam's books and notes?' They were my first hope to find critical information regarding the designs. Mutthur smiled, and from his cupboard, removed a large bundle wrapped in coarse muslin cloth and set it down before me.

The bundle contained copies of all the Vedas in Malayalam including one *Sthapatya Veda*. Kala's grandfather was a devout and well versed with Hindu scriptures, Mutthur revealed. Highly organized too, I assumed, spotting two timeworn notebooks – one in an orange cover and the other, in light brown.

I picked both and flipped through their pages; they were in surprisingly good condition and contained texts, calculations, geometric figures and drawings of all possible cross-sections of a boat. Much like our 'Mechanical Drawing' books. Fortunately, he exercised one more good habit. Of marking dates whenever a fresh topic began. Hence, without much difficulty, I gathered how old the texts were. The first entry in the orange notebook dated back to 1994 and the last one referred to the year 2000.

'When was Gopalan's boat built?'

'Seven or eight years ago, I think. It was Asari's last.'

'98 or 99,' I estimated the year and leafed through the notebook till the end with Mutthur's aid as it was all in Malayalam. The boat drawings mentioned in it seemed to match the proportions and dimensions of Gopalan's boat. Feeling a thrill crawl up my spine, I checked the brown notebook too. It had details of the years between 1985 and 1993.

Our boat was forty years old.

'Did Kala give you anything else?'

'That is all she could find.'

We had met a dead end. No details regarding our boat existed anywhere. Nevertheless, I picked the orange notebook again and studied its content.

'It mentions *Sthapatya Veda,* along with some equations and quotations from the text,' Mutthur pointed to one of the pages.

My gaze swung to the thin copy of Sthapathya Veda.

The scripture was the most striking component in the study of boat-design that I had dug up in past one week. It was, all in all, a set of architectural and planning principles related to the construction of buildings. It described numerous equations and formulas based on the ancient Vedic Mathematics, and defined various proportional aspects for a structure to be built; in theory, for buildings but in practice, used frequently to construct just any physical structure of significance in ancient India, including boats.

Making sense of those equations, however, proved to be an excruciatingly slow process. Since the text was in Malayalam, I had to rely entirely on Mutthur whose graduation in Humanities didn't help me either. Having struggled for nearly two hours, I threw up my hands.

'We need to find an alternate way,' I said, closing the notebook. 'Let us go out for smoke.' Mutthur just nodded and followed me outside.

'You know, there are three types of engineers,' I said, lighting a cigarette as we grabbed our chairs in the warehouse. 'First are the ones we address as "Geniuses". They secure fitting results, *and* they always know the *things. Things* that ensure them an A-lister post-grad school or a top core company instead of a random IT firm,' I drew in a long puff.

'Second are the "Workhorses". They aren't geniuses and hence, work hard, mug day-in and day-out, throughout their engineering to compete with the "Geniuses". They also excel,' I paused, pondering over my good ol' days.

I belonged to none and fell in the third category of this name-calling "we": the Ignorant Souls, never the Geniuses, but always living in the delusion of being one. Often, it'd be too late for us to realize the truth and be the Workhorse either.

Mutthur gave me a bewildered stare, probably waiting for me to explain in clearer terms. I didn't blame him. We had never had a conversation between two of us alone. So, we had no measure of each other's cerebrations. I took a long drag on my cigarette and returned to my college days.

We missed classes, had no clue about our subjects whatsoever and presumably had only one night like this to crack the mantra of attaining 'passing marks.' Topping a class was not just a LOL, but rather a ROFL. Hence, we used reverse engineering – the real engineering where we'd deduce things backwards; to find the best possible and timely solution and ensure we didn't fail.

To hell with 'complete' understanding or 'perfect' solution; the world was in a state of constant change, regardless. Nothing was permanent. Like Robin's dinosaurs.

'What's our final goal, Mutthur?' I asked.

'Gopalan,' he uttered rightly. No-hoper hadn't lost the hope, yet.

'Yes, and to defeat him, we need to make our weapon strong and potent. Let's go and understand his weapon first,' I said, and once back in Mutthur's room, straightaway began with Gopalan's boat.

Mutthur had followed my instructions faithfully, so we had various perspectives of the boat available to us. They served an important purpose; tallying the dimensions, equations and calculations mentioned in the notebooks, we could compare theoretical and actual designs. With the tabulated data, we'd create a graph of deviations.

This graph was a must because in real, the Asaris on the basis of strong intuitions took many design decisions during the traditional process of boat making in Kerala, Mutthur told me. The graph would also help us decode certain equations and conditions we were unable to crack - a significant head start.

I went to 1997, the year Puranjal Vallam was built. One of the formulae yielded the ratio of the length to the width of the boat within a precision range of one-eighth of an inch, further explaining the impact of variations on the structural stability. Based on these calculations, I created a few rough cross-sectional drawings. We laboured through the entire night and by morning, were able to scrape through the orange book. More or less, I understood what kind of data we required to proceed further.

Satisfied and exhausted, knowing we had much work to do in the day, we broke for a small nap. As soon as we woke up, our engineering would start with measurements.

The boat shone brightly under the sun. The morning had arrived with storm clouds but fortunately the rain gods had called them back, giving us a breather for the day. Mutthur had summoned each of his oarsmen, and all of them were present.

'How many people can this boat accommodate?' I asked, casting a long glance at the Odi-vallam.

The interior of its hull was divided into small thwarts that ran through its entire length in two rows except towards the ends due to tapering where three chambers each, in a single file were constructed. The boat had no stern, and both ends were actually bows with spiral hoods. *Cool.* Reading so much on boats, I was finally sounding technical.

'Maximum forty-four,' Mutthur replied.

'And Gopalan's boat can accommodate fifty-two,' I recalled from the designs. 'How much difference can eight people create in a similar boat?'

'Significant. Remember the day you attended our practice? We had clocked three seconds faster at full strength of fifty,' reminded Mutthur. 'And two of you were not even oarsmen. So you can imagine.'

Capacity of the boat had to be extended, I noted down my first point. I handed Mutthur one end of the tapeline and proceeded to measure out the dimensions of the thwarts at various cross-sections, followed by height and the radius of the curvature on each side of the hull. My final measurements would be the weight of the boat, the wet surface area at its full capacity and the current displacement of water; to determine the hydrodynamics of the boat and hence, optimise its speed and the dead-weight.

'I need the wet surface area of Gopalan's boat as well,' I said, with my readings in place. 'Could we ask Kala for one more favour?'

Mutthur folded his arms across his chest and let out an exasperated sigh, 'How is she going to do that?'

'She is a celebrity. All she has to do is to take one more boat ride with the crew to boost their morale for the upcoming Nehru race,' I winked.

'I hope their morale doesn't get a boost in real,' he said, bemused at my latest demand. Worst, he had to comply.

'Take the boat out of the river and flip it,' I demanded more.

The real engineering of the boat lay at its base that determined its speed, balance and manoeuvrability. A narrow keel ran through its whole length and had a function to split the water stream into two as it moved in a straight line and kept the boat stable. I must take measurements of the oars as well.

'I'm done here. Let's go back,' I announced like a pro satisfied and exhausted with his job.

'Should we take a ride in case you require speed readings?' Mutthur asked. I stared at him.

Where do I find a speedometer for his boat now?

'No point. Currently, I'm focussing on design. So, let me not waste any time,' I insisted. When time is a concern, you have to concentrate on specifics and avoid things that have no apparent significance.

And the only thing that bothered me now was: How would I decipher a bunch of equations and calculations to get my measurements accurate in such a short span of time?

The Kissing Circles

****

Adish Mathew loved Java, the supreme knowledge. He loved it so much that he considered it his heaven-bound duty to spread the gospel of Java amongst the ignorant and non-believer minds, and convert them into believers. He was, after all, a computer engineer.

Sitting in the library, he keenly observed the two ignorants sifting through the bookshelves, picking and flicking through the arrayed titles. One of them, the tall one, beheld a book on core management in IT, and the other flipped through a Design software manual. These two had deviated from the true path. The boat was a priority, agreed. But not at the cost of their jobs.

His father was right. The judgement day was six weeks away. They ought to be brought onto the correct path. Didn't matter if they held other views. Their salvation lay in the "Power of Java", the book currently lying in front of him.

As soon as Rajesh joined him, Adish whispered, aloud. 'You know, Java is such a powerful language that you can code anything, absolutely anything.'

'Provided, you know what you want to do.' Rajesh spoke, with a half-smile as Manoj too, quietly grabbed his chair, his eyes dug into "The Management Bible". It was futile, Adish thought; revealing them Java at the current juncture. He decided to go back to the basics.

'How did your C++ test go?' he asked Rajesh.

'Pretty good. Shelja commended my code. Even better, it compiled and ran. Thanks for your support, man. I appreciate. I really do,' said Rajesh.

Adish felt vindicated. He was at least, able to evince the light of C++ to Rajesh. Java wasn't too far. 'What problem did you solve?' He asked.

'Nothing complex. A small mathematical problem.'

Adish curled his lips, loathing his 'mathematical' choice. Pure mathematical problems corresponded to machine level dynamics and hence, preferred languages other than Java. Though Java was inherently capable of giving similar results if handled with intelligence, he'd reckon. 'Why mathematical?'

'Every problem in the universe is mathematical. So don't fret.'

'Okay. So what was the problem?'

Rajesh flipped back a few pages in his notebook and then nudged it towards Adish. 'Kissing Circles. Ever heard of it?' Adish leaned forward and saw three circles drawn on a page, having no clue whatsoever; neither about the figures nor the peculiar name.

'Descartes' theorem,' Manoj chipped in, without shifting his gaze from his book. Adish gaped at him; feeling left out again but didn't despair. Java could wait.

'What's that?' he asked, sliding his chair closer to inspect the three circles touching each other, externally.

'These tangent circles are *the kissing circles*,' said Rajesh, a grin erupting on his face, as he again picked up the pen and labeled the circles as "Rajesh", "Adish", and "Manoj". Adish gave out a suppressed smile while Manoj managed a mere frown.

'The theorem states that for any set of three kissing circles, we can inscribe the fourth circle, tangent to each of them,' said Rajesh and traced a small circle in the space enclosed by the three adjoining circles, 'the radius of which, is given by a quadratic equation.'

'And who is the fourth circle?' asked Adish.

A slow smile came on Rajesh's face and he scribed "Mutthur" on the inner circle. A profound silence followed as the three stared at the drawings.

'You said Java could do anything,' Rajesh leaned forward.

'Yes, of course,' said Adish, sitting upright.

'Ok, there is a snag. There are just too many equations and calculations to work out, and I have neither any boat simulation software nor time to manually quantify the correct dimensions for the boat,' said Rajesh, exasperated. 'Can you create something... like an interface program to help me?'

Adish shut his eyelids and mulled over the requirement.

'What are you looking at?' Rajesh said to Manoj who glanced at him over the top of his book. 'This fourth circle needs our help.'

Manoj put the book down. 'A quadratic equation always has two solutions; real, imaginary, same or different, but two. This is one solution,' he pointed at the smaller circle, and picked up the pen, 'there has to be another.' Inhaling a deep breath, he drew a large circle, circumscribing the three kissing circles and wrote "DigiSys" on it.

Rajesh shook his head and turned to Adish. 'Are you in?'

Pondering over the matter, Adish still had his eyes closed. He couldn't set his foot in Mevalloor. He couldn't be of any help, otherwise. This was his chance to contribute, but the simulation program might consume weeks. 'What man? I can't believe this,' Adish heard the mutterings outside.

He opened his eyes as Rajesh rose to his feet and walked off. The large engulfing circle was now staring at him. *They should learn from you,* his father's voice echoed in his head.

He must seize this moment to show his real worth. Java's too.

'It might take a while for me,' he whispered, bending over the notebook.

'If you do it alone,' he heard Manoj speak and looked up. His eyes were fixed on the notebook too. 'I have an idea for you.'

Manoj Bansal's

The Design of God

****

'Bansal! Where're you going, fucker?' Chaudhary called out from the fountain as I strode out of the MPAE academic block with Preetika and headed to the canteen. I had purposely ignored the quartet of him, Mady, Supriya and Pulkit.

'Hey guys, what are you up to?' I said, keeping my distance from them. Their wet clothes screamed out their intentions.

'Celebrating the end of the third year. But how come you're so dry, man?' said Mady. The four closed in and surrounded me before I could escape. Next moment, I hung in air, ready to be flung into the fountain.

'Fuck you guys. Leave me. Save me Preetika,' I pleaded, but she had already moved fifty steps back, tittering. Well, at least she hadn't lent them a hand. So much so, for guarding her from that lecherous GG who took me as her boyfriend and kept his hands off her. My desperate eyes darted around for help but fell on Arpita who had stopped by, curiously waiting for my outcome. Damn you fuckers. Not in front of my crush.

'One, two, three,' Supriya counted and SPLASH!

The water slapped me full in the face; seizing me from all around. My specs were gone, and everything turned all hazy. Water filled my lungs as I struggled to rise to the surface but sank deeper instead. It was as though my body had turned into a heavy sack of sand getting heavier as water wetted it. I couldn't breathe.

'Save me God, save me.' I uttered a yelp and out of nowhere, a hand appeared and descended upon me. I threw my hands in wild desperation, trying to grab it but failed clutch it.

I woke up, gasping for air but dry and safe.

'Fuckshit Adish, you're a genius, dude,' Pandey cried over the phone, standing at the edge of the bathroom door. 'You're a real circle,' he said and hung up. 'Wake up Bansal! It is 6:45. We have a test today. Bansal!' he crowed again, without looking in my direction and shut the door. I was back to being 'Bansal' again.

The clock read 6:40, I checked. *Lying asshole. I have five more minutes.* I clutched the edge of my bed sheet and pulled it over my face.

Angry and frustrated on a day that looked so bright and promising in the morning, I paced back and forth in my room, casting my mind back to the day's happenings and cursing that shithole GG, Gagan Gupta.

The test had gone well. For the first time since my Social Studies exam during the tenth standard, I was genuinely satisfied. Every test or exam I had taken since then, had been marred with this dissatisfaction – the feeling of "Could've been better, much better if only" types. Though, it being an open book test had helped. I understood how the real world would work now onwards.

Gone were the days when we raced through our books and notebooks, trying to memorise each solution. Here, the info you required was right in front of you. In fact with engineers, it had always been the case. All inventions had originated from pre existing tools.

Following the test, we had a session with P Sundaram, the Asia Pacific business head to hear his views on the newest feather in CapVirgo's cap.

'With the acquisition of M.B. Consulting, we hope to usher in a new era in CapVirgo's growth story. I agree that opportunities are limited in the new vertical for our current IT workforce but they do exist,' he had revealed during the one-on-one session.

Ironically, it was M.B. Consulting, the top consulting firm in Europe, that had made the CapVirgo DigiSys merger possible.

Yeah man, Karma is a bitch. It comes full circle.

As Sundaram left, Rajan Dandekar, our management faculty came to me, and spoke, 'I see a genuine opportunity for you. I've worked with M.B. consulting and the area they shine brightly is brand management and business transformation. Make sure you fill the preference form for Phase Three with management heavy details.'

Had I been the Spons-Secy of my college fests, my resume would've been so strong. Damn you GG. The blast from the past had whipped me hard.

I had run from pillar to post to find sponsors for our cultural and tech fests for three years in running. But when my turn came in the fourth year to grab the Spons-Secy post, his third-year Fatass girlfriend stole it from me. Why? Because she took a fancy to that self-obsessed GG – a self-proclaimed Mr Popular bronze medallist – and let him be her arm candy.

Oh no dear, I wasn't being a sexist. I was stating a fact. Or else why'd she date an ugly duck – an electronics nerd with five IIM calls post-prelims, besides a job offer from Intel.

Huh. I meant why on earth would an organizing committee's president indulge in hanky-panky with a Fatass having a GRE score of 780 in her trial attempt and probably heading to Penn state, next year. Bloody, we weren't even spared the seeds of wild imagination that rumours of them being caught in the act by the hostel warden sowed in our innocent, chaste minds. The whole hostel had gone to sleep at ten, after the Shahi-Paneer dinner that night. Fuck man, the Fatass *was* a nice curvy bod. A Jury-picked Miss Popular Gold medallist.

Though, I knew the real reason that sucker blocked my ascent. It was Preetika. Crazy fellow he was. F*uck you. Fuck you.*

'You okay?' Adish poked his face through the door.

'Yeah, man. Come in.'

Adish walked in but not alone. Following him was a guy in his squeaky, shining black shoes, brown trousers, white shirt and hair oiled and neatly swept back.

Mutthur! I was floored. With the coconut odour.

'Wow, you look cool man,' I let out a hoot. 'Kala must see this side of yours if she hasn't.' Mutthur blushed. 'What brings you here?' I asked.

'To discuss the final design,' he said.

'Final design?' I was flummoxed. These suckers had reached the final design stage, and didn't bother even sharing with me. True, I had stayed away in the past week while Adish had worked on the simulation program that he named MAVA after his father, and Pandey too, had immersed himself into the design.

Still man. Not an excuse.

Adish should've told me, at least. That moron forgot it was I who had suggested him to propose the simulation project to our group. If not for me, he would've spent not less than two weeks to finish his god damn code. Huh, selfish self-centred pricks.

'Where is he? His phone is switched off,' Mutthur said.

'I don't know. He is gone for like, two hours,' I said dryly.

Just then Pandey appeared.

'Where the hell were you?' I demanded.

'I was on a con call,' he said. I stared at him for further details. 'MIT,' he said with a raised brow.

M…I…T…! 'You were in con call with Arpita?' I asked in utter disbelief. The winner's expression on his face told me I was spot on. 'Fuck man, she doesn't even respond to me whenever she is online, and she had a con call with you. From Boston and that too, for two hours,' I was hugely upset.

'There has to be a difference between a crush and a junior,' he smirked. *Crush? Hers on him? What else could he be hiding?*

'*Yem my tea*? You have a friend in *yem my tea*?' Adish, true to his habit, let out an 'astonished Malayali' response to the 'best foreign word' for engineers and felt proud as well.

'Shut up for a moment, Adish,' I said and turned to Pandey. 'She had a crush on you? Seriously?' Pandey winked.

Bullshit. But what if it was true? My body sagged.

'Your phone was switched off,' Mutthur spoke, reminding us of his presence too.

'Oh yes, the battery went dead. Sorry,' said Pandey.

'Tell us the complete story,' I said, no more willing to be left out.

It started a week back.

While browsing through the MIT OpenCourseWare, Pandey had stumbled upon some research papers on boat designs. So, he emailed Arpita to seek her help in digging out as much relevant information as she could. By a stroke of luck, she'd been working in conjunction with M.E. department on a Hydraulics project. She connected him to Andrew, her mentor, pursuing his PhD in boat design. When Andrew gathered that Pandey required his guidance on an "Indian" boat, he literally jumped on the opportunity. Sharing extensive data and insights with Pandey, he even ran simulation experiments at the MIT to give further inputs on increasing the boat's efficiency.

And today, they had discussed and locked the final design.

'I could never foresee this boat would reach MIT one day,' Adish spoke softly, teary-eyed and mouth wide open in awe. I didn't blame him. Pandey's tale did sound like a dream.

'I guess now we have our final design. But before we discuss the changes,' Pandey turned to Mutthur, 'have we found someone who can make the suggested modifications to the boat?'

Mutthur nodded. 'There is one. Kareem Chetta.'

Kareem Rashid, not the famous one, but a "designer" in his own rights, nonetheless. Kareem was one of Aleppy's most skilful workers, and did frequent repair jobs on commercial Kettuvallams, Mutthur told us. The perfection in his woodwork was quite unmatched. But the most stunning aspect of Kareem's being was that he'd been the first non-Malayali an Asari had ever accepted in his stead. Seven years ago. The Asari was none other than Kala's grandfather. Unfortunately, the Asari died a year later and since then, Kareem had devoted his skills to the houseboats.

'Where the hell did you find him?' I asked Mutthur.

'Mohammad Kutty dug him out,' he said.

'Brilliant. Now, let us discuss the design,' Pandey came straight to the point. He extracted few A4 sheets from his bag and spread two of them on the bed in our view. Boat designs.

'The right one is Gopalan's boat and the left one is ours. As we know, our boat is smaller and a little heavier due to considerable dead weight. It also lacks the customary symmetry of Odi-vallams that you see in Gopalan's boat. Both these factors in our boat lead to an additional drag that slows it down,' he quickly recapped our countless discussions during the past one week. We all nodded.

'Now the changes,' he said, putting another paper in front of us. 'The biggest change is in the seating cabinets of the boat. We'll have to restructure the middle section to adjust six additional people. This will increase its capacity to fifty. Luckily for us, the compartments of our boat are bigger than the newer ones so we have scope.'

'I have forty-six oarsmen. Forty-eight by a stretch. Where do I find the other two?' Mutthur asked.

'Take them. They are weekend professionals,' Pandey winked at Adish and me. 'Now we have fifty people on board, we should gain at least five seconds as per our calculations.' Mutthur nodded.

'Now the second and the most difficult step - shedding the excess weight,' Pandey proposed. 'We need lighter crew so your men must lose a few kilos, each.'

Adish coughed, and I couldn't control my laughter. 'Now you will starve them too,' I said.

'In case you do invite the extra crew on-board, the maximum extension I can allow to the current dead weight is fifty kilos,' he offered. Mutthur scratched his chin at his insane demand. Take it or leave it,' he pressed. Finding no way out, Mutthur nodded.

'All said and done, how do we solve the problem of increased drag that you mentioned,' the engineer inside me asked.

'Good question Robert,' said Pandey. 'This one is tricky. To counter the drag, we have to make our base symmetrical. Now, we could've scratched some wood out, but we have to be careful with the wet surface area. So a wooden overlay-,' he said, drawing a thin layer along the periphery of the boat's frontal half, 'like this might work for us.'

'In total, how much could we gain?' asked Mutthur. It was the most relevant question of the evening.

'Let's say between twelve to fifteen seconds,' said Pandey. 'And yes, with little shorter and narrower oars, proper polishing and repairing of the bottom keel, which is not at its efficient best, we can add two-three seconds more.'

'Eighteen in the best case,' Mutthur said in a pensive tone.

'Lord Jesus, eighteen will be a miracle,' said Adish.

'This would require a lot of money.'

'I told you, we'd contribute,' said Pandey, looking at Adish and me with apprehension. We both nodded. Irrespective of whether we were an active part of the project or not, we had made the pledge to Pandey.

'You don't understand. It may require around one and a half lacs, which is beyond our initial estimate. Much beyond,' said Mutthur. 'And we don't have that much money on us. Do we?'

We gulped at the enormity. Mutthur was correct. Initially, Pandey had hinted at minor changes but by the look of the final design, the task seemed substantial. Perhaps, in his zeal to modify the design, Pandey had ignored financial constraints. 'Welcome to the real world, Engineers', the designs mocked us.

Back to the square one, I muttered Bajrang Bali's name, praying for strength.

'Nevertheless, I will meet Kareem to seek his opinion on the cost breakup,' Mutthur said. 'Then we can decide which changes to keep and which ones to ditch.'

'The weight loss doesn't involve any financial implications I suppose,' Pandey hadn't abandoned the hope yet.

'Okay, what if we get somebody to sponsor the boat?' I said.

Silence was all I heard, as three stumped mouths gaped at me.

The Sunday Church

****

Is God a figment of our imagination or are we a figment of God's imagination? Who can tell? Yet, 'God is one and eternal' is the prevailing belief. So how do two people praying together, perceive the eternal God when one of them believes in the Trinity of the Father, the Son and the Holy Spirit and the other believes in the Trinity of Brahma, Vishnu and Mahesh? Perhaps they'd think the Father creates, the Son preserves and the Holy Spirit is the Shakti that transforms.

Krishna and Christ, the spiritual twins, sat together in the Paramdhama or the Paradise, gazing down at their subjects. Years ago, to preserve humanity, they had journeyed to the land of Mortals - to bestow wisdom on them. But soon, they deduced that human minds had turned too convoluted and interpreted entirely different versions of them.

So now they preferred to bide their time in the supreme abode until the Day when the Trinity would pronounce that the time was ripe to impart few more lessons to their most intelligent (or rather the most idiotic) creations.

On Sunday mornings, they'd let open their windows, ease into their armchairs and watch the live, human drama unfold on Channel 'Planet Earth' while relishing green tea.

'You're a master-soul Krish. Thanks for the gift,' Christ admitted, sipping tea.

They used to indulge in Somras wine before Krishna introduced the tea, brought especially for Christ from Kamrupa. Krishna first tasted the flavour during the grand victory celebrations post his fierce campaign against Narakasura and knew Christ would fancy his new find. But that it'd replace the wine altogether, he hadn't presumed even in his wildest dreams.

'All thanks to Muhammad. Had he not decreed against wine, it wouldn't have been possible,' said Krishna.

'I agree. Hope when the DAY arrives, we are detoxed enough for the next world-cycle.'

Years ago when Muhammad decreed against the consumption of wine on Earth, the two avowed to set an example and proposed prohibition in the Supreme Abode too, until the DAY. Every life-force should enjoy it together, they reasoned. Thank heavens, they were soon sent a worthy replacement in the form of dark green leaves from the Brahmaputra valley. And now they both savoured a daily cup, enhanced with honey and lemon of course.

'I was impressed with that Moses' kid,' said Christ.

'Who, Mark?' said Krishna.

'Yes. I felt rejuvenated seeing his dedication to preserving his parents' memories. We do have hope, Krish. We do.'

Krishna leaned in, smiling, 'And what do we make of these two, sitting there on the second last row,' he asked, pointing towards Manoj and Adish inside St. Peter's Jacobite Syrian Church.

'Good chaps. They're recommended by Hanuman and Thomas.'

'Today, they seem to have doubts that we might not exist.'

'Because we aren't answering their prayers?'

'Yup.'

'Hmm. But we did want them to think that way, didn't we?'

'Yes, we did. Where is the fun otherwise?' Krishna's steepled fingers and tight-lipped smile weren't lost on Christ, however.

'I see a little mischief brewing inside your head. What is it?' he narrowed his eyes. It soon struck him. 'Oh Jesus,' he cried.

'Aah, such delight when you call out your own name.'

'Yeah, I still remember the Champakulam incident.'

'One of my favourites!'

And with that, Krishna closed his eyes and tipped his head back to the head rest of his chair and, with Christ, took a trip down their memory lane as if the incident had happened yesterday.

Pooradum Thirunal Devanarayanan – the Chempakasseri king, was a great devotee of Krishna. He had intended to build a new temple at Ambalapuzha, advised by his royal astrologers on divine inspiration. Soon a Balakrishna deity was sculpted. A day before its installation, the Tantri Namboothiri noticed, the idol hadn't turned out to be flawless and had a small swelling on its left side that rendered its installation inauspicious. An alternate idol was urgently needed as per the rituals or else misfortune would befall on the kingdom.

'You had given the idol that little tweak, didn't you? So that they seek another idol,' Christ chuckled. Krishna winked. 'And the one available, was the one you had bequeathed to Arjuna.'

'Parthasarathi.'

'You know Muhammad has a strange liking for Arjuna?'

'Well, they both have so much common - wars, persecution and the fact that through their mortal bodies, the supreme knowledge was delivered.'

'Fascinating, isn't it?' Christ was filled with admiration.

Now back to the story,

With deliberation, the high priests concluded that the sacred idol at Karikulum temple in Kuruchi should be brought to Ambalapuzha for installation.

Through the Pamba river, the king's men travelled in a grand Palliodam, singing bhajans all the way to meet the Parthasarathi idol, the one with a whip in right hand and a conch in the left. Acquiring the idol, the king's men set forth on the royal boat for the return journey. While returning, darkness fell, and as advised earlier by the king, they took shelter for the night at a Christian homestead - the house of a loyal subject and the king's confidante,

Itty Thommen of Mappilassery. Mappila literally meant 'son in law' and was used for the immigrants to Malabar whether they were Christians, Jews or Mohammedans.

Itty Thommen and his family received the king's men with great enthusiasm and honour and offered them a place to spend the night. The idol was also kept with the same respect it'd derive in a Namboothiri household.

In the morning, the king arrived at Mappilassery with many devotees and priests. The idol was worshipped in a little ceremony at the Mappila house, and people of all faiths attended the feast. From there, the idol was carried to Ambalapuzha in a large boat. On the way, the king and the deity received a grand welcome by the people of Champakulam. On their request, he agreed to place the idol for a day in the Kalloorkadu church so that the people and the priests could honour it before its consecration and installation at Ambalapuzha temple.

Seeing so much love and affection showered by his Christian subjects, the king felt gratified and declared that an annual water carnival be celebrated to commemorate this religious amity on the same Moolam day when the idol was kept in the Mapilla house.

Even today, people believe, Krishna resides not in the temple but in Mapilla house on this day. Before the race commences, the temple priests enter the room where they venerate the lamp along with the cross, and the statues of Christ and Mary.

Finishing their tea, the spiritual twins decided to leave for their daily chores. As they rose, their attention steered back to Manoj and Adish.

'They're still praying,' Christ remarked. 'It is not just the boat race you see, that is at stake.'

Krishna smiled. 'May the Trinity fulfil their wish.'

'In the name of Father, Son and the Holy Spirit and men, may the grace and peace of God the Father, and love of Jesus and communion of the Holy Spirit be with you,' the Padre said.

'Amen,' chorused the mass attendees.

The Sunday prayers had run for exact two hours – the longest Manoj had ever spent in a God's house. By the time the Padre culminated it, he felt as if he had endured a crucifixion. He wasn't sure if Rajesh rightly declined their proposal to attend the Sunday Mass, citing too much travel.

'You know, I was mulling over this sponsor thing,' said Manoj, as they walked out of the Church. 'You guys have so many rich NRIs. We should be targeting one of those big fishes, instead of wasting our energies on itsy-bitsy local sponsors.'

'NRIs,' Adish blinked. 'And where do we find them?'

Manoj glanced around as if looking for an answer, rubbing his nape, 'What time is it?'

'Twelve thirty.'

'Twelve thirty?' Manoj slackened his jaw. 'No wonder I feel hunger pangs.'

'But where do we find an NRI sponsor?'

'Adish Mathew,' Manoj gave him a bitter smile. 'First, find me a good restaurant. I cannot think.'

'Veg restaurant? Hard to find here,' said Adish, inspecting the area around the Church. 'Let's try near the temple.'

'Try and try to succeed, King Bruce. I don't want people to say we could not get a breakthrough just because you couldn't locate a damn restaurant,' Manoj gave a harsh squint. 'And see, if you can also find Pandey's Kerala Lights.'

'Excuse me,' said a voice in their direction. They turned their heads and their bodies quaked. 'We met in Kochi, right? At the antique's shop?' enquired Vazhoor Chandy, ignoring the visible disbelief on their face.

'Yes, I think. You intended to buy our boat,' said Adish.

Our boat. Vazhoor raised his brow. 'Yes,' he said. 'I was in a hurry that day so could not hear you out. If I recall correctly, you needed that boat to participate in Vallamkali. Didn't you?'

Manoj hadn't missed the eagerness in Vazhoor's voice, and the stress on "Vallamkali" as he spoke.

The sun advanced on the tropic of cancer, turning the day hotter and sultrier as Rajesh stood outside the Technopark gate, watching auto-rickshaws pass by. No sooner had Manoj and Adish left for the church than Rajesh regretted turning down their invitation. Feeling despair he conceded that he couldn't stay alone and came out of the hostel. But where'd he go? He was still unsure.

Half-drenched in sweat, he got bored with the tug of war inside his head and called out for the auto that now approached him. His voice wasn't alone, though. It had a female echo. He glanced aside and saw her, hurrying out of the gate. The Auto stopped midway from them. Briefly, their eyes locked in confusion. Who should lay the claim? Male chivalry won as Rajesh smiled and gestured at Shelja to go ahead. She acknowledged with a wide grin and boarded the auto. But before it moved, she popped out her head.

'I'm going to Trivandrum. Should I drop you somewhere or else you might have to wait longer,' she said.

Rajesh contemplated his options. An arresting female, offering a lift to a broken hearted guy on a hot day was like an oasis in the middle of the desert to a parched man dying of thirst.

Real desperate men don't say no to such divine interventions. Rather they jump on it, Manoj had opined once.

'I'm also going to Trivandrum,' he affirmed his destination.

'Ok, hurry then. I'm already late for Sunday church,' she said. Sunday church, Rajesh mumbled as he took his seat beside her. *She was a devotee.*

'I'm also going to a temple,' he decided to be a devotee too. For today. Nothing wrong in it. He argued with his inner self.

'Nice, which temple?'

'There is this big one, I'm forgetting the name-' he prodded his head, feigning forgetfulness.

'Padmanabhan temple?'

'Padmanabhan temple? Is it big? Yeah, could be,' he said, feigning remembrance now, but staying non-committal.

'It's near our church.'

'That's the one,' he confirmed. An hour-long one-sided 'Sunday Temple-Church Auto-ride date' with Shelja was now secured. Instantly, his bristling male hormones simmered down, and his mind seemed appeased. Even if it was for a day. He wondered what else was in store in the name of God. He had never been a firm believer in God nor had he much regard for destiny.

Just a coincidence, he told himself. A pleasant one, though, he agreed.

'It seems everyone owns a private church in Kerala,' he said, noticing numerous churches on their way. 'Are you also going to your private church?' he jested.

Shelja smiled, 'Yes, it's a family church. But we don't own it.'

Rajesh laughed. 'Your family lives in Trivandrum?' he said. She nodded. 'Ahaan, you're a local too. Nice.'

'Yeah, but not anymore. I'm based out of Chennai. Though, I hope to move out once this training is over.'

'We don't have many choices, do we?' he said and received another smile. 'I thought you were leaving last week itself.'

'I was, but the new project they offered didn't excite me. It was again in Chennai, so I declined.'

'Can you do that?' he was astonished. 'How?'

'Well…,' she hesitated.

'Don't worry. I'll guard your secret,' he raised his fist over his chest. She laughed. *Girls are fond of guys who make them laugh,* he had recently read.

'I told them, my fiancé works in Hyderabad so I'd prefer a project there.'

'Fiancé? Are you getting married?'

Stop the damn auto, right now.

'No, no. I'm not. Not so soon. Please,' she dismissed my fear with a snort of laughter. 'It was a lie. Hyderabad has a few exciting projects you see.'

Relief washed over Rajesh as he eased back on his seat.

Slow down the auto, bhaiya. Why are you in such a hurry?

'I see,' he said. 'How long have you been in DigiSys?'

'Two years.'

'Two years. So you're no longer under the bond period. Free bird, huh. That's why you have the balls to lie.'

'You're from North India right?' she said, trying to control her laughter.

'Yeah, from Delhi. Why?'

'You've just joined a company, and you already feel so bonded.'

'Because we're free-spirited,' he declared.

'Or because, you're commitment-phobic,' she suggested.

'Hello! Nothing like that. We're truly committed. Just that we don't commit easily. And I don't think one should, at least not under the fear of a bond. For us, it has to be gradual and mutual. Whether in a profession or a relationship.'

Shelja smiled at the reason and turned her gaze outside. No further conversation ensued between them for next few minutes, but Rajesh continued to think about her. On their first interaction outside the office environment, she had proved to be an affable person. With her sitting so close to him, almost touching, he could sense the warmth exuding from her body. It was a familiar sensation – the one stirring him at the moment.

He'd felt the craving before.

Diverting his gaze outside, he brushed off *her* thoughts before they could depress him. Their auto had touched the periphery of the city now.

'You plan to spend the whole day with your family?' he said.

'Not whole but yes, we'll have lunch together and then I'll head back to the hostel.'

Her lunch would be over by two-thirty or max-to-max three in the afternoon, which meant he had four hours to kill, he calculated. *What would he do until then?* His male hormones pushed him hard, craving to spend as much time with a female as he could, to heal his bruised self while his mind discounted the possibility of going back to the hostel, alone.

'There's your temple,' Shelja pointed towards a large temple wall, few hundred meters away.

'And church?' Rajesh asked, getting off the Auto. He couldn't spot any.

'That is another two kilometres. I thought of dropping you first. See you,' she waved, and before he could respond, the auto lunged forward.

'Hey, you forgot to take my share of the fare,' he shouted from behind.

'Well, thanks for the chivalry, but next time,' she said, sticking her head out.

'And when is that next time?'

It remained a query as Shelja pulled her head back in.

Inside the auto, a wide grin had appeared on her face.

Adish and Vazhoor stared at each other in complete silence.

A few minutes ago, Manoj had nudged Adish to explain the boat story while he focussed on the food thali spread before him. But now, he cursed himself on allowing Adish to spew every damn detail in the first place. The eagerness on Vazhoor's face had disappeared, and it seemed drained of colour as if bitten by a venomous snake. Manoj squinted at the empty plates.

Thankfully, he'd polished off every scrape of food on his plates.

On the other hand, Vazhoor was struggling to digest the new

fact; the boat he deemed a piece of history, had turned out to be a worthless wood. When he had bumped into Adish and Manoj an hour back, he thought he had met a team, which could ride on the boat's glorious past and make his dream come true. *Glorious past, damn it.* How could he be so naïve?

'That hideous old man lied to me,' Vazhoor muttered, scratching his head. 'He said, it was a legendary boat.'

'Oh, it is *legendary*, sir,' Adish said proudly. Vazhoor lazily raised his brows, still puzzled at his enthusiasm. 'Twenty years ago it qualified for the *finals* of Kumarakom vallamkali and came *seventh* in the championship.'

Vazhoor stared at Adish, speechless. He wasn't sure if he should be elated with the fact that these kids saved his few lakhs or kick their butts at the brazen salesmanesque glorification of a piece of crap.

'What did you want from us? Manoj asked.

'Umm, nothing. I thought the boat was a winner so maybe if I get a team I can sponsor…,' Vazhoor's voice trailed off mid-way as he chewed upon his words. 'Never mind. My impression was wrong. Both, the boat and its team are certified losers,' he said.

'You wished to sponsor?' Manoj gasped. Vazhoor bid his time for what seemed an eternity and responded with a nod. 'Why the hell did you have to broadcast everything?' Manoj muttered to Adish who swallowed hard at the reproach, and looked at the food instead.

High time he used his mouth to eat while Manoj talked.

'Sir, I understand your concern. But let's assume, you put your money into this highly capable team and lend your brand to this little but incredible boat. Suppose, with an MIT-backed design, it emerges a winner. Suppose, they all become big. Then guess, who gets the free entry into the big league,' said Manoj.

'Free,' Vazhoor broke into hysterical laughter.

Manoj carried on, undeterred. 'Actually at one fourth of the price you were willing to pay last week,' he leaned forward and dropped his voice, 'you get the boat, the team and your brand circulating at *every* future event. Shouldn't you just grab it?'

Now he was talking to a marketing brain, Vazhoor thought. The grin disappeared and a serious, thoughtful face emerged. A sound business advice always made him attentive.

'By the way, what's the name of your brand,' Adish asked, between the mouthfuls.

'Kerala Lights,' the gleam was back in Vazhoor's eyes.

Rajesh's response had been well rehearsed and simple:

He was eager to study the design and architecture of Kerala's religious buildings and after his visit to the Padmanabhan temple, he had set on to see the churches in the neighbourhood. Of course, what a *coincidence* it'd been that he met Shelja at one of those.

While Shelja had accepted his explanation without casting a doubt, he still hoped she didn't mistake him as a stalker.

On second thought, he indeed behaved like one.

Or else how would he explain running around for an hour to locate her church in a two-kilometre long peripheral vicinity of the temple?

If only he had asked the name of her church instead of offering his share of the fare.

'I plan to visit a bookstore post lunch. So, I'd be leaving around the same time you would. We can go back together. I'll also have company and a chance to show off my chivalry too,' Rajesh said, trying to push his luck further.

'I'm not sure. I might get late so don't wait for me, please,' she said flatly. 'But yes, if I don't, I'll give you a buzz.'

'Yeah, sure. My number is-' he blurted out the digits without any delay and no sooner had she left than he realized he hadn't asked for hers. What if she forgets to call? He feared. But there was nothing he could do now. He'd have to wait.

Sticking around the Church for a while, he noticed it was the most unusual church, he had ever seen. It wasn't white but gravel red in colour and had an extravagant four-storey high tower-like gothic structure. Must be very old and in desperate need of a renovation, he reckoned, noticing its frail condition.

In contrast, the Padmanabhan temple he had visited in the morning was the richest temple in the world – a fact he had earlier mistaken for the much-publicised Tirupati Balaji temple. Yet he hadn't found it a bit profligate but much closer to the traditional art and ambience, unlike North Indian temples. Simplicity was what he had observed, time and again in Kerala.

It'd been long ago since he had last gone to a God's house, he recalled; almost an year since he visited their local deity's temple near Jim Corbett National park, on his mother's insistence. It was after he had secured that super offer from Ramsek Technologies. 3.25 lakhs per annum gross! Could his breakup be due to his refusal to accept the local deity's gift?

Today, on a single Sunday, he had visited two Global biggies; Lord Vishnu in Padmanabhan temple, and Christ in St. Joseph Church. His thoughts once again drifted to Shelja.

He was still not at ease with the idea of hanging around. His conscience had already declared his acts as mere stupidity and sheer desperation, leading to stalking. Not that he had never acted likewise. However, he could hardly be blamed for believing that he was doing it for the first time. He had suffered a very, very tragic break up a few weeks ago and ideally, he should be despising women to the core, the way he despised *her.*

He shrugged his shoulders to brush off her memories, again. Sudden hunger pangs reminded him he hadn't eaten anything today. Feeling weak and dizzy, he foraged outside the church only to be disturbed by his phone, vibrating inside his pocket.

It was Manoj, much to his disappointment.

'We have Kerala Lights.'

'How many packets, man?' Rajesh exclaimed. A mere mention of Kerala Lights had lifted his spirits.

Silence fell on the other side.

'Yeah, man. That too,' Manoj broke it finally.

'Where are you guys?'

'Kerala Lights factory on the outskirts of Trivandrum.'

'Whoaa, you smoked out the entire factory for me? I love you, man. I'm in the city as well,'

'What are you doing here? You said you weren't interested?'

'I was missing you guys. Now, tell me the address, quick.'

Kerala Lights

****

Vazhoor Chandy could never fancy the cigarette business his father set up in 1969; to rehabilitate the *beedi* workers after their infamous October lay off in 1968, and the subsequent agitations that forced the state and the central governments to lock horns.

While most of the workers had joined the newly floated Kerala Beedi Workers Central Coop Society (KBWCCS) - a government undertaking, many others had chosen to forgo *Beedi* in lieu of the more refined *Cigarette* that promised a "better future". The brand of Kerala Lights had become a household name since then.

But things changed in 2004 when two large manufacturing units of Kerala Lights in Kollam were destroyed during the December Tsunami. Why God had chosen Kollam and Alappuzha on the Western Coast when Tsunami had intended to destroy the Eastern Coast of India, was beyond Vazhoor's understanding.

By then, he had already made good a business of his own in Oman – producing unique Frankincense based cigarette lighters for Eastern European and South Asian markets. Frankincense or Olibanum was an aromatic resin extracted from Boswellia trees. It was nature's most expensive gift to the arid lands of Oman, and the most valuable source of income before oil made it to the front-page headlines.

Working with a firm that provided refilling fuel for pocket lighters, Vazhoor had met the second love of his life, Olibanum, during a candle-light dinner in a restaurant; he'd gone there with his wife to celebrate their marriage anniversary. He was contemplating on their future in Oman when the waiter arrived with an aroma filled lamp and placed it on their table.

It was the great Omani scent, the waiter told him. As he lit his cigarette and experienced one of the unique moments of his life, the idea of a cigarette lighter with Frankincense scent struck him.

For next six months, Vazhoor focussed his energies into an ambitious business plan. Easy and cheaper availability of fuel meant low costs as far as non-refillable lighters were concerned, and he foresaw the demand for lighters growing manifold in coming years. To top it off, Frankincense would provide him with an exclusive edge, he believed. And yet, it didn't quite seal him the deal. Rather it was the brand name he had chosen for his product that his investors fancied the most.

"Kerala Lights Lighters" apparently alone had the ingredients to grab the Omani market. Statistics backed their belief: Sixty percent Malayalis constituted the Indian diaspora in Oman which itself was twelve percent of the country's total population, meaning there were one million people of Malayali origin. Even at a conservative estimation of twenty-five per cent of smoker's rate, he had *two-point-five lakh* consumers ready to consider his brand – an astounding number for a Start-up, especially when the name "Kerala Lights" had already been leveraged, as Malayalis were familiar with the brand.

Within a year from making that discovery, Vazhoor Chandy dispatched the maiden lot of his lighters into the market. Two years thence, Oman listed lighters in their exports journal for the first time. Buoyed by his success, Vazhoor was considering the idea to expand the manufacturing beyond Oman when Tsunami welted the Indian shores. His father soon took ill, presenting him an opportunity to look at the Indian market in different light.

The cigarette economy was faltering as anti-smoke drives hit Kerala, and cheaper brands bombarded its markets. He deduced that no matter which brand of cigarette people bought, they'd always need something to light it with. He was ready to launch Kerala Lights in its unseen avatar in India.

Vazhoor's idea made perfect sense to Manoj as they traipsed through the factory corridors.

Kerala Lights' factory lay on the outskirts of Trivandrum. Spread over fifteen acres, it was a big, closed compound. On a Sunday, the factory bore an empty look but on working days, it had six hundred people working in two shifts; that, of course, in the past when it manufactured cigarettes. Now, a large part of the factory had been converted into an assembly line with enormous automated machines capable of producing three thousand cases of lighters a day. Cigarettes to Cigarette Lighters, the business transformation of Kerala Lights had been complete.

'I had planned the launch on the first day of *Chingam*, the Malayalam New year, which is two days after Nehru Boat Race,' said Vazhoor. 'It would've been a perfect launch.'

'That's why you were fishing around for your own boat and a team,' Rajesh said conclusively. Vazhoor nodded with a grin.

Manoj had cracked it, Rajesh believed. And once he shared his detailed MIT scholar backed designs too, he had no doubt that Vazhoor would consider the offer a diamond deal. The day had been so remarkable, and he still couldn't believe the turn their fate had taken.

'Gentlemen, tea is served in my cabin. Let's talk over the deal upstairs,' said Vazhoor as his assistant called him to notify.

'You'll have to excuse me for a minute,' Rajesh said, showing his little finger, and hurried away to the loo. As soon as he stepped in, he pulled out his phone. It had vibrated so many times inside his pocket, but the intensity of the discussion had held him from reaching for it. One message from *her*.

I hope you have deleted our intimate pics from your phone. If not, please do it soon. I don't wish to ruin things with Rohan.

'What the hell? She's gone all the way to the third base with that *Chutiya*, and she is worried about her first and second base pictures with me?' he cursed. Should he tell *her* that he'd posted them on a porn website with title, 'Delhi girl showing her tits.' That would upset *her* big time. *But what if she lodged an FIR?*

He shrugged aside the dangerously cheap idea. He still loved *her*, he reminded himself as he clicked on the image folder and browsed through their pictures once again. *She* looked so hot and innocent. How could *she* turn out to be evil? Feeling aroused, his hand moved to unzip his zipper.

Flashes of *her* making out danced before his eyes, and his hand stopped. He tried to picture *her* with Rohan but couldn't. He'd never seen him. He never cared. Disgusted, he closed the folder, still undeleted and hopped to the next message. It was from Shelja.

Hey. Shelja here. Sorry, I will get free by five. You carry on.

The text was sent at two, and now it was four thirty, he noted. He'd been in the factory for over three hours.

Hey, some personal work came up in Trivandrum, so I am still stuck here. How long you are going to take? He typed and paused.

Should he send it? Wouldn't he come across as a despo? His thumb wiggled over the keypad. *I love Rohan,* her voice pounded in his ears again. *Yes, he was a despo,* Rajesh pressed the "send" button. The message delivered within seconds.

Waiting for Shelja's reply, he brooded over the day's events. He'd never been a firm believer in destiny, and yet, there was no denying the fact that they had indeed received God's blessings having set out in the morning to find Him.

Was Shelja too, His blessing? He wondered, reflecting on his afternoon hypothesis, seriously this time. His heart desperately sought a pattern, but his mind forthwith enjoined him from treading that treacherous path.

His phone vibrated. Shelja had called.

'I thought you had left.'

'No, I had to meet someone.'

'Okay so where are you?'

'I'm at,' Rajesh paused a little, 'near this Kerala Lights factory. A place called Vazhutha something.'

'Vazhuthacaud?'

'Yes exactly.'

'Then you are not too far from me.'

Of course, not.

'I was planning to leave. What about you?'

Rajesh looked at his watch. 'I'll be free in five minutes.'

'Cool then. See you at the St. Joseph Church at five.'

'I'll be there, but please do wait in case I'm late. I'm not familiar with the roads, and it is tough negotiating with Auto drivers.'

Shelja laughed at his honest admission and told him she'd wait.

'I guess we should get going. We have so much to do and so little time,' said Rajesh, bursting into the cabin to wrap things up. His gaze fell on the tea, and the biscuits and his hunger returned. No, he couldn't take a chance.

'Absolutely, you have my word and of course, my money as well,' Vazhoor Chandy said, with a wink.

'Thanks a ton, sir. We assure you that we shall create a great campaign,' Manoj rose from his chair.

'Let's meet on Tuesday, because I am leaving for Oman on Wednesday. Share with me your branding strategy, and collect your cheque,' Vazhoor said with a satisfied smile.

'Done, sir,' Manoj shook hands with him.

'For you Rajesh, I have a gift,' said Vazhoor, opening the drawer of his table. He took out three packets of cigarettes and tossed them over to him.

'Kerala Lights?' Rajesh couldn't be happier.

'The stock is officially over now.'

The Dhamma

****

After the God's design had promised to change their collective fortunes, Vazhoor Chandy left for Oman to attend to his family and pending business matters, leaving Manoj with the advance cheque and the task to strategize the promotions and rebranding of 'Kerala Lights'. A surprised and relieved Mutthur couldn't find words to express his gratitude towards his Northie friends.

Kareem had also appreciated the altered design and had shown eager enthusiasm, working on his master's creation. Though, he cautioned that the modifications demanded time, and if done in a single go, might not leave Mutthur's team enough time to practice. Kareem, therefore, broke down the changes into phases: First and foremost, they'd expand the seating capacity. Then, based on a week-long testing at full strength, they'd fix the issues of base stability, if any. Once done, rest of the alterations could be brought about, in parallel to the practice.

Meanwhile, at the campus, it dawned on the three circles that the second phase of their CLP would be over soon, and they were yet to fill and submit their preference forms.

Resting his head against the headboard of his bed, watching his friends struggle with the form, Rajesh mused about Shelja. Riding on Sunday's fortune, things had moved fast with her; besides taking lunch and breakfasts together at the hostel canteen where he *coincidentally* arrived at the same moment as she did, they had even met outside the campus at the café once.

Shelja had truly brought in a breath of fresh air into his life and Rajesh was glad that they had moved beyond the decorum of *senior-junior associates.* And subsequently after he'd shared their Kerala Lights project with her, a sense of admiration had built up in her eyes too. *That magical pair of eyes, embellished on his mind forever.*

'I haven't even seen the form yet,' said Rajesh.

'Oh yes, why would you?' Manoj said in a sarcastic tone and turned to Adish. 'Let us go to the café, Adish and have some coffee. That might jumpstart our brains as well!'

'Am I missing something?' Rajesh narrowed his eyes with a hint of self-doubt as Manoj mentioned "Cafe" for the third time today. He hadn't shared anything with Manoj yet. Though, he had often quizzed Rajesh about leaving so early for the breakfast these days. *Had he sniffed out his little secret called 'Shelja'?*

Manoj stared back as well. *Yeah, your secret is out, fucking mongrel,* he spoke under his breath. Rajesh raised his brows. 'I think I have to practice some Malayalam. Of course, with Adish. He is so beautiful, isn't he?' Manoj added with a smirk.

'Why are you dragging me into this, Mister India?' Adish retorted. 'He knows your secret, Rajesh.'

Manoj glared at Adish for spilling the beans.

'How the fuck…' Rajesh quavered. 'How did you find out?'

Manoj laughed hard. Adish smiled too. The sheep was out in front of hungry wolves.

'Oh dear Watson, this man thought he had his back covered. Poor chap, isn't he?' Manoj sneered, looking at Adish. 'You remember the kissing circles crap he spouted that day? And how depressed he was on Sunday morning? While we tackled Vazhoor, this fucker was on a date. In fact, he cared more for his cigarettes. That's why he abandoned us for a romantic bus ride.'

'You…you guys…were on the bus?' Rajesh struggled.

'You're not that unlucky or else you'd be dead by now,' said Manoj, sounding like a typical Hollywood villain. 'But that's not the point. The point is…you lied. You lied to us.'

'Listen, dudes,' said Rajesh, guilt-trapped. 'I am…sorry.'

'And you're not forgiven,' Manoj shook his fist at him and went back to filling his form. 'This is so confusing. What do I write?' He had heeded to the suggestion of Rajesh Dandekar but the task had felt too heavy now.

'What are you so worried about?' Rajesh peeped into his form. 'Don't take it seriously.'

'I'm concentrating on this form and not your trainer, you imbecile moron.'

'I was also referring to the form.'

'Use object nouns in your speech to be more specific about your subject,' Manoj gritted his teeth. 'And yeah, this matter is serious. Therein lies our future.'

Rajesh grimaced. They were along the right lines, thinking of their future and purpose. For few weeks, he had a purpose too – the boat and while working on it, had forgotten everything else. Meticulously, he had tabulated every single observation and sent the final data to Andrew too, who wished to include their case study in his MIT thesis. But now that the task was over, his aches and pains had returned.

'Are you not going to fill it?' Adish asked Rajesh.

'What do I write? You guys have set goals while I have no clue whatsoever,' he said.

Manoj sighed and moved his fingers on the cursor pad of the laptop that lay beside him. 'A piece of information for you,' he pushed the laptop towards Rajesh and showed him an image on its screen. It was a newspaper article:

'CapVirgo-DigiSys go fast and high,' read the headline, followed by the subheading, 'With a major airline and a Formula one team as their partners, CapVirgo-DigiSys dive into unchartered domains.'

'I don't know what options it may unlock for you but imagine what if it does? You could be working with Boeing or a cool F1 team. Who else from your batch could be doing that?' Manoj spurred. 'Now fill this damn form.'

Rajesh grabbed his form and scoured it. 'It is confusing,' he said. 'Let's go to the cafe and crack it together.'

Mutthur took his usual refuge in the warehouse and toddy as soon as he finished his routine check-up of the paddy fields. The hybrids were growing at the predicted rate. In one and a half months, the crop would be mature for a harvest. His own fate, though, would be sealed in a fortnight.

A week had passed since Kareem had taken over the boat. He still needed four more days to fix the seating section, leaving barely a week for Mutthur to prepare for the Nehru boat race. They'd be grossly unprepared, but Mutthur knew that the opportunity to face a stiff competition couldn't be missed. At least, they'd be apprised of how well the boat had shaped up.

'How many times have I told you to light the lamp at dusk?' said Vasudevan, as he entered. 'It is a bad omen to stay in the dark after sunset,' he said, picking the lamp that hung on the wall. 'Matchbox?'

'Use this,' Mutthur stuck out a pocket lighter.

Vasudevan stared at the glittering fire device, confused and snatched it from Mutthur. 'Have you taken up smoking?'

'Oh come on Chetta. No,' said Mutthur, making a face. 'It is a gift. From Vazhoor.'

Vasudevan fiddled with the lighter for a while and then lit it. A sweet aroma surrounded him. 'What is this scent?' he asked, forgetting to illuminate the lamp.

'That's the speciality of the lighter, some Omani material. Hugely popular in Gulf. Vazhoor believes it is going to be in demand here as well.'

'I told you that ample opportunities exist there. You should go.'

'Opportunities are coming home,' Mutthur smiled. For a while, only Frankincense made its presence felt.

'Are you fine with a cigarette company giving you money?' his brother's voice had a sudden anguish. Mutthur knew he referred to their father's lung cancer. The doctors had claimed it was due to his chain smoking.

'Lighter, not a cigarette,' Mutthur said.

'What's the difference? When you sell a cigarette, you want people to smoke. When you sell a lighter, again you want them to smoke. Same,' Vasudevan offered his blunt analysis.

'You have a point. But what about a choice, Chetta,'

'Okay, then what about those people's choices who think we shouldn't cultivate paddy and instead, fill our lands with rubber.'

'You're right, again. We all have choices, but then it is also us who ought to choose what we believe in. Not for ourselves but for others. Father chose the curse, and he burnt his life with a matchbox, someone else burnt our boat with a beedi, and we? We choose to shun it with a lighter.'

Vasudevan remained quiet, his eyes were closed. One couldn't make out if he was under the influence of Mutthur's reasoning or Frankincense.

'I've chosen my Dhamma,' said Mutthur. 'Now, I need you to understand and support me.'

Vasudevan opened his eyes. 'You mentioned that our men needed to reduce weight for the race,' he said. Mutthur nodded. 'That's the toughest thing to ask of them. They work, they eat and they do both in abundance.' Mutthur nodded again.

Vasudevan sighed, deliberating the matter in his mind.

'Engage them in coconut plucking. Most are fishermen and aren't used to it. Every day's climbing up and down might help.'

'But that would still mean too many coconuts. Where do we sell them?'

'Let our men consume half. The water will fill their stomachs, leaving less room for solids. And the rest, let them sell away.'

'We won't earn anything.'

'Don't worry. The paddy looks good,' Vasudevan said, gazing outside. He lit the lighter again and smelled the aroma. 'Just make sure the village participates in the competition. Our father shall feel proud.' His brother's eyes were closed again.

Mutthur hadn't missed the tears in those eyes.

The Choices and the Dilemma

****

It was a breezy Friday evening, and Rajesh sat in the Café, waiting for Shelja to arrive. Another week of CLP had culminated.

Depending upon their inputs, associates had been assigned modules for phase three, which included similar courses for everyone, except for a few courses that differed as per the preferences of the associates. Manoj had two modules related to management; 'New Age Business Strategy & Value Management Principles' and 'Business Process & Change Management'. Sitting in their hostel room, he must be leafing through the entire study material to align Kerala Lights into the similar direction, Rajesh thought.

'How do I make the campaign IT relevant?' Manoj had asked Rajesh in the afternoon.

'Introduce a website,' Rajesh had cheekily suggested.

Manoj had cringed.

For himself, Rajesh had two subjects of interest - 'Understanding Structural Designs in Transport Industry' and 'Production Planning & Lean Shop Floor Solutions'. Besides, he had taken a brief course on CAD - the design and modelling software - too and without any delay, had transferred the boat data to his assigned system in the CAD lab.

His tests on the modified seating arrangement had shown satisfactory results. Much to his relief. However, upon verifying his measurements based upon his calculations and simulations on MAVA against Andrew's results, a few discrepancies had surfaced regarding exterior and bottom structural changes. This had made him anxious as Andrew wouldn't be available for a month. He had dropped him a detailed email, though.

His phone beeped. New message from Shelja, he checked.

I will be there in five minutes. Order black coffee for me.

His lips parted, letting out a deep breath. Knowing she was on her way, he flopped back into his chair and chewed on his other worry. Eight days had remained for the Nehru Boat Race and the boat hadn't arrived yet.

Their participation looked dicey. Worst, what if his design wouldn't work? The possibility bothered him consistently. He hoped for the boat to arrive latest by the next evening so that he'd have the weekend to study the suspected discrepancies.

He forgot to order her coffee. Damn. Black coffee?

Rajesh wrinkled his nose, disagreeing with her choice today. Personally, he preferred Cappuccino. He called out to the staff and quickly placed an order.

'You take so much time to decide,' Shelja said, walking in.

'I was in a mood to be lazy,' he sank deeper into the chair.

'Which means the boat is still under the hammer,' she took her seat across him.

'How do you know?' asked Rajesh. While her deduction puzzled him, the fact that she remembered, pleased him too.

'Otherwise you'd be all worked up and nervous,' she winked as the waiter put two coffees on the table. 'Their service is quite fast. Isn't it?' Rajesh loved the way she spotted these little details.

'You're right Miss Holmes. Honestly, I'm damn nervous,' he said, picking a sugar sachet and noticed she sipped hers without. 'You don't add sugar?'

'What's the point of black coffee if you do?'

'I don't know. I find it too bitter.'

'Well, everything can't be sweet. Isn't it?' She sipped her coffee. 'What makes you nervous?'

'I was afraid. I mean...what if we fail?' he said. 'What if I fail?' he rephrased.

The moment Shelja heard the dreaded F word, she wondered if their pleasant rendezvous would sail into the gloomy waters but thankfully, Mutthur called up, relieving both of them of their fears for the time being. The boat had arrived, and now they could discuss themselves, the perfect thing to do on a balmy evening.

Though, she had made a note to herself. She'd ponder over his fears later. What if Rajesh failed?

Vazhoor had sounded exhilarated. And it had worsened Manoj's fear surrounding the timing of the launch. If the design didn't work, the launch could fail. Though he had kept his concerns away from Vazhoor, and as a strategist had insisted upon choosing a more propitious occasion. To ensure positivity around the brand rather than any negativity or ridicule.

How could they miss the biggest regatta in the world? Vazhoor had scorned over the phone. 'If you wish to sail deep into the sea and discover pearls, you ought to ride on the bigger waves. Or else you'd never cross the shallow waters,' he had said.

Manoj had spent the entire evening thinking of the matter while finalising the logo and promotional plans on Adish's laptop. Vazhoor's marketing and brand manager Mohan Perumal had asked him to submit his suggestions by the night. His assistant was already waiting downstairs, at the hostel gate.

Plugging in the pen-drive and putting the files on transfer, he lay on his bed exhausted. *Once he hands over the data, he'd catch some sleep.* Humming an old Lata Mangeshkar song that depicted his own jumbled up mind, he reflected on the present situation of his life. Ceaselessly balancing their job training along with the boat, he felt like threadbare sugarcane; squeezed by a juice machine. And he hadn't slogged even half as much as Rajesh, who juggled his official schedule with the extreme design work.

Hats off to this guy. But where is this bugger?

He realized Rajesh had been absent since evening. Must be with Shelja, he concluded and felt his lips stretching into a half-smile. However bad he felt about Rajesh lying to him, Manoj did feel joyous to see him return to normalcy.

'Like poison treats poison, a girl is an antidote for another,' he'd told Adish earlier. 'Just a matter of weeks. Once he is allocated to a project Pandey will return to his old self, with or without a girl,' he had added with utmost seriousness.

'Malayali Christians are very orthodox, particularly we Syrians. Marriages outside our community are a rarity. And Rajesh, being a North Indian Brahmin, beats them all,' Adish had said.

Manoj couldn't have laughed harder.

'Marriage? You crazy? She is nothing but a pity shoulder for him.'

'Did he tell you?'

'He hasn't realized yet.'

A ping from the P.C. notified him the transfer was complete. He picked the pen drive and went downstairs to hand it over to the young, lean man who stood outside the hostel. An evening drizzle had made the weather breezy and pleasant, Manoj noted, casting a glance on the rustling palm fronds while Perumal's assistant shook hands with him and took his leave. He should go for a stroll, Manoj decided.

Not that he didn't recognise Rajesh's desperation. He did and was completely on his side. Last two months had changed the way he perceived girls. Especially, since the day he cognized his *averageness*. Uums had been a *factor* in his transformation.

Such broodings were intermittent, though, and inflicted his mind only when he listened to the song "Chak de" on repeat mode. Rest of the times, he'd picture her as Katrina and himself as Govinda dancing around, trying to convince her of his worth. He'd definitely go and watch "Partner", releasing two weeks later. "Chak de" too, which was due next Friday. He hoped Bollywood films were shown in the local theatres here.

He had reached the mart when Rajesh called and shared with him the big news. The boat had arrived at Mevalloor.

On the professional front, his choices were simple, straight and devoid of any confusion.

Adish was happy with the generic modules he'd been assigned after he had picked product development as his focus area. It was his personal life instead, where he felt trapped in a dilemma.

He remembered what Rajesh had said a few weeks ago.

First, you should know what you really want to do.

He knew what his choices were. *Yes, he did.* Deep inside, he longed to be on Thiruneelakhandam, singing the *Vanchipattu*. He could hear the music loud and clear, and feel the rhythm in his heart. Just that, he couldn't find the courage to make those choices. He was helplessness personified.

On one end, were these two daredevil Northies; spurned by his own folks and yet, trying their best to salvage his village's reputation. On the other, was he; a wimp who couldn't even step into Mevalloor. Yes, he did chip in by creating MAVA, but that was just a few lines of code, something he didn't consider a noteworthy contribution.

His agony grew unbearable.

He missed Antony sometimes. Not sometimes, he corrected himself. He missed him all the time. And now, when he saw Antony's image in Rajesh…for, his part in the whole struggle had been selfless, he didn't wish to abandon Rajesh when he needed his support the most.

Standing in front of the washroom mirror, Adish prayed to Jesus to mitigate the cry of desolation that inflicted his soul. Only the Lord could save him. But didn't the Lord say, *God helps those who help themselves?*

His father would be leaving for Yemen and as usual, he had summoned Adish to receive his customary sermon.

He must talk to his father and clear the air around his friends, he decided, staring into the mirror. It was indeed true that on the crust, he was a splitting image of his father. But inside, he couldn't be more oppugnant. Suddenly, the face in the mirror broadened as if the glass had turned concave.

'What are you up to, son?' A booming voice reverberated. It was his father, staring back at him with an impish grin. 'I told you to stay away from them.'

'Dad…they're not as bad,' Adish spoke into the mirror, almost pleading.

'Since when have you started to question my judgement? Have I not always been correct about your friends?' he mocked.

Clutching the rim of the washbasin, Adish swallowed hard. 'That is what you must know,' he gathered some courage. 'You were never correct about Antony nor are you right about *him* now.'

'How dare you?' came the peremptory reply. 'Okay fine. Let us assume I was wrong on both the accounts, Antony and Rajesh. But tell me, son,' the voice softened, 'have I been wrong about you as well? You know what I mean?' It burst into laughter. Adish shuddered from head to toe.

His phone rang.

'The boat has arrived. We're going to Mevalloor,' said Rajesh.

'I'm off to Kochi.'

The First Disappointment

*****

Manoj Bansal was in high spirits. He had identified an ideal spot to place the logo on the boat.

'Just beneath the hoods on either end,' he pointed towards the boat. 'Also we can create a narrow strip of a slogan for the hull on both sides. Something like, Kerala Lights – Fire in the Water.'

'Sounds good enough for Vazhoor,' said Rajesh, his clammy hands clawing up his throat. Nervousness daubed his face. He had reviewed the alterations thoroughly and recorded his observations as soon as he had reached the river. And the moment oarsmen had pushed the boat into water its relative stability had given him a clear indication that his fears were accurate.

His task wasn't over. Though his main worry, at present, was the oarsmen who appeared as bulky as they did before. Losing mass had proved to be a Herculean task. Twenty kilos, they had sacrificed in total. Ten kilos, Kareem had added to the net weight of the empty boat.

Waiting for the four extra men Mutthur had summoned for a full strength trial, Rajesh did a quick calculation: These extra men meant an addition of at least two hundred and eighty kilos. The ceiling was set at forty so arithmetically they were off limit by two hundred and thirty units. As the four heavyweights approached, Rajesh broke out in cold sweat. The situation was indeed panicky but he kept his calm.

The practice soon commenced. Rajesh boarded the boat along with the oarsmen while Manoj decided to wait at the embankment and watch the crew ride away until it disappeared at the curve. Knowing it was in transit for a while, he eased onto a rock nearby, gazing at the calm river and the surrounding ecosystem.

Monsoon was on a retreat and Muvattupuzha had receded from its peak flow, exposing few meters of moist bed around its edge. Unbridled grass had now grown on this tract, providing a sanctuary to the hunting kingfishers. Few minutes had passed when he heard someone call out his name.

Narayanan's familiar figure stood behind, holding a bottle.

'Thiruneelakhandam,' he said, taking his seat on the adjacent rock. 'You know the meaning of its name? Manoj shook his head. 'Thiruneelakhandam means sacred blue throat,'

'Blue throat?' Manoj was curious. 'Any connection to Lord Shiva?' Narayanan smiled and offered him the toddy, which he duly accepted. Smelling fresh and combined with a story, it seemed a splendid idea to while away until the boat returned.

'Full connection,' said Narayanan. 'It refers to Shiva's throat that turned blue after consuming the poison which appeared from the churning of the Ocean. But the boat's name actually derives from an elephant temple dedicated to Shiva.'

'An elephant she is, indeed,' said Manoj, in between the two swills of the potion.

'Only his father knew how to ride her,' Narayanan laughed fondly at the old memory.

'I hope Mutthur succeeds too.'

'He wouldn't know how to.'

'Why?'

Narayanan motioned at Manoj to pass him the toddy. 'For ten years his father rode that beauty. Commanded her, guarded her and nurtured her,' he said and paused. Taking a swig, he turned his gaze towards the bend and raised a brow. 'Then it consumed him.'

Narayanan's riddles didn't make much sense to Manoj but he didn't interrupt. He recalled the story of Narayanan's troubled life Mutthur had shared with him: Narayanan was his father's deputy and his most trusted friend. But post mishap, he confined himself to his hut, refusing to see his friend much. His alcohol intake too, crossed unmanageable limits, and within a year the council ostracised him. Surrounded by books, Narayanan had remained unwed and an outcast, considered good for nothing by his own family.

What an oddity, Manoj thought.

A whimsical and improbable notion hit him. Could it be possible that Narayanan was *in love* with Mutthur's father? The man didn't look like a gay, though. *How do they look anyway? Like they show in the movies?* He wondered and glanced at Narayanan who grinned back, downing swig after swig and licking his lips. Manoj felt his muscles getting tensed, ready to lope as his eyes swept around to find the thick Rubber forest looming a furlong away. They were alone, and no one would hear his cries.

Fuck, toddy had hammered his mind.

'I guess Mutthur will be kind to her. These people never treated her with grace, but here she is. Back to save their whipped arses,' Narayanan cracked up.

Exhaling a long breath, Manoj made a quick sign of the cross and waved at the boat headed towards them.

Yeah, it was back. At least to save his.

They had returned to the hostel after a drawn-out tiring day, and four sessions of training and mock races. The first results of the new design were now out before them.

'We managed to cut three seconds,' said Manoj.

'The target was five,' Rajesh reminded him.

'But that's with fifty oarsmen, right? We had forty-six today and rest four were like, hefty passengers. If we have oarsmen within our weight range, we can gain few more seconds,' Manoj reasoned, having learnt the design requirements by heart now.

Rajesh gave him a fleeting smile. 'My concern is the middle section,' he pointed out, again grim-faced.

'What about it?'

'We had altered this section to increase crew capacity which in turn has rendered the boat little unsteady. We'd need to counter this imbalance or else the boat may flip if pushed too much.

Manoj swallowed. 'Didn't you consider this scenario earlier?'

'Frankly, we presumed it wouldn't have an impact, but now I cannot ignore it. I guess we should forget Nehru Trophy and instead, focus on the qualifier.'

'Whoa, what are you saying, man? Vazhoor will kill us.'

'If your boat fails, your brand fails too. Then, he sure will kill us.'

'Fuck man. I feared the same. What do we do, now? Do we tell Mutthur?'

'Let us not bother him with any of the technical stuff. Let him practice. I'll modify the design before the next set of changes.'

Agreeing with a small nod, Manoj lay down on his bed. For the first time in many days, he didn't have much to do. He could go to Uums' room and spend time there. Her roomie would be stepping out in an hour, leaving the room all to herself. More than a month and still, the opportunity he'd lost in Aleppy hadn't knocked his door again. *The coming weekend might prove different,* he hoped. Uums did seem excited about the boat carnival, though.

Where was Adish? He wondered. Adish had carried the Laptop back to Kochi with a promise he'd bring it back and never had Manoj waited for someone so desperately.

Laptop or Uums either would do.

'You tharki asshole!' Adish stormed into the room and put down his laptop on Manoj's bed. 'What the fuck have you been doing to my dad's laptop?'

'The turtle wins the race,' Manoj sucked in a quick breath.

Adish threw an angry glance at him and clicked open a folder. Turning the laptop screen towards Manoj, he spoke.

'Do you recognise this?'

'Oh fuck, here they are,' Manoj was ecstatic, finding his lost treasure. 'I thought I'd lost them. Thanks, man. These are the best ones I had,' he said and played one of the videos.

Adish glared at him in an eerie silence, wishing he possessed a butcher's knife.

'What? They are Indian babes,' said Manoj.

'My dad thinks I watch this stuff, and that's what I have learnt from you,' blurted Adish. Manoj fell quiet while Rajesh's laughter filled the room from the other corner. 'Look at this, man. It is so, so weird,' Adish turned to Rajesh, crestfallen. 'How could he do this to me?'

Manoj's head spun, unable to comprehend his anguish. Agreed, that big Chinese dude was…weird but damn. They were supposed to ogle the milky white NRI *hottie* and not him. Bloody she was the new Internet porn sensation; the star of the millenium, some had even suggested.

Look at her curves and the size of her implants, Manoj almost yelped. 'I am sorry if your dad got upset,' he tendered an apology.

'That's the whole point. Dad didn't seem upset at all. Rather he felt gratified. He even granted me the permission to attend the Nehru boat race.'

Manoj gaped at Adish. 'You should thank me then. Had it been my father, he would've thrown me out of the house.'

'Thank *you*?' Adish was baffled. 'You don't even get it. Do you?'

'Pass me the laptop,' Rajesh said.

'See, wasn't I telling you? That NRI babe is a real lush,' Manoj winked, handing him the Laptop.

'I have to work on my changes, fucker,' Rajesh said, sneaking an extended peek at the video. 'She is hot. I see why your dad was bloody impressed,' he said, bursting into laughter with Manoj.

Adish ignored. 'You are working on further alterations? What about the Nehru trophy?'

'We discovered some issues with the boat's stability today.'

'How am I going to explain it to Vazhoor?' Manoj shared his dilemma.

'Tell him, this year's race falls under Rahu Kalam. Inauspicious. Or some similar crap. He seems superstitious like you. I bet he'll buy it,' Rajesh winked.

'I am not superstitious. There is a science to it.' said Manoj, offended. Though, he did see some merit in Rajesh's idea.

'I just hope the new Malayalam year brings us better luck, and we get past the qualifier,' said Adish.

'When is your New Year?' Manoj asked.

'On the day of qualification race, 17th August.'

An idea had germinated inside Manoj's brainbox.

The Nehru Trophy

****

Vazhoor Chandy was obviously not on the cloud seven; being unable to crash through pearly gates of Nehru Trophy in view of the current astrological development. But Manoj had convinced him to postpone the launch until the New Year. In the process, he'd learnt a valuable lesson in management:

When you run out of logical reasons to persuade someone, use emotions. And if that doesn't work either, instil fear using religion or superstition to justify your rationale. Belief or no belief, he'll accept it with a closed mind and open heart.

Expectedly, Vazhoor had bought his idea of introducing the product on an auspicious day. To be honest, Manoj hadn't exactly lied. He did study Vazhoor's Kundali. His stars were certainly not lying in the favourable house. At least not for the next two months. Though as per Vazhoor, the bigger contributing factor had been the village council.

'Better to sort them out before the launch,' he had advised.

Anyhow the launch date had been pushed ahead.

Rajesh worked overtime throughout the first half of the week and managed to find few solutions after Andrew responded to his email with some crucial details. It'd be the last time Andrew could be of help. He'd be away in the Alps, trekking for the next two weeks. Once their modified design was locked, Rajesh decided to rush to Aleppy.

'You sure? It's a weekday, and you cannot take a day off,' Manoj was surprised when he shared his plan of bunking the training.

'Vivek will manage. He is the HR CR.'

After an exhaustive discussion with Mutthur and Kareem

in Aleppy, it turned out they couldn't use the boat before next Tuesday; Rajesh told Manoj upon his return. Their fate was sealed as far as Nehru Boat Race was concerned. Though, Kareem and Rajesh had more or less sorted out the boat issues.

'So you're adding wooden strips to the base near the ends,' said Manoj, nibbling through his breakfast on Friday morning. 'But wouldn't it increase the overall weight? Something you are desperately trying to cut down.'

'Yup, it would. But the good news is when I applied principles of buoyancy to the boat's modified structure and played with the volume of the hull and the wet surface area, I could ascertain that we'd need a little less wood than we had estimated earlier.'

'Okay,' Manoj nodded, though only half of the chatter made sense to him.

'And the better news is, Kareem is going to use the lowest density coco-wood planks, extracted from the coconut tree core.'

'Is there anything in Kerala which coconut cannot do?' Manoj chuckled.

Rajesh laughed. 'Your logo done?'

'Not yet. But I've furnished them with some references. And they have liked one. Let's see,' said Manoj.

'I heard the company is arranging an official trip for us to see the Nehru boat race.'

'Yeah, funny. Isn't it? I thought we'd be participating. We have to go regardless,' Manoj took the last bite of his Idli, 'to study how sponsors use events here to market their brands.'

'I'm not sure if I wish to come.'

'Didn't you want to record observations for further revisions?' Manoj seemed confused.

'I have formulated the final set of amendments. Can't keep modifying forever,' Rajesh had a hint of dejection in his voice. 'I wish we had more time.'

Manoj had seen him slog day and night and felt he was being

too hard on himself. After all, it wasn't his fault; the eventuality of that night. Besides, what more could he do in any case?

'You deserve some time off, bro. Come with us and enjoy the trip as a spectator. I'm sure you won't regret,' said Manoj.

'I might go to Munnar.'

Manoj gawked at Rajesh. The word had exploded on his head like Diwali's *Cock Brand* atom bomb. Harmless but spine-chilling. His pity for Rajesh transformed into contempt. 'Munnar,' he gritted his teeth.

'Yes, as you rightly suggested. I do need to take time off from this boat thing.'

Manoj feigned a smile. He was devastated. *Earthquaked.* And he hadn't told Rajesh yet that he was banking on him for company; Uums' boyfriend would be joining her in Aleppy.

'Shelja has requested, too,' Rajesh divulged, sheepishly.

Shelja! He had been betrayed.

Tricksters. Traitors. He gets to enjoy Munnar with a Chatur Naar while I slog alone in Aleppy, Manoj cursed, sinking further to the nadir of despair.

'I guess Adish would be going with you now that he has his father's permission,' said Rajesh, trying hard to stifle his laughter.

A joke about Adish couldn't amuse Manoj anymore.

It was not just Kerala's natural heritage but also the whole design of its civilisation and cultural legacy that had him mesmerized for last two months. With a universal village-like appeal, almost non existing cities and a narrow web of roads that the locals blamed on non-acquisition of land (though it also meant minor traffic); Kerala appeared ordinary in terms of modern development. Yet, its cine-stars donned their mundu with utmost pride, including in large roadside hoardings, never once caring for the gibes from the North Indian community, which often mistook it for a *lungi*.

Manoj had realized why.

In last two months, he had come to see this single element, mundu, uniting people of all faith and economic status and going beyond the rural-urban divide that was so apparent in the rest of the country. This unity instilled brotherhood and harmony; the testimony of which now peppered in front of him in the form of thousands of sturdy oarsmen and visitors gathered up in the same white wrap-around from all corners of the state.

A strange emotion came over him, as he stood in the Nehru Pavilion at Aleppy, witnessing the grand celebration of Kerala's history and culture on the second Saturday of August.

Near about five hundred garlanded boats, in eight categories of varied sizes floated in the Vembanad Lake to kick-start the Vallamkali season. From twelve to one twenty, the crew was anything in between. An extravaganza it was; a sight he'd never seen before.

Each of the oarsmen wore a coloured vest with a sponsor's logo while each boat bore the sponsor's or owner's name, Manoj noticed. The whole venue was full of banners, posters of different brands and their kiosks.

'Now I see why Vazhoor was so keen to launch his product here,' he mumbled, as four snake boats hissed through the waters towards the finish line. The sound of Vanchipattu - the traditional boat song grew louder as seconds ticked away.

'The regatta receives at least thirty thousand people annually,' said Adish.

'Thirty thousand,' Manoj exclaimed. 'That means ten thousand potential customers. Damn. I wish the alterations had worked in the first attempt. We lost a golden opportunity.'

'I wish the boat hadn't burnt in the first place,' lamented Adish.

Manoj couldn't agree more. If it didn't, he would've been a satisfied man. Or a man at least. Looking at the stationary Ketuvallams parked at the edge of the venue to give an exclusive view of the race, he wondered if one of them housed Uums and her boyfriend, engaged in the act he narrowly missed six weeks ago. The thought of her being with someone else and *not* him piqued him beyond measures.

'Anyways, our main event is after Onam. We better be ready by then,' said Adish

'But it won't lend Kerala Lights such a massive platform,' said Manoj, wistfully at the forfeited opportunity.

Loud cheers erupted from the pavilion as the first lot of four snake boats arrived to complete their heat. True to their name, these long and sleek watercrafts - almost double the size of Thiruneelakhandam - resembled giant serpents gliding through the water.

'That fucker Pandey has no clue what he is missing. Oh and by the way, wasn't he the one who keeps yapping boat...boat all the time? Where is he now? Bloody loser.'

'Why are you going bananas?'

'Because I hate hypocrites,' Manoj sneered, still smarting from Rajesh's betrayal of the bro-code. *The guy even forgot how I put Uums aside when his girlfriend ditched him. Asshole,* Manoj muttered under his breath. 'I'm off to take a round of the venue,' he declared.

'I'll stay,' said Adish. His eyes were fixated on the next set of boats approaching, Manoj discerned. He nodded and ambled away for a thorough inspection. Though, it wasn't Adish's eyes but ears, focussing on the boats or to be precise, on the *Vanchipattu.*

His two Northie friends had been exemplary, Adish thought. More than a professional greed, the risks they had taken by sidelining the CLP and engaging in Mutthur's cause, demanded conviction and emotional commitment. The number of participating boats had further declined this year, he noticed. In such times when their ancient tradition suffered for lack of interest, will and funds, people like them were a new beacon of hope.

Damn! How could he not be on that boat? He contemplated a rebellion, but soon his shoulders drooped again. Their training ended on the weekend preceding Onam, which meant he'd be receiving his first project brief on the race day.

What could he do? How could he make a difference? Adish wondered, mumbling the lyrics of Vanchipattu. It was the most efficient song ever made to define the rowing patterns and had been used by the teams since time immemorial.

Playing a crucial role in a boat's performance, the boat song directly determined the pace and vigour of the oarsmen. The oars ought to complete the loop in the same duration and at the same instant to move the boat forward with maximum speed. It meant the looping trajectory that would start at a pre-determined high point over the water surface, follow a curve to go beneath the water till a fixed depth, and return to its initial point, had to be a Constant in space-time. Hence, oarsmen required a syncing device. Besides, they needed focus and motivation.

Boat song served both purposes. In its absence it'd be impossible for the fifty-odd crew, sitting at a hair's breadth on a slender boat, to row in perfect sync. Each boat had specialised singers called *Nilakkars* on board as the song had to be sung faultlessly as well.

Four years ago, he'd been the Nilakkar on Maruthi Vallam.

Could he improve the efficiency of their oarsmen? He racked his brain while his eyes darted around, seeking an answer but he knew well it'd transpire from within. His sight fell on Gopalan and his boat dawdling in the warm up area. Odi-vallams would be next in line, once Chundans finished their heats.

A preposterous idea sprang inside his head.

What if he rewrote the song to change the rhythm slightly? Or perhaps, composed a new boat song altogether?

Rajesh Pandey's

Our Campus Love Stories

****

I find hills most alluring. Perhaps, owing to my genes. My family belongs to the state of Uttarakhand, and we are called Pahadis, meaning 'from the hills'. Kumouni pahadis to be exact.

Fierce, honest and brave and yet on the surface, Kumounis appear to be calm, laidback and God fearing peaceful creatures who'd never wish any ill upon anyone. And unlike other North Indian communities, their loudness quotient is almost zero. They are never greedy, except for tea. And if you could dispense them with four-five teacups a day, rest assured they will fight for your life. They aren't one of the most decorated regiments in Indian Army for nothing. Indian Army, the place I wished to be. Until I misplaced my SSB call letter.

Naturally when Shelja invited me on a hilly trip, it hadn't excited me much. Well, when you've trekked through the snow laden peaks of Himalayas all your life, you tend to believe you've beheld the greatest of the mountains.

However, Munnar broke my notions.

If Aleppy was nature's painting you could touch, Munnar was an illustration you could smell as well. Hills after hills covered in thick blankets of tea gardens under overcast sky, the cold climate holding the fragrance of tea-leaves pervaded by the aromatic flavour of green cardamom; I wondered if anything could be more hypnotising than nature's pulchritude unfurled before me. Few droplets of rain and your North Indian masala cardamom tea would be ready. Was I missing Nehru Race? Not really.

Manoj would be cursing me though. Six weeks ago, I was

the source of sorrow in many lives. But his pain had been the most agonising. I could envisage his trauma as Uums enjoyed the backwaters with her boyfriend in a similar houseboat where I had ruined his only shot at fulfilling the most elusive quest of his life. He had remained a virgin. He'd never forgive me if he ever discovered the truth. Nor for that matter would Mutthur or Adish. And how would Shelja react?

I shivered at the dreadful thought.

In few days I had grown fond of her, and I was glad she had also felt at ease with me. Last night and the whole day today, we had continuously talked, sharing things from our lives as if the Pralay would consume us the next day. So engrossed we'd been that we didn't feel any fatigue, during our expedition to the tea estates. I gathered two most important details - she was vegan, and she was single.

A Single Vegan Malayali Syrian Christian. Adish would be traumatized as she had shattered almost every Malabari norm. Perhaps why she'd been so uninhibited, for she considered me a norm-breaker too; a North-Indian Brahmin relishing non-veg. Well, I didn't tell her that I was actually a conformist as Pundits residing in hills of North were more often than not meat eaters. Some other day. Today, the day had been so good. The night had promised to be better.

Yet, I lay in my hut, holding my phone and caught in one of those weak teary moments when you browse through your past and cynicism cripples your mind. You cannot fathom why you're not good enough for her and whether you'd be adequate for someone else too. How could you trust anything and anyone? Including you.

The place we were spending the night at, had two big lawns and in one, a large bonfire was arranged for a recreation tonight. The party had begun, and I could hear the songs blaring from the speakers. It brought back the memories of that night.

'Are you coming?' Shelja's text shook me out of my muse.

You have not come so far to mourn inside a damp, musky room, I reminded myself and stepped out.

While people danced, sang and played games around the bonfire, the wannabes continued with their skirmishes to outdo each other in their pursuit of *happyness* - Shelja. Including the familiar Nikhil Lal and I, as we sat across, stealing desperate glances at her.

Men are a strange species, vying for every female as if it were their life's singular purpose.

My thoughts returned to *her*, wondering how many chased *her* everyday. At the same moment, I caught Shelja's eye. For a reason unknown, despite our budding friendship, we were acting rather strange. Or was it just I? I couldn't pinpoint, but a sea of anxiety rose inside me.

To avoid any distraction, I moved to the other lawn, away from the celebrations. Not much time had passed when I heard her voice. 'You abandoned me with those guys, eh?' Shelja complained, walking up to me with arms folded across her chest.

'You've been handling them well for ten weeks.'

She smiled. 'You're a sharp observer, I must say.' I smiled back. 'Could we walk together? I'm little anxious,' she said. *Pleasure would be all mine.* I nodded.

While we walked in quietude, she decided to initiate the conversation. 'So, how did you like Munnar?'

'It's heavenly. In fact, in my newly formed opinion, nothing is more beautiful than a hill covered in tea shrubs and the scent of cardamom. It cannot get any greener. You know I…I love green.'

'You do? But I've never seen you wearing any green.'

'You're a sharp observer too, Miss Holmes.'

Shelja smiled. 'Sharp observation would be when I say, you have a taste for blue.'

I gaped at her in disbelief. God, she was correct.

'Green would look good on you. Let us say, a lime green shirt with forest green trousers.'

'And a cherry red tie with ginger coloured boots.'

'And the cocktail for the evening is ready. Wow!' she laughed.

'That's how I was dressed for my first campus interview.'

'I was joking,' she said. 'But you aren't, right?' She stopped laughing. I shook my head. 'Oh, my God. Didn't they just reject you on the ground of your jungle book guise?

'They rejected me anyway.'

'So your first wasn't DigiSys.'

'It was Infosys.'

'Oh, I'm sorry. Must have been demotivating.'

'To an extent, yes. But I'm glad it happened, or I would've never met someone who adored green Martians.' We both giggled.

'So what went on in your interview besides green?'

'My birthday,' I said. Shelja sucked in a quick breath. I continued, 'I was nervous. Hadn't prepared well. So when they asked me to introduce myself, I said – I am Rajesh Pandey, 22-year-old, 3rd year Mechanical Engineer and today is my birthday'.'

She caught her breath. 'What?'

'Yup and next, what do I see?' I added, 'These two guys rose from the chairs and extended their hands towards me. And said, "Happy Birthday".'

She cackled with an impish glee. 'Oh my God, they wished you before rejecting you.' Now, Shelja had this strange laughter that set her off into convulsions making funny guttural sounds. I had never seen anyone laugh so freely.

'When is your birthday?'

'18th August.'

'18th August? That is next weekend,' she said with a hint of excitement. 'Thank God you're here. I can catch you for a treat before you disappear.'

'Where would I go?'

'I don't know,' she said casually and looked away. Her

excitement was gone. Silence gripped her again. A self-conscious silence.

'What about you?'

'What about me?'

'Your interview.'

She smiled, 'Not as spicy as yours. I got selected at the first go. But I must tell you that I was lucky to be even interviewed.'

'How so?'

'If you remember, we had to fill out a lengthy application form online as the first step for recruitment for DigiSys.'

Yup, I too had endured that pain. DigiSys had this fetish with annoying, never ending complicated forms. I had almost decided not to apply. But *she* had insisted. DigiSys had a massive facility in Gurgaon. I nodded to Shelja.

'There was no second chance if the session timed out while filling the form. The internet connection at home was erratic, but somehow I managed it. And two days later, when the recruitment team visited the campus, my application stood rejected. I was not shortlisted.'

'Why? Low Marks?'

'I was among the top three of my batch,' she sneered. Top three. Ahem. 'Anyways, I went and enquired. At first, they were not ready to consider my plea, but I persisted. They finally disclosed I had answered one of the questions incorrectly, and I wasn't alone. Total forty applicants had been rejected on identical grounds. The number was just too big. So obviously, it was the question that was incorrect.'

'You fought your way through.'

'Of course,' she grinned. 'I had to stand up for myself, no matter what. I couldn't let any reason ruin the chance I deserved. I needed the job - for my father. He had undergone a bypass surgery, and we had no steady income. Being the eldest of the three siblings, I had to set the right example.'

She felt overwhelmed, I could sense from her choked voice.

Baring your soul and letting someone in your personal world needed some spine and she seemed to have it in abundance. I deemed myself lucky, just to be walking beside her.

'You are a brave girl,' I said.

'Nothing in comparison to you. I'd never choose to work on that boat, leaving my job aside.' Her solicitous tone suggested she meant what she said.

Silence fell between us again but with certain calmness now.

'It is so calm here,' she echoed my reflections. 'You know, I like hills more than the sea. Here, I could feel someone is around. Not disconcerting and keeping his distance, but always assuring that he is right there to guard me.'

Again a facsimile of my musings. What was happening?

'But tonight is lot calmer and unusual, and it's not because of the hills.'

'Then?'

She paused in her steps. 'I'm not sure,' she said. A different anxiety washed over me. I yearned to touch her, sensing her anxiousness too. I clasped her hand in mine. She didn't resist.

'Come with me.' Pulling her by the arm, I took her into a dimly lit corner, right behind the huts. Secluded and away from the prying spirits of the fellow associates, we stood there peering into each other's eyes, frozen in time. I placed my trembling arms around her waist and pulled her closer in slow motion. Her breathing quickened as her palms rested on my shoulders, her fingers drawing me closer, too. Barely moments later, my lips fused with hers and locked in a soft and wet embrace.

Even as we pulled away to catch some air, my arms held Shelja still and my eyes traced the contours of her radiating face. Suddenly our grips went loose, and we both stepped back. The *moment* had passed. Her eyes bore a mysterious nonchalance now. I was confused because I saw her differently too.

But before I could know why, she'd turned around and left.

Thekkady, as it is known locally, is the Periyar Tiger Reserve - one of the many tiger reserves in the country. And right through it, flows the mighty Periyar, Kerala's largest river and lifeline.

The journey from Munnar to Thekkady took us three hours and during that stretch, she behaved like nothing had happened the previous night. Man, had she any fucking clue how dazed I had been by her mystifying disappearing act?

Until the morning, she had made no communication while I had been rattled, blaming myself over and over again for pushing things too far. True that she had also participated but how could I be such a female grubbing shmuck? How could I defile a goddess like her?

To screw with my sanity further, I tried hard to figure out the reason behind my intense yearning to pursue her. I prodded myself the whole night, pacing back and forth in the same lawn braving the cold, but failed to gain any clarity. As it turned out, there had been nothing for me to be contrite.

The Reserve was bumbling with picnickers today. But the possibility of a tiger sighting was low and that too in the afternoon, we were told. To bide our time we took to a bamboo raft straight from the chronicles of early man's history. A raft was the oldest form of river transport, man had devised. And in doing so, he had unwittingly discovered the concept of density i.e. total mass of an object divided by its volume. The hollow bamboos had introduced 'buoyancy' that had further invented the engineering of boat hulls, several millennia ago.

'Are your fantasies only limited to boats?' Shelja interrupted my brown study. How would she always know?

'Nope. I do fantasize about other things,' I said. 'For example, the subject of my single-minded focus last night was you,' I blurted.

'I am glad it was,' she smiled again, effectively revealing her thoughts. But I wished to construe them no more and screw my head again. I was all right being an ignorant.

A flush of adrenaline tingled through my body as I read the title of the magazine I held in my hands. Scaring me further was a grinning hairy God-man with a Rudraksha garland around his neck, plastered on its cover. I ran my eye over the title again: *Vashikaran – a guide to hypnosis and subjugation.*

What the hell was it? And what was it doing on my bed? The answer came to me the very next instant. Manoj Bansal.

Now, this fucker did have some weird habits that were beyond my grasping. Especially, his beliefs in *tantra-mantra.* I usually ignored all his singularities but Hypnosis? Subjugation? Man, he had surpassed every 'what the fuck' limit. The captions on the magazine were in Hindi, I realized, which rendered it highly unlikely to be sold anywhere in Kerala.

Meaning, he'd been carrying it all along.

Damn, I'd been living with a psycho-Tantrik. I whisked through the book and ran across several pen markings on certain pages. Intrigued, I began to pore over them one by one.

How to subjugate and win over a married woman, the first page offered. *Savita bhabhis?* Seriously?

It explained the interpretation of different signs a woman would drop; from the kind of colours she'd wear in your presence to the time of day she'd speak with you the most, and the food she'd offer you in her husband's absence. Sanskrit Mantras followed the prognosis along with cures in the form of voodoo magic potions and rituals. I flipped further.

One separate chapter described the categories of women based on a scale of difficulty to subjugate. It covered all kind of situations that could arise between a man and a woman. Yet another page taught you how to make a girl dump her current lover and become your girlfriend. And then the next one said, 'Turn yourself into her lover without her breaking up with her boyfriend.'

Bansal must be acting by either of these two chapters. I could even picture him chanting, *Om Heem Kleem Chamundai Vichhai,* moulding dough dolls of Uum's boyfriend and inserting pins into the nether regions of his body.

'What a sick book?' I threw it away on his bed.

Since human psyche is capable of orienting itself to its surroundings, mine too considered varied possibilities: Do these things work? If they do then shouldn't I take its aid too? Should I subjugate her to dump her new guy?

The idea didn't excite me enough. I picked the book again.

There was one chapter of my interest - How to conquer the heart and mind of a "single" girl?

It had the same categories of women ranging from the 'ones who hated you' to the 'ones who were smitten but hadn't submitted yet'.

Speak the name you have set your heart on, it asked.

Shelja Thomas. The answer came straight away.

'This girl is charming and friendly. She even shares her innermost feelings with you,' it read. 'She has been intimate with you (kissing, smooching or even intercourse) but hasn't admitted to being in love with you.' Not yet.

Was it pointing towards Shelja? I read further.

'This girl has already enslaved you to her will and hence, is the most impregnable. Difficulty level - 10.'

Was I enslaved? By Shelja? Had she read this book too? Was Bansal her accomplice? I shook my head and sifted the mantras and the magic potions, carefully. The main ingredient was raw tealeaves. *What the fuck? Munnar!*

So, I didn't go there. I was led there. Everything was planned. I stood still, quietly gulping down my breaths. The door flung open, and Bansal barged in, bellowing to someone on the phone. Or was he fighting?

'I'm from Meerut. Do you know *what* Meerut is? No-one would know how and where you disappeared, you piece of constipated shit,' he threatened. My 'what the fuck' moments were not over yet.

He listened to the caller impatiently for a while and spoke one last time before he hung up. 'You can do nothing dude. Nothing! You can only fart. Like you did in Aleppy...Oh, yes. She told me how much she wanted to throw you in the lake. So keep a watch over your smelly arse and girlfriend. Do not blame me. Got it? Now fuck off.'

Amazed and curious, I stared at him with arched brows.

'Uums boyfriend. I gave that *Chutiya* an earful,' said Bansal.

Uums' boyfriend! My mouth opened to repeat but paused midway, wide open.

'Don't worry. She is under my control, and if you want, I got some tips for you as well,' he winked and let out an evil laugh, pointing his finger at the book I held.

I realized my precarious situation and came straight to the point. 'I don't care, you inconsiderate prick. Just tell me. How do you subjugate a man? I mean this book cannot be just about female subjugation, right?

'What?' he furrowed his brow. 'You like men now?

'No. Not that way, dickhead,' I cringed. 'I was referring to Gopalan. Suppose we cast a spell over him and seize control of his mind,' I said, in conspiring tone. 'We can bring him to his knees. Even manipulate his will to row slower and lose the race to Mutthur. What do you say?'

Manoj broke into a smirk. 'You are a champ, dude. Evil personified. Why the hell did I not think of it earlier?' his eyes gleamed with a certain regard for me. 'Let me check if I can find something,' he said and grabbed the book from me. *Sucker had taken the bait.*

'Okay, here is the trick - a magic potion. Like the ones in Harry Potter films,' he tapped his fingers around an imaginary crystal ball like a witch. This guy watched too many fantasy movies. 'Ideally, I'd need a lizard's tail, but since we're in Kerala, a crab's tail would do as well.'

I couldn't believe my ears. Bansal had unearthed a spell. This guy was crazy. Yet, I wouldn't be complaining if he could make it work in real. One thing baffled me, though.

Do crabs have tails?

Prayers

****

Mutthur sat with his crew, discussing their strategy after the drill while Kareem and his team launched into their evening ritual of polishing and scraping the base. The bottom of the boat had to be as frictionless as possible; the task would take another four days. Mutthur hoped the boat-work to finish before the qualifier on Saturday, but the odds seemed low.

Mutthur's other worry was the "alterations" that hadn't worked to his satisfaction. On the other hand, his crew had toiled tirelessly in their daylong practices. They had given him as much support as they could, even managing to shed few excess kilos. Though they were still eighty kilos off target, that too with two oarsmen short of the full strength. So much effort might be enough for the qualifier but to beat Gopalan in the race, it was not.

Unless Adish, the Nilakkar, returned.

Mutthur remembered the crucial difference Adish had induced four years ago. Moreover, he could get Manoram back at the oars too. This way, they could gain at least three more seconds.

Every single second mattered.

It reminded him that Kala would reach the temple by seven. He hadn't seen her for a week. Her father had forbidden her to meet him and today, she must've gathered immense courage to sneak out. Mutthur rose to his feet and a few minutes later, he and his little boat, were no bigger than a blob on the horizon, travelling upstream.

Kala waited behind a small dome, some distance away from the main temple. Today, she had snuck out with an excuse to pick flowers for the Malayalam New Year rituals the next day and at most she had thirty minutes to spend with Mutthur.

The evening prayers were being doled out in the temple premises amidst clanging bells. Talks regarding her marriage had already begun between her and Gopalan's families. If she were to believe Lakshmi, her sister in law, her father would announce her engagement with Gopalan on the Chatayam day, which was also the race day.

Her heart choked with immense sadness. Kala knew her father had no inclination to wait until Mutthur proved his mettle. He had never cared. Yet, he lingered over his decision; perhaps so that he could mock and ridicule Mutthur. But why he saw the redemption of his defeat twenty years ago in Mutthur's loss and humiliation, she couldn't fathom.

She did trust Mutthur and his unflagging love for her; he'd do anything for her. But to prevail over Gopalan? It'd be beyond his mortal strength. Only an intervention of Gods could provide a panacea, but Lord Vishnu seemed to be in no mood to listen to her prayers.

Could Lord Mahabali do something? Since childhood, she'd heard tales of the great benevolent king. He was her last retreat.

'Lord Mahabali, this year when you descend onto the earth, I shall be waiting for you. In hope that before you ascend back to heaven, I unite with my love. Or else I shall depart alongside you,' she mumbled with her eyes closed while tears rolled down her cheeks.

She opened her eyes and saw Mutthur approaching. Promptly, the Nair woman inside her took charge. Mutthur's strength lay in her trust in him. Her tears must not weaken him; she reckoned and wiped them off. She wasn't going to reveal that if he failed, this Onam would be her last, and tonight would be the last time he'd ever see her, alive.

The moment Mutthur arrived at her side, he pulled her into his embrace. She felt all her worries and pains had disappeared and she had indeed found her heaven. Her tears flowed uninterrupted, creating a moist spot on his chest.

'Don't worry Kala. Lord Mahabali shall unite us,' she heard Mutthur say. The temple bells had started to ring, and she could never hear what he added further. 'In life or death,' he had muttered.

Adish Mathew had his own tryst with destiny. Just when he planned to slip away for the trial on Saturday, he had received a call from his mother. The whole family had arranged an outing to Idukki dam, the largest dam in Kerala. It opened to the public every year during Onam, for a month.

Twelve days remained for Kumarakom boat race, and he was running out of time. Sagged into his study chair under the weight of his own indecisions, Adish once more reached out to the sheet tucked under a paperweight on his desk, tentatively. He had spent his entire week penning down the new song, which he believed would change the rhythm, resulting in more rowing per unit time and hence, a considerable increase in boat speed.

However, he realized, he had just a weekend to test the new rowing pattern and get the oarsmen accustomed to it by the time the race day arrived. Any further delay ran a risk of cramming too much into their brains in too little time and thereby, creating confusion.

That weekend would be lost to Idukki. His hopes now rested on divine intervention. He closed his eyes and prayed to Lord Jesus to rescue him.

At the precise moment, many miles up north in Kochi, Sarah groaned with pain in her lower abdomen.

Adish Mathew's

The Qualifier

****

'You were to go on your family trip?' Rajesh asked me as I entered their room in the morning.

'Sarah wasn't well so we cancelled the tour,' I said.

'What happened?' asked Manoj, concerned. *Why was he always interested in her news?*

'Viral,' I lied, and it was none of the two reasons my mom had shared with me. First was that my father had postponed his return by a week. And I didn't quite buy it because Mom hated to alter her plans, with or without him. The second and probable reason was her 'Ladies monthly issue.' During that period, extending to five days, neither my mom would take up any strenuous activity nor would she let Sarah. They wouldn't even go to Church. And Idukki meant both; long-hops and a nearby Church visit. Some other day, I might've had reservations against the taboo. Today, I was happy. I got to join my friends on our Mevalloor trip.

Mutthur stood outside the house, waiting for us as we arrived at the colony four hours later.

The Malayalam New Year had begun yesterday, marking the first day of our ten-day Onam festival. The figurines of King Mahabali and Lord Vaamana had appeared at the entrances of most houses along with a circular carpet of marigold and thechi (ixora) flowers in the courtyards.

'That's Pookkalam. It had lain yesterday, and now one ring of flowers will be added to it every day until Onam, the day it takes its grandest form,' I explained Manoj and Rajesh as we exchanged greetings with Mutthur.

The nine council members had already assembled at the embankment overlooking the factory of Hindustan Newsprint, the most famous landmark of Mevalloor when we arrived at the venue. Dark clouds congregated above us, threatening to hide the blazing afternoon Sun, much to our relief.

'The oars haven't been shortened yet?' I asked Rajesh, pointing at the long handles Mutthur and his crew held as they boarded the boat after greeting the council members.

He shook his head. 'Mutthur didn't wish to take any risk. So they deferred it for post qualifying.'

My hand reached out to my pocket to pull out the paper but stopped. It could wait as well.

'I love this tag line. Fire in the water.' Vazhoor Chandy was ecstatic, sure now that his money was cast into good use. 'I tell you, boy. You're wasting your time in a Software company,' he said to Manoj. 'I have an offer for you. Join Kerala Lights as deputy operations and marketing head and you will go a long way.'

Manoj looked perplexed. Hunger perhaps, had clouded his wits.

Meanwhile, the boat song reverberated around us as Mutthur and his team waited at the centre of the stream for the whistle to go off after two rounds of practice. Two council members had already vamoosed to the finish point to note down the final timing.

Mutthur turned his head in our direction and forced a nervous smile as we raised our thumbs to wish him luck. A lot depended on him today.

O... Thithithara thithithai
Thithai thaka thei thom

The singers began the boat song; the energy levels surged, and oars rose to their starting position, resting inches above the surface of the water.

We waited with bated breath. The whistle blew finally, and the oars struck the surface of the water in split second, pushing the giant boat forward.

I closed my eyes and prayed while Rajesh and Manoj kept their fingers crossed. The boat gained momentum gradually. The rhythm of the oarsmen began to synchronise, as they imitated the song cues, pushing and accelerating the boat downstream.

Our eyes followed the boat. We could see Mutthur put all his concentration and power into providing the backward stability to the boat with his long oar as they advanced towards the great bend.

'I hope it holds,' said Rajesh. With its recent most modifications, the boat looked more stable but how much, only the bend would tell.

In next few minutes, though, the boat laid our concerns to rest and vanished with ease beyond the curve. After waiting for a few anxious minutes, Mohammad Kutty received the call from the two council members who were present at the finishing point.

'Three seconds faster,' Kutty pronounced the result, with a joyful shout. The council members gave a collective sigh of relief and a smile broke across their lips while we, the three hobbits hugged each other. The first round had been won.

'You've done it, guys,' Vazhoor patting our backs. Of Manoj and Rajesh, actually.

'No, sir. We have done it,' said Rajesh, putting his arm across my shoulder.

Such humility had been a rare aspect of the Northies, but I was glad we were amongst the rare to receive it. It had to be my turn now, I resolved and pulled out the paper from my pocket.

'What is it?' asked Rajesh.

'A new boat song I wrote. Should improve the efficiency of the rowers,' I replied.

'Brilliant, man. We are closing in. Mutthur is going to be damn happy.'

Outside, the rain clouds had dispersed after a sudden burst. But inside the warehouse, a storm brewed in our hearts. It stung me to see Mutthur holed up in a corner, lost and defeated, his eyes lowered to the ground. It had been a while, but nobody had spoken yet. I hated Gopalan for it.

As usual, the scoundrel had provoked and ridiculed Mutthur and his team as they retreated to the start point, and had harped about his team still being ten seconds faster in the Nehru boat race. Mutthur had subsequently arrived in a foul mood, heading straight to the warehouse without uttering a word.

'With my old boat I had a hope but with this waste, I can do nothing,' Mutthur broke his silence, tipping his head back. Ten seconds was indeed an impossible task even with my new, untested song.

'Who did this to me Rajesh? Who did this?' asked Mutthur, clutching his arm. Rajesh cringed in pain but sat still.

'You're hurting him,' I said.

Mutthur loosened his grip. 'I am sorry, brother,' he said, with a lump in his throat. 'It is not your fault.'

'It is, Mutthur,' Rajesh muttered. 'I am the scourge of your unhappiness. Your boat caught fire because of me.'

I interpreted his dilemma. Had he not been in that condition, Mutthur wouldn't have stayed in Aleppy that night. 'Mutthur was there because you are his friend. The curse might've befallen anywhere.'

'No Adish, you don't get it. The boat burned because I was there,' he said. I had misgivings about the way his voice wavered. He stood up and turned to Mutthur. 'That rum bottle was mine.'

Rum bottle? The same bottle that was found lying on the charred boat? I exchanged incoherent looks with Manoj and Vazhoor while Mutthur had his gaze pinned at Rajesh.

'I was inebriated that night. I felt miserable, and I wanted to drink more. So I carried the rum bottle to your boat where it toppled and spilled. Then...,' he paused and hesitated to speak further. Disquietude gripped us. 'That cigarette, my cigarette, it flew from my hand and dropped on the boat as I tried to get off, clutching the anchor rope with both ends. I don't remember what happened next except-' he paused.

The boat burned.

The revelation stunned us all. An old Malayalam proverb might have equated our situation to those dogs who gathered under the palm tree to crib and moan but received coconuts on their heads instead. Visuals of the fateful night danced before my eyes; Mutthur wailing helplessly while the blaze incinerated his boat.

'I'm sorry Mutthur, but I had to tell you. I can no longer live with this guilt.'

'Guilt!' Mutthur spoke in a hoarse voice and his icy cold stare seemed like a lull before the storm. 'Is that why you helped me?'

'No Mutthur. That's not true. I mean yes, I do feel guilty but,' Rajesh trembled with emotions, 'the reason I helped was you, my friend.'

'Friend? Do you people even understand friendship?' Mutthur spat, rising from his place. 'Now, you see Adish what kind of self-centred opportunists they are?'

Seething with anger, he had switched to Malayalam for his outburst. Perhaps, to burn the first bridge between him and the two Northies. His direct words echoed my father's apprehensions, though. To be frank, my own usual notions had given place to mistrust too.

'Worse, they believe they can walk over us, ruin us and then troop away, faking guilt,' he continued and in a fit of rage, grabbed Rajesh by his collar. I saw the faces of Rajesh and Manoj, full of trepidation.

'Mutthur, I'm sorry,' Rajesh opened his mouth to speak, but a slap from Mutthur cut him short.

The anger had turned into violence. Stupefied, we gave vacant stares to each other as silence fell in the warehouse.

'Mutthur,' I pleaded.

Mutthur looked at me with tears welling up in his bloodshot eyes. Getting a grip on himself, he let go of Rajesh and stepped back. A hapless Rajesh hunched up on the floor as small as he could. Tears pooled in his eyes too.

'How could you, Rajesh?' I said, shelving my own conclusions. Having re-played that entire night's scene inside my head, I agreed that it was indeed an accident. Or at most a mistake.

'First he defiled our deity by throwing liquor over it and then burned it. It is not a mistake but an unpardonable sin,' Mutthur howled at me and started to snivel.

'Calm down, Mutthur,' Manoj whispered but received the same resentful look.

'Mutthur are you fine?' Dhaniya's voice boomed from outside, followed by a knock on the door. More people had arrived.

'Everything is fine,' Vazhoor shouted back. 'This may go out of hand,' he cautioned, and rightly so. If our Malayali folks waiting outside even got the sniff of the real matter, Rajesh and Manoj would find themselves in trouble. *You just don't mess with Malayali pride in Mallu-land.*

'Take your friends away,' Mutthur spat in a bitter voice. I peeped into his accusing eyes. There was no concern; only hatred and anger. I turned to Rajesh, clutched his elbow and motioned to Manoj.

'Come with me, you both,' I marched them out of the ware-house where Dhaniya and other oarsmen stood bewildered.

'Where are you going?' asked Dhaniya, seeing us leave.

'Let them go. They have no business being here anymore,' Mutthur's voice thundered from inside. Dhaniya squinted with a wrinkled brow, studying our faces for a moment. Then, he stepped inside the warehouse.

Without delay, I pushed them through the narrow road, never looking back once. Their business here was indeed over.

Manoj Bansal's

The Friendship blues

****

There are days in our lives that just refuse to come to an end.

Today had been one.

It'd been a while since we returned to the hostel, and we had barely spoken. Adish had stayed in Mevalloor, by Mutthur's side. Deserting Vazhoor and me in the no man's land. Baffled with Pandey's afternoon whammy, we had no idea how to react.

I, particularly, couldn't get why he'd chosen to hide such an enormous secret from me, his closest buddy for last two months.

Since the day we took that Kerala Express ride together, we had shared our fears and concerns. Fuck, we had even shared underwear and toothbrush once. Okay, time for my own little confession; it was I who had used his. But hey, that wasn't the point. The point was, every friendship has its limit - a threshold of sanity. Today, Pandey had breached it. He had violated the sacred bro-code. The point was, if he knew my secrets, including the ignominious ones, if I could put my trust on him, then why... why the hell he couldn't entrust me.

'I'll take a brief stroll,' he spoke as we wrapped up our dinner in glum muteness. A night stroll was our daily routine to improve digestion. But he had hardly eaten anything. The lone chapatti on his plate hadn't lost much except for its severe mutilation here and there. However, I refused to intervene and simply followed him outside.

The sky appeared clear as Edavapathy had started to withdraw from Kerala. It reminded me that the upcoming week would be our last in Trivandrum.

'I agree I should've told you,' he muttered as we walked, still avoiding an eye contact.

'What did you achieve by telling the truth now?'

He slowed down and glanced over his shoulder at me, puzzled.

'I don't know. I had to speak the truth,' he shrugged.

'And ruin everything for us?' I stopped. Pandey let out a baffled sigh, perhaps speculating why did I not ask him the reason he *hid* the truth rather than why he *unveiled* it.

'Are you aware of what you've done?' I said, in a harsh tone. 'Mutthur was disappointed, yes, but then he put his trust on you because you gave him hope and belief. Hope, which rescued his spirits and belief that carried him so far. And then, you fucked up both.'

Pandey remained silent, but I was sure he was listening.

'And what about Vazhoor? He was relying on me, not you,' I said. 'Chuck him, what about me? You know I never wanted to be involved, but I did because I thought....well, okay let's deal with it. For friendship's sake. I had a hope, Pandey. And now it's gone. Obliterated! All for your moment of truth.'

I was furious, again. I didn't care if it was an accident or he burned the damn boat deliberately. What I believed was, actions spoke louder than the guilt. And if he didn't reveal the truth then, he had no business telling it ten days before the final race.

'Who gave you the fucking right,' I screamed in exasperation. 'Do you have any idea how terrible it feels when things end so abruptly, having come so far?'

'I do,' he folded his arms and inhaled a deep breath. 'Six weeks ago, my relationship came to a similar end.'

'What? What the f...,' I was baffled. 'For God's sake man, there are things beyond girlfriends,' I yelled. He had managed to blow up my fuse as well. 'Life is not just about girls, *bhenchod*.'

My whole world was coming to an end, and this guy was still mourning over his ex when he already had a new chick. Could there be a bigger loser, hiding in a closet?

'I thought I'd failed when I realized DigiSys was my last resort. I was staring at a life of perpetual mediocrity and agony,' I began my tale. 'The trauma of CAT still haunted me. And when I bumped into you in the train, I saw my mirror image, except for one little difference,' I paused, to muster up the courage to come out of the closet of my own loser truth.

'You faced up to your problems with a stout heart unlike me,' I said. 'I saw the light. Things were not as bad as they appeared. This place did have something for me, a meaning. A purpose. In a flash, I had focus and direction, both. Earlier I was deluded, presuming an entitlement of sorts owing to my IQ of 140.'

'You have an IQ of 140?' Pandey raised a brow. 'Mine is lower. 137.'

'I know that fucker. But that's the point. IQ is irrelevant if not backed by efforts. And that I learned from you, and from Adish. You know his IQ is 125. But in efforts? Man, he beats us all,' I said. I never thought my "Institutional pride" would ever let me speak such words for Adish but it did. A wry smile broke on Pandey's face too.

'I too, resolved to make my best efforts,' I let out a suppressed laugh, reflecting on my past events. 'And then...' I shrugged and went quiet. Pandey stared at me, with dry eyes.

I didn't expect him to provide me with any answers. He had none. And frankly, I didn't care anymore. One more week and it'd all be a memory. Nothing more, nothing less.

'I'm glad Adish chose not to dip his spoon in this Coconut soup for engineers and stayed clear,' he said.

'Yeah, glad he opted for the outer circle and not the inner one.' Pandey chuckled at my remark. 'I'm going up,' I said.

'I'll stay here for a while,' he said.

I nodded and turned to leave but stopped, spotting a lean, human figure emerge from the hostel gate. It approached us. *Shelja Thomas.* How could I not recognise her?

That's why he wished to stay downstairs. That's why he kept

silent and let me blabber. Fucker, he wasn't even interested in talking to me.

'You know what? Stay wherever you fucking wish and don't step into the room tonight. I'm severely depressed and feel like an utter loser, because of your dumb, low IQ acts,' I muttered angrily and walked off, crossing Shelja on my way as she threw a smile at me, and I sent a wide grin back.

Why would he want me around when he had her shoulder?

The Birthday revelations

****

After Rajesh and Manoj had departed, Vazhoor Chandy returned to the river to spend time with the deserted blue elephant, Thiruneelakhandam. His heart was filled with empathy, having established a strange relationship with it unwittingly.

Had his deal with Mark gone through, this awe-inspiring wooden artefact would've been resting at his Trivandrum factory. He had felt so downcast that day, when one after another all his hopes were quelled because of these four young lads. And then by God's providence he had run into them again at the Church.

Vazhoor waded through the shallows to the side of the boat. New wood had been used in the middle of hull interior to create smaller chambers and near the base on either end of hull exterior that stood out like streaks of mahogany clouds across an azure sky. Running his hand over the otherwise shining hull surface, well-polished with Sardine oil and ash, he noticed an epigraph, carved below the rear hood. *Jacob and Sara, 1962.*

'Here you are,' Adish called out from behind.

'What is this inscription about? Any idea?,' he asked, as Adish joined him.

'Jacob and Sara's incredible love story,' Adish began to narrate the story. 'It was the year when the two lovers eloped on this same boat, against their family's wishes,' said Adish. 'It was a kind of a water marathon where he and his friends drove the boat, and the villains chased them through the Vembanad till Kochi. They could never catch them.'

A puzzled frown appeared on Vazhoor's forehead. 'With this speed, it is quite hard to believe that they could evade their pursuers. Why did they elope?'

'Sara was a Syrian Christian so you can imagine the kind of resistance she must've faced for marrying a Jew. Her parents feared she'd be lost to them if she migrated to Israel with her husband. But Jacob never left his birthplace in the east. Even for the lures of an exotic West. He stayed here so that she could always be near her family. Though, her family didn't reconcile until weeks before her death. When she died – and she died in peace, Jacob arranged for her to be buried in a Syrian churchyard near a Jewish cemetery and breathed his last in Kochi; so that his soul could rest in eternal repose, next to her.'

The story brought tears to Vazhoor's eyes. He realized why the old man was unwilling to part with his beloved. A tender smile appeared on his face. Wiping his tears, he rubbed his fingers through the carved letters. The wood felt different. It was cold and damp due to the rain.

As he took a few steps back, his sight fell on the logo and the logline, 'Fire in the water', running on the side. He smacked his palm onto his forehead and glanced at Adish.

Guys, you have been such fools.

Sitting on the bench in front of the Technopark gate, Shelja had a hard time convincing Rajesh that the whole boat burning incident was a misfortune. He could do nothing more to alleviate his and Mutthur's pain. Rajesh felt less agitated, though, he hadn't yet accepted her reasoning.

What would be the situation in Mevalloor? He was worried. The hatred and bitterness Mutthur had hurled at him whirled inside his mind. He had kept checking his phone, but the call list showed no new entry. He noticed the time. 11:40. In next twenty minutes, he'd be turning twenty-three. Would anyone remember? Would *she* remember and call to wish him?

'Aren't these mosquitoes biting you?' Shelja asked.

Rajesh glanced over his shoulders. A hapless Shelja was

scratching her right arm. 'Yes a bit,' he said, noticing the two guards who stood at the end of the deserted road, peering at them.

'Let's just go to my room until your friend calms down. I've had malaria once and trust me it's terrible.'

'Isn't it late? You roommate must be sleeping.'

'I don't think so. At least not in my room,' she said with a smirk. 'She is out.' Rajesh smiled wryly and rose.

The hostel bore an empty look, near ghostly in contrast to the weekdays when it'd be bustling with people well past midnight.

Fifteen minutes to go. His imagination once again drifted to *her*. Like a forgotten but un-erased memory languishing in his sub-conscience, *she* had reared *her* head like a serpent from the netherworld. He shook off the feeling as they walked up the stairs, but the swirling clouds of past emotions gave no indication of clearing up.

'Come,' Shelja spoke as she opened the latch. They both entered the room. It was well-organized, typical of girls, he deduced and thanked God she never visited theirs. If she did, she would've kept a safe distance from him.

'You may sit as well,' she said.

'Sure. Which one is yours?' Rajesh examined the two beds while Shelja blinked. 'Oh sorry, didn't mean otherwise,' he said and sat on the one next to the window.

'That's mine,' she smiled and sat across, on the other bed.

How could he think of her when he was with Shelja? And what validation he sought from her in the form of a birthday wish? Doubt arose inside his head like a monstrous squid as he battled its one tentacle after another.

'Okay. Not sure if I should bring it up but I think I will,' he said, wanting to clear at least one doubt right away. 'Because whenever I'm disturbed, I have this bad habit of stirring every single hornet's nest and in turn, worsen my situation,' he said and paused. Should he risk the chance? Yes, he decided. 'It's been bothering me for a week and-.'

'You wish to talk about 'that' night?' She cut him short.

Had he screwed up already? How could she always read his mind? He cursed, and congratulated himself under his breath. He could join Bansal now, and the two losers could celebrate his birthday, together.

She still waited for his answer, though. He nodded at last.

'I should say then,' she said, getting up. Was she going to slap him? He leaned back. 'I don't know how it happened and whether what I did was right or wrong' she hesitated, pacing back and forth.

Her voice was disturbed, he could sense. Was it because her past was dark and traumatic or even worse? A broken engagement with an ex who cheated on her?

'But I do know Rajesh, what it was like,' she spoke. His name flew with comfortable ease from her mouth, he noted. 'It felt so good, that I didn't know how to react. I was confused. And why wouldn't I be when I was kissed for the first time,' Shelja confessed.

'First time? Seriously?'

'Of course,' she said. 'I told you I'd never had a boyfriend.'

'No, I mean you didn't feel guilty, right?' he gasped.

'No. Why should I?' she shrugged. His eyes shone, locked on her for details. 'I've never been with a man before. And how would I? I studied in a girl's convent school. Then, college was all about securing a job, the first year in job was all about surviving and learning and second was all about earning and saving. In fact, sometimes I wondered if I was different. You know different?'

'Well, yeah if this different meant that different,' he tittered and hesitated. 'Are you different?' he asked, nervously.

'No, I'm not. You helped me break the notion.'

Rajesh took a big sigh of relief. 'So you were not upset because of me?'

'Are you crazy? I loved it,' she said and realized she spoke too soon. Rajesh rose from the bed and walked up to her.

'Thank God. I never wished to take advantage of my situation and your feelings and hurt you,' he said, gazing deep into her eyes, her big eyes he was so besotted with.

'But I won't mind taking advantage of you,' she leaned over and whispered, her arms and lips reaching out for him.

For the next few minutes, soft moans filled the air.

'Wow! Definitely better than the last one,' Shelja winked as they parted their lips to catch some fresh air.

'And a lot longer,' Rajesh smirked.

'Hmm. I guess it is time,' she said.

'For?' Rajesh dreaded she'd ask him to leave.

Just then his phone rang.

'Come up, you shithole,' Manoj whispered over the phone.

'What happened?'

'Vazhoor Chandy happened. So, get your ass over here. Now!'

Manoj was nervous, damn nervous, sitting scared stiff on his bed. Vazhoor had refused to divulge any details about his visit, but he was sure Vazhoor had come on a recovery spree.

He'd heard how dangerous South Indians were, regarding their money matters. Particularly Malayalis. Today on two instances, he'd seen that rage too. Mutthur's men had nearly thrashed them earlier in the day, and now Vazhoor sat across on a chair, cross-legged like a Filmy Don holding his Frankincense oozing lighter. To make his situation more dreadful, a man-Friday accompanied him; a henchman who looked equally menacing with his broad frame, big moustache and dark eyes.

Manoj cursed himself more than ever now for making Vazhoor a part of the deal. 'I hope they didn't notice you. They are very strict here,' he said in a timorous voice, taking note of the two polybags held by his assistant.

'You mean Menon?' Vazhoor gave a chortle. 'Don't worry. He is an old friend.'

Manoj gasped. What if Vazhoor had told Col. Menon about his engagement outside DigiSys? He was in hot waters now, all thanks to Rajesh and the moment he saw him enter, he couldn't control his anger and erupted. 'Where the hell were you, fucker? We've been waiting for so long.'

Crossing his arms, Vazhoor raised his brow and lowered his chin. Manoj tittered and corrected himself in a soft voice, 'He's been waiting for so long.'

'What's the matter?' asked Rajesh.

'Thought, I'll show you a little magic,' Vazhoor let out a big smile and gestured to his henchman who handed him one of the bags. Vazhoor put his hand inside the bag and pulled out a rum bottle. 'That's your brand, right?' he said, placing the rum on the side table and snapped his fingers.

The henchman brought him the second bag as well. Vazhoor removed two logs of wood from it and laid them on the floor near his feet. Another finger-snap apprised the man to leave the room and shut the door behind. Rajesh exchanged a confused look with Manoj who could hear his pounding heart now.

'Let's begin,' Vazhoor said and poured the rum over the logs.

'What the hell are you doing?' Rajesh was baffled.

'He is doing what you did to Maruthi Vallam and his money,' Manoj yelped, terrified. 'And he is Colonel Menon's buddy, you fucker.'

'Relax boys. The suspense will be over soon,' said Vazhoor and drew a cigarette from the Kerala Lights pack kept on the table. It had few sticks left. 'I see you are quite economical with its consumption. I like it. Smoking kills.'

Rajesh didn't respond while Manoj shuddered. Like any normal being, he had tabulated the best ways to die. Death by fire had never featured on the list.

Vazhoor lit the cigarette and took an overlong puff. A whiff of smoke joined the fragrance floating in the air, seconds later.

'Sit down, Rajesh. You have suffered a lot,' he offered. Rajesh quietly did as asked. 'Do you believe in destiny?'

'I'm not sure,' said Rajesh.

'I wasn't sure either until I met you people.' Vazhoor said and dropped the cigarette on the log.

'What are you doing?' Rajesh and Manoj screamed in unison and bent forward. The cigarette simply lay on the top of the log. Vazhoor put the lighter near the log and ignited it again. A thin, blue flame appeared that extinguished in a few seconds too. They gave each other a blank look.

'A dry log it was,' said Vazhoor. 'And you assumed you had burned down an entire boat soaked in rain.' Rajesh didn't know how to respond. 'That's the problem. Too much theory, too many films and no practical,' he mocked.

'That means it is highly unlikely that I-,'

'Completely unlikely if I may correct you,' Vazhoor said.

Rajesh slumped to his bed, soaking in the incredible moment of relief. He had carried the weight of his guilt for two months in his heart and finally, it'd been lifted. He felt a sudden giddiness now.

'Come in,' Vazhoor called out. The door opened and instead of man Friday, Mutthur and Adish entered.

'For a moment I forgot what you did for me. Without you, I would never have hope, even with my old boat,' Mutthur said.

'We still have hope, and we won't give up,' said Rajesh.

'I tried hard to keep out of this inner circle, and instead concentrated on the outer one. Well, I failed,' Adish said, drawing out the paper from his pocket and handed it to Mutthur. 'I've written a new boat song for the team. It should contribute.'

'Without you, it cannot.'

'I'll help the team prepare tomorrow onwards.'

'Wait, we're yet to solve the mystery of the burning boat. Who the hell torched it?' Manoj asked.

'Could be anyone.' Vazhoor said. 'It doesn't matter. What is important is the truth. The truth of your bond and friendship, and the truth of Kerala Lights that impelled me to believe in you guys and destiny.' He picked up the rum bottle, raising it to his mouth and slugged the rum straight back, down his throat. It burnt. He flinched.

'Also the truth of 18th August,' they heard a female voice.

Shelja stood at the door, holding a cake in her hands.

She remembered! Rajesh was amused.

'Whose birthday is it?' asked Adish.

'Kerala Lights,' said Rajesh.

It was a small happy family of Kerala Lights celebrating that night, and the happy family believed things would just be fine.

Indeed.

Adish Mathew's

The Final Call

****

It was perhaps one of the most tumultuous Monday mornings of my life, after the weekend that had ended on a high note.

The new boat song had worked. In just two days of unremitting and enervating training sessions that stretched from the dawn to the dusk on each day, we'd been able to strike off three more seconds. It had given the crew joy at last and to Mutthur a reason to feel inspired again. He still had eight more days to make the most of it. *How many did I have?* Just a weekend more. The reality struck me hard.

I realized I wouldn't be here for the race. Starting from coming Monday, it'd be our last week of the CLP. And Sunday would be the last day for me to help the crew practice.

Sitting at the gate, cursing my luck I shared my dilemma with Manoj who seemed equally disheartened while Rajesh had resigned himself to the other corner. Knowing I hated cigarettes, he always maintained a distance while smoking. Such heedful gentleman he was, reminding me always of Antony. I'd miss him.

'Three months here and the least we deserve is to attend the festival. Fuck man,' Manoj interjected my thoughts while Rajesh blew the last of his smoke rings before our buses arrived. 'But you're a local. Can't you get a two day festival leave?'

'I asked Delphin. He said only after we've been allocated a project, we can apply for any leave.'

'What about sick leave? People fall ill, don't they?'

'Oh yeah, and what do I tell my family? They are aching to host a farewell party for me.'

'Tell them you're not relieved, say, till Tuesday. Let the company assume you're unwell and join wherever they are placing you, on Wednesday instead. Problem solved.'

'You mean I should just go absconding?'

'I wish. Nah, forget it,' Manoj dismissed the counsel with a wave of his hand.

'What if they don't relieve you on Friday?' said Rajesh, done with his cancer stick. I shrunk back in fear and anticipated another philosophical catechism about life. He smiled like a calm assassin. 'Tell me, honestly. Do you really wish to participate?'

Well, I had mulled over the same, many a time. The truth was, I wasn't sure. Damn.

The bus arrived soon and the swollen queue of associates geared up for their quotidian struggle. Few things hadn't changed in past three months: Hordes of people, trying to invade the bus, pushing each other in a hope to grab a seat. Even if it meant a single minute's reprieve.

A pitiable state we'd been reduced to. No matter what, this melee of each mile had become our destiny. With no escape or respite.

Being the blessed one I sat and glanced around. The "likes" of me wore a proud smile while the "unlikes" hung their head in despair, albeit with determination. Rightly so, because post this alluring transient, we'd be back to the equality only an engineering corporate life could offer you; standing in another queue to punch in our ids and disappear behind the campus walls for one more day.

The fight was out of my hands. *I must reconcile myself to the fate*, I thought. Suddenly, my limbs felt heavy and shoulders drooped as I dragged the mangled heap of sadness - my body, into the Dark Tower, as Manoj would put it.

Inside, fellow associates had gathered up in the central lobby, facing a grinning Delphin Perumbavoor who held a copy of the latest circular.

'Associates,' he greeted. 'As you're aware, your relieving date is Friday. But since, you've been here for three months, DigiSys believes that it'd be grossly inconsiderate to devoid you the joy of Onam, our unique festival. Hence, you shall now be relieved on Wednesday. Your final rating test, however, stays as scheduled on Friday.'

Jesus had granted me the wish.

'Any more excuses?' Rajesh shot me a look.

'I am going to play my part, come what may and you two, will help me out,' I made up my mind. 'Because I don't know how to tackle my dad.'

'On one condition,' Manoj scratched his chin. 'If only we're watching the evening show of *Chak de* together.'

'A Hindi film?' I shuddered.

'It's a perfect movie to motivate you.'

'I am already motivated.'

Manoj guffawed. 'Doesn't matter how brave a fowl acts, it will always cower in front of a wolf,' he said. 'Not that I called your father a wolf,' he added sheepishly.

"Chak De" became the first Hindi movie I saw in a theatre.

It wasn't bad. The way it told the story of an underdog women's hockey team rising to the zenith of dreams had left me dreaming too. I particularly cherished the part where the goalkeeper rebelled against her family. Eventually, they welcomed her whole-heartedly after she returned victorious. *Victory reforms so many hearts.*

But the minute I had stepped into the hostel, and received a call from my mother, the reality bit me once more.

Apparently my family had gone one-step further post Idukki debacle. They had planned an Onam holiday package after my father confirmed he'd be back on Friday: Picnic in Idukki on Saturday, Onam in Mevalloor on Sunday and a grand farewell in Kochi on Monday. Then I'd be dispatched to Trivandrum by

Tuesday evening, leaving me no chance to partake in the race. Sure, it was my father's idea to please my mother.

There would be no red-carpet treatment waiting for you, Adish.

'Have you told them, the final rating test is on Friday?' asked Rajesh. I warily shook my head. 'Good. Let's make a master plan,' Rajesh leaned back with steeple fingers and lowered his head, like a scheming gangster.

Listening to the ticking of the alarm clock, I waited in silence for him to unveil his proposition.

'First, your family goes to Idukki without you, so that you're free to carry out the God's mission,' he spoke in his signature theatrical style that was always so persuasive. I guess he stood a real good chance in Bollywood. He had smashing looks too, his biceps almost ripping his sleeves apart.

'They've already cancelled the trip once. If I refuse, I can assure you that my fate would be worse than the hell's fire. My mom simply hates it if someone messes around with her plans,' I explained.

'Exactly. That is why she is the pawn who'll checkmate our tyrant king,' he said, conspiringly. Now my mom was a pawn and my father, a tyrant. King nonetheless. Hmm. I could pass this one over. After all Rajesh had a golden heart.

'How?' I asked.

'You'll tell your parents that the test is on Tuesday and it requires an extensive two-day preparation,' he said conspiringly. 'Assuming your father doesn't ring up DigiSys to confirm.'

'He shouldn't,' I wasn't sure.

'That ensures you a free race day.'

I swallowed hard, 'Then?'

'Second, you'll intimate only your father and that too, not until Friday night,' he said. 'Your mom is already irritated with him. Well, who isn't! And I doubt he'd risk irking his wife again. No man in his right mind should,' he said, turning to Manoj who was busy texting. He shook his head and focussed on me again.

'Besides you'll sound the way you do - an ideal career oriented son who keeps fretting about his job.'

'Do I sound like that?' I was offended.

'Yeah, you do,' Manoj chuckled. 'But that's not the point he is making. The point is, if you sound the genuine you, they will believe you and go ahead with their plan without bothering you until Tuesday.'

I fidgeted in my chair. 'And if they don't?'

Rajesh shrugged, 'Then, they'll stay in Kochi and again won't trouble you. Except, of course on Onam.'

'What if my dad comes to Kumarakom?' It'd be my worst nightmare.

'That's quite farfetched. If he had any affection for Vallamkali, he would've let you participate,' added Manoj.

How did they decipher my father's psyche so well? I had only one doubt. 'I may not get enough time to prepare for the test.'

'I'll take care of that,' Manoj said, leaving me bemused. 'There was this guy in college – Rajat, my hostel neighbour. Before every exam, he'd explain me the gist of important sections and problems and helped me clear many subjects. I guess it is time to give something back to the society. I'll assist you in revising faster and make you a memory card to tell you what lies where in the books, since it'd be an open book test.'

Manoj Bansal was a messiah.

What if my father got a whiff of my participation later? The answer though, laid in my question. Yes, he'd definitely find out from one source or the other. I had no escape.

'Ok. What if my dad comes here, to visit me?'

'You have so many issues, *bhenchod*,' the messiah swore, irritated.

'Well if he does, Bansal will use his Vashikaran Mantra to subjugate him,' said Rajesh.

'What mantra and subjugation?' I was scared.

'I'd need a frog. But let me caution you. If I don't get the right specimen, it may go wrong as well,' said Manoj.

'Hey wait, wait. No frog, no mantra and no subjugation of my dad, ok?' I pleaded. Rajesh chortled at my plight.

'Don't worry. Mevalloor is less than half the distance from Kochi. I'll ask Vazhoor to keep a vehicle ready,' Manoj proposed.

This settled the plan for me. Now all I needed was to pray, wait for the best Friday and act my old usual self while speaking to my father.

Thiruvonam

****

North Indian Hindu festivals like Diwali and Holi had never necessitated them to wake up so early in the morning and take a bath. But Onam had been a different experience.

Just last night they had witnessed a strange ceremony. As evening prayers had come to an end in the temple, a boat had arrived at the *ghat*, playing loud music with people dancing on the deck. At its middle, stood a man in king's guise with another one holding a large umbrella over the king's head. Once the boat was anchored, the king received a grand welcome by the priests and locals alike.

'Who is he?' Manoj had asked.

'He is King Mahabali. He has descended onto Kerala and now he will be here for four days,' Mutthur had said and shouted, 'Jai Mahabali'. Soon similar chants erupted from all corners inside the temple. The demon king had arrived to meet his subjects.

Rajesh and Manoj had come to Mevalloor to celebrate Onam and since it'd be their final visit, they had decided to immerse themselves in local rituals. The first had been an early morning's dip in the Muvattupuzha.

Surrounded by scores of men, dipped in chest-high water and praying with closed eyes, the two were reminded of the public bathing in the Ganges at the *ghats* of Haridwar.

Once cleansed, they returned to the Sankunni house where festival activities had already commenced. Their eyes begged for more sleep, but it was out of question as the whole residence was being cleaned and decorated. Defeated, they offered to help instead.

'You can assist in making Trikkakara appan,' Mutthur said and ushered them to the courtyard where Vasudevan was painting some conical figures moulded from clay. 'They represent gods in diverse forms. We are going to place them at every prominent corner of the house.'

'I'll help in Sadhya preparation,' said Manoj, looking at the mud stained Vasudevan. He walked to the kitchen while Rajesh sat there, intrigued by the clay gods.

Once the figures were coated with a layer of red, Vasudevan picked up a bowl containing a white paste. 'We will now smear them with this paste of rice flour,' he said.

'Ah, that's why it is called Appan,' said Rajesh, excitedly. 'In North India, especially in Uttarakhand, we create Aipan during festivals. They are also decorative designs, prepared from the rice and flour paste on a solid red base, which is either a wooden plank or floor. It's same everywhere.'

'Why don't you draw your North Indian designs here as well?' said Vasudevan.

Rajesh hesitated, 'You won't mind?' Vasudevan shook his head with a warm smile and told him he would rather welcome the idea of North Indian infiltration into their South Indian festival.

After all, they were all the same.

The Pookkalam attained its grandest form adorning the yellows, pinks, reds and whites. Appans turned out unique and beautiful, half of them with North Indian designs. Lamps were kindled, Sadhya had been cooked, and a grinning Adish had joined them as well. And why not? His ploy had worked flawlessly and for once, he'd been daring. Not only he'd abided by Rajesh's strategy but had bunked the CLP on Wednesday and Thursday as well.

'People do fall sick by eating in a Punjabi Dhaba. Especially the unsuspecting Malayalis,' he had reasoned, albeit in the presence of an incensed Manjot, but before he could hurl his

Punjabi *profunnyties*, Adish had scurried straight to Mevalloor to take part in the drills.

It was now time to proceed to the temple. With loud, rhythmic shouts of joy, the men carried the ata, a dish prepared as offerings to the God and strode out of their houses. Rajesh and Manoj also joined them, dressed in white Mundus and white shirts Shelja bought them as gifts before they took off for Mevalloor.

As they marched towards the temple, large swings caught their sight, hung on the high branches of trees and decorated beautifully with marigold flowers. The young kids were busy swaying, gambolling and trilling their favourite movie songs.

'They are called Oonjal,' Adish pointed out.

The community elders, assembled in the temple, welcomed Rajesh and Manoj; delighted to see them donned in their traditional attire. After the flag had been raised in the courtyard, the head priest began the prayers and offerings to please the deities, which went on for good two hours. Another long *aarti*, dedicated to Lord Mahabali, concluded the proceedings.

The folks eased into their seats in the courtyard afterwards. The grand Onamsadhya satiated their stomach followed by recreational hoedowns to fill their heart and soul. Women, dressed in white sarees with a golden border, stood in a circle holding each other's hands and sang devotional songs while the male members clapped and extended the chorus. It ended with young Aadil Kutty, Mohammad Kutty's son and the latest addition to Mutthur's team - a standby, who recited a heartfelt rendition.

When Mahabali, our King, presided over the land,
Free from deceit, devoid of sickness
People were truthful, people were gladsome.
When Mahabali, our king, held sway over the minds
People, like paddy grains, formed a casteless nation

While his father cheered, Basheer Kutty, stood up and cleared the lump in his throat to speak. 'We all have gathered here to celebrate our great harvest festival, Onam. May Allah bless us with a healthy produce,' he said and was met with resounding cheers. He shifted his gaze to Rajesh and Manoj.

'You see, people ask us Malabaris, or rather us Mappilas – I mean Muslims and Christians,' he said, pointing at himself and Adish's grandfather who smiled back at the old Basheer. 'Why do we observe a Hindu festival with such zeal and enthusiasm?'

Rajesh and Manoj exchanged a look as Adish translated Basheer's speech to them. He was correct. The question did cross their minds.

'Because we understand the distinction between our religions and our historical culture and we respect both,' Basheer said. 'Onam is our foremost tradition. It is about us - our peasants, our families and our brotherhood.'

The gathering clapped on his profound words of harmony.

'Day after is the day of Vallamkali in the honour of Saint Sri Narayana Guru who taught us equality. Our Odi-vallam that brought prestige to our village twenty years ago is going to enter the waters once again. I remember when my son rode the great boat as an oarsman and Mutthur's late father, was his captain. Today, it is my grandson under the tutelage of Mutthur,' Basheer paused and smiled at Adil Kutty and Mutthur.

'Back then, we cared for participation and pride. Today, we have reduced our tradition to a mindless and ruthless contest. Let us pray our children open the minds and hearts of our people once more,' he concluded and sat down. The priest took the cue and blew the conch.

Chants of 'Jai Mahabali' filled the surroundings.

Winding up the Onam ceremonies, Medavoor Nair retired to his room for some rest. The next two days would be forbidding, and he hoped to find all the strength from Mahabali. The future of his beloved daughter was at stake.

Sitting in his recliner, he threw a glance at his father's portrait hung on the opposite wall. Standing proud in a pearl white beard and long hair in the picture, the Asari had devoted his whole life to the boats and their study. His feats with building them were still considered legendary in the whole of Kuttanad.

Quite not the fact, though, as far as racing boats were seen; as winners. None of his father's creations had ever won a prize. And he had built twenty Odi-vallams in his life - including the one Mutthur rode. It was Asari's first wood job, some forty-five years ago and it had proved to be faulty on all except two occasions.

First, when Mohan Sankunni steered it to the seventh position ahead of him in the most prestigious Kumarakom race and second, further twenty years down, when Asari employed the boat for his friend Jacob and his wife Sara's rescue. That was before he'd even finished it. Otherwise, it had refused to perform. How? None had a clue.

The history seemed to repeat itself as Medavoor saw those events merge. Two days later, another Sankunni would ride the elephant to stake his claim on his love. It'd be next to impossible task for him, though. In all probability, Gopalan possessed the best boat his father had ever built. Puranjal Vallam was far superior to Thriuneelakhandam Vallam, in terms of speed.

'Are you awake, *Appan*?' Medavoor heard Kala calling out for him, and opened his eyes. Kala stood at the door, draped in a mundu saree, looking like a flower bud.

He'd always been proud of his daughter who often reminded him of his late wife. Like Kala, she too was beautiful, fierce and independent and yet, loving and doting. After her untimely demise due to Acute Hepatitis, he'd brought up Kala single-handedly. He had remained her only parent.

'Yes I'm awake,' he adjusted to a comfortable position so that he could see her.

'Chetta and Lakshmi are going to Kottayam for the fair.'

'Are you going too?'

'No.'

'You should. It is a festival.'

'Am I allowed to go out only on festivals, and that too under your or Chetta's vigil?'

'One day, you'd appreciate what I'm doing for you.'

'One lonely day, you'd bewail what you are doing to me,' Kala said with a cold smile.

Medavoor could perceive that for all her devotion to him, she had turned stony and detached. Despite him forbidding her from seeing Mutthur, neither had she cried nor shouted or threatened to run away. She had fought him, staying calm and wooden. And now she'd added that frigid smile to her armoury too.

'Had your mother been alive, she would've explained you better,' said Medavoor.

'Had she been alive, she would've reminded you the history of Nairs better,' said Kala, defiantly. 'Particularly Nair women.'

'That history is past, Kala. It's become a myth. But if you insist then you must quote the history correctly. Nair women chose rightly when it came to men. They knew. But you, clearly don't,' Medavoor was agitated. 'I'm trying to save you from making the biggest mistake of your life.'

'I wish I could save you too.'

Medavoor tightened his hands into fists, then loosened them, shaking his head. 'I haven't committed to Gopalan yet. I'm waiting for Mahabali to decide. I hope you accept his decision at least,' he said, leaning back in his chair. His daunting eyes disappeared behind their lids once again.

The discussion was over.

Mahabali's Gift

****

Sunday night, Adish Mathew's family gave him a hearty farewell for the final exam before he presumably left for Trivandrum. In reality, along with Rajesh and Manoj, he'd sneaked into Mutthur's house and emerged the next morning, dressed as one of Mutthur's aides after his family departed for Kochi. His local appearance had left Rajesh and Manoj in splits. But Mutthur seemed more than glad to meet his old *Changathi*.

Leaving Manoj and Rajesh at his house to rest, Adish and Mutthur had made a dash for what was going to be their final day of preparation.

'I think we can stretch for two more rounds, but we shouldn't push beyond. Let us conserve our energies for tomorrow,' Mutthur told Dhaniya during the mandatory break as the picked up their tea and medu-vada.

Today's session had been lengthy and upstream and on an ideal day i.e. if you were riding a Chundan, these light snacks would be a mass feast, organized by some wealthy soul. *Well, a generous NRI had already contributed for his lost cause.* Mutthur wasn't sure how he'd pay Vazhoor back, for his tomorrow's fate was more or less a foregone conclusion. Someday things might change perhaps, he thought, looking at the white sky.

Edavapathy had receded from the rice bowl and days turned hotter, humid and tiring again, but his men had held together. The song had worked, giving them considerable swing in the final timings. It had caused much relief to Adish, not to mention Manoram who looked elated holding the oar once more.

'I've always agreed to the old adage. "Not everyone who takes a stick becomes a drummer",' he told Adish, who was busy munching the beef patty with his tea. Toddy was prohibited until the race to keep their focus intact. Married oarsmen were tossed enough hints to refrain from coitus, and all of them had religiously obeyed the mandate.

Adish nodded after he polished off his snack. He hadn't felt so much hunger in a long time. 'I think we're going to put up a tough fight,' he said.

'Hope so. Your new song has certainly lifted our spirits,' said Manoram.

A sudden noise veered their attention to downstream.

'Such a shameless man. I'm sure a Peepul tree will soon grow out of his ass,' Dhaniya cursed, at the approaching Puranjal Vallam.

The boat arrived and stopped near theirs. 'Hey Mutthur, how is the practice going?' asked Gopalan.

'You'll discover tomorrow,' Adish said. 'We have surprise for you.' Gopalan gawked at Adish as if he hadn't heard correctly. Then broke into a peal of laughter.

'So tomorrow the crows will bathe and turn into cranes,' he spoke to his tittering crew and jumped from his boat. Wading through the water, he came up to the shore where Mutthur stood, and snorted, 'But why wait until then.'

'Why are you so eager? Are you afraid?' Adish sneered.

'Afraid?' Gopalan spat at Adish. 'I don't mind waiting, you fool. I just wish to save him the embarrassment.' He again turned to Mutthur. 'You must be a peabrain to think this forty-five year old trash would win you Kala, eh.'

Mutthur remained silent, having chosen to ignore him.

'Okay fine. If you wish to live in your fantasyland, why should I care? Just make sure this rotting boat doesn't cost you any of your limbs like your father,' Gopalan mocked and turned back. Then, he heard Mutthur speak.

'You're really proud of your limbs, huh?' Mutthur tiptoed towards Gopalan, drawing back his sleeves and baring his arms.

Gopalan blinked, and Mutthur's clenched fist landed on his face, resulting in a satisfying crack and a casualty of a tooth or two, perhaps. Gopalan stood there dumbfounded holding his jaw, his nostrils frilling like a mad bull and blood oozing out of his mouth. With a howl, he launched himself upon Mutthur.

Rajesh awoke after the most refreshing nap in days, in fact, months. The wooden clock on the wall read four thirty. The sun typically set around six, which meant one and half hours of practice still remained, he estimated.

One and a half hours to gain as much as they could.

Post sunset, they'd leave Mevalloor and head to Kumarakom. As per the plan, he and Manoj would rent a hotel room for the night while Adish and Mutthur would arrive with the boat and the crew, early in the morning.

Manoj still lay asleep snoring to glory, Rajesh checked. Waking him would be too much pain, he knew from his experience, so freshened up in the attached bathroom to leave for the river, alone. Picking his phone that was put on charging via P.C., he looked for new messages. He had one from Ruhika.

Hey, I am online. Come on Yahoo, her text said. It had arrived ten minutes ago from her international number. 'So, Ruhika is back in Ukraine,' he concluded. It had been three weeks since he had a chat with her and today, she had specifically messaged her.

He weighed his options. A quick natter wouldn't make a heaven's difference, he decided and logged into the messenger. Ruhika was online. *She* was online too. So was the sinking feeling.

His hands trembled. Should he write to *her*? He clicked on *her* id to open the dialogue box. Just then, it notified him that *she* had gone offline. Or maybe *she* had selected the invisible mode, seeing him online? Was *she* ignoring him? Fuck, why should it bother him?

'Hey, wassup? Long time.' Ruhika typed.

'I'm good. How are you?' Rajesh replied promptly and then went on to tell her how he had missed talking to her.

Ruhika told him about the places she visited in India; she'd been to Indore, Sanchi and New Delhi post her brother's marriage. Rajesh too shared with her the details of Onam celebrations, and the mundu.

'Seriously? You wore a mundu? I don't believe you.'

'Let me show you my pic,' he said and shared one picture. However, he avoided any mention of on *whose* insistence he'd donned the Malayali attire. He didn't feel the necessity. Well, to be honest, he'd sensed a growing soft corner in Ruhika for him, quite visible in her most recent messages.

He wasn't sure how she'd react.

'You are looking so hot, dude,' she wrote. 'Mundu would be fun, don't you think so?' She said, adding wink and heart smileys.

'Hahaha. Thanks.' Rajesh knew where their heart-to-heart was heading. The last time they got naughty was more than a year ago; when he was single. And now, he was single again. 'I was about to leave for the boat practice.'

'Oh yes. You were designing a boat, right? How's it coming out?'

'Pretty decent. Hopefully, it will carry us through.'

'Are you still wearing the mundu?' she asked. Rajesh felt a sudden tension building inside his underwear as memories of their old sessions came rushing to him.

'Yes,' he said. 'Won't you show me your India pics.' Wink Wink. He hadn't had *conversational sex* in ages.

'Of course, I would. Wait,' she typed. Obediently, Rajesh waited for her to upload her pictures. Ruhika was not conventionally good looking, but he liked her face cut and perceived her proportionate body structure quite alluring. 'Can't upload. Some problem at my end.'

'Mail me,' he wrote impatiently, keeping an eye on Manoj too, lest he woke up. What about Shelja? Her thought finally presented itself. But he wasn't cheating on her. They were still in the zone called 'friends'.

'I mailed. See and tell me what you like,' she added winks again.

His left hand squeezed and adjusted his crotch to ease the strain while his mailbox opened. Her email was at the top of the pile; with attachment. However, there was one more entry that called for his attention. It was from Andrew, sent an hour ago.

Rajesh clicked Andrew's email open. It was unexpectedly lengthy. As he sifted through its content, his face turned ash white.

Ruhika's pings flashed on the taskbar but right now, he couldn't care less and continued his perusal of the email.

'How could I ignore this shit, fuck,' Rajesh pulled his hair as he finished reading the most explosive shit he'd ever read. He quickly wrote an apology to Ruhika, without reading her new messages, said goodbye and logged out. The stress inside his mundu had climbed straight to his head now.

'Wake up asshole,' Rajesh gave Manoj a violent shake.

Manoj woke up with a start, fear plastered over his face as if shaken by an earthquake. 'What the fuck happened?'

'Get up. We don't have time,' Rajesh spoke through gritted teeth with all seriousness and urgency. Manoj gave him a curt nod before jumping out of the bed. He knew they had to run.

'Is he sure?' asked Manoj as they rushed to the river shore. After he'd gathered full details on Andrew's email on their way his sleep, perforce, had vanished from his eyes.

'Well, he seemed convinced about at least one aspect – the speed,' said Rajesh. Manoj nodded. If Andrew was right, it could prove to be a game-changer. But as Rajesh said and Andrew mentioned too, there were two sides to the coin. First was speed and second-.'

'Its rear balance needs an urgent vetting,' Rajesh added.

'But we have no time, dude. The race is tomorrow.'

'I know, man. Fuck. I wish there was *some* mention of this boat in Asari's notes. It has become an inscrutable maze.'

'Wait,' Manoj halted in his steps. 'Do you see a link that may connect Andrew's deduction, Jacob's adventure and Mutthur's father?'

Running his fingers over his lower lip, Rajesh gave him a blank look. 'Holy shit!' he widened his eyes. 'You're a genius, *bhenchod*.'

'I guess we must talk to Narayanan,' said Manoj, pointing at his hut. 'Thank god that guy speaks Hindi. I just hope he isn't sloshed.'

Narayanan muttered in Malayalam from inside his hut as they knocked on his door. But before they could respond, the door opened, and Narayanan appeared. To their relief, he looked sober and didn't smell of toddy.

'Tell us the story. How did you come eighth?' Manoj said.

Narayanan laughed. 'You come here to hear that story?' asked he. 'Queer times indeed. No one made such request before,' he mumbled again in Malayalam and a slow smile irradiated his sunken face. 'We had discovered her secret,' he said. 'Mohan Sankunni and me! Let me tell you how,' he said and beckoned them in.

'What is wrong with you Mutthur? Is this the way to sort out matters?' Mohammad Kutty frowned in disbelief as Mutthur slumped to the ground, enraged at his helplessness. A scuffle between him and Gopalan was the last straw Kutty had ever wanted the Council members to witness as they amassed on the shore to check on their team's rehearsals and now, stood tight-lipped, surrounding them.

Following Gopalan's diatribe he'd wanted to teach him a lesson, Mutthur had told Kutty defiantly. Kutty understood the under-currents Mutthur felt, but he also knew had he not intervened, the competition next day would've seen not one but two boats less. Such savages the two skippers had transformed into.

'Get up Mutthur. Forget him and concentrate on your practice,' Kutty growled. Gopalan had receded from the view so there was nothing for him to worry about. He talked to Rajagopalan, insisting him to withdraw the council members from the venue and not bother Mutthur and his team for the rest of the evening. Rajagopalan acceded to his request and motioned at the council members to move.

'Is there any hope, Adish?' asked Mutthur, alone with his crew now.

'Do not be afraid; do not be discouraged,' Adish muttered a verse from the Bible. Just then, they heard a squeal.

Rajesh and Manoj rushed towards them, along with Narayanan. Mutthur cursed. The drunkard was the last person he fancied at the moment.

'We have some news,' yelled Rajesh but as soon as he came to a halt, an eerie quietness hit him. 'What happened?' he asked, panting heavily. Adish narrated him about the brawl with Gopalan - the cause of Mutthur's ultimate worry. Rajesh smirked.

'Forgive that fellow God, for he knows not he carries a false belief,' Rajesh recited the biblical verse too and giggled.

'Good for us. The shock of a drubbing would be greater for him tomorrow,' added Manoj, with earnestness and broke into laughter too.

'Have you guys been drinking toddy?' Adish was bewildered.

'Ah, he doesn't believes us, precious,' Manoj hissed. 'Tell them, Pandey.'

'You know, two magical words turned Coca-Cola into the great Coca Cola? One day somebody suggested, 'Bottle it'.'

Adish cringed, 'Fuck the riddles, man.'

Rajesh grinned, 'Oh boy. You do sound a daredevil now. Anyways, I say to you Mutthur, three words, "Switch the ends".' Mutthur twitched his face, unsure if he heard him right.

'Come. I'll show you,' said Rajesh and waded up to the boat. He pointed to the either ends of the boat and asked. 'This is the front end, and that is the rear, right?'

Mutthur nodded. Rajesh continued, 'But if you realign the boat's direction and make its rear end as the leading end when you row it, you may gain few more seconds.'

'How's that possible?' asked Mutthur, bemused.

'It is possible, Mutthur. Because this is exactly what your father did twenty years ago,' Manoj joined in. 'The proof lies in the seventh position your village achieved that year.'

'It was no fluke or a coincidence, Mutthur,' Rajesh added.

Mutthur was silent, unable to comprehend the facts. Rajesh gestured at Narayanan to step forward.

'They speak the truth, Mutthur,' spoke Narayanan, gazing at the inscription of 'Jacob and Sara' and narrated him the story. Since they always practised in the river and used either end for only one direction – either upstream or downstream, they could never detect the speed disparity of the two alignments. They always assumed that the differential timings were because of the river flow. Or perhaps, they never observed. But that year, a couple of days before the race day, he and Mutthur's father stumbled upon the secret of the boat; one alignment was faster than the other.

'That's why I was so baffled while studying its design. The weight distribution, the seating arrangement and the wet area, nothing was in balance which was quite odd for an Odi-vallam,' Rajesh told Adish while Mutthur and Narayanan exchanged the secret in Malayalam.

'So my father rode it this way,' said Mutthur, moving his hand over the rear hood. 'Then why did it not produce the same result again?'

'No one knew,' said Narayanan. 'After your father's accident, he didn't want anyone else to get hurt. So Mohan chetta never spoke up. He took an oath from me too that I'd never disclose the secret to anyone.'

'My father's accident?' Asked Mutthur, his past now flashing before his eyes. He had never seen his father walk. And everyone assumed it had been his fault.

Narayanan nodded, wearily.

'The gain in speed wasn't without consequences,' Rajesh told Adish. 'Which means, this end had lesser backward stability. So if you'd push it too much, it could-.'

'Flip,' Adish interjected him.

'We were so happy with our finish that we kept pushing it hard in the Muvattupuzha while returning. And then it flipped at the bend,' Narayanan revealed to Mutthur. 'Unfortunately for us, your father wounded his leg badly and,' he became quiet.

Silence engulfed Mutthur. Yes, that's what happened to his father before he lost his leg and resigned himself to smoke and liquor in the privation of life and hope, and yet never turned bitter.

'And after the revamp, the speed variance is even greater. But most importantly, the backward stability has probably improved too,' said Rajesh.

'So, if we ride the boat reverse, we can refine our timings by five-six seconds. That's brilliant,' Adish said. 'But can it flip?'

Rajesh swithered. 'Well, technically yes,' he said.

'I can't endanger my people's lives,' Mutthur mumbled, wading to the other end and put his palm over the front hood. 'We are going to race the same way we have practised. And I'm sure, we won't be finishing last.'

'We don't care whether we finish last or first, Mutthur. We want to defeat that Gopalan,' Dhaniya said. The crew hadn't spoken yet, but they had heard all.

'Dhaniya is correct, Mutthur. Here is our chance, for our pride and your love,' Manoram joined in too.

'I lost my father, maybe not because of the boat but I did, and I know the pain,' Mutthur said. 'How could I be unmindful of the consequences of my selfish needs and put anyone's life at risk, Dhaniya?'

'Your father was not selfish either. He just didn't know. But you do,' said Narayanan. 'Besides our boat did not overturn in the Vembanad but in Muvattupuzha.'

Mutthur stayed quiet. Narayanan was right. But how could he be sure that the boat wouldn't act same in Vembanad? Perhaps they hadn't pushed it too hard.

'I steered the boat with your father at the rear. Maybe, it was the lapse in my concentration that I couldn't gauge the flow of the river. Not that I was supposed to. But still, for twenty years I cursed myself. Every single day. Yet, I feel in all my conscience that you should reverse the boat. And if you don't trust my judgement, ask your oarsmen.'

Mutthur threw a glance at his people. He knew if he turned the boat, each of them would stand by him. They always had. But that didn't mean he was allowed to put their lives at stake. He was their captain, and his foremost duty was to ensure their well-being.

'Reverse the boat, skipper,' Manoram spoke with resolve. 'And if anyone fears for his life, he may step off because you are going to lead us the way your father did. With pride.'

Nobody moved. No noise came either.

'Take this leap of faith, skipper,' said Dhaniya.

'You said, we require two oarsmen at the rear,' said Mutthur, to Narayanan. 'Will you join us?'

'With gratitude, my captain. Let me be your fiftieth oarsman,' said Narayanan, teary eyed and ready to board his beloved boat.

'Jai Mahabali,' Adish screamed. The crew repeated in unison. 'Let's make the most of our remaining practice.'

'Guys, we still don't follow Malayalam. Can somebody please translate what is being decided?' Manoj pleaded.

'Mutthur is reversing the boat,' Adish grinned.

Raceday

****

'Wake up boys,' Vazhoor knocked enthusiastically at their door. It was the launch-day of Kerala Lights in its new avatar; also, the first time when he'd see his new logo adorning the main arena of a competition.

'Open the door, Bansal,' shouted Rajesh from inside the washroom.

'Today is the last day,' Manoj grumbled and gritted his teeth beneath the sheets. 'If anyone, fucking anyone dares disturb my sleep tomorrow onwards, I swear I'm going to chop his head off.'

'I have gifts for you,' Vazhoor grinned as Manoj unlatched the door and noticed him wearing an XL vest printed with the 'Kerala Lights' logo in the centre; a small red lighter with a sleek orange flame drawn in the shape of a boat, placed in a manner that it formed 'i' of the 'Lights'. Pride took over the sleepiness in his eyes and his chest swelled, finding his idea embellished on the yellow vest.

Half an hour later, they sat in Vazhoor's suite overlooking the Vembanad Lake. With a stockpile of promotional merchandise, it resembled more of a warehouse now. Hundred pairs of sports vest and shorts lay in large cartons; fifty for the boat crew, ten for the assisting team and rest for free distribution. Besides, there were caps, flags and of course, the star product - Frankincense lighter.

'The idea is simple. I want each of our supporters to wear this T-shirt at least if not the shorts,' said Vazhoor. Manoj raised a brow on the mention of 'supporters'. 'And this cap too, okay?' He picked one of the caps and wore it.

You resemble the retired monkey of a circus in this cap, Manoj recalled one of the dialogues from a popular Hindi movie while his team - Mohan Perumal, his assistant and two marketing interns - bobbed their heads. 'And they should be holding this flag in one hand and the lighter in other,' added Vazhoor, going through the flags and complimentary lighters packed in low-cost but beautiful and sturdy cases.

Rajesh picked one to inspect and scratched his chin, 'Why did you get 'Smoking Kills' stamped on it?'

'Manoj's idea,' said Vazhoor. 'A brilliant one I must say. To grab the attention. Rajesh curled his lips in acknowledgement while Manoj took in a deep breath of pride. The day had started on a good note and he hoped Bajrang Bali would continue to pour his blessings.

'We're going to distribute them at every stall outside the temple, be it food or lemon soda or the CD-cassettes or even books stalls,' he said. Entry of cigarette lighters was strictly prohibited inside the temple area. The marketing team nodded again.

'Good, we are ready then,' Vazhoor babbled, bouncing his knees. He inhaled, exhaled but his heart refused to slow down. He raised his left wrist and glanced at his watch.

'Where is Kerala Lights?'

Shree Kumaramangalam Temple had been abuzz with activities since morning. Outside the temple compound, booming sounds from Nadaswarams and Thavils created an emphatic environment while inside, in Garuda Mandapam, the high priests offered prayer and flowers to the deity Sri Subrahmanya Swami in remembrance of venerable Sri Narayana Guru. Next, the crew of the participating teams stepped, one by one, into the Mandapam – a square roofed dais for the rituals - with assorted flower petals and a brass lamp on a plantain leaf to seek Guru's blessings.

Waiting for their turn in Nalambalam - the temple courtyard, Mutthur stood with his men as his eyes seared around to catch a glimpse of other teams. Gopalan's team was next, to light the lamp and offer prayers. Kala was nowhere to be seen though her father was present, preparing the plantain *thali*; unlike last year where Kala had mounted the rituals and applied vermillion on the forehead of every oarsman from their crew.

Draped in a golden *Kasavu* bordered off-white mundu saree, she was performing *archana* when his sight first fell on her.

Mutthur had never seen anyone so divine and so blissful, and was instantly smitten. And when her eyes had turned towards him, the twinkle in her gaze vouchsafed she hadn't disliked him either.

Where was she? Was she alright? He felt an impulse to go to her father and enquire her whereabouts when Medavoor Nair glanced in his direction. Their eyes locked for a moment, seemingly accusing each other of being the nemesis of her happiness. However, a tired calmness on Medavoor's face assured Mutthur that Kala was fine. His gaze soon shifted to Gopalan and his crew as they entered the dais to perform 'archana', all charged up.

Kuttanadan punjayile, thai thai thaka thai thai thom, Gopalan's team chanted.

No quandary troubled Mutthur now. He recalled their previous day's rehearsals that had brought them within two seconds of their arch rivals' timings, lifting his spirits once more. By all measures, he was ready for the final battle.

A narrow stretch of Vembanad Lake in front of Kumarakom boat race club was chosen as the racetrack with a total length of two kilometres between the start and the finish points. For the entire distance, the channel was partitioned with bamboo logs into two lanes. Single tiered, temporary pavilions for visitors were erected on both sides, adjacent to the finish post. In one of those pavilions, sat Rajesh and Manoj, alongside the assist team, all dressed up in Kerala lights vests.

The lighters had already been distributed, and thankfully had generated anticipation with tag its line "Smoking Kills". But the vests were yet to be dispensed as people had just started to fill in. It was twelve, Manoj checked. The race was scheduled to commence at one-thirty, and the artists had already begun with their presentations. The first one, Garudan-Thookkam or eagle hanging, performed on the beats of the orchestra of five instruments called Panchavadyam, had just finished. And its dancers, dressed up as eagles dangling from a shaft hooking their skin on the backs and calves, had left them cringing in phantom pain.

The next line of artists came wearing large headdresses similar to the Kathakali dancers. Their faces were painted with elaborate patterns in red and orange; each relating to different deities. Carrying swords and shields, they showcased an exemplary ritual dance called Theyyam.

'For the first time I respect the fact that I joined DigiSys,' said Manoj as they watched the performers, mesmerised. At the back of their mind, though, was Mutthur. Five minutes or so was all he'd get.

Rajesh shook his head. 'How absurd a racing competition could be?'

'And cruel,' added Manoj. 'You keep practising for hours and days and weeks and months, probably years if you're in Olympics and then, few seconds decide if you win some or lose everything.'

'So unlike cricket, isn't it? Where you're in field for hours and hours while your fortunes and emotions swing like a see-saw.'

'I agree. By the way, what do you think our chances are in the twenty-twenty world cup? You think Dhoni is a right choice?'

'Honestly, this whole twenty-twenty idea repels me. Still, I believe the team is young, brimming with confidence. Cannot be worse than the previous one! What do we have to lose anyway?'

'I hope Mutthur does a Dhoni today. Remember Pakistan?'

'Dear people, the boat procession is here. It will proceed to the start point now,' the announcer declared as boats began to gather one by one in an extended row. A flag with a number printed on it fluttered at the rear of each.

'Our boat number is seventeen,' Manoj was suddenly perturbed. 'And today is twenty-seventh, meaning nine.'

'Of the eighth month,' said Rajesh.

'Oh yes, I didn't realise. And the year is nine too. Thank God. The sum is still eight. It is Tuesday and Vashikaran on Gopalan should help too.'

'What?'

'Yup, I found his broken tooth yesterday and...'

'And?'

'I cast a "Slow down before the finish" spell.'

Just then Rajesh's phone rang. Shelja had called.

'She's there at the entry point,' said Rajesh as he hung up following a monosyllabic chat with her that comprised of 'okay.' He got up and waited for Manoj to rise as well.

'It is almost a kilometre,' said Manoj, sniffing his intention.

'We will grab something to eat as well.'

'Okay, let's go. Just for the sake of friendship,' Manoj straightened up, reluctantly.

In the middle, Odi-vallams waded towards the start point, amidst a loud cheer. The pavilions were overflowing with spectators now, with many more occupying the grassy embankments on either side.

In the qualifying round the boats were going to race in pairs, the announcer divulged the rules. The pairings were decided as thus:

All twenty-eight boats were divided into two separate tiers, based on their previous year's performances. Tier one had fourteen top ranked boats from last year, and tier two had ten bottom ranked boats alongside four new boats in the competition. A draw picked one boat each from the two tiers to make the required pairs.

Top eight teams with best timings would then qualify to partake in the final race to decide the winner.

Clutching a black leather pouch, Vazhoor Chandy hurriedly returned to his seat as boats made their way to the other end of the tract. His team had finished distributing the vests. Only one – an XXL size, had remained as they couldn't find anyone large enough.

Except for the one person who sat next to him, he noticed.

The man appeared uncomfortable in his chair and squirmed, shifting his buttocks frequently. Unbeknownst to Vazhoor, he was none other than Mathew Varghese; Adish Mathew's father and MAVA's grandfather.

'Any problem with the chair?' asked Vazhoor.

'Yes, brother. Frauds they are. They sell tickets so costly. And don't provide proper seats. But you see, I had insisted. The view is quite clear from here,' Mathew said.

'I agree,' said Vazhoor.

Eight boats had already glided towards the start point, by now. Kerala Lights would be arriving soon, Vazhoor kept a watch. 'We have a team in the competition,' he said. 'Kerala Lights.'

'Isn't that a cigarette brand?' Mathew said. 'Strange because I heard Kottayam plans to be a smoking-free zone.'

'We don't produce cigarettes anymore. We manufacture pocket lighters now,' Vazhoor pulled out a lighter from his pouch and flashed it before Mathew who acknowledged the tag line with a curious grin.

'So they allowed you to sponsor one of the teams,' he said. 'Which village team?'

'Mevalloor'

'Mevalloor?' Mathew narrowed his eyes. 'That's my village. I'm from Mevalloor,' he said, with a hint of excitement. Vazhoor sensed his opportunity and promptly pulled out the XXL vest from his bag.

'Then you must support them,' he flashed the vest.

'I'd love to,' Mathew grabbed it and wore. A perfect fit. Vazhoor was pleased. His task was finally over. He could now watch the race and cheer for his team sans any distraction. He turned his gaze to the lake. Thiruneelakhandam now approached.

'Here is Kerala Lights,' he squealed with delight, unaware of the antithetical emotions building up in his neighbour's stomach as the boat passed over their view. 'Led by captain Mutthur and motivated by nilakkar-,'

'Adish,' Mathew cut him with a whisper, squinting at the boat. His eyes widened once more and shouted again, desperately. But the boat had passed already, and it was unlikely that Adish heard him in that commotion.

'Yes, Adish Mathew. Do you know him? Of course, you do. You're from Mevalloor,' Vazhoor chuckled.

Baffled, Mathew clenched his jaw. 'What is he doing here?' he demanded.

'Ah…he is the lead singer. Such a fantastic chap, I tell you. An IT engineer, and still holding such passion and respect for our culture. But his father… he is such a horrible ass.'

'I know. But what the hell is he doing here?' Mathew asked again and paused. 'Did you just say his father is an ass?'

'Of course or why else would his poor kid lie to him?

'He lied?' Mathew's face reddened. 'He lied to me.'

'Why would he lie to you? You aren't his father,' Vazhoor laughed and then his jaw slacked. The coincidence had knocked him like a Mike Tyson's southpaw. Sheepishly, he stared at Mathew who appeared to have grown huge fangs like an angry two-horned monster from a mythological film. 'Are…you? Mathew?' His lips quivered.

'Yes, I am,' Mathew leaned forward with a clenched fist. 'But who the hell are you, Mr Cigarette seller?'

'I am not a Cigarette seller. I'm a Lighter seller.'

'I don't care,' Mathew bobbed up from his chair. 'I'll deal with you later. First, let me whip the arse of my moron son.'

Vazhoor leapt to his feet and threw his arms out, blocking Mathew's way. 'What kind of father are you? You should be appreciative of him,' he pleaded and pushed him back to his seat.

The last pair of boats had passed by, which meant the race might commence anytime. The start point was two kilometres away and going by the old man's obese frame, he'd require at least twenty minutes reaching there; Vazhoor worked out the complete trajectory of Mathew's flight to save his son.

He must delay him as long as possible.

'Look, Mr Mathew. Think with a cool head. Your son is such a great talent and above all, he has the will to carry his traditions. Why don't you let him?' he beseeched through gritted teeth. 'And it's not as if he's quit his job. It's a holiday today, damn it.'

'Is your son participating in the race as well?'

'No, I don't have a son,' Vazhoor said. Mathew stared at him, considering his next response.

'The first pair of number 3 and number 12 has lined up behind the start line,' the announcer revealed.

The race was about to commence.

'My son will not participate,' Mathew barked, getting up from his chair with clenched fists. 'Now, get off my way or I'm going to cripple you.'

Adish's heart pounded fast. He heard his father's voice calling out his name. His frightened eyes scoured the race venue around but could not find a trace of him, though.

'What's wrong?' asked Mutthur.

'I think I heard Achan,' Adish said. For all his newfound bravery, he still wasn't sure if he'd stand his ground or be back to the coconut tree if indeed his father turned up at the race venue.

'It's nothing but your fear. You've taken a big step Adish, and this fear is dragging you down. Don't let it affect you,' Mutthur tried to comfort him. 'And if he is truly here, it is a good sign because I've never seen him give a damn to the boat,' he winked. Adish couldn't help but smile at his words. It was something Rajesh had mentioned too.

An announcement informed they were paired with number six. It stood two rows ahead; Adish descried and was none other than the last year's winning boat, Daniel. It was also the longest boat in the competition while theirs was one of the shortest. True, their new design ensured their numerical strength was at par with any other boat yet, whether it was still sufficient to outstrip that monster, he couldn't say. Last year, the margin between them was twenty-six seconds.

Damn, it was going to be the toughest race of his life.

A loud cheer brought his attention back to the starting grid. Five pairs had already left one after another, as organisers did not wait for each pair to finish the course. They merely required a safe margin between two successive lots and hence the pairs were being released every second minute.

'Number 9 and number 2, please proceed to the start line. Number 16 and number 7, you are the next,' announced the speaker. As Number 7 approached from the warm up area, Adish instantly recognised the familiar face standing tall at its rear.

'Hey, Mutthur. If not for that Kutty, I would've broken your neck,' Gopalan snickered as his shining black Puranjalparamban halted briefly beside them. 'But worry you not. Today, I shall do worse to you by breaking your pride. First, I'll vanquish this old rotten boat of Kala's grandfather. Then, I'll snatch his Muru Chundan and Kala as my prize.'

Wanting to crush Gopalan's puny head beneath a bulldozer, Adish's whole body flushed with fury. He felt a press of Mutthur's palm on his shoulder; *keep your calm Adish*, Mutthur seemed to convey.

'And I forgot. There are four new teams this year. I hope you losers beat at least one of them and not embarrass your village again,' Gopalan sneered and barked at his oarsmen to head towards the start line.

'Scoundrel! I'll break this *Kandi Theeni's* neck,' Dhaniya said.

'Leave him Dhaniya. He is trying to provoke us because he is scared,' said Mutthur, as Gopalan's crew positioned their oars in mid-air and waited for the whistle. 'Let's gear up. We are next.'

Medavoor waited restlessly for Gopalan's boat to appear at the bend. Because the channel ran too narrow, even the slight bend made sure that the incoming boats could be seen only for last eight hundred meters or so. The sixth pair had completed their heat, and the seventh was a few hundred meters away. The leading boat in this pair was last year's runner-up. This year too, it showed exceptional speed through the water.

In few seconds, his wait was over. Gopalan's boat appeared at the bend, leading its rival boat but only marginally. It was a new, smaller boat and in surprisingly good shape; Karichalthira was its name, on Goddess Kali. It hadn't lost much speed at the bend and now, was defying Gopalan's boat any respite.

As the seventh pair crossed the finish line and Gopalan's pair closed in as well, cheers from the stands grew louder. The oarsmen pushed hard as their oars enacted circles in a perfect pattern. Gopalan steered the boat at the rear with his stretched out oar, supported by Thomas, his deputy. Medavoor held his breath as both the boats zoomed ahead, scrambling to conquer the other one. But Gopalan's experience soon spoke as his team began to widen the gap.

Medavoor released a long breath. 'Come on boys. Do it. Top eight beckons you.'

The person sitting next to Medavoor stared at him. 'Are you kidding? Seems like a thirteenth or fourteenth position to me,' he said.

Medavoor gave an ugly twist to his mouth, 'what do you know?'

The person laughed and sat upright. 'I've won it twice my friend,' he said, and sunk back in his chair.

'Almost there,' Mathew Varghese panted as he sprinted towards the start line where he could see his son's diminutive silhouette on the blue monster that was lined up next. And now, when he looked at the boat closely, he remembered seeing it before. When he was young. Once, Mohan Sankunni had taken them on a sail; him and his college friends who were visiting Mevalloor. No time to reminisce, he shrugged off the memories. The boat and the race didn't matter to him. He just wanted to pick his idiot son and leave the venue as soon as possible.

'Get ready, number 6 and number 17,' the man with the whistle announced. Mathew hurried up and began to run before he realised he was too tired. He made a mental note to join a fitness centre and lose few kilos but first, he must salvage his son. Mathew prayed to Jesus to hold the whistle from going off until he reached the boat.

'We're almost there Adish,' Mutthur said, moving to the rear alongside Narayanan. The reverse countdown had begun. It was time for a little pep talk.

'I always thought the purpose of this race was to win my love,' Mutthur spoke. 'But I was wrong. This race had always been about our people, our village and you, my friends.' His words worked magic on his men and adrenaline gushed through their veins. Mutthur continued, 'Thiruneelakhandam was the most stellar boat we ever had. But we turned it evil. Now it deserves its redemption. May we all redeem ourselves with it.' The oarsmen shouted in unison, and their oars went up in air.

Kareem had finally shortened the oars.

'Let's hope my father...your fathers...every other father in our village is proud of the *real* us. Let the song of our flight and freedom begin,' said Adish, with his eyes closed. Few metres away his father stood, transfixed. Despite his best efforts, his son rode on that boat once more, against the backdrop of their cheering supporters.

'Lend him just five minutes, Mathew,' Vazhoor spoke behind him, panting heavily. He had followed him. 'Five minutes of his own life. He isn't doing it for himself. At least not today.'

Oh Mahabali, blessed we are
For you giveth us the Periyar

Adish intoned the opening verse. A collective hum poured out of the crew's lips.

With all the strength we get from thee,
Today, we prepare to go to war

'hum…hum…'

Mathew turned to Vazhoor and then towards his son, who had begun his song. His son did have a soul-stirring voice; a voice he never took notice of. A deluge of emotions erupted in his heart as Adish raised his tempo.

For your pride, show the valour

The oarsmen echoed the cue. 'For your pride show the valour.'

Mathew looked at the faces of the oarsmen who echoed his son's cues. They looked invigorated and their chants turned intense. A deluge of emotions erupted in his heart as Adish upped the ante further. With great difficulty, Mathew Mathew muttered his son's name.

Adish opened his eyes and froze. His legs went weak, and lips stopped reciting the song. Dizziness engulfed him and the world around him blanked out of existence, except for one reality; his father who stood before him.

Adish, he heard his name again but realised the tone of his father bore no anger. Rather, it had anguish.

'Time to move,' the starter confirmed and blew the whistle.

The oarsmen brought their oars down, and water splashed in circles, as both the boats pushed forward. The number 6 crew quickly caught their rhythm and surged ahead. Mathew noticed their harmonised movement and the contrasting silence and chaotic rowing on Thiruneelakhandam while his son stood stupefied, staring at him. Realisation dawned upon him. It was not his son's but his own trial today. He could not fail.

'Adish,' he said, in a pressing voice. 'Sing. Do it for me.' But Adish stood still, unable to comprehend.

'Your father is asking you to sing, Adish,' Vazhoor shouted too.

'Sing, my son. Sing,' Mathew yelled again.

Adish heard him this time. He closed his eyes and thanked Lord Jesus. With a deep breath inside, he began.

Kuttanadan Punjayile
Thithi thai thiki thai thai tho

Mutthur roared, 'Raise your oars.' Each of the crew whooped in unison. Swiftly, the oars fell into the correct rhythm as if under the command of their master Nilakkar. Mutthur and Narayanan manoeuvred on either side at the rear, providing the necessary balance as the other oarsmen pushed with all might and sallied forth. They were roughly two boats' length behind the number 6.

While Vazhoor was conspicuous by his absence, Rajesh and Manoj were back in the pavilion along with Shelja, wondering what happened at Mutthur's end. As per the running commentary, their boat had already taken off from the start line.

Towards the middle, the action couldn't be tenser. Gopalan's boat looked increasingly in good shape as it made its way towards the finish post. The competition seemed tougher than what they had pictured. Yet, if Mutthur succeeded in reining the new alignment, it could still be a touch and go. Everything depended on him. Manoj crossed his fingers while Rajesh shifted his gaze back and forth from Gopalan's boat to the bend.

Not too far away Medavoor Nair sat on tenterhooks, with his stomach in knots. He had never felt so worked up. According to him, Gopalan was doing a brilliant job in the middle but the neighbouring man's remarks had successfully sown seeds of doubts in his mind. Though, there was still no way Mutthur could eclipse him, at least not with the current alignment of the boat, he believed. Yes, he knew the secret, for his father had shared it with him post Mohan Sankunni's accident. Medavoor remembered how broken a man his father had become, blaming himself repeatedly for the tragedy.

He had kept the secret buried in his heart. Firstly, because he didn't want anyone to point fingers at his legendary father and, secondly, Medavoor had espied Mutthur's recent practice sessions and deduced that his team had achieved tremendous progress in last one month. With realignment, Mutthur could pose a serious threat to Gopalan, which he could never allow.

Fifty meters away from the finish, Gopalan's boat was around three boat's length ahead of their rivals now. But before it could cross the line, a loud cheer erupted in the stands for the two boats that currently negotiated the bend. The next pair had arrived. Nevertheless, Medavoor concentrated on his team and as soon as it finished with a comfortable margin, he turned his relaxed gaze towards the forthcoming pair.

With barely a boat's length gap between them, the two approaching boats were locked in a fierce contest. One of them was Thiruneelakhandam aka Kerala Lights from Mevalloor. Medavoor Nair's jaw dropped.

'And then, they begin the momentous war of their life...in their beloved boat...all thanks to their beloved Kodunappa who is watching over them, from a distance.'

'For your pride, show the valour.'

The boat song emanating from Mutthur's boat instantly reminded Medavoor of his father.

'Wasn't it the slowest team last year?' the person next to him exclaimed. The sight was certainly something no one could ever imagine. 'This is what I call a bloody good fight.'

The clamour in the stands grew deafening. And sure, it wasn't for the defending champions who led the race, marginally. It was for Mevalloor's oarsmen who challenged the number 6 neck-to-neck, right behind. 'Kerala Lights', it seemed glittered like the native flower thumba poo in the afternoon sun.

Had Mutthur stumbled upon the secret? Even if he did, would he risk it? Medavoor wasn't sure. It was indeed a difficult choice to make between the love of his life and the lives of his loved ones. Whatever it was, he didn't feel comfortable. And the reason was the sudden guilt of not having shared the secret with Mutthur. He dreaded that Mutthur might meet his father's fate. Even when he never approved of Mutthur, he couldn't overlook Mutthur's dedication to their culture and values - a rare sight in today's world. And if anything were to happen to him, it would mean a terrible loss to his community.

Back, where Rajesh and Manoj sat, the atmosphere had turned electrifying.

'I cannot believe it Pandey. The blue Appu has become white Shadowfax,' Manoj exclaimed as Rajesh held Shelja's hand tightly in nervous excitement. Manoj shook his head, 'You a genius fucker.'

Less than five hundred meters remained. Toiling hard against the top draw, the oars aboard Kerala Lights made perfect circles with lighting speeds. And there was more sweat on the oarsmen of 'Daniel' than the water splashed on them by their oars; sweat owing more to the tension and less to the physical effort.

The chants of 'Kerala Lights' percolated through the air now.

In the middle, Thiruneelakhandam scudded through the water as if propelled by a divine force. While, it had been a blood-rushing spree for Mutthur's crew, they had transformed into a surging tide nonetheless. For the first time in their lives, they didn't feel intimidated by the reputation of a top team ahead of them. Lusting nothing less than a coup now, they pressed harder as they sighted the finish post, barely two hundred meters afar.

Having never experienced such a high speed, Mutthur could barely sustain the rear balance. He felt indebted to Narayanan who had joined at the last moment or else the boat would've toppled by now. Dipping his long oar further, Mutthur threw a furtive glance towards his left and realized Narayanan stood still, holding his oar firmly and staring intently at his feet.

'Narayanan?' shouted Mutthur. Narayanan looked up, alarmed and gave him a prompt cautionary nod. But before Mutthur could decipher the meaning of the silent riddle, he felt it beneath his feet. The wobble. Mutthur gasped and swung his fear-struck gaze first towards his feet, then at Narayanan and finally, at his crew, all in a split second.

The tempo of Adish's voice was at its peak, resonating with the rhythm of synchronised oars. His oarsmen had shrunk the gap between the two boats further and now, their front end was in line with the rear of number six. In stands, chants grew louder, and more people screamed "Kerala Lights." Brushing aside the fear in the midst of that galvanizing noise, Mutthur changed the position of his oars. Then, for a moment, he heard his father's voice:

That's a trap, son. Do not succumb to it.

'Am I daydreaming? Are these guys seriously going to beat the defending champions? Oh Lord Jesus, it is incredible. They are my bet for the final round,' the person beside Medavoor screamed in excitement. A smile broke across Medavoor's face for the first time, but next moment his worry increased manifold.

A Hundred meters left now.

Do not let it happen, son!

His father's voice turned fraught. Mutthur's mind, as if wafting through 'tau' – a parallel dimension of time that seemed to move at one-hundredth of the speed of 't' – the time dimension his physical being existed in, scanned and rescanned the relentless countenance and fervid eyes of his men. Each of them rowed fervently, swaying from one side to another, and pushing harder and harder with each stroke while keeping a close watch on Daniel, the number six. They had eaten away ten feet more of the deficit. Never before, Mutthur had seen them thirsting so much for a victory.

It is not transcendental passion, son, what you see!

The baleful voice grew louder as the wobble intensified beneath his legs. Mutthur felt he was riding not a boat but a monster; the same monster who had consumed his father. And now its jaws could swallow any of his men. Mutthur glanced over this shoulder at Narayanan. He'd stopped sculling and tautly held his oar, immersed in water at an acute angle as if desperately trying to keep that monster at bay.

It is not underwater, son, nor is it on the boat.

They were fifty meters away.

Where was it, then? What was it? Mutthur's mind vehemently searched for an answer. Then, he realised. It was the earthly greed. Without thinking twice, his tongued uttered orders to his oarsmen to slow down. No one heard him.

'I said *halt*,' he shouted again. In an instant every oar stopped in a reflex action; their movement reversed, the next moment. As the boat slowed down, the crew's adrenaline-fused minds fathomed what exactly happened.

'What did you do? We were only fifty meters away,' Adish screamed.

Mutthur blinked. 'Finish the race slowly.'

From the stands, everyone saw the number seventeen slow down abruptly as number six surged ahead, few meters away from the finish. Seconds later, a relieved number six crossed the line and cheered. But the audience's baffled gaze was fixed on number seventeen, crawling towards the finish post.

Rajesh exchanged a bewildered look with Manoj.

'Are you sure it was Gopalan's tooth?'

'I...think so.'

'Come on guys. It's not some motorboat that the engine went out. Something happened there,' Medavoor's neighbour made a biting remark.

Medavoor rubbed his eyelids. Like everybody else, he hadn't anticipated such an anti-climax, either. Mutthur's wail to command his men to halt still reverberated in his ears. His neighbour was right. Something must have happened there. And he must find it.

Medavoor rose up and left the pavilion.

'Five minutes are over,' said Mathew as he lumbered towards the other corner, breathlessly. Vazhoor smiled. 'How do you think our boat must have fared?'

'Hard to guess, but the way it took off, it must have performed some miracle,' said Vazhoor and winked. 'Not that it hasn't yet. Look at you.'

Mathew shook his head, 'I have to lose more.'

'Why did you make us stop? They were the defending champions,' said Manoram.

The crew sat still in the boat waiting for the last heat to finish. Rajesh and Manoj stood there alongside Adish, equally bewildered at the outcome.

'We could've been in final round,' Dhaniya said

'Or we could've been under water,' Narayanan spoke. Every head turned towards him. 'I know what he felt because I felt it too. And not for the first time,' he added. A collective gasp escaped from the people around. Narayanan shifted his gaze to Mutthur. 'Your father didn't stop.'

Mutthur swallowed with difficulty and stood up. 'I know you are disappointed, but I'm not,' he said. 'Look at what we've done. Had we ever heard our names being chanted in those stands before? Today, we did. We fought with the fastest team and yet, didn't give them an inch.'

'We were faster. We could've won,' Manoram interjected.

'Winning doesn't always matter, Manoram. Sometimes not losing becomes more important. And I didn't want to lose any of you, the way I lost my father,' said Mutthur, his voice choked with emotions.

Each of the crew was conscious of the fact that he had probably lost the love of his life forever, and still it was they who occupied his mind right now. They knew Mutthur spoke the truth because he'd never been afraid for his own life.

'This is the end of the qualifying round, and now we shall announce the eight finalists,' the commentator declared from the central podium.

'Let us see where we finished this year. I bet we're in the top twenty,' Dhaniya humoured.

With a rejuvenated smile, they all held each other's hands and closed their eyes to mumble a silent prayer before the results were announced.

'I hope it's not lost yet,' muttered Rajesh.

'Number eight, St. Mathew,' the commentator pronounced the last team amidst loud cheers from its supporters. Where it came as the first relief to Mutthur, Gopalan was crestfallen. He kept stabbing his finger into his deputy's chest while Medavoor Nair carried a deadpan expression on his visage. He wasn't consoling Gopalan, Mutthur observed and a faint smile ran across his lips.

'Not over yet,' Gopalan shrugged his shoulders and ran towards the podium.

'Rascal,' Dhaniya cursed. 'Let me also go and check,' he said and scurried into the same direction.

Medavoor plodded up to Mutthur's crew. 'My entire life I've seen boats and oarsmen and captains. Hell, I once stood where you stand, now,' his voice sounded heavy but soft. 'However, I've never witnessed an end like this, before. And I am sure no one else present here, has either.'

Mutthur listened to him silently, uncertain of how to respond. *Should he reveal the secret?* He wasn't sure.

Medavoor leaned slightly forward, his eyes fixed at Mutthur, 'You knew the secret?' He whispered. Mutthur gaped at him, startled. Medavoor broke into a smile, 'And yet, you chose not to go all the way. So unlike your father.'

'My father didn't know. I did,' Mutthur said defiantly.

Medavoor inhaled deeply. 'I knew your father,' he said. 'He was cut-throat competitive, unparalleled. Even if he had known, he would have gone for it. I assumed you would do the same.'

'We're twelfth, Mutthur,' Dhaniya screamed with joy.

'I've beaten you, Mutthur,' Gopalan pumped his fist in the air. 'We're tenth,'

Mutthur gasped and swallowed the news and turned back to Medavoor who seemed to ignore Gopalan's frenzy and kept looking at Mutthur.

Mutthur gave out a wry smile, 'Sorry to disappoint you.'

Medavoor shook his head. 'You didn't disappoint me son,' he said softly. 'Because I was wrong. You proved to be as fiery an oarsman but above all, a true captain, who held his team above his own want.'

First he addressed him as son and now Mutthur perceived

incredible warmth in his voice too – an emotion, Medavoor had never exhibited before.

'You saved not only your people but also the boat, my father and me, not to mention my daughter,' said Medavoor. It was the warmth of a father.

'So I win Kala,' said Gopalan as he joined them, his chest bursting from euphoria.

Medavoor turned to him. 'No man can ever dictate who wins a Nair woman, Gopalan. The right stays with the Nair woman,' he said as Gopalan blinked rapidly. 'And we know what her heart aches for.'

'But,' Gopalan stammered but could barely speak further.

Mutthur looked around, his breathe caught in his throat. With a triumphant cry he dropped to his knees, his head tilted up and arms stretched skywards. Tears of joy rolled down his cheeks.

His team erupted in joy and began to recite the new boat song that resonated through the venue. Once more the visitors' attention veered towards the team of Kerala Lights.

They were celebrating despite breaking down at the last second and finishing twelfth after they had challenged the defending champions.

'Why're they so overjoyed?' one visitor asked another.

'I have no idea.'

Of course, they had none. But Rajesh and Manoj understood every emotion on display at the moment. Well, some days you just don't need anyone to translate the human emotions transcending race, region, religion, caste and language.

They were the feelings of friendship, love, hope and bonds.

Overwhelmed and choking with emotions, the three circles walked up to Mutthur, their fourth circle and enveloped him in a tight embrace.

They had won.

Rajesh Pandey's

A Night to Remember

****

I was born on a Wednesday; my mother would always remind me. Once again it was a Wednesday when I felt reborn. Our CLP had concluded, appraisals had been conducted and allocations were made but first and foremost, feedback forms and unsettled dues like hostel, bus, laundry and canteen were all filled and filed. Tonight was a night of celebration in the B bar.

Unexpectedly, Vazhoor Chandy and Mathew Mathew had joined too. Actually, they'd planned a farewell but at Adish's behest, arrived here instead. And it seemed the 'Rubber Baron' and the 'Lighters Czar' had become friends. But nothing in comparison to Bansal and Adish; both were headed to Mumbai now, for their respective projects. Whereas I'd leave for Bangalore.

'This is what I call real friendship dude. First, it was the same batch and now the same city. Wow,' I said.

'It's easy for people like you. Had I known he'd be posted to Mumbai, I would've skipped the damn interview. In any case allocation in FinServe isn't worth much, an ugly moronic job.'

Manoj sounded dejected, realizing he got lured in the name of management based opportunities to FinServe. Though, he had his doubts since day one and hadn't really cared whether he made it through or not. He already had his eyes set on the next CAT.

'But I'm so happy for you, man. Boeing! Cheers to you,' he said, and we picked up our glasses to raise a toast.

My worries had eased today, though I was totally nervous in the morning. We had learned at the beginning of the week that an urgent opening in design process had opened up in the

Bangalore based Boeing project. The opportunity seemed good. The only issue had been anomalous job timings and a brief session with the Boeing project leaders; a requirement received directly from the top management. I had applied.

'The project is first of its kind in Indian IT industry and hence quite delicate. It's still in initial set up stage and therefore demands associates who are willing to put in extra hours. Probably one of the weekends too,' Arun Niranjan, the design process lead, had informed each of the interested candidates before the individual sessions had begun.

He was impressed with the extracurricular boat project I had shared with him. 'You've worked on mechanical designs of cars in college and here, on a small boat too. Pretty excellent. But our project concerns not design, but coding and testing of several complex modules that would aid Boeing's design engineers. There is vast difference,' Arun Niranjan made a direct point.

'I know sir-.'

'Call me Arun, please,' he interjected.

'Sure, Arun. Being a mechanical engineer I held the same opinion when I first came here. But soon I realized I had a purpose. The purpose of a bridge. Let me explain,' I said and drew my three kissing circles of equal size and named them as 'Design', 'Code' and 'Bridge'. 'These are the three elements that are essential to create a correct design, defined precisely by the contribution or let's say radius of the three.'

I drew the large circle circumscribing the three and named it, 'product'.

'If even one of them is absent, the product circle can take any shape, a highly deplorable situation.'

'That's true,'

'I can learn.'

'I'm sure,' Niranjan closed the session with a smile.

That's how I bagged the Boeing project. Thanks to Robin.

'What has gotten into them? FinSoft is going to be no better,'

Manoj broke my musings. I followed his gaze to Adish who danced wildly in jubilation alongside his father and Vazhoor. Manoj shrugged and emptied his glass. 'What was your dad's reaction?' he asked.

'Dad was all right, but mom! She freaked out the moment she heard I wasn't coming back to Delhi.'

'Ditto with my mom! She couldn't believe her son betrayed his own words that he'd be back following a three-month picnic.'

'I love my friends,' Adish screamed from the other corner and continued to dance. He was the one, enjoying the most, tonight. And why not? That brave bugger had bagged product development and above all, a renewed father.

'I wish Mutthur were here too,' said Manoj.

'Yeah, I had invited him, but he said he'd feel out of place. But he'd come to the railway station with Kala. To see us off.'

'Cool. By the way, Uums is coming along. To Mumbai,' Manoj said, pushing up his spectacles. I stared at him, incredulously. 'We applied together.'

'I thought after that night, she would've changed her mind.'

'Changed?' he chuckled. 'Dude, she is so thrilled and excited. She is dying to taste the nightlife and freedom of the city.'

'Freedom? With you?' I asked, puzzled.

'Of course.'

'Your Vashikaran is working, I guess.'

'More to come tonight,' Manoj winked at me as the DJ played Bryan Adam's 'Let's make a night to remember'. I had heard the song recently. On the houseboat. 'Where is your heroine? You said she'd join us.'

'She must be reaching in some time,' I said, fiddling with my phone. She hadn't called yet.

'So what is it like…between you two? Anything serious?'

'I don't know exactly. Shelja is a terrific girl. And it's all great between us. Just that I fear another heartbreak.'

'Heartbreak, again? Dude, you just had one.'

'No, not that. I mean what if I break hers.'

'Why would you?'

'Because, maybe I'm not over *her* yet.'

Manoj laughed. 'It takes only a few seconds to erase unpleasant memories from your phone, mailbox and Orkut,' he said. How the hell did he figure that out? Did he try his Vashikaran on me?

'I've seen you peeping into your past,' he cleared my doubt. 'Just like you've seen me doing-.'

'Hey, fucker, I haven't seen anything,' I cut him off midway.

He laughed. 'That's not the point. The point is I see no reason for you to carry the torch any further, and keep peeping into the dungeons of your past. Your present is better. Much better,' he stressed. 'Remember dude. Markets are down. There aren't many buying options. And you're not the only stakeholder.'

Bansal was right. I had no reason to cling onto my past. But was Shelja my present *and* future? I wasn't sure. I didn't even know if I featured in her future plans. Though, if I did, "Distance" would still be the bigger issue for me. Once bitten, I'd always be shy.

'What're you doing here, boys?' said Vazhoor, joining us at the bar for a refill.

'Bansal baba is doling out wisdom in heaps,' I said.

'I can vouch for that. It has benefitted me a lot. I hope it helps you too,' said Vazhoor. 'My only regret is that he didn't take my proposal seriously.'

'What proposal?' asked Manoj.

'What do you mean by what proposal? I had offered you to join Kerala Lights as deputy operations and marketing head. You could've forged your future boy. I feel pity when I see you wasting your skills in IT. You must read Dr. Kalam.'

'What?' Manoj was bewildered. 'I thought you were joking.'

'Have I ever joked?' Vazhoor tilted his head towards me. I simply shook my head. 'Here you go.'

Manoj gaped at us, one by one. I was mystified too. It seemed an earnest offer to me and it could change his future, *but still.* He was outbound for FinServe, and we had our train berths reserved for tomorrow. A tough call to make.

As Vazhoor filled his glass and turned to leave, Manoj spoke, '

Are you serious?'

'Neither I was drunk that day, nor I'm today. Not yet,' he said with a smirk and took his leave to join Mathew Mathew.

'That's a strange situation,' I gathered few words. 'But I must say it is tempting.'

'It is an unknown territory but,'

'Where you are headed, that is unknown too,'

With an 'hmm', Manoj looked down and stared at his glass for an overlong moment. 'What do you suggest?' he asked.

I inhaled, exhaled, and repeated the breathing pattern. I needed to be sure. What I'd tell him now, could very well decide the course of his remaining life. 'You know dude,' I said. 'People like us need a right moment and a right place to make a decision that could change their lives forever.'

'Hmmm,' he said, seemingly mulling over my suggestion. 'I've made new plans,' He turned his gaze to an animated Uums; her head swirled, and hair swayed wildly as she danced to Eric Clapton. I raised a brow. 'She had a small break up a few days back.'

'I thought you were using "make the girl submit to you without a break up" Vashikaran mantra.'

'I know. One wrong ingredient,' he slammed his fist on the table. 'The Crab didn't work. But that's not the point. The point is, I chalked out a plan for myself. Two years' work experience, CAT, and then MBA. Preferably in marketing. I'll get a brand manager's profile.'

'Pretty much what's Vazhoor offering you, eh?'

He blinked. Tapping the table with his fingers, he threw one more glance at Uums who beckoned him. 'I guess you're right. Let's make it a night to remember,' he winked at me and stood up. 'And I hope the night carries the right moment and right place for you too,' he pointed at the entrance and bounced towards the dance floor to join Uums.

Shelja was in the house, wearing an elegant black dress. As she turned, I noticed her deep V back and her hair tied in a bun. My heart skipped a beat but before I could catch her attention, Nikhil Lal blocked her way. I didn't know why but I began to laugh, and my eyes darted towards Manoj and Uums.

Being a guy, I understood how desperate we could turn out to be. The social structure, parental thrusts and subsequent mental barriers in our country meant the ratio of the girls interacting in a public environment was pretty skewed, particularly in technical courses like engineering. Which implied there was far more competition amongst the boys. And it increased manifold once we came out of the education phase and entered the professional circuit; the ratio skewed further. Perhaps, in coming years the situation might change; the inherent patriarchal social structure crumbles, more and more girls opt for technical courses to gain independence and security, and the government from the future launches a program - *'Make her an Engineer'*.

Unfortunately, today wasn't that day, and until aforesaid future arrived, the male engineers must bear the curse of desperation. And in such an environment, how could any girl hope to fend off advances from so many guys around her?

'Hello,' her voice broke my train of thought. 'Where're you lost?'

'Nowhere! I was waiting for you,' I glanced at her from top to bottom. 'You look different.' Drop dead gorgeous, I meant.

'Different, as in good or bad?' She took the stool Bansal had occupied earlier.

'The way people are making a beeline for you is proof enough that it is good.'

She gave me a smile. A mysterious smile, like Menaka, adequate to sway the most resolute minds from the path of *brahmacharya*;

And I was no Vishwamitra. 'What are you drinking?' her magical voice coaxed me out of my broodings.

'Trying whisky today.'

'How's it?'

'I like it.'

'Ahaan! Let me try as well.'

She caught me by surprise, 'Really?' I asked.

'Why not,' she seized my glass for a swig and flinched as soon as the alcohol hit her taste buds. She looked so hot doing that.

'Dressed to kill and a peg of whisky down,' I remarked. 'Any special occasion?'

'Yup, there is,' she took another swig. 'Not bad. I like Whisky, yaar. Though, I prefer beer the most. And I hate wine...,' her words slowly dissolved into thin air as she went on and on with her interminable list of liquor preferences. The only thing I could see was her childlike innocence. *Was I in love with her?* I was.

The DJ switched to the Hindi songs.

Ek main aur ek tu hai, aur hawa mein jadu hai
Aarzu bekabu hai, rah na jaaye baat baaki...baaki...

I couldn't delay it any longer. I cognized that the place and the moment were right there, right then. I just had to stop worrying about the consequences. In front of me, was a present I simply couldn't ignore, at least not because of distance. Bangalore was anyway located centrally in South India, and Shelja would never consider working beyond Godavari.

Fuck all logic. I was in love with her. And that was more than enough.

'I'll be back in a moment,' I stood up.

'Are you leaving me here, all alone?' Shelja asked, making an angry face. 'You always do that.'

'Nope. Going for a moment so that I don't leave you later,' I winked at her and raised my little finger.

'Oh, shoo then,' she said.

I went straight to the toilet and locked myself in. I opened the image folder on my phone. I scrolled through her pictures once more and deleted the first one.

Nothing. I felt nothing. No pain, no regret.

The rest too, followed into the trash. A sudden calm washed over me. Yeah man, it took just a few seconds. I went to the inbox and erased her messages too and finally, removed her number from my contact list as well. My phone and my life were clean slates again. My heart raced faster as I moved about feverishly inside the small cabin, like a teenager anticipating his first date.

'Have you booked your tickets for Bangalore?' she asked when I joined her again at the bar.

'Not yet. Tomorrow may be,' I said. Manoj and Uums were no longer on the dance floor. I wondered what he'd decided finally.

'I have few friends there. Let me see if they could find you a decent accommodation.'

'I'm going to miss you,' I blurted out.

'Why?' She had a deadpan expression on her face.

'Because you won't be there.'

'What would you do if I was?' Again deadpan.

It was unexpected, and I felt my insides quivering.

'Is it such a difficult question?'

I had to tell her. No point waiting. 'No actually,' I gathered some courage. 'It's the easiest question of my life, and I have the answer ready. I will love you,' I said and held my breath.

She remained quiet, giving away nothing. Perhaps, she hadn't expected me to speak out those three words. Not so directly, at least. She could be an excellent poker player.

'I think I'm in love with you,' I rephrased.

Shelja shrugged. 'I told the HR that my fiancé is shifting to Bangalore for a new job. So I wish to be allocated a project there.'

Fiancé? Her fiancé? And that too, shifting to Bangalore? This makes no sense.

It all started to revolve in front of me as the same sinking feeling returned. I couldn't utter a single word. My head spun, and legs went weak. She was engaged. She was bloody engaged. The words rang loud in my ears. Instantaneously, I heard her making those strange sounds she called laughter, with her hand over her mouth.

There was no ring on her finger.

Damn. How could I miss the plot? The fiancé of course. Blood surged to my limbs, and my nerves calmed down. Despondency gave way to exhilaration as her laughter too transformed into a wide grin. 'Do you *think* or are you *certain* that you're in love with me?'

'Sure as hell.'

'Then prepare to love me from Thursday onwards,' she said. Those were the most beautiful pair of eyes I'd ever seen in my life, and the oval face and the ponytail and those soft lips that parted to utter those magical set of words. Nothing else mattered at that moment.

Not even Manoj's SMS to notify him the latest: He'd take up Vazhoor's offer and stay back in Kerala; Uums just patched up with her boyfriend; and nevertheless, Manoj would be spending the night, their last, with Uums in her room.

For me, though, it was the first of our new lives.

Acknowledgements

****

So, dear reader, our small journey finally comes to an end, one we had undertaken, together, few hours or days or probably weeks ago depending on how big a pain in the ass the book proved to be. But together, we have done it. I congratulate you on being the chosen one to have made it to the end, and from the bottom of my heart, a “Big Thank You”. Let us thank the people now who made our conversation possible.

My almamater, NSIT Delhi, the institute that embraced me into this Engineering Universe; active or inactive, I'd always be an engineer, for “once an engineer, always an engineer”.

Tata Consultancy Services, the organization responsible for my first brush with the God's own country. Without them, there would be no story.

My parents and my inspiration. They always taught me to take pride in my true self. The reason I could share the empathy of my characters.

Stenzin Tsesdup and my other beta readers, who patiently poured over the initial drafts (always hoping them to be the final one), and provided me with invaluable inputs, feedback and suggestions: Vikram Chaudhary, Pooja Agarwal, Zaeem Khan, Priyank Jain, Robin John, Melvina, Sudhir B Iyer.

Every work of fiction needs real inspiration. Here are few, who inspired the different facets of this story and its characters, and above all motivated me to turn my thoughts into a book: Ashish B, Puru S, Shashank N, Sumit N, Sumit B, Rahul G, Pulkit M, Anubhav K, Vady H, Rajat M, Suparna B, Mridul K, Naveen K, Tushar D and Monica G.

My incredible Begum and an unremitting editor, Meher Haque. Without her hardship, persistence and pursuit to finesse, this novel couldn't even be half as good (i.e. if it was). She managed to put aside the shockers she always believed were the biographical elements of my engineering past, and concentrate on the content instead. Fighting over grammar and language, it felt more like raising a baby than putting together a book, parents banging their heads over what the kid should grow up to be. Nonetheless, I am glad the mother ended up grooming the kid more than I could ever dream of.

Subhash Nathan, my Malayali friend and alter-ego, who shared immense data from the history, traditions and culture of Kerala. He is currently writing his own Novella, a beautiful story, set in Himalayas (my turn to turn a beta reader now). I wish ourselves all the luck.

My publisher Ajay Setia and his team, Abhijeet Singh and Sneha at Invincible Publishers who read and re-read the drafts without ever asking to cut down even a single paragraph, keeping complete faith in me. For a first time Author, that means a lot especially, when what you have written is neither a Mythology nor a Thriller, and yet runs for over 90,000 words.

Last but not the least, technology and Internet that helped me understand the various dimensions of the art of fiction writing that aided in my transformation from a Filmmaker who creates stories for viewing to an Author, weaving stories for readers.

Thank you